THE SLEEPING PHOENIX

Best Wishes!

THE SLEEPING PHOENIX

Patrick J. O'Brian

iUniverse, Inc.

New York Lincoln Shanghai

The Sleeping Phoenix

iUniverse books may be ordered through booksellers or by contacting:

iUniverse
2021 Pine Lake Road, Suite 100
Lincoln, NE 68512
www.iuniverse.com
1-800-Authors (1-800-288-4677)

This is a work of fiction. All of the characters, names, incidents, organizations and dialogue in this novel are either the products of the author's imagination or are used fictitiously.

ISBN-13: 978-0-595-40231-1 (pbk)
ISBN-13: 978-0-595-84608-5 (ebk)
ISBN-10: 0-595-40231-3 (pbk)
ISBN-10: 0-595-84608-4 (ebk)

Printed in the United States of America

This is for Gregg Winters
1957–1991
Devoted father, brother, & son

From Molly Winters, Gregg's wife:

Gregg raised his right hand and took the oath to be the best police officer he could be; and for over four years he did just that. Gregg loved his job, and as dedicated as he was to being a great police officer, he was even more dedicated and committed to being the best husband and father possible to the boys and I.

Gregg was not only a father to our sons, but he was a Daddy. On the guys' day out, Gregg and Kyle would dress in matching sweat suits and spend the day together after picking up Gregg's paycheck and eating lunch at McDonald's. He always told Brock that as soon as he was old enough to eat french fries he could come too.

Gregg's lifelong goal was to be an officer, and he proudly wore his uniform as he upheld the thin blue line of justice. He gave his life for what he believed in. Gregg touched many lives. And that is the one regret I will always have; Gregg's sons will never know what a gentle, caring, compassionate, loving man their dad was.

As Kyle said to Gregg on the night he passed away:
"Have good dreams, Daddy. We love you."

From Terry Winters, Gregg's brother:

Gregg was not only my youngest brother, he was also my best friend. Whenever I needed anything he was always there for me. Gregg was a caring person. When he was around we always had fun.

When Gregg was about nine-years-old I was working at a grocery store and every payday I would take him out and buy him a toy or something he wanted. Gregg looked up to me and I'll never forget him crying when I got married and moved out of the house.

Gregg became a police officer because of me. Before I got promoted, Gregg and I went on several calls together, and I was always proud of the way he handled himself. I don't think I ever told him that. I thought he would be around forever. Little did I know that everything was about to change for my family.

The phone call I received from Muncie Police dispatch the night Gregg was shot still haunts me. I couldn't believe it. Gregg was a good street cop and always wore his bulletproof vest. Later I found out that he didn't have a chance to protect himself because he had been shot five times in the back of the head.

I miss Gregg and I hate the fact I have been a deputy chief for ten years and Gregg has not been there to share that with me.

Thanks to Brad Wiemer, Carol Pyle,
Mark Adams, Nannette Bell,
Rob Mead, Joy Winslow, and Jeff Groves
for their contributions.

Thanks to Kirk Mace, Jim Evans,
John Lancaster, Brent Brown, Terry Winters,
Ric Oliver, and Mike Rost for their
assistance on the cover.

Special thanks to Kendrick
Shadoan at KLS Digital for creating
the cover, handling photography, and
putting up with me.

Other novels by Patrick J. O'Brian include:
The Fallen
Reaper: Book One of the West Baden Murders Trilogy
The Brotherhood
Retribution: Book Two of the West Baden Murders Trilogy
Stolen Time
Sins of the Father: Book Three of the West Baden Murders Trilogy
Six Days
Dysfunction

Current, past, and future projects by the author can be seen
on his website at:
www.pjobooks.com

CHAPTER 1

▼

Clay Branson watched his wooden practice sword block his opponent's swing in the center of his personal training facility.

Already exercising a taboo by not watching his opponent, he knew the skills of his uncle were nowhere near his own, so he studied Bill's technique, rather than predict his moves.

Ten years older than Clay, Bill Branson was the youngest of three brothers.

Experience and youth gave Clay distinct advantages.

Another swing of Bill's practice sword came at his throat from the side, but Clay deflected the blow, then gave two quick swings, which his uncle parried.

Not that Clay was arrogant, or underestimating any adversary by passively fighting, but Bill wanted to learn the ways of a Japanese shogun the way Clay had during his stint overseas. What Clay learned was a handed down version of the art taught several hundred years back, but he was still considered one of the most lethal men on the planet by those who knew of him.

Bill said nothing, his blue eyes boring into Clay, attempting to study his expression. Already his uncle had come a long way, no longer displaying the fear that he was going to be beaten. In all likelihood, Bill knew he was going to be defeated, but only from lack of experience, and a lack of discipline Clay had long since vowed to maintain.

"You're being unusually quiet," Clay noted.

"No talking," his uncle mimicked the words Clay often stated to keep Bill focused on the task at hand.

After all, they were simulating a sword fight that would likely end in death if it were the real thing.

Clay grinned inwardly, but gave Bill no satisfaction for the sarcastic remark.

At the rear of Clay's house, he had built his personal *dojo*, which was little more than a replica of the facility he used during his stay in Japan. Along the walls were weapons of all kinds, hung amongst bright red and gold trim to adorn the eggshell color of the walls and floor.

Circling one another in the center of the room, swords held outwardly, each wearing practice uniforms of crimson red, neither flinched, or even batted an eyelash.

Bill's neatly parted hair had become disheveled during their first two entanglements, which Clay allowed to end in draws. Above his lips was the brown mustache that matched his hair color, while his thin-framed glasses appeared lightly fogged.

He refused to get corrective surgery, citing several recorded medical mishaps, and contact lenses didn't work with his particular prescription.

When Bill finally struck, Clay reacted defensively, because Bill had given no indication with his eyes, his expression, or even through the visible muscles in his hands, that he planned to attack.

Clay used his wooden *katana* to block several blurred slices and jabs, proud of his uncle's progress. Bill has mastered many things, including regulating his heart rate, masking his intentions, and proficiently using a sword.

At least for defensive purposes.

Around them was a second level, accessed by nearby stairs. It looked somewhat like an opera house balcony, which loomed above the training area. Though Clay had never found much need for it, the upper level provided more area to train within.

Now Clay found himself backed toward the steps, though in no danger of being killed by his uncle in the training sense.

He was disappointed that Bill did not dedicate more time to training, or practicing his skills. It was a downfall of Western life, he supposed. Bill had his own life to live, and there was little practical use for swordplay or assassination techniques in Muncie, Indiana.

Clay reached the fourth stair, then flipped sideways to the floor below, never using a hand for any kind of support, or as a spring. He hit the floor running, quickly cutting off the stairwell as a means of egress for Bill.

Now an uncomfortable look crossed his uncle's face. Bill had never battled on the unstable terrain of stairs before, and this was exactly what Clay wanted. By no means was he trying to cheat for a quick victory, but he wanted Bill to understand that battles knew no bounds when it came to setting.

Regaining his composure quickly, Bill seemed to realize he had the high ground, but appeared openly unaware of how to use it.

He defensively held his sword in front of him, backing his way up the stairs. As he was in mid-stride, Clay aggressively swung his sword in a manner that deflected his uncle's weapon. In the same motion, he thrust his own wooden sword upward, bringing it to rest beside Bill's neck in a most dangerous position.

Bill started to let his sword limply drop toward the ground, but in a flash, raised it to block the wooden blade from touching his neck. He had learned that the fight was never over until the blade touched him.

Both swung at one another, each countering their attacks as they stepped in sync up the stairs. Clay prolonged each lesson a little more, and he was about to bring this one to a close, particularly since they were both due to work within the hour.

He waited until they locked swords, with Bill's facing the wall, as opposed to the open bannister, then forced his uncle's sword against the wall. In one swift motion, Clay whirled in such a way that he drew himself around his uncle's side, switching sword hands in the process. He let the wooded blade rest against his uncle's throat this time.

The move was meant to let his uncle know the lesson was over.

"Point taken," Bill said, loosening the grip on his practice sword.

"You did well," Clay admitted, letting his uncle out of the precarious position before leading the way down the stairs.

"I know you're just letting me feel better by dragging it out."

"That may be partly true, but your confidence and focus are *so* much better."

He turned to see Bill shrug almost indifferently.

Bill didn't know it, but he was already capable of killing an average man with a blade. Clay prolonged the battles more each time, but mostly to study his uncle's improvements. Clay was no true master of what most people called *ninjutsu* in the sense that he didn't consider himself a very good instructor.

Also, his limited time in Japan never gave him adequate opportunity to perfect the techniques he learned. He also felt denied, because he felt there were certain disciplines he was never taught.

They returned to the normal portion of Clay's house through a small hallway that led to the kitchen. Bill worked out with him most every morning before work, often bringing a change of clothes with him.

As the director of maintenance at Ball Memorial Hospital, Bill had a day full of stress and demands. Clay's position as part of a drug and gang task force on the city police department was no less demanding.

"You going to shower?" Clay asked his uncle, grabbing a fresh bottle of water from his refrigerator for each of them.

"I'd better. I've got a meeting with the big bosses first thing today."

"Tim's out of town today, so there's no big hurry for me to meet up with the boys. Take your time."

Bill took a sip of water, giving his nephew a quirky smile.

"When do I get to learn the fun stuff?"

"When you start working on your discipline. I need your mind as strong as I've made your body."

Bill soured openly.

Clay's answer meant hours of meditation, physical techniques that stemmed from the mind, and the spiritual methods used for combat. Though some people thought the spiritual aspect was a useless stimulant at best, Clay knew it developed skills to predict the enemy's movements, and heightened the senses.

He suspected Bill was never going to devote time to perfecting such skills, but he liked to nag him anyway.

"I just want to throw a throwing star once in my life."

Clay sighed aloud.

"Do it wrong, and you wind up with half of it lodged in your wrist."

Bill appeared content with waiting, despite his comment.

He had been patient through the initial exercises, which required lots of weapons manipulation, stealth, and heightening his senses. By no means were they fun or exciting exercises, but Clay knew they were essential.

"You'll throw one in this lifetime," Clay promised. "You're coming along just fine."

It felt strange talking to a man ten years his elder as though he were a child needing encouragement.

Bill nodded, then left the kitchen to shower and change clothes.

Having a student gave Clay incentive to maintain his own training, which he had to admit was lax the past few years.

His job allowed him little spare time, but he dedicated a few hours a day to training, especially after the incident the year before. A battle to the death with his old nemesis taught him a valuable lesson that wars never truly stopped, no matter how far he moved, or how safe his surroundings felt.

The world had changed since the days when men used swords to kill one another, but the art was not completely lost. Clay suspected he still had enemies hiding in the shadows, which was one reason, at thirty-four years of age, he had not married while living in the States. It was also the reason he taught Bill techniques that might save his life.

Bill had nearly become a casualty the year prior, when Clay's arch enemy brought terrorists to Muncie. He wanted to know his uncle had a fighting chance if such problems arose again.

He was due to meet Ed Sorrell and Rod Maynard within the hour to plan their day's events on the task force. With their sergeant, Tim Packard, in Cincinnati for the day, Clay was expected to take temporary command.

Maynard replaced Chris Hamilton, who didn't live up to Packard's expectations. Their task force didn't always follow police procedure, or even the law in some cases, so Packard needed officers who followed his orders rather than standard protocol.

Stepping outside, Clay took in the May sunrise, knowing it was just after seven o'clock. It was going to be a fairly warm, humid day, but Clay didn't plan on enjoying any of it. He hoped Packard enjoyed his day off, but suspected the sergeant was going to regret making the trek to Cincinnati.

It was uncharacteristic of the man to volunteer for something that put him in the middle of a busload of kids. Perhaps spending time with his daughter overwhelmed Packard's common sense, because Clay never pictured himself dealing with rowdy kids heading toward a theme park.

Taking off his practice uniform shirt, he returned to the comfort of his house, ready to meet Sorrell and Maynard within the hour.

CHAPTER 2

▼

Tim Packard had never been so relieved to reach Great Realms in all his life. Though he had been with his family to the theme park several times, his head had never felt like it was due to explode any second.

The bus ride of nearly three hours was virtually a personal hell, because the teachers did little to quiet the students, and he wasn't about to speak up. Several teachers had looked at him, expecting him to use his police authority in some way, but he wasn't about to be labeled the mean parent.

When his twelve-year-old daughter, Nicole, came home one night asking him to chaperone their trip to the theme park, he readily agreed.

Every night since, he had dreaded the trip, regretting the impulsive decision. His wife's nagging for him to spend more time with the family resulted in his rash thinking. Sarah meant well, but there were better ways for the police sergeant to prove he was a good husband and father.

When the bus reached the park, it took a few minutes for the teachers to explain the rules to the eager students. Since the park was open specifically for school trips on this Thursday, it closed at six in the afternoon.

Students needed to report to a teacher or chaperone by that time.

Season pass holders were also welcome, but Packard didn't see many cars in the parking lot.

When Packard walked with his daughter toward the entrance, he heard several screams from above as a roller coaster near the entrance dropped riders from a high peak. He watched the cars roll along the track, thinking he was going nowhere near the taller rides.

How do I let myself get talked into these things? he wondered as he stood in line for the tallest ride the park had to offer.

Beside him, Nicole glowed with anticipation as they waited for their turn on Skydiver. The ride, little more than a large purple cylinder with fifty seats, took guests 300-feet into the air, then dropped them straight down.

Some sort of hydraulic brakes kicked in during the last few seconds of descent to slow the ride from an actual crash, but Packard remembered hearing rumors about people falling out of it when their overhead restraints failed.

Urban legends about faulty theme park rides were common, but he seemed to remember an incident from a few years back about a boy falling out of a metal coaster when it went into a loop.

The newspaper article didn't give much detail, but it said the boy fell from the loop's crest, landing on the metal track below. Apparently the fall was from around three-stories in height, so he probably died on impact with the track, but the coaster itself struck him when it came out of the loop.

Packard turned his thoughts to the metal detectors at the front gate. It seemed the threat of terrorism reached everywhere, even to the areas where people were supposed to think of only a fun retreat.

"You going to be okay, Dad?" Nicole asked, a somewhat sinister smile on her face.

She prided herself on talking him into riding the most fearsome ride in the park.

Taking off his glasses, Packard momentarily used his shirt to clean them.

"I'll be fine, kiddo," he replied. "I'm just hoping you get this out of your system. The ol' man can't take these rides like he used to."

Momentarily, he heard screams from above as the circular station that held fifty guests at one time dropped from its summit. Packard looked up, seeing legs sticking out from every direction as people tested the weightless feeling the drop provided by letting themselves be pushed upward against their restraints.

It looked like a ladybug with a hundred feet coming down to earth with a mammoth pole at its center to provide stability on the lift upward.

Packard guessed they were about three trips away from taking their turn on the thrill ride. He felt his stomach tighten with anxiety, wishing he had never agreed to ride it, but too proud to back out in front of the hundreds who had filed in behind them.

He vowed he wasn't going to scream like a school girl when he took the plunge, but something told him he was going to have his eyes closed most of the way up.

"I can't wait to see the rest of the park," Nicole commented. "Can we go on the Twister after this?"

Packard groaned lightly.

"Uh, we'll have to see if I live through this or not."

When Nicole made good grades the year before, the entire family went to the park. Packard spent most of the time with his young son in the children's portion of the park, while Sarah and Nicole braved the big rides.

Taking a deep breath to calm himself, Packard wondered how Clay was doing with the task force. He didn't expect them to carry out too much activity without him, but Clay had been known to surprise him before.

Looking upward as the next batch of riders slowly rotated around the center tower during the ride's ascent, Packard shook his head. He vowed the next time he used a personal day at work, it was going to be for something he truly enjoyed.

*   *   *   *

Rod Maynard sat beside Ed Sorrell in their unmarked car, down the block from an abandoned automotive repair shop on the city's south end.

He was new to the task force, but eager to make an impact, and to please Packard.

After coming from a small town, almost rural, police department a few years back, he took a lot of hazing about being a farmer cop. Despite being an assistant chief at his previous department Maynard had trouble earning respect.

Until Packard recruited him for the task force.

Maynard's only hesitation stemmed from rumors the mayor wanted to shut the division down for lack of funding, but Packard had presented overwhelming numbers to the city council. When they saw how much crime was down, and how many arrests the sergeant's team had made, they told the mayor to rethink his budget allocations.

Assured he was welcome, and in no danger of being booted to another assignment, Maynard came aboard.

Nicknamed 'Bulldog' because of his slightly wrinkled face and completely shaved head, Maynard warmed to the nickname more quickly than the other forms of hazing he endured. Barely making the state pension board's age cutoff six years prior, he now found himself in his early forties without a rank in his new department.

Looking older than his actual age sometimes hindered his ability to bond with his fellow officers. Some called his look weathered, which Maynard attributed to the abundance of farmwork he did as a teenager. He continued to work the land at his father's farm several miles east of Muncie at the beginning and end of every crop season.

He and Sorrell had watched Clay duck behind several buildings, which were surrounded by overgrown brush, then disappear completely.

"How does he do that shit?" he asked Sorrell from the passenger's seat.

"Do what?"

"Just disappear."

Sorrell shrugged.

"I heard some shit about him being trained over in Japan," Maynard said, trying to answer his own question.

"We don't speak of that," Sorrell said with a serious tone, his eyes fixed on the garage. "Sarge says we're, uh, to say nothing to no one about that."

Maynard raised an eyebrow.

"Then it's true?"

Sorrell shrugged with an elusive look, being coy.

Maynard had heard stories about dead bodies at a partially renovated apartment building the year before, and even something about a decapitated body, but blew them off as hearsay. Officers talked about Packard covering up for Clay, but they never seemed to know specifics, and Maynard wasn't patrolling on the night in question.

A combined task force comprised of state and federal officials immediately took charge, so no local officers witnessed the supposed death toll at the hotel last year.

Except for the one officer who discovered it, and he was sworn to secrecy by the feds. No amount of prodding ever got a word from him, so the officers figured his employment was threatened if he spoke about whatever he saw.

Returning his attention to the task at hand, Maynard recalled Clay saying something about a tip that the garage they were observing being a coverup for a drug ring. Though the task force had curbed much of the trafficking between Gary and several other major ports, they hadn't stopped it completely.

Maynard was just along for the ride so far, but he hoped to do more than make simple arrests soon. He was ready to start seeing some of the larger action. Packard always talked about catching small fish to find the bigger ones, but they had yet to confront any major players in the drug circles.

"It's not regular procedure just to let Clay run up there like this, is it?"

Sorrell turned from his pensive stare at the garage.

"No."

Maynard had yet to fully assess what Sorrell did for the team. A thick man with hair usually shaved down to his scalp, he had to be muscle for Packard's operations. He had extra training in tactical driving, and he was handy with a shotgun, but Sorrell was by no means light on his feet.

Maynard would never describe him as bumbling, but Sorrell walked with the equivalent speed and grace of a possum. He drank on weekends, was rumored to run around with other women, despite being married with two kids, and had a tendency to make serious judgment errors.

Still, he followed orders and had a propensity for keeping vigil over his fellow task force members, both professionally and personally.

He seemed to understand the hardships Maynard endured when he first joined the Muncie Police Department, sharing a few of his own stories with the new team member. It turned out Sorrell came from a rural background growing up, so they had at least one thing in common.

During the past year, since the death of Clay's cousin, fewer hairs grew back when Sorrell shaved his head. Maynard also noticed more gray whiskers replacing the otherwise brown hair on Sorrell's chin. He had grown in a full goatee, which members of special teams were allowed to do on their department.

In some aspects Sorrell took after Packard, and in others, like Mitch Branson, whom he had partnered with for years. He now adopted a tougher image, wearing different clothes and talking more lingo like his sergeant.

In some ways he seemed vastly improved, even during the short time Maynard had worked with him.

"Clay won't do anything without us," Sorrell finally said. "He knows Packard will get pissed if we make any moves without him. And the chief would, uh, get upset if any of us flew solo on these things."

Though he had made strides during the past year, Sorrell occasionally stuttered when he spoke. Self-confidence was his greatest enemy according to Packard, because the man certainly wasn't mentally slow.

Maynard remembered a time when the younger officer barely said two words, so the fact that he spoke to colleagues in complete sentences was an achievement. He suspected something from the man's childhood kept him from speaking, whether it was a form of discipline, or perhaps even abuse.

Being on the task force had saved Sorrell's job, and perhaps his life, in several ways. When an officer can survive undercover work and other hazards drug enforcement presents, he or she gains respect from peers, and vast knowledge.

Each of the officers had a portable radio with him, which they had to use, because the unmarked car contained absolutely no features that allowed it to be identified as a city vehicle. At this point, they were simply waiting for Clay to call them over the air.

A moment later, he spoke his first words over a tactical channel only they and the county task forces were privy to.

"Ed, I've got movement in the garage," he reported. "They're moving something out of there right now. And it seems to be in bulk."

"Do you have a visual on their cargo?"

"Negative. It's all packed up."

Now they had gone from a tip about stored drugs to something being moved out of the garage. Maynard knew he had no legitimate input on their decision, but he was itching to see some action. He wished Clay could verify some illegal cargo, allowing them to spring into action.

"Give me a minute," Clay said over the radio.

Maynard sucked in a deep breath, waiting for something to happen. He envisioned a large truck on the other side of the garage, remembering it had three large bays when it was a business. They were staring at the rear side, where overgrown weeds blocked their view, accompanied by old, rusted barrels. It was the only safe observation point where they remained hidden from local occupants.

"You think we'll get to go in there?" he asked Sorrell.

Biting his lip almost nervously, Sorrell seemed a bit less enthralled about the idea of barging into a warehouse. At this point, neither dared radio Clay, because he might be inside the lion's den.

Maynard shifted uneasily in his seat, checking himself over to make sure his gun and cuffs were where they should be. Patting his sides, he realized his gun wasn't in its usual spot.

"Goddamn you guys for making me do this," he said, looking under the seat for his gun.

"Do what?"

"Wear my fucking chaps to a drug bust."

Sorrell snickered.

He whistled a Village People song, prompting Maynard to smack his arm as he located his holstered firearm under the seat.

Packard used one of his informants to set up a deal with a very untrusting dealer at the city limits. The dealer had dealt with a mysterious buyer he knew by reputation only. Since Maynard rode motorcycles regularly, owning just about every kind of leather accessory ever invented, he found himself volunteered to act the part. It seemed the buyer was some sort of loner biker type, so the group coached Maynard on how to look and act.

He wore his chaps, leather jacket, fingerless gloves, and bandana to work, riding to city hall on his Harley-Davidson. Clay and Sorrell immediately told him to get into the unmarked car because the dealer postponed the deal on their voice pager. Instead of giving him time to change, Maynard's colleagues drove him to the garage, acting on a hot tip.

"You two *could* have let me change," he informed Sorrell, implying they intentionally rushed to keep him from grabbing normal clothes.

It seemed cruel jokes had a place in every police department, because his new team loved making fun of him whenever the opportunity presented itself.

"After we get done here, we can see if the Deuces Wild is open."

Sorrell spoke of a known gay bar in the downtown area.

"Fuck you," Maynard said. "That's all I have to say to you until I get a change of clothes."

From the corner of his eye he saw Sorrell smirk at the remark. At least someone found a source of entertainment while they waited for Clay to report.

Refusing to give Sorrell any more ammunition for jokes, Maynard folded his arms, staring out the window. One side of his chaps creaked, prompting Sorrell's mouth to open.

"Don't," Maynard warned. "One more word and I shove this up your ass."

He held up his firearm, waving it slightly so the younger officer saw it.

Sorrell cleared his throat, obviously suppressing a laugh. He turned his head the other way, giving Maynard the satisfaction of at least a few quiet minutes inside the car. Sighing inwardly, he wondered how much worse the day could get.

CHAPTER 3

▼

Packard felt positive he was going to vomit before suffering the displeasure of having the metallic harness dropped over his shoulders and the safety belt run through his crotch. He was now close enough to know exactly how the ride worked, almost intimately.

He watched the ride rise for the last time before he was due to sit beside his daughter. An image of seeing people milling like ants far below him crossed his mind, then vanished. His left leg nervously twitched as his mind wandered to anything except the ride.

"How has work been?" Nicole asked, thankfully breaking his concentration.

"Not too bad," he answered, giving her a questioning look. "You've never asked about my work before."

"I know you don't like to talk about it."

"Yeah, well, there's a reason for that. Your mother doesn't want you to hear about all the stuff I do."

She responded as though he was about to reveal all, to spite Sarah.

"And *I* don't want you to know, either."

Her expression slumped.

"I'm old enough to handle it. If you whack people or something, you can tell me."

Packard chuckled.

"I don't run around shooting people, Nicky."

"Mom says you deal with the worst criminals out there."

"Yes, I do, but it's easier to outsmart them than have shootouts with them."

An inquisitive grin crossed her face.

"Do you ever get scared?"

Packard gestured uneasily.

"Not really," he answered. "Out there, I'm in control of what happens to me. On a ride that takes me halfway to the sky, that's another story."

"It's *fun*," Nicole insisted.

"If you say so," he replied, purposely giving her an uneasy look. "I don't know how your mother had any hair left after riding these things."

The Skydiver was in the part of the park designed to house the largest thrill rides. A centralized concrete lot cobwebbed off to several paths that led to different extreme rides.

Being a chaperone wasn't so bad, he decided. It wasn't like he had to follow kids around, or make sure they were staying out of trouble. In a theme park it was their nature to ride rides, buy junk food, or swim in the water park. He basically got a free pass to spend the day with his daughter.

Packard was about to ask his daughter another question when a muffled boom came from overhead. Sounding somewhat like a shotgun blast, the noise was enough to draw his attention upward.

Along with everyone else around him.

He heard a scream of genuine terror, not like those produced as a natural reaction from a brief scare. Looking up, he saw a seat falling from the rotating cylinder, with a person still strapped to it.

About halfway down, the screaming stopped, which likely came from the shock of such a traumatic, unthinkable event. Packard recalled hearing something about how the human mind shut itself down in extreme situations.

Like impending death.

Knowing what was about to happen, he pulled his daughter against his chest, shielding her from a horror even he wanted to avoid.

Still, he was compelled to look, wondering what had gone so wrong that a complete seat had fallen from the ride. As the seat and its passenger hit the concrete walkway less than twenty feet away, Packard grimaced as blood and brain matter spattered everywhere around him. Bloody pieces of flesh and gray globs of cranium struck several horrified people, as though the fleshy chunks were slush hurled by a passing vehicle. Everyone appeared incapable of movement, simply stunned by the scene before them.

Trying to keep his daughter from looking, Packard began walking away from the line before park employees, and authorities, arrived. The last thing he wanted was for Nicole to be permanently scarred by the disturbing sight.

She struggled against his embrace, as though wanting to see what had occurred, but he knew she didn't really want to see. Visions like that tended to burn themselves into impressionable minds, sometimes to the point that they never recovered.

"Don't look, hon," he told her in a hushed voice. "That's not something you want to see."

"Oh my God," Nicole sobbed, obviously knowing what had happened.

Based on the sound he heard before the seat fell, Packard wondered if foul play might be involved. He led his daughter away from the tragic scene as people flocked to see what happened. He was only halfway across the large concrete lot when park officials, security, park police, and an Ohio State Highway Patrolman passed him in a rush.

He swallowed hard, almost feeling as though he had done something wrong, but thankful it wasn't him, or Nicole, in that seat. He had narrowly escaped death before, but this was different, almost as though an act of God had saved him.

Trying to imagine how the girl's parents were going to feel disturbed him even more, so he tried to put such thoughts out of his mind.

As far as he was concerned, his day at the park was done. He would be surprised if the entire park didn't shut down, but anything was possible.

Looking behind him, he saw the ride stopped around halfway up the tower. Though he couldn't see much detail, he knew the riders were terrified. Some shrieked, while others seemed to stare down in horror, wondering how such a thing had happened. Then he saw the vacant spot where the seat had dislodged.

Stopping where he stood, Packard noticed a dark spot in the middle of the space, along the purple paint. He let Nicole free from his embrace now that a wall of people stood between them and the dead girl.

"What's wrong?" his daughter asked.

Thinking the seat malfunction was no accident, he wasn't about to reveal that to his daughter, or talk to the authorities. If it was just him, he would tell all, but he wasn't dragging Nicole through any torment.

"Nothing," he finally answered her concern. "Let's get going."

She didn't argue, and as her teacher approached with several students, he gave her a look equivalent to the somber mood his heart felt.

"Was it—?" Nicole's teacher asked, apparently already knowing about the accident.

"It wasn't anyone we knew," Packard revealed, knowing none of Nicole's classmates were in line before them.

"Did you see it?" she asked.

A solemn nod of his head gave the answer.

He was about to suggest they walk further away when his cellular phone rang at his side. Plucking it from the holder, he noticed a message along the Caller ID box indicating it was a private number.

In no mood to answer the call, he decided it might be something important, though any other development seemed to pale compared to seeing a young woman lose her life.

He excused himself from the group a moment, stating the call might be important. Nicole seemed content to tell everyone about the event she barely saw.

"Packard here," he answered once he flipped the phone open.

A silence filled the line momentarily.

"So glad to finally speak with you, Sergeant Packard," a man's voice with a foreign accent said over the line.

It sounded Asian in nature, but Packard was never very good at deciphering accents. To him a Boston accent sounded similar to one from Chicago.

"Who is this?" Packard demanded, realizing instantly from the tone that this was no social call.

"Someone who wants to see you stay the entire day here at Great Realms."

"You'll excuse me if I decide to leave with my group in a few minutes," Packard stated more than asked.

Again, a second or two of silence.

"Then what if I told you the accident you just witnessed was no accident at all? And what if I told you there were lots more of them to come if you decided to leave the park?"

Packard felt his body tense. He glanced at his daughter, and her classmates, beginning to suspect he was in the middle of something that stemmed from the prior year's events.

Something he had no control over.

"What *exactly* do you want from me?" he asked sternly.

Now the voice was icy cold from the other end. There was no need for shouting, or demands, so the Oriental voice simply stated what it wanted.

"I want you to call Mr. Branson, Mr. Sorrell, and Mr. Maynard, and have them here within three hours. No weapons, no outside help, no police, and no tricks."

Packard instantly suspected he was being set up for slaughter with his three task force members. He was in no position to argue, but he had little right putting their lives in danger without their consent.

"And if I don't?" he decided to push the issue.

"Then not only will I kill anyone in this park I choose, including your lovely daughter, I will murder your task force, their families, and *you* at the times and places of my choosing. Here, I will offer you the opportunity to save some lives, including your own."

Packard doubted the sincerity of such an outlandish offer.

"How do I know you're for real?" he questioned. "Why are you doing this?"

"A year ago your men eliminated a group called the Koda. Let's just say I oversee a similar cell that has a vested interest in your health."

"So you're a terrorist," Packard heard himself mutter.

"Ticktock, Mr. Packard. In three hours, I'll know your decision."

An abrupt click reached the sergeant's ears, and he had a major decision to make.

And little time to make it.

He knew the Koda was a terrorist cell interested only in profit. They took jobs for the sake of money, making them more mercenary than terrorist, except for the fact that countless innocent people died at their hands.

Now he faced a crisis that appeared entirely personal. There was no financial gain killing people in a theme park, so revenge had to be their motivation.

Looking to his daughter, he wondered if he possessed the ability to keep her safe. He also wanted to know that he wasn't leading three men to their deaths if he called them. Clay was a problem solver, but he couldn't protect an entire theme park full of people.

Fuck, he thought to himself. He had no time to waste, but he had absolutely no plan of action. Feeling helpless, he looked at the group of students with distressed looks standing before him. Figuring he had time to deal with them momentarily, he went through his phone's index, finding Clay's name near the top.

Hesitating before pushing the send button, Packard felt strangely disconnected, as though in a dream. He knew calling his men was the complete opposite of police procedure, and calling them meant placing them in extreme danger.

He felt certain local authorities had ways of maintaining silent vigil if he contacted them, but park security wasn't nearly as well-trained. Most of them were teenagers. One wrong move gave the terrorists an excuse to begin systematically murdering park guests. Obviously they already had someone, or more than one person, infiltrating what little defense the theme park put forth.

Packard realized only one realistic choice existed if he wanted to keep casualties to a minimum.

Exhaling through his nose, he turned from the group, pressing the send button on his phone.

*   *   *   *

Just off the corner of Willard and Shipley in Muncie, Clay had made his way through several large bushes undetected, then to a large side window of the garage.

Peering inside, he saw six men moving wooden cases of what he suspected were drugs or weapons. Either way, he knew Packard had picked the wrong day to go on vacation.

Except for several wooden crates about the size of small footlockers, the garage was barren. Greasy film lined the windows, while the concrete foundation appeared covered with a thin layer of dust, only now disturbed by fresh footprints. The building had obviously been vacant for some time.

Clay was in no position to decide whether or not to call for backup. He had no proof of any wrongdoing, short of possible trespassing. To top it off, this was based on a tip. He had no idea where the tip came from, because one of his fellow officers had passed it on to him, probably from an anonymous source.

Many times, tips came from irritated people who wanted to cause trouble for their neighbors, or from senior citizens who overreacted to kids in their neighborhood. Warrants were not available from judges on hearsay, and simply stopping by a drug lair was dangerous without sufficient backup, so Clay wanted some facts.

Packard knew the intricacies of search and seizure, while Clay understood little more than he did as a patrolman. He was no ranking officer, so the call was never his to make. He sensed he was witnessing something big, that required immediate action, or their chances of catching the bigger fish were doomed.

He waited until the six men walked outside for a break, then accessed a window that pushed inward rather easily, quickly slipping inside undetected. Though outwardly cautious, the six men talked about several subjects, appearing more concerned about anything passing by in the streets. Clay realized they were using a rental truck of some sort, like those used to move furniture.

From his vantage point he couldn't see a logo on the truck's side.

Clay listened, making his way over to one of the boxes, using a nearby rusted hammer to pry the lid of one open. He glanced outside, finding the men preoccupied, then looked into the box. They were making idle talk, so he ignored their words, focusing on the crate's contents.

Despite the garage having no working electricity, enough natural light entered through the windows to allow him a view of stacked plastic bags inside the crate.

"Crack?" he wondered aloud, finding a white residue beneath the surface of each bag.

He lifted one, finding it close to the weight and texture of dried cookie dough. In his mind, there was no doubt the garage served as a layover point for crack cocaine, but these were moving men. If he wanted the bigger fish, as Packard always put it, an arrest at this location did little good.

It was an opportunity to damage their supply, and take months worth of product off the street. Another look at the six men let him know they were antsy, and with only a dozen or so crates left to move, they were probably about to finish the job at hand.

With most of the old garage's interior obscured by shadows, he made his way toward the window to slip outside before they detected him. As he neared the window, the worst possible thing that could happen did.

Clay had turned off his radio before entering the building, but mistakenly thought his cellular phone was in vibrate mode.

When its distinct chirping sound chimed, letting him know he had an incoming call, it drew the attention of six men as well.

Knowing he was spotted, Clay didn't even look their way. He dove through the window instead, dashing down the weed infested walk beside the garage as they scrambled to gather their weapons.

He heard one man bark orders for two of the men to find and "take care" of him.

Reaching a short fence toward the back of the garage, Clay leapt atop it, but instead of jumping over, he made a different leap, up to the roof.

His worst fear at the moment was contact with poison ivy, because he had an idea of how to deal with the two henchmen. Before they were within range, he plucked his phone from his side, seeing it was Packard calling him.

Packard was not one to call for simple conversation, like talking about the weather, or how his day went. On the other hand, he was on vacation.

Now that he knew who the caller was, he flipped the phone open and shut to sever the call. He then muted the phone's ringer, to ensure no more distractions came his way. The thought that Sorrell and Maynard had seen the activity crossed his mind. He didn't want them coming to his rescue against six armed men.

Clipping the phone to his belt, Clay heard the two men reach the short fence he had used to climb to his current position. Knowing they were going to cross it, he decided to act now, to prevent his two colleagues from making a mistake.

Sprinting to the end of the roof, he jumped down, catching the rooftop edge with his hands to steady himself. Like a gymnast, he swung his legs outward, catching the first thug squarely in the chest, throwing him back about ten feet.

Clay landed on the ground with catlike poise, immediately sending his right leg out in a straight kick that caught the other thug off balance, removing the gun from his grasp. Sending a stiff elbow into the man's forehead, he stunned him, then rammed the back of his head against the bricks, ending their brief skirmish.

The first henchman had lost his submachine gun in the brush. When Clay came his way, he decided to return to the safety of his four remaining buddies.

Not about to confront five armed men by himself, much less break the rules of his department, Clay had little choice but to find Sorrell and Maynard. He jumped the fence a second time, continuing through a nearby yard until he found his colleagues waiting for him in the unmarked car.

He climbed into the back seat, finding both of them craning their heads to see what news he had.

They had seen nothing of his plight.

"What's the plan?" Sorrell asked immediately.

"To drive us out of here before we get shot," Clay answered hurriedly, suspecting the five remaining men were either going to hunt them down or hastily leave the area.

"What?" both asked with surprise.

"I kind of stumbled on their crack operation."

"Fuck," Sorrell muttered, starting the car as the moving truck they had been loading the crates into screeched around the corner ahead.

In the opposite direction.

"Uh, do I follow it?" Sorrell asked.

Clay had their safety and the welfare of other officers to worry about. They were not equipped to combat automatic gunfire, and there was no time to summon the SWAT team.

"From a distance," he answered, still contemplating what he wanted to do in the longer term.

Clay now knew the company logo on the side was a moving company located in most cities. Tracing it might be difficult, but not impossible.

His phone vibrated at his side, prompting him to take it up.

Ironically, it was Packard again.

"Hey, Sarge," he answered as Sorrell stayed a few blocks behind the large truck, moving at a relatively slow pace.

"Clay, I don't have time to explain things, but I need you three in Cincinnati right away."

He had no doubt Packard was serious, but there seemed no logical reason why Packard would actually need them down there for anything.

"Can I ask why?"

"I think your buddy Sato had friends."

Clay felt a chill associated with the name his sergeant stated.

"They killed someone on a ride down here," Packard reported. "They called me on my cell phone, Clay. They know about *us*, and they knew I was coming here. And they threatened to randomly kill people if you three weren't here in three hours. Which is now closer to two hours and fifty minutes."

Requiring a few seconds to let the overwhelming amount of information sink in, Clay took a deep breath in through his nose.

"Who called you?"

"I don't know. He had an Oriental accent, but he was very deliberate in his speech."

"Anything stick out at you?"

"He said 'ticktock' to me."

Clay stiffened, thinking it was impossible that the voice might be another adversary from his past, but one closely related to his arch nemesis whom he'd killed in battle a year prior.

"I'll call you back in five minutes," he said after regaining his composure.

"They may be monitoring this line."

"Okay. We'll deal with that. We're on our way."

Clay shut the phone down as Sorrell turned to look at him.

"Get that license plate number," Clay told Maynard, pointing to the moving truck. "We have to break this off."

"Break it off?" Maynard exclaimed, as though they were supposed to use an unmarked car to pull over five heavily armed men.

"We don't have a choice," Clay explained calmly, despite Sorrell turning to issue him a stunned look.

Sorrell often expected him to singlehandedly handle everything, even more than he trusted Packard to.

"What's up?" he asked a few seconds later.

"We're heading to Cincinnati."

Maynard said nothing, simply giving a dumbfounded look to Sorrell, then to Clay.

"It seems the terrorists we dealt with last year have friends. And they've already killed someone at Great Realms, then demanded Tim bring us there or they would kill lots more."

Openly unhappy about the situation, Maynard gave a heated sigh.

"I didn't have anything to do with that shit last year," he stated. "What if I don't *want* to go along and get slaughtered by these pricks?"

"Then lots of innocent people will die," Clay replied. "I can't *make* you go, Rod, but do you really want the blood of hundreds of people on your hands?"

"No. But I don't want to walk in there and get shot in the head, either."

"If they simply wanted us dead, they would have done it already," Clay continued with a calmness that seemed to unnerve his companions. "No, they want something more from us."

"Like what?" Maynard almost demanded.

"Last year they tried to make us look like failures. I think they'll try to do the same thing."

"Which means if we go, they'll just kill more people? That sounds counterproductive."

Maynard's argument was sound, but Clay knew how his enemies thought. It had been years since he last saw most of them in Japan, but his master had failed to drive the corrupted nature from several of his prize students.

"And if we don't stop them today, they just annihilate us at will and move on to do the same thing somewhere else. Rod, I've already got a plan in the works. You think I'd be heading to Cincinnati, or asking you to, if I thought I was going to die today?"

"You've got your Japanese samurai thing, Clay. Ed and I aren't bulletproof and impervious to torture."

Ignoring him, Clay addressed Sorrell.

"Head south, Ed. If Rod is going to puss out, we have lots of room to dump him off along the way."

"I'm *in*," Maynard insisted. "I just hope you know what you're doing."

"So do I," Clay said under his breath, picking up his phone to dial another number.

CHAPTER 4

▼

Bill Branson had the displeasure of attending several meetings a day as the head of maintenance at the local Muncie hospital. When directly related to his job, he participated, paid attention, and interacted with his colleagues.

Other meetings were simply supervisor gatherings used to discuss current and potential policies throughout the hospital. What could easily be covered in a brief memo was often dragged out for an hour in a dull, windowless conference room.

He was in just such a meeting when his pager buzzed for the second time at his side. Taking it up for a look, he noticed the number for his own office, meaning his secretary needed him to call. This time there was a '911' after the number, meaning the need for him to call or return to the office was urgent.

His staff knew better than to contact him with petty issues, so he excused himself from the meeting, stating his department had some sort of emergency, then walked out.

His position allowed him unquestioned credibility.

Any number of things might be wrong at the hospital, requiring his attention. Water main breaks, supply issues, power outages, and elevator malfunctions were just some of the critical things Bill's people maintained and repaired.

Without a cellular phone on him, he decided to forego his portable radio, because his office was easily within walking distance. Though somewhat thankful to be out of the arduous meeting, Bill suspected he was about to discover something that required more work from him.

"What's going on?" he asked Jeanie Slocumb, his secretary, a few minutes later when he opened his office door.

His office manager and secretary had desks that actually shielded his own office space behind them.

Jeanie pulled a note from her desktop, virtually flinging it at him hurriedly.

"Your nephew called," she informed him. "He said it was extremely urgent that you call. Some kind of family matter."

Bill immediately thought of his brother, but knew he and Clay weren't very close. Still, Clay wasn't one to call him at work.

"Thanks," he said, then slipped around the doorway to his own office, plucking the phone from its receiver after seating himself.

Not knowing Clay's cell phone number off the top of his head, he dialed it from the sheet of paper Jeanie gave him.

"Hey," Clay answered the phone with a rushed voice.

"What's the matter?" Bill asked, not wasting any time.

"I need your help, Bill. In a big way."

Clay spent the next few minutes explaining the situation to him, so far as he knew it.

"So you're actually going into the belly of the beast?" Bill questioned Clay's judgment after the narrative.

"Yeah, but only because I'm counting on you to bail us out."

"What can I do?" Bill questioned, unable to imagine how he might be of service to his nephew, despite wanting to help Clay any way possible.

"It's time to put some of your training to the test. I need a few of your radios, a weapons pack from my house, and some inside information."

Standing, Bill reached over to close his office door all the way.

"I'm not sure I understand."

"I need you to use one of your trucks from the hospital and disguise yourself as a maintenance man of some kind. If you can get into the park, you might be able to infiltrate the employment records, or get around to see where the bad guys are."

"You think they're working at the park?"

"How else could they have rigged a ride to blow up just minutes after the park opened? They're getting in there somehow, and so can you."

Bill swallowed hard. Clay requested he do something he felt completely unready to do. After all, he had a career, a marriage, and very little training from Clay about infiltrating buildings.

"I'm not much of a computer guy," he said, not wanting to let his nephew down. "I can only do so much, even if I get in."

"You *will* get in. Our lives depend on it."

Clay said something to one of the other officers with him before continuing.

"Once I get to the park my calls are probably going to be monitored, so we need to have a plan ready by the time I arrive. Basic communication and that sort of thing."

"It's been years since I've been to a theme park, Clay. What the hell am I supposed to pose as?"

"They probably have in-house guys to repair the rides, so maybe a computer tech, or a phone guy. You'll think of something."

"You're so inspiring," Bill muttered sarcastically. "I'll call you once I'm on the road."

"Thanks, Bill. I owe you one."

"More like three, if we live through this."

Hanging up, Bill wasted little time carrying out the first phase of his plan. He stepped from his office, informing his secretary he was going home for the day because of a family emergency, then walked down the hall to snag a shirt that went with the navy blue work pants at his house.

He planned on being overly prepared, just in case a better idea came to him.

Walking into the storage area, he found an old work shirt with the name "Tony" on it. Left by an employee who recently quit for another position, the shirt would suffice. He took it, stuffed it into a nearby sack, and proceeded to the sign shop, which was one of the numerous shops included within his department.

Though they typically manufactured metal signs and decals, the shop also did lettering and vinyl signs. As he walked inside, his mind scrambled for an idea of what to put on one of the utility trucks the hospital owned. Gaining access to a vehicle was no problem, but marking it well enough to fool park security was a completely different issue.

"Need something, Mr. Branson?" Jim Baldwin, the only employee in the shop, asked him as he walked inside.

"Have you seen Mike about the job on the seventh floor?" Bill asked almost casually, knowing the sign department had as assignment coming their way.

"No. I can see him now, if you like."

"Please."

Baldwin gave him a funny stare, since it was highly unusual for Bill to personally walk into any shop and address the employees personally. Usually, he waited until they came into his office, or had one of his assistant managers deal with the laborers.

Now alone in the shop, Bill looked frantically for something useful. He found magnetic lettering, which looked too large and bulky to use on a truck. An idea struck him as he touched the lettering. One of the interns who parked beside him in the garage had a computer business on the side. His car had a vinyl sign on either side, with a business name and phone number in colorful lettering.

Snagging two portable radios from their chargers on the way out of the shop, Bill had a suspicion he might be able to pull off the improbable and gain access to the park.

But then what?

He had at least a few hours to formulate a real plan because he still had to travel to Clay's house. Why his nephew wanted handheld weapons was beyond him, but he suspected the terrorists might share training similar to his. Clay's final battle with Sato had been honorable, using only handheld weapons the year prior, but Bill had little faith in the honesty of terrorists.

He planned on bringing at least one firearm along for his own protection, hoping this entire plan of Clay's didn't land him in jail.

Packing his accessories into the bag, he headed down the basement corridor toward the closest exit. The whole story sounded too much like an action movie to be real, but he knew firsthand from the year before how Sato's group operated. He also knew he was the one thing between the terrorists and their objective.

Feeling less than confident about his abilities, he took a set of stairs upward, seeing sunlight through a window. The glare nearly blinded him, but it was the first natural light he'd seen since arriving to work.

His body felt numb, as though part of a strange dream he had no control over, which wasn't so far from the truth in his mind.

He had complete faith in his nephew, which was the only reason he risked everything to head toward Cincinnati. Bill hoped Clay's plan spared innocent lives at the theme park, and prayed the terrorists had no idea he was Clay's backup plan.

CHAPTER 5

▼

Packard's worst fears quickly unfolded before his eyes.

Not only was the park not closing, but his daughter and her classmates were staying. By now most of them had masked their horror toward the tragic event with gossip about what might have caused it.

If only they knew, the father of two thought to himself.

Completely torn, he felt obligated to guard Nicole, but wanted an opportunity to explore the park, and begin looking for clues. Saying anything to the chaperones simply made him look bad, or raised questions about what he knew.

"What's the matter, Dad?" Nicole asked as they stood near the park's entrance.

Around them, the main strip had half a dozen large water fountains that sprayed water upward, surrounded by a pool and a decorative metal fence like some people use in their yards.

Shops and small restaurants, along with some seating, lined the sides of the main strip, surrounding the fountain area.

"Other than the obvious, I guess nothing's wrong."

"You're acting weird. I know you see stuff like that all the time."

Packard shook his head.

"I *don't* see stuff like that all the time. You watch way too much TV."

"Maybe. But you're still acting weird."

Turning toward the front gate, Packard noticed more people filtering through the metal detectors, then the turnstiles as they presented their tickets. Most were probably completely unaware of the alleged accident from the previous hour.

Subconsciously paying attention, he had noticed the park security sectioning off the Skydiver area, closing the ride down completely. Most of the people in line, or on the ride itself, were whisked away for questioning, and he saw someone walk by with a badge he suspected was a coroner.

Apparently the girl was with a group, because about a dozen people convened near the ride, talking to park officials. Many of them broke down in tears, but Packard doubted any of them were family members. Their torment was due to be long, starting with the shocking news they would likely receive within a few hours.

"We're waiting for the rest of the kids and chaperones to return," a female teacher informed Packard.

"Then heading home?" he asked with more anxiety than he cared to show.

"Probably. Several students witnessed the accident, and they aren't holding up very well."

"Yeah. I can sympathize."

Her look softened considerably as she tried forcing an understanding grin.

"I suppose you're more than ready to get out of here," she said.

He didn't dare tell the truth that he planned on staying behind. If he said anything before the last moment, a hundred questions would fly his way.

Simply giving a nod, Packard wondered how long it was going to take for the others to return. Since he wasn't far from food or shopping, he decided to see if he might cheer up his daughter.

"I'm going to take Nicky to the shops," he informed the teacher. "We'll just be over there."

He pointed to let her know the area.

"That's fine. It'll probably be a little while before the other kids get here."

Packard suspected they were going to be more than a little disappointed their day was cut short, but if the truth ever came out, they would count themselves lucky.

"Let's take a walk," he said to his daughter, leading her toward the shops.

"Did you call Mom to tell her what happened?" his daughter inquired.

"No."

"Then who was on the phone with you?"

"I talked to Clay for a minute."

"And?"

"And what?"

"You were on the phone three or four times."

Nicole had reached an age where no answer seemed satisfactory, and lying only prolonged the stream of inquiries. For her sake, however, he needed to lie.

He had yet to manufacture an answer when they reached the closest ice-cream stand.

"Does this have anything to do with what happened last year, Dad?"

Intentionally giving her a strange look, he shook his head negatively.

"Why would you ask that?"

"I just don't think that ride would fall apart on its own. Something happened to that seat."

Instead of replying, he ordered them each an ice-cream cone. Leading the way over to a number of tables, complete with seating and patio umbrellas, he took a seat.

He didn't feel much like eating, but for Nicole's sake, he needed to act like nothing aside from the obvious was wrong. No good plan had come to him, because he felt like a sitting duck. Unable to look around, Packard had no idea who was friend or foe inside the park. He intentionally looked for anyone of Asian or Middle Eastern appearance, but most of the workers looked like high school kids.

Even the security force consisted of kids who generally fell short of college age. Only once had he seen an armed officer with a park uniform different from those on the security force. He saw no opportunity to get around the caller's orders, especially if the man knew his three officers.

He hoped Clay had some sort of plan, but even he had little idea who they were up against.

Clay had called back, but relayed little information to him. The three were on their way, and Packard had given them the quickest route possible, since he visited the park once or twice a year.

"Do you think something happened to that seat?" Nicole asked after a few minutes, apparently not content since he failed to answer her question.

"I don't know."

"You heard that explosion, the same as everyone else. You don't have to protect me, Dad."

He let a smirk slip.

"No, I guess I don't. But I still like to."

Finishing his cone, he wiped his mouth with a napkin.

"Something went wrong with that seat, but I'm no expert on how those things work."

"Dad, I heard an explosion."

"How do you know the metal didn't just buckle loose? That can make a lot of noise, you know."

Nicole crossed her arms as she gave him a look that said she didn't buy one word of what he was saying.

"You're too much like your mother."

Deciding to let him off the hook, Nicole changed the subject.

"I can't believe they're making us leave because of that. All the other schools are staying."

"Maybe it's for the best."

"We drive all the way here, stay ten minutes, then get gathered like concentration camp prisoners at the entrance? They could at least let us get in one ride."

"Nice comparison there, dear. We'll be able to come back here some other time."

Packard didn't feel much like talking, but he wasn't about to tell his daughter to hush, fearing he might alienate her. At the moment he didn't want her out of his sight, so he kept the conversation going.

"You're not being very compassionate, considering someone just died right in front of us," Packard informed his daughter. "I can't believe you'd still want to ride something."

"You seem to think it's one big accident, even though they check these rides daily."

"How do you know so much about theme park affairs?"

"I watch Discovery Channel."

"Ah. Smart girl."

Nicole finished her snack, then returned to the conversation.

"I do feel bad for that girl, but it just stinks. We've been looking forward to this trip since March."

Packard understood. The kids had raised money for the trip, and he recalled competing against several other officers to sell the most candy bars for Nicole. They had also performed well on their state tests because the trip provided motivation. If she found out the accident, and the reason she was about to go home, was directly related to a revenge plot against her father, Nicole would use that as leverage to come back later that summer.

If I live through this, Packard thought.

A few minutes later Nicole's friends returned to the front gate, so she looked to him with anticipation in her eyes.

"Go ahead," Packard said with an airy wave of his hand.

He felt fortunate to have spent so much time with her already. Nicole had reached the age where friends were important, which meant sleep overs, shopping, and lots of time away from parents.

With a sullen grin, he watched her walk toward her friends, seeing them all hug after apparently learning the tragic news. Again, Nicole began explaining the incident to them, putting a brave face forward.

Turning away from them, so it didn't appear he was staring, Packard eyed the shops, then returned his gaze to the front gate. People continued to enter the park, oblivious to the terrible news, or completely unconcerned.

He wondered when the news people might show up.

Then he saw it. Above the entrance gate, which housed several shops to either side, since it was one building, was a second story. He suspected corporate offices were housed there, or perhaps meetings took place in conference rooms.

What really got his attention, however, was someone holding a pair of binoculars only a few feet behind one of the large windows that seemed to comprise the second level. Packard barely caught a glimpse of what the man held, because he turned away so quickly.

He was unable to see any details concerning the man's build or face, but thought for certain he was wearing some sort of park security uniform.

Packard stood up for a better look through the tinted glass, but the man did not turn around, and vanished from sight within a few seconds. Wondering where the access point to the upstairs might be, he quickly dismissed the notion of doing anything that might look inappropriate while his daughter was nearby.

A few minutes later the rest of the students, teachers, and chaperones returned. Packard walked toward the group, still trying to formulate exactly what he wanted to tell his daughter's teacher.

He pulled her aside as the students protested the decision to leave. Some of the teachers looked reluctant to leave the park now that the students didn't seem upset. People still entered the park at regular intervals.

"What's the matter?" Miss Austin asked him once they were separated from the pack.

He thought her first name was Jill, but wasn't positive, so he decided not to address her personally.

"You're not considering letting the students stay, are you?" he asked as casually as possible.

"Well, they don't seem very traumatized by the whole ordeal, and we *did* drive all the way here."

What she said was logical under normal circumstances.

"What happened on that ride was no accident," Packard decided to reveal.

Shock registered on her face.

"Are you sure?"

"*Positive*," he assured her. "It is definitely best that you get the students out of here right away."

She nodded affirmatively, but slowly, letting his words sink in. After starting to turn, she squared up with him, giving a concerned look.

"What about you?"

"I have to stay," Packard replied. "Don't worry about me. I have a way home."

"If you're wanting to help the authorities, we can wait for you."

Packard shook his head.

"No. Get the students out of here now. I'll feel much better if I know Nicky is on the way home."

"Who could have done such a thing? And how could they have gotten anything past the metal detectors?"

Packard hesitated. She was inquisitive, but asking the right questions.

"They had help. And I'm pretty sure it came from the inside."

More than a little surprised, she seemed to have no response to his words.

"For your own safety, get them and yourself out of here," he implored. "I'll deal with whatever's going on around here."

Miss Austin gave him a brief nod, apparently understanding they might be watched, because she appeared hesitant to look around.

"Do you want to talk to Nicky before we leave?" she asked.

Packard hesitated, deciding he might never see his daughter again. Putting her life in any danger was not an option, either.

"No. Just tell her I love her."

He knew he wasn't putting forth a very good front, but the sooner the group left, the better his chances of finding the people responsible became.

The teacher looked hesitant, as though she knew his position wasn't everything he had stated.

"Are there any other messages you want to send?"

"No," he answered emphatically. "Go ahead and get them out of here so I can take care of what needs to be done."

She nodded, turned to leave, then spoke with several teachers, who immediately began ushering the students toward the exit gates. He turned to tend to the matters at hand, then glanced back, finding his daughter staring at him with grave concern.

Slowly blowing her a kiss, he walked out of her view before she had a chance to react, seeing a teacher step her way to intercept her.

Despite a huge burden being lifted from his mind, Packard realized he remained trapped in a theme park with thousands of people. Looking around, he saw smiles, kids skipping along gleefully, and employees oblivious to the fact someone who worked with them was a terrorist.

"It has to be someone on the inside," Packard muttered to himself, looking at his watch.

His officers had under two hours to arrive, but if Sorrell was driving, he doubted it would take nearly that long.

CHAPTER 6

▼

Jack Turpin's day wasn't going as smoothly as he originally planned.

Agents of the Federal Bureau of Investigation had it easy on television. In a fictional world there was no time to show what a pain in the ass airline flights were, or the difficulty of securing a rental car at the last minute.

Solving the case was always straightforward, as was an impending arrest. In truth, nothing proved quite so simple, but Turpin's new job description made life a bit easier for him.

A few years over fifty, he had actually retired from the Houston Police Department in Texas, serving a tour during the Gulf War in Iraq from 1991 until the following year. Some of his colleagues affectionately called the stint his working vacation, because he left his department while overseas, returning to police work almost immediately upon his return.

His unit was called upon once again, which effectively ended Turpin's career in law enforcement when he was honorably discharged from the United States Army Reserves. A peacekeeping mission in Iraq landed his entire unit in the hospital after they were overcome by a chemical agent.

Strangely enough, everyone recovered, though the military revealed few details about their health or the investigation into the chemical mishap. Physically, Turpin felt and appeared fine, but the secrecy prompted him to visit his doctor for a blood test.

When the results came back, the retired police officer learned his blood had been chemically altered by the chemical compound. By no means harmful to him, the chemicals from the accident left a strange new cell that attached itself to his red blood cells.

Assured he wasn't going to die, but couldn't be cleared medically to return to work for the police department, Turpin found himself at an impasse. Though the FBI had strict rules about hiring processes and requirements, an experimental group of rogue agents was under the command of Alan Stewart, the assistant director of the Los Angeles branch.

Turpin came to work for Stewart, always pondering in the back of his mind if the government hired him to track his activities rather than threaten him.

As Turpin walked toward city hall in Muncie, he didn't think the term "rogue" quite described the nature of his work. True, his activities were not closely monitored, and he had little reason, or need, to report his activities to supervisors, but he wasn't exactly given free run of the country either.

In number, there was a maximum of five rogue agents at any given time. They were assigned the worst of cases, depending on their specialty. Some sought out the most violent criminals, sometimes bringing them in singlehandedly, while others tracked down serial killers across state lines.

Turpin possessed several specialties, most stemming from his combat service. He was an expert in firearms and explosives, knew quite a bit about communications, spoke fluent Spanish, and was an avid motorcyclist.

His first wife was the reason he spoke Spanish, but it also came in handy during his career in public safety. Her parents were from Mexico, so she constantly spoke her native language. Turpin decided rather quickly he was tired of being left out of the loop, so he learned. He always suspected his in-laws talked badly about him, so it surprised them when he understood what they said one day, and had a comeback for their pointed remarks.

Entering city hall through the door closest to all of the patrol cars, he approached a desk sergeant, presented his credentials, and asked where he might find Clay Branson.

"He's on a task force," the black sergeant answered. "Want me to try raising him on the radio?"

"Please," Turpin answered with a courteous nod.

By no means had the move from Texas to Los Angeles been easy for the agent. He still wore his Stetson hat and cowboy boots regularly. Owning a touring-style motorcycle and two horses wasn't as easy in a state he considered far more liberal than his own, but he found a home outside city limits with no nearby neighbors.

Today he had no hat with him, but the black leather cowboy boots gleamed from a fresh shoe shine at the airport just a few hours earlier.

Rogue agents tended to dress a bit more casually when possible, but his agenda bordering the noontime hour required him to wear a dark suit. Turpin didn't have time for people to question his authenticity or slow him down based on his appearance.

Looking into the glossy desktop, his brown eyes spied his graying fringe of dark hair, accompanied by a peppered mustache with only a handful of surviving black hairs. Turpin worked out regularly, so he remained in excellent physical condition, drawing stares from women of all ages wherever he went. He attributed the attention to his attire instead of his personal grooming, finding few people disliked a cowboy.

After three marriages he was no longer the marrying type, but he was prone to the occasional fling, or brief relationships. He had what he called an on and off relationship with an assistant district attorney in Los Angeles. They had spoken during several court cases, had dinner, and compared their careers.

On what Turpin called layovers, he stayed at her place for a night or two between assignments. He had done commercial trucking before joining the Houston police force, which was a contributing factor to his wayward nature.

Turpin paced the floor a moment, waiting for the desk sergeant to report something. Only the sound of his boots clopping against the floor kept him company.

His impression of Muncie was like most cities he visited. It held a little bit of everything a person needed, but lacked the flair big cities displayed. Of course he usually buried his nose in government maps and printouts while driving or flying, so he seldom viewed much scenery.

Before an answer came from the desk sergeant, the elevator doors behind him opened, revealing several men in white uniform shirts. Since street officers wore dark blue uniforms, almost black in color, he assumed the two men before him were the top brass.

"Chief Ron Salyer," a younger man with a full head of black hair said, offering his hand toward Turpin. "And this is my deputy chief, Gerald Carter."

"Special Agent Jack Turpin."

Turpin shook hands with each of them, wondering if he needed to check with the desk sergeant or not.

"I'm not accustomed to such a reception," Turpin said, realizing his Southern accent probably sounded a bit thick to them.

Occasionally people had difficulty understanding him at first. Northern states had their own accents which he loved hearing when he visited the Boston or Chicago areas.

"We overheard the radio traffic, and thought we might be of service," Salyer said. "We were just on our way to lunch if you care to join us."

"Thanks, but no," Turpin answered. "I'm just in town long enough to meet with your officer."

Turpin didn't realize the sergeant had stated an FBI agent was looking for Branson. Perhaps the chief had simply inferred it from the radio traffic, or happened to have good timing.

"Is this a personal visit, or business?" Salyer inquired.

"Business," Turpin replied hesitantly, sensing he was being probed by a man who probably had his thumb on everything.

Micromanagement came to mind as the term Turpin heard thrown around his precinct in Houston several times regarding a deputy chief who monitored everyone virtually all the time.

Salyer stood before him a moment, saying nothing, as though expecting the agent to elaborate.

Turpin did not.

"Well," Salyer finally said with an informal salute meant to be a wave good-bye. "It was good meeting you, Agent Turpin."

"Thanks, Chief," the agent replied, making it obvious he was ready to be left alone.

Turpin knew enough about Clay Branson, and the prior year's events to understand why the chief of police might be concerned. Locally there were lots of unanswered questions, and even more speculation.

His reason for seeking the young man had nothing to do with those events, or his membership in the drug task force.

"Any luck?" he asked the sergeant once the chiefs had exited through the double doors for their lunch hour.

"Nothing. I can't raise any of them on their radios."

"I kind of made a special trip for this," Turpin revealed. "How can I get in touch with him? *Soon*."

Replying with a corkscrewed face that indicated it might not be so easy, the sergeant sat down at his computer, then accessed a program that listed everyone on their department. It also seemed to list every other local police and fire department, as well as emergency medical personnel working for the county.

Within a few minutes, Turpin had a sheet of paper containing the names and every available phone number and address for each task force member.

"I saw three of them here this morning," the sergeant said. "Packard wasn't with them, but I think he's on a personal day."

"Any idea where they were going?"

"Hard telling. They operate pretty freely."

Turpin could relate to free reign.

"Thanks very much for your help," the agent said before heading toward the double doors.

As he exited city hall, he found the chief and deputy chief talking beside a dark sedan. Upon seeing him, they ceased communication, both entering the same car.

Turpin suddenly felt like a marshal in the Wild West, entering a town full of desperados and bandits. He wasn't forthcoming about his reasons for seeking out Branson, but he didn't have to be.

He seated himself inside his rental car, looked at the list, and wondered exactly where to begin. Even task forces typically answered their radios, unless they were in a zone requiring complete silence.

Those instances were typically few and far between, so he wondered what the task force was doing.

*   *   *   *

Packard wasted little time making his way back to the Skydiver, which was now shut down, with red and yellow scene tape all around it. Since it was in the open, comparatively speaking, tape was about the only way to keep people out of the area.

Though the layman probably wondered what so many security officers and park officials were doing there, Packard recognized telltale signs that a coroner had arrived. Several blankets covered the cot the ambulance service would use to remove the body, and though they were trying to be discreet, Packard knew more truth than any of them.

He viewed the ride a bit more closely now, realizing what he thought was a spot where the blast had occurred was actually just a worn spot where the seat made contact with the main structure. Several technicians observed both the spot and the chair itself, which had remained mostly intact. One side of the metal seat appeared crumpled, because it took the brunt of the impact, along with the rider.

Everyone seemed somewhat casual about how they went about their work. Perhaps they were practicing discretion, but the police sergeant thought they were a bit too laid back.

Packard worried it might take hours, perhaps even days, to determine a blast of some sort caused the malfunction. Scolding himself for dwelling on things beyond his control, he studied anyone nearby wearing a park uniform. He looked for anyone who might be of foreign appearance or descent.

Events from the previous year had taught him the enemy could be American, or even female. Some people had a price, even at the cost of their loyalty or patriotism. Packard had only a voice on the phone as circumstantial evidence, but he knew the man wasn't working alone.

Even so, he doubted an influx of international workers could infiltrate a family-owned theme park. Of course they probably didn't have to if the right person was able to get them inside at any given time.

Failing to find anyone who stood out, Packard examined the scene one last time, seeing nothing new. In the park's hurry to protect their image, he wondered if their internal investigation might be compromised.

Realizing he should have feared more for his own safety at this point, Packard devoted his nervous energy toward finding answers. He knew the terrorist group was not going to act until the other three officers arrived, and even then, he doubted they would attract attention until the perfect time.

Walking away from the area, he realized he was somewhat unfamiliar with the park's layout. While his daughter knew every eatery and ride's location, he usually stumbled around until he found what he was looking for.

Without trying to appear obvious, he cautiously surveyed the area around him as he walked, wondering if he was being monitored. It occurred to him that keeping tabs on him in the park, and researching his home life had to be a very involved project.

Clay seemed somewhat reluctant to tell him details over the phone, but he suspected the young officer knew who was behind the scheme. For the time being, Packard could only kill time and wonder what his future held.

As he passed a cotton candy vendor, his cellular phone rang at his side.

Again, the ID stated it was a private number calling him.

"Packard," he answered.

"Sergeant Packard?" a voice with a soft, easy drawl asked from the other end.

"Yes."

"My name is Jack Turpin. I'm with the FBI. I've been trying to reach one of the officers under your command this morning, but haven't had much luck. I hear you're on a personal day, so I hate to bother you."

Packard's mind raced with possibilities. If this man spoke the truth, Packard was unwilling to reveal too many facts, because the call might be overheard.

If he was lying, he might be part of the terrorist faction determined to bring the task force to the theme park.

Either way, he needed information, or proof of the man's identity, but talking for a lengthy time was no option.

"Which one are you looking for?" Packard asked, trying to be civil.

"Clay Branson. Any idea where I can find him?"

"Well, I'm at Great Realms just outside of Cincinnati, so I haven't been around the boys at all today."

"Little vacation, huh?"

"You could say that."

Packard looked around uneasily, seeing no eyes aimed in his direction.

"How did you get this number?" Packard inquired, deciding to test the agent's authenticity.

"A desk sergeant at city hall gave me all of your numbers."

"Any particular reason you're needing Clay?"

Turpin remained silent a few seconds.

"That's between me and him, sir."

"I see. I'm in a bit of a pickle here, Agent Turpin. I'm sure a G-Man like yourself knows a little something about technology."

Again, a few seconds of silence.

"I'm not a computer expert by any means, if that's what you're getting at."

"No. Nothing like that. What are the chances someone could pick up this particular phone conversation on a scanner?"

"Slim to none. If your cell phone is a newer model, it's probably digital. They have a band different than those picked up by everyday scanners."

Packard had to know the entire truth.

"But it is possible, isn't it?"

"Perhaps," the drawled voice returned. "There are places in Canada and overseas that make such devices, but they're illegal. Why are we discussing this?"

"I'm in a theme park with potentially hundreds or thousands of phones. What are the chances of this particular conversation being overheard?"

"Maybe one in a thousand. Probably less likely than that. Again, why are we discussing this?"

Packard decided there was no harm in disclosing a little bit of something to the agent. If he was legitimate, he might be of help, and if he was dirty, then it was already too late.

"If you want to talk to Clay, you're going to have to come here. He's on his way, and we have a situation brewing. I suspect someone in your position probably knows what happened to us last year, and if you do, what we're about to get into is much, much worse."

"I know a little something. If you can promise me Branson will be there, I can be there in two hours."

"He will be."

"Good enough. Hope to see you in two hours."

"Looking forward to it," Packard answered with as comforted a voice as he could offer.

He still felt uneasy about talking on the phone, but if Turpin was right, it seemed fairly safe. After all, there were any number of people using phones and short-range radios.

Unless, of course, his frequency had already been locked in by a scanning device.

"Shit," he muttered, wondering if he had just done a completely wrong thing.

CHAPTER 7

▼

When Clay led the way to the front gate, he looked around suspiciously, wondering if the task force was being monitored.

Kids skipped ahead to the metal detectors with their parents, obviously ready for a day of fun in the sun. Clay couldn't help but wonder if some of them might be dead by the day's end.

Maynard and Sorrell had agreed to approach the gate separately, but Sorrell lacked funds for a ticket, and his wife had the credit card, so Clay and Maynard chipped in for his ticket fare.

During the trip Maynard found opportunity to remove his leather chaps, but complained about having to wear heavy boots all day. His shirt and black riding boots gave away the fact that he rode motorcycles, but slight discomfort was going to be the least of his worries.

By staying separate the officers hoped to avoid detection, at least long enough to meet with Packard and create some sort of plan.

Clay had also contacted his uncle, and though Bill was far from thrilled about being involved in their dilemma, he was only half an hour behind them in traffic. He seemed to have a good idea about getting into the park with Clay's requested supplies, using a truck marked with a computer technician's label.

Sorrell had suggested several angles Bill might use since the park was building a new metal coaster, and most every shop had credit card machines. Clay didn't consider his uncle a smooth talker, but Bill was rational and intelligent enough to talk above someone's head long enough that they would likely give in.

After stepping through the metal detectors, Clay continued to observe everyone around him as he replaced his wallet and his keys to their rightful pockets.

His wallet had a replica of his police badge in it, which he wasn't certain was a great idea if trouble came their way. Their authority was limited to their jurisdiction, and their word wasn't worth much in another state.

Clay presented his ticket to a lady seated at the turnstile, then walked inside, his eyes taking in the view of a huge observation tower at the opposite end of the water fountains and the pool that contained them.

Along the sides he saw shops and restaurants of every kind, but he wasn't about to take a tour of the facility. He hadn't been to the park since childhood, and the main drag didn't look much different. A makeover in the form of brighter colors and new displays was something new, but the view appeared much the same.

Maynard and Sorrell were eventually coming in behind him, but they had already planned to meet at a pizza place beyond the observation tower. It was enclosed, providing them an opportunity to speak privately before the terrorists issued further demands.

Doing his best to casually stroll down the main strip, Clay watched families being badgered by employees with cameras, though they left him alone. It was the park's way of making money by having people pay for memory photos of their trip, just in case they didn't pack a camera of their own.

Since he was alone, they didn't ask him to stop for a photo in front of the water fountains and observation tower.

He wondered how Bill was going to fare, but his primary concern remained when they were supposed to meet up with Packard. The sergeant relayed information that the terrorist on the phone said he would know if the three officers arrived. Clay wanted to know if this was true, so he held off instead of calling Packard.

As he passed the observation tower, which was taller than any building in Muncie, he stared upward, seeing two separate elevator cars travel up and down simultaneously with guests. The tower was visible from the highway for miles around, supported by huge metal columns at its base, which allowed guests to walk beneath much of its steel structure.

Using Sorrell's directions, Clay reached the restaurant within a few minutes, seating himself inside. He carefully observed the area around him, noticing nothing strange about any of the people. Most were with families, and no one outside the pizza parlor seemed to be faking busyness.

Part of Clay's overseas training involved an uncanny sense of nearby danger. Usually, he knew when physical danger drew near, but ill will was a different case.

He had an idea who the mastermind was drawing them to the park, based on what little Packard was able to tell him. He was a Korean man named Chung-Hee Kim who came to Japan as one of the many stragglers Clay's *sensei* taught.

Like Sato, he had impure thoughts about life in general, and seemed inclined to take an easier path, instead of working for the things he wanted. Though he never showed their master his true intentions, the man seemed to know better.

Clay was his master's favorite, and he made no real secret of that. Sato killed Clay's wife and child in Japan, which in essence ended Clay's tenure there. He searched for Sato, losing touch with the clan, and its members.

He suspected Kim had likely joined Sato in mercenary efforts, but failed to understand why any loyalty would exist beyond their business ties.

As Maynard entered the parlor, Clay reflected upon Kim's first name, which meant "righteous" when translated from Korean. Ironic, Clay thought as he watched Maynard order a slice of pizza and a Coke from the counter.

Maynard caught the quirky look Clay shot him when he seated himself at the table.

"I might as well have a decent last meal," the officer stated.

"We're all walking out of here alive if I have anything to say about it."

After chomping into his slice of pizza, Maynard eyed him with a bit of suspicion.

"You know something about this, don't you?"

"I think I know who's behind it."

"Is it related to what happened last year?"

Clay looked outside, seeing Sorrell drawing near the restaurant. He seemed to be eyeing everything around him, which made him look openly nervous.

"I think the man behind it was a business partner with Khumpa."

"Is he trained, well, like you?"

Now it was Clay's turn to shoot a less than friendly expression.

"Rod, it's in your best interest not to bring up my extensive training. The more you know about me, the more danger you put yourself in."

"Oh, like sitting in the middle of a theme park with terrorists threatening to kill everyone around me?"

Maynard's sarcasm was wasted on Clay, and as Sorrell sat down, he seemed to sense the tension around him.

"I don't think I was followed," Sorrell reported.

"Your gawking tourist act wasn't very believable," Clay stated.

Sorrell ignored him, staring at Maynard, who was biting into his pizza.

"I was hungry," Maynard said defensively. "And Clay here was just about to tell us who wants us dead."

"No, I'm not," Clay said. "I just want you both to know I *think* I know who he is. If I'm right, he's very dangerous, and probably has friends like Khumpa did."

"What do we do?" Sorrell asked.

"We wait for Tim to call us. They're directing everything through him for some reason. And if they knew he was coming here today, they probably know everything about all of us."

Maynard finished his pizza slice, wiped his hands, and felt instinctively for the gun usually at his side. They had all left their weapons in the vehicle, and when they paid for parking at the first entrance, they had Maynard cover himself in a blanket in the back seat, so it wasn't obvious that three men arrived in the same car.

"I feel like shark bait," he admitted.

"Our advantage is they want us *here* specifically for something," Clay said. "We have to figure out what it is and give Bill a chance to uncover their motives before we do anything."

"No offense, but I'm not sure your uncle is exactly an adventurous kind of guy," Sorrell noted. "What if they arrest him when he tries to get in here?"

"Then we're fucked, and he knows it," Clay replied. "No matter what, he'll find a way in."

*　　*　　*　　*

As Bill approached the park in the hospital truck, he decided deliveries had to be in a special part of the park for two reasons.

One, the main entrance had canopies like toll booths, which were low, not allowing for larger vehicles to pass.

Secondly, he noticed a separate drive for an employee entrance, which he assumed was also where deliveries and repairmen entered the park to avoid public detection.

Pulling hesitantly into the drive he thought about his future, and what a difference prison was going to be compared to living in a brand new house, larger than most in his community. He packed several firearms, a fair amount of his nephew's handheld steel weapons, and about a dozen computer parts he borrowed from the hospital to pull off the charade.

Very little activity occurred around the employee entrance, mostly because it seemed to be a simple concrete drive that lasted half a minute. He spied a guard shack in the distance, swallowing hard as he tried to bury his nervousness.

"Good afternoon," the guard said with an easy grin when Bill pulled to a stop, rolling down his window.

Thank God he's friendly, Bill thought, smelling hotdogs from within the guard shack. It seemed so quiet the man probably had little to do except eat and greet.

"Same to you," Bill replied, putting forth the best smile he could muster. "I'm here to repair the digital camera systems on a few of your rides."

A glance inside revealed monitors flipping between several different views. There were eight monitors in all, and they seemed to focus on external aspects of the park, as well as wooded areas, probably at the edges of the park property.

He also noticed several photos inside, including one of the guard with a person Bill assumed was his brother, in military attire.

Clay had taught him to be cautious of his environment, and to an extent, Bill always remained wary. Now he knew how to take in his surroundings with a single glance.

"Ever been here before?" the guard inquired.

"Negative," Bill answered.

"Do you have an invoice with you?" the guard asked, trying to be cooperative, but getting a bit more serious.

"No. Look, I just drove almost three hours to get here. I've got the parts with me, and it'll only take me an hour or so to fix the things. That's money your park is losing if they aren't working properly."

Still, the guard seemed reluctant to simply take his word.

"Without an invoice, or some sort of authorization, I can't just let you in."

"Then call your boss, or whoever handles the photography stuff."

Bill held up some of the parts he had borrowed from the hospital. In reality, they were discontinued parts for old security monitors, but they looked brand new, and highly technical.

"They don't run when these are burned out."

The guard grunted skeptically, beginning to turn toward his phone.

"It wasn't even this hard getting things done in the Army," Bill added just above a whisper, hoping to get a bite.

He did.

"Army, huh? When did you serve?"

"Enlisted in 1989, and got out last year. Now I work for my brother fixing computers and digital equipment."

"Gulf War vet?"

"Negative. My unit never got deployed."

"You're lucky. I spent the better part of two years over there."

Though not exactly eating out of his hand, the guard had lightened up somewhat. Bill decided to give himself a way out, just in case the guard was planning on calling someone.

"Look, I can get to a copy shop and have my brother fax me the work order," Bill said, acting both casual and understanding.

"Don't worry about it," the guard said, pushing a button for the gate. "I just wanted to make sure you were on the up and up since I hadn't seen you before."

He handed Bill a map of the park which was different, and perhaps better, than those handed out to guests. It had all of the behind the scenes buildings and facilities.

"Which rides are you working on?" he inquired.

"One of them is called Slinger," Bill replied, recalling the name of the ride relayed to him by Clay.

"Ah. It's right up here," the guard said, pointing the way along the map.

The gate continued to remain in an upright position, where it would likely stay until the guard pushed the button a second time.

"Much obliged," Bill said with a brief wave before driving ahead.

As thorough as the park appeared with metal detectors at the front, they seemed to have total disregard for checking employees and temporary workers. Once inside the park, Bill felt like a kid in a candy store. He could literally drive anywhere and check out virtually anything.

Outside the buildings, anyway.

If not for the map, he would have no idea which buildings were used for the carnival games or managerial applications. Knowing he was out of his element, he pulled to the side of the road, studying the map a bit more carefully, trying to decide where employment records might be kept.

His charade wasn't going to work with park managers, so he needed to be cautious about where he dared tread. A feeling of hopelessness passed over him. He wasn't Clay, and he felt his nephew had asked something impossible of him.

"I'm not as good as he thinks," Bill muttered to himself.

A work truck passed by, bringing him out of his trance. The truck contained park emblems on the side, and for a moment he thought it might stop. He envisioned the driver grilling him about why he was there, then calling the authorities.

But the truck passed without incident, or even slowing, and he studied the map once more.

Deciding he didn't want his borrowed truck in the open any more than necessary, Bill started looking for a place to park where it would remain out of view. One way or another, things were going to get bad by the end of the day, and he needed to keep himself distanced from the terrorist activities in every way.

That included any evidence left behind, or people seeing what truck he drove. The last thing he needed was implication that he had joined a terrorist cell.

Still, he needed to navigate the park within reasonable lengths of time.

As he looked up from the map he spied a park police car pulling up the drive behind him.

He cursed under his breath, trying to reach a practical decision without panicking. Time was against him because he had little doubt the officer inside the vehicle had spotted him.

CHAPTER 8

▼

Packard hadn't heard from Clay, which concerned him somewhat as he glanced at his watch.

He wasn't worried that his officers weren't coming, but the feeling of not knowing anything ate away at his mind. Being in control was something he was accustomed to, and not knowing a thing about the situation around him was unnerving to say the least.

The conversation with Turpin bothered him on several levels, especially if the call was overheard. It also gave him reason to avoid calling Clay.

If the terrorists wanted them at the park badly enough, they would call Packard in due time, particularly if his time expired.

Which it just about had.

He had toured most of the park, mentally noting areas where employees ducked behind gates, where he thought the park's fire and police departments might be, and areas that might be targeted.

His walk had taken him through the main park area, and into the kiddie area, which also held rides and food booths. It seemed the park grew busier by the minute, but wasn't as crowded as Packard had seen it during previous visits.

Currently, he stood beside a maze of waterfalls, sprinklers, and plastic tunnels, which comprised a splash and slide attraction in the children's area. Several parents had passed him, shooting him strange stares, as though he might have a child fetish.

Groaning to himself, he walked toward a souvenir shop when the phone at his side finally rang. He plucked it upward for a view of the screen, seeing it was a private number calling once again.

Though he questioned which private number it might be, he wasted no time in answering the call.

"Packard."

"Hello, Sergeant," an Asian voice said. "I see our time is up."

"And?"

"And you're standing there alone. Haven't your men checked in with you?"

Packard looked around, wondering how anyone could spot him amongst the hundreds of people. He saw no one observing him, and no one else standing by himself.

"They're here," Packard said confidently, seeking a response from the caller.

Saying they were not there served no good purpose, so even if he was incorrect, it might buy time enough for them to make their way inside the park.

"How would you know they are in the park when you're standing around hundreds of children, and they are ordering pizza just past the White Water Splash?"

He knows, Packard thought, his worst fears realized. Their every move was somehow being monitored, and they probably weren't aware of it. Perhaps Clay knew something more, since he had a weird sense that allowed him to know about things, seen or unseen, around him.

At least this guy hasn't mentioned the FBI agent, Packard thought.

If his phone conversations were private, they still had one advantage.

"Since you know *all*, what do you want me to do?" the sergeant inquired.

"I want you to meet with your men and wait for me to call you back."

"Then what? You want us to jump on a roller coaster you have rigged to explode?"

"Hardly. I have much bigger plans for the four of you."

Packard continued to look around, seeing no one who paid particular attention to him.

"Is revenge for Khumpa worth killing innocent people to you?"

"You think in terms of black and white. Not only did you murder a good friend and business partner of mine, but you nearly crippled my income."

"Income which comes at the expense of murdering, maiming, and extortion? You'll pardon me if I don't lose sleep over your loss?"

An insincere chuckle came over the line.

"Your favorite officer has something called loyalty. He learned it in the same place I did, then he turned against his own kind."

Packard gave an irritated sigh.

"I think your perspective is a bit mixed up. But we'll play your sick little game until you show your true colors. Then everyone will see you for what you are."

"They'll see what I want them to. Join your men, and I'll be in touch."

An abrupt click reached the sergeant's ear. He clipped the phone to his belt once again, then started walking toward the pizza parlor. Though unfamiliar with some of the park, he knew the restaurant because his family had eaten there a few times.

He passed through the oncoming crowd, brushing against several people on the way. As he walked, he realized he was not only weaponless, but he was in no way dressed for adventure. Wearing cutoff blue jean shorts, sport sandals, and a golf shirt, Packard was fit to work on his tan, not chase terrorists.

Much less battle them.

Somehow his every move was being monitored, but Packard had yet to see how. If security cameras were inside the park he didn't see them. Occasionally he saw video surveillance around some of the carnival games, but they were more of a theft deterrent than a security measure because their prizes were left in the open.

When he finally reached the restaurant, spotting his three officers seated at a table, they looked openly glad to see him. He had no good news for them, but at least they were going to endure whatever plan the terrorists had together.

Taking a seat between Sorrell and Clay, he waited for one of them to speak first.

"I hope you have a plan," Sorrell said.

"I don't have any idea what's going on," Packard replied. "I'm hoping Clay might enlighten me about what we're up against."

Clay quickly informed his sergeant about Kim, their similar training, and what he knew of the man's relationship to Khumpa.

"Comparatively speaking, how dangerous is this guy to what we faced last year?" Packard asked when Clay finished.

"He's more intelligent than Khumpa, and highly vindictive."

"Not good."

"If there *is* any good news, it's that he's not very skilled. He doesn't do bombs, he's not tactically trained, and he wasn't very good with a sword."

Maynard held up a finger, indicating he wanted to say something at this point.

"So if he has a sword, and I don't, I shouldn't worry?" he asked. "Or perhaps I can fend him off with a tree branch?"

The officer's sarcasm went ignored by Clay, but Packard decided to take control of the situation.

"Rod," he scolded his officer.

"Hey, I'm just asking for the sake of my own safety," Maynard said defensively, despite Clay burning a hard stare through him.

Packard wasn't about to have his own group bickering if they were about to fight for their lives. Though Maynard usually made pleasing the sergeant a top priority, he tended to think more freely than the younger officers because of his age and experience. Packard didn't want zombies working for him, but he had little patience for squabbles amongst his people.

"You need to cool it, Rod. I know you don't want to be here, and that you had nothing to do with the events last year, but thousands of people are counting on us."

Maynard started to reply, but thought about it, holding up his hands defensively instead. Packard knew the officer had nothing to do with the prior year's events, and probably felt like he was endangered for no good reason, but anyone who watched the news understood what their city survived.

"We're about to get instructions on what's coming next, so this may be the last opportunity we have to talk," Packard said. "Any ideas, Clay?"

Giving an uncertain shrug, Clay seemed oblivious of what his old acquaintance was capable of doing.

"I can't even imagine why he picked this setting," he said.

"Then maybe that's what we need to find out."

"But that would actually require us telling someone what we're doing," Maynard added. "We can't exactly approach people for help."

Sorrell looked uneasy.

"What if it was something that happened here before? Last year's problems were motivated by revenge against Clay, and that, uh, jackass they wanted freed."

"That's true," Clay chimed in. "They could wait for any time, any place. Why here?"

"It would have to be a park mishap, maybe even something they covered up," Packard concluded. "Getting people around here to live up to their mistakes would be next to impossible."

Maynard gave a sigh.

"Most of the workers are kids. This is probably the first summer here for most of them."

"Then wherever we have to go, we inquire about accidents, major terminations, or past terrorist threats," Packard ordered. "Something has to be there."

Even to him, it sounded strange to inquire about such things from employees, but he was desperate for answers.

"What if they just picked this place because it's public?" Sorrell questioned. "We could be wasting our time completely."

Packard wanted to bring up the FBI agent's call, but time barely permitted them to discuss the topics they had covered. He doubted Clay knew the man, which offered no help to Packard in deciphering whether or not the agent was legitimate.

Their discussion was interrupted by the phone ringing at Packard's side. He gave his officers a solemn look, then reached for the phone to discover his options.

If there were any.

✶   ✶   ✶   ✶

For a moment, Bill thought the security car was simply going to pass him by, but when it pulled directly behind him, turning on its lights, he tensed.

Images of being cuffed and dragged off to jail ran through his mind, but he still had a valid reason for being there, and the initial guard's blessing.

Unless it was all a ruse.

Rolling down the window, he studied the officer as Clay had trained him, looking for anything that might tell him if the officer was friendly, or an enemy. It potentially gave him ideas for connecting with the man, lying if necessary.

"Hello, sir," Bill said when the man reached the side of his truck.

"Problems?" the officer simply asked.

A white man about Clay's age, he seemed somewhat guarded, as though studying Bill for some reason. Though Bill doubted he was aligned with the terrorists, he needed to act out his part, planning for the worst.

"I'm here to work on a few rides," Bill said, holding up the map. "I was just trying to figure out where I'm going first."

Glancing at the map, the officer nodded.

Wearing a black uniform, complete with badge and name tag, he also had a fully stocked gun belt around his waist. A golden stripe ran up each leg to offset the black coloration. His dirty blond hair was cut short, and his face seemed to display a somewhat cocky nature.

"Just thought I'd better check and see if you needed a guide," he said after a few seconds of examining the map, and Bill. "We're kind of leery of newcomers since this morning."

Bill put forth his best confused expression.

"What happened?"

"Just a little accident. Nothing to worry about."

The officer seemed to examine everything about the truck, including the inside. Bill's equipment was beside him, and a probing of any depth would reveal that the tools were useless for fixing any kind of machinery or rides. Keeping his cool, Bill observed the man, deciding to make conversation.

"I'm supposed to work on the Slinger," he said.

"That's just up the road and to the left."

Looking over his truck, the man seemed fixated by the sign on the door, raising the hairs on the back of Bill's neck.

"Where's that area code from?" the officer asked without looking up from the magnetic sign fixed on the door of Bill's truck.

"Delaware County in Indiana," Bill replied, trying to be vague without acting like it.

When the officer's head moved upward, for his eyes to meet Bill's, his look was unflinching and serious.

Almost deadly.

Bill saw the man's eyes, but more importantly, he saw the right hand shifting toward the man's firearm.

"Is that anywhere near…Muncie?"

A danger light flashed in Bill's mind, and he realized this man was sided with the terrorists, because there was no other reason for him to be so curious.

Or to reach for his firearm against an unarmed man.

Reaching for a sheathed short sword beside him, Bill prepared himself for the worst.

"Why do you want to know?" he asked, slowly pulling the weapon toward his side.

"No particular reason," the officer replied, beginning to take half a step backward, undoing the latch on his holster.

Making a decision that he figured might save his life, Bill threw the door open, slashing downward at the officer's right arm with the sheathed weapon. Likely breaking the man's wrist, the move kept the man from drawing his semiautomatic pistol.

As the man hollered in pain, Bill kicked his side, then punched him directly in the nose, drawing blood with the blow. A quick leg sweep from Bill knocked the officer defenselessly onto his back.

In desperation, the man went for the radio console pinned to his uniform shirt at the shoulder. Releasing the sword from its protective cover, Bill severed the cord linking the radio unit to the transmitter with a quick slicing motion that spared the man's flesh.

Now sheer terror showed in the officer's eyes, but Bill knew this man was nothing more than a mercenary, working for an evil group that meant his nephew harm.

Pinning the man to the ground, Bill placed the sword dangerously close to the man's throat, in complete control of the situation, though surprised his training enabled him to overpower a trained officer so easily.

Clay was right.

"Who are you working for?" Bill demanded.

"The park," the man answered hurriedly.

"No. Who are you *really* working for?"

Hesitating, the man seemed reluctant to answer from a deep fear, but not the fear of having his throat slit. Making his point clear, Bill moved the blade close enough to touch the man's flesh.

"I want an answer."

"If I tell you, they'll kill me."

"If you tell me, you have a chance to leave here alive and never look back. I don't plan on being anywhere near this merciful with them."

"I'm not telling you," the officer sneered. "You kill *me*, you sign your own death warrant. There's enough of them here to take you out without anyone ever knowing."

Now it was Bill who was incensed.

"They kill an innocent girl this morning and the only thing you can think about is your sorry ass?"

Bill pushed the blade lightly against his throat, knowing any more pressure would slice through the tissue as easily as it might a tomato.

"You're no killer," the officer stated arrogantly. "If you kill me, you can't hide me, and they'll come looking for me."

"Awful sure of your spot in the pecking order," Bill replied. "I'm not a killer, but I can't have you jeopardizing what I'm doing here."

Still not quite sure what he wanted to do with the officer, Bill spied a vehicle passing through the front gate, coming his way. It wasn't a police vehicle, but Bill could not afford to be spotted wrestling down a park officer by anyone.

An arrogant grin crossed the crooked officer's face as he saw Bill's dilemma.

"Now what?"

Bill tossed the sword behind him, then struck the man across the bridge of the nose with his elbow, knocking him senseless.

He was able to drag the man behind his truck before the vehicle passed them. Obviously the driver was in a hurry, or not very curious, because he or she didn't bother to slow down.

Perhaps the strange ability to sense danger was rubbing off from Clay, but Bill felt something wasn't right, or safe, once the car passed. Rolling toward the road defensively, from instinct alone, Bill heard a metallic click.

Regaining his feet on the other side of the truck, he peeked above the bed, seeing the officer point the gun in his direction. He hadn't radioed for help, so his intent was obviously to eliminate Bill efficiently, to rid the terrorists of any distractions.

"What are they paying you to murder innocent civilians in your own country?" Bill asked, safely ducked behind the truck.

He peeked under the vehicle, watching the officer's feet.

"I'm not murdering anyone," the officer answered. "My job is to protect their investment, and make sure no one gets in here who shouldn't be."

"Whatever helps you sleep at night, I suppose."

Knowing the man wasn't about to call for backup, Bill decided his best chance was to make a break for the woods that surrounded the passenger side of his truck. Guessing most of the park police were trained official police officers in local communities, he suspected he might be shot at, and possibly wounded.

If he was lucky, however, the officer might pursue him without using the firearm, which would openly alert others to the chase.

Bill waited until the officer rounded his side of the truck, then darted into the woods, weaving left and right in his stride to avoid gunfire that never came.

After finding cover from a large tree, Bill dared look behind him, seeing the officer in hurried pursuit. Without weaponry, now deeper in the woods, Bill doubted the man would think twice about putting a bullet in his head.

From what Bill observed the officer had not spotted him, but he was about to deduce Bill's location, because the area provided few hiding places. Clay often preached that Bill needed to keep some kind of weapon on him at all times. Even something as subtle as a shuriken inside a belt buckle, or a knife strapped to his legs might suffice in a pinch, but Bill thought it was impractical.

It was simply another lesson from his nephew he regretted not following.

A quick look around revealed no useful objects nearby. Small pebbles, a few fallen tree branches, and some strewn garbage were the only things available. None of them seemed capable of solving the dilemma he found himself in.

Before any of his training, the thought that he was about to die would have overtaken his rational mind, and left him paralyzed with fear. Now, facing grave danger, he kept his composure, reaching upward for a thick tree branch.

Pulling himself up from the ground, Bill listened intently for the officer's footsteps. He positioned himself away from the man's view, prepared to risk some physical injury to ultimately save his life.

Able to keep his body around the tree, out of view, Bill waited until the guard quickly scoured the area, then darted his way in what he thought was an attempt to catch up to his quarry. When he neared the tree, Bill swung his legs out, trying to control where his feet struck the officer.

His timing was a bit off, but his knees struck the man's right hand, knocking the gun free. Letting his momentum carry him through the full swing, Bill landed on the officer, flattening them both against the ground.

This time the man's arms were free, and he clawed upward at Bill's face, but the older man clasped his throat with one hand, constricting his airflow.

Gasping desperately for breath, the man fought and grasped at Bill's arm, leaving the aggressor only seconds to decide whether or not he wanted to end this man's life. Evil or not, Bill thought death was a harsh penalty, and being a religious man, he didn't want to take another person's life.

But if the officer lived, Bill would be looking over his shoulder the entire day.

Putting off the ultimate decision, he struck the officer on the neck, rendering him unconscious. Clay had shown him an interesting pressure point which Bill mastered with several hours of practice on a replica torso and head combination. Basically, it shut off substantial blood flow to the brain by pinching the main artery.

The artery's closure came undone within a few seconds, keeping the victim from dying or suffering major damaging effects.

As the officer's eyes rolled back into his head Bill scooped him up, darting up the hill with the man over his shoulder. After assuring himself the area was clear, he bound and gagged the man, then threw him into the trunk of the patrol car. The keys were readily accessible inside the vehicle, and a remote control key chain allowed him to automatically open the trunk.

About to close the trunk, he spied the emergency pull cord which allowed anyone locked inside to get out. A common feature on newer cars, it became a burden for Bill. Using a small blade, he severed the wire just above the handle, making the wire impossible to grasp.

He now had to dispose of the patrol car, but there were no good hiding places around. Knowing he needed someplace where the car would not be seen, and the officer's muffled pleas for help would go unheard, he looked around, then turned to the map for guidance.

Several places stood out, the closest being a storage area for company vehicles. There, the car was certain to blend in, but Bill needed to ensure no one was working there. Since the park was probably partially staffed for the special student day, he hoped his luck might continue.

As he climbed into the car, starting it, he also hoped no one spotted him driving a park police cruiser.

CHAPTER 9

▼

Packard received his orders with little enthusiasm because his group was being split up, leaving them more vulnerable than before.

The voice had requested he send them each to a specific location, which he marked on the park map with a pen. There, they were each to pick up a cellular phone which kept them in contact with the voice.

Each of them had their own phone, which allowed them to maintain contact with one another, though Sorrell's had a low battery. Packard felt less concerned about using his phone since he observed so many other people using cell phones and two-way radios.

His only concern was that his phone emitted a certain frequency, which might be easily monitored if programmed into an illegal scanner.

Even so, he wondered if the terrorist leader had time to monitor a scanner, or if he was busy scurrying to ensure his plan went perfectly. Packard couldn't picture any desperation on the villain's part, since everything seemed too well thought out.

Hidden cellular phones in designated areas indicated the plan had been formulated for weeks, perhaps months, ahead of time.

As he walked toward the area he was ordered to visit, Packard wondered just how many mercenaries Kim had on his payroll. If he had park employees working for him, as Packard suspected, stopping him was an unimaginable feat.

He now relied on Clay's knowledge of the man, which was limited, considering his officer hadn't seen Kim in virtually a decade. Knowing Bill was possibly somewhere in the park gave him little hope because he didn't see the hospital supervisor making much difference in their overcoming the odds.

Even if Bill managed to get inside the park, access to most of the buildings was probably restricted. There was no one to trust, for Packard or Bill, and if the terrorists were nearly as clever as they seemed, they would expect a trick from someone linked to the officers.

Packard passed several children who skipped along with cotton candy and ice-cream, noticing their less enthused parents lingering behind. He hoped his daughter was safely on her way home, praying he saw her again.

A fleeting thought told him to call his wife because she deserved an explanation. Packard needed to tell her why Nicole was alone on the bus, but feared she might contact the authorities if he told her about the terrorists. For now he decided not to call Sarah.

He heard screams in the distance from roller coaster riders, and carnival music from the merry-go-round as he passed. Understanding the reasons why Kim split up his group, he failed to see the point in sending them to four different areas of the park, if not to kill them.

Clay had noted that Kim was more dramatic than Khumpa had been. He speculated if Kim wanted them dead, they would have already met their ends.

"Not that he doesn't ultimately want us dead," Clay had said, "but he'll draw this out as long as possible."

Those words crept through the sergeant's mind as he approached what appeared to be a dead end at the end of a concrete walk, except that the remains of a metal roller coaster loomed behind a partially covered sign.

Several metal barricades stood at the ride's entrance, along with several large trash cans. Packard wondered why he was told to come here, and strangely enough, to pass through the gates. Nothing except trouble was due to come his way if he entered.

"Whirlwind," he muttered the ride's name to himself.

Stopping short of the gate he looked around, seeing no one close by. Down the path, toward the main drag, people walked by, but no one came his way. Turning, he observed the coaster a bit closer, noticing sections had already been removed from the metal ride. He wondered if this was the ride where the tragedy occurred a few years back.

Urban legends ran wild about theme park rides, so he questioned the validity of the story. Still, the ride appeared in excellent condition for being almost twenty-years-old. He knew the age because the ride was there years ago when he traveled to the park with several police buddies and their wives.

Unity within his department seemed a thing of the past. Everyone now had their own agendas, political party alliances, and circles of friends. A time existed when a task force might stick together on and off the clock. Family picnics, drinks at the bar, and softball tournaments were virtually a thing of the past.

When Packard dismissed his three officers from any function they often went their own ways until he saw them the next day.

He suspected their lack of a bond might be harmful, considering their current situation. Slipping through the front gate with a cautious look around, he took in the view of the coaster, incomplete with railings gliding skyward, having no end to them.

Nothing obvious struck him, making him wonder if he was being set up to be nabbed by the security officers.

Several dump trucks sat nearby to tote the metal scraps away, along with a crane, a metal crate, and two utility trucks, which indicated workers probably weren't far away.

He glanced at the launch bay, where the line once formed for the coaster, and the metal gates ensured they entered the ride in an orderly fashion. It appeared fully intact, leading Packard to believe another ride would launch from the bay eventually, or it served a contemporary purpose, like a shady break area.

Entering the bay, he stood there a moment, listening for any activity. Hearing none, he stepped around the side, startling a construction worker who was taking a bite from a sandwich.

"Sorry," Packard quickly apologized to the bearded man, his mind racing for an excuse why he was in a restricted area.

"It's okay," the man replied, quickly swallowing his bite. "You get lost?"

He appeared to be in his early thirties, and not very concerned that a park visitor had strolled into his area.

"My daughter and her friend said they wanted to get some photos of this thing before it got torn down," Packard lied as smoothly as possible.

The man seemed to buy it.

"Haven't seen anyone," he said.

"They probably changed their minds."

Packard gave a wave, starting to leave, but turned around, deciding this might be his one opportunity to gather information. No one else was around, so he could talk individually to the construction worker.

"You know why they're tearing this ride down?" he inquired.

"A few years ago I guess a kid fell out of it," the worker replied, offering Packard a Pepsi, which the sergeant accepted, wondering why this man was being so cordial.

Perhaps he had an hour-long lunch break with nothing else to do.

"The park got sued, but they ended up winning, so I'm not exactly sure why they decided to tear it down."

Packard felt a strange tingle when the man said the park won the lawsuit. Such a verdict likely meant the rider was somehow at fault, and the equipment never failed, contrary to popular opinion.

"What are they doing with the parts?"

"There's what I guess you'd call a graveyard of pieces and parts off one of the trails. They're talking about using the cars and part of the track for a new ride they're putting together over the winter. They might change their minds and auction it. You never know with these things."

"You guys put up the new rides?"

"Nah," the man replied with a chuckle. "They call in the big boys for that. We just disassemble the things and dump 'em."

"So what really happened to the kid who died?"

"I heard he squirmed his way out of the seat so he could get his arms up and fell out on one of the loops."

Packard saw three loops remaining, two of which were as tall as several buildings he had seen on the Ball State University campus in Muncie. Death from such a fall was inevitable, particularly if the metal track was built directly beneath the loop.

"How do you squirm out of those things?" Packard wondered aloud. "The shoulder harness holds you in."

"Those kids can find a way."

"But why?"

"Ah, the thrill of it. Some of those kids can't enjoy it unless it's a life and death situation."

Finishing his sandwich, the worker reached into his shirt pocket to fish out a cigarette. He offered Packard one, which the sergeant declined, since he had quit a year earlier.

Watching the man light up, Packard wondered what he was doing here. There had to be a reason why Kim sent him specifically to this ride.

"You do other work around the park?" he asked.

"I do maintenance around here. Me and one of the other guys on this detail work here full-time, but the other guys were hired just for this job."

"I bet you have some good stories."

The man shrugged.

"Nothing much ever happens here. Kids get lost sometimes, we have rides break down from time to time, but nothing drastic. It's not very glamorous behind the scenes."

"Yeah. I know the feeling."

Packard decided to leave the area because he had no other questions, and he didn't like being in an area where he might get in trouble.

"I guess I'd better get to finding my daughter," he informed the man, who finished smoking, crushing the cigarette butt against the wooden plank floor of the launch bay.

"I'm sure she's fine," the worker said in a strange tone, as though he actually did know something about Nicole's whereabouts.

Packard stiffened, but said nothing, reading the man's expression. He appeared as casual as ever, but now the police sergeant wondered if the man was a hired gun for Kim, or merely a chance encounter.

An uneasy feeling came over him as he walked away from the ride, feeling like nothing was accomplished. Looking up as he exited the barriers, he spotted a surveillance camera atop a nearby concession stand, aimed loosely in his direction.

If it was set to a wide-angle shot, he had just walked into the frame of whatever monitor the video fed to.

"Fuck," he muttered, wondering if Kim was setting him up for something.

Either way he didn't have time to ponder his situation. Ducking his head toward the ground, he briskly walked past the camera, more confused than ever.

✳   ✳   ✳   ✳

Little doubt remained in Clay's mind that Kim had formed some diabolical plan to discredit the task force before he attempted to murder them. Before separating to their designated areas, Packard walked with him to retrieve his phone, exchanging information with his younger officer.

He knew Packard was heading toward a shut down ride, and Clay was ordered to sneak into the woods directly beneath a ride called Expedition. Deciding to deviate from his command just a bit, Clay wanted to experience the ride first. Being a roller coaster on a steel track with wooden beams, he suspected it might give him a great view from above before he embarked on his assignment.

In addition to gathering information, the walk toward the ride's launch bay provided an opportunity to chat with the most important person he knew at the moment.

"Hello?" his uncle's voice answered after two rings.

"Bill, what do you have for me?"

"I'm inside. The guard at the entrance bought my story, but I had a little snag with a park police officer."

"And?"

"He's locked up in the trunk of his patrol car, hidden away from everyone."

"Good man," Clay complimented his uncle.

"Clay, he was on Kim's payroll."

Though not shocking, the news felt far from encouraging.

"This scheme is better orchestrated than I figured, Bill. You're going to be my only hope of getting to the bottom of it."

"It's going to be tough. There's no one I can trust."

"Obviously."

"Where are you?"

Clay walked along the metal hand railings weaving toward the launch bay, now under the cover of trees, fabricated scenery, and a tin roof overhead to protect guests from rain. Stopping to let people pass, he took a look around, seeing no one observing him.

"I'm separated from the guys. Kim ordered us each to different locations of the park."

"That's not good. What are they having you do?"

"It looks like they're incriminating us by having us enter forbidden areas of the park. I'm about to jump on a ride called Expedition."

"A ride?"

Clay paused, looking around once more. Seeing nothing suspicious, he sauntered toward the enclosed bay, hearing a recording meant to add to the ride's theme. It said something about the mine shaft being closed, and the last expedition disappearing, never to be seen or heard from again.

Comforting, he thought sarcastically.

"I'm supposed to go to the woods under the coaster, but thought it might be prudent to get an overhead view first."

"Smart lad."

"I had some good parenting from a certain uncle. Look, I better go before they suspect something. They have to be monitoring us somehow, so I'm not taking any chances."

"Call me when you get the chance."

"Will do."

Clay clicked the phone off without uttering another word, then continued toward the ride. He reached the gates as a group of people exited the ride, and nine pairs took their places in the seats.

The wait was evidently short, because no line had more than four people waiting. Clay picked a line that would place him on the next available car as the attendants checked the lap bars on the car currently seated in the station.

Another car was already waiting behind the station, which meant there were two or three sets running. In turn, that explained the short lines.

A few minutes later Clay found his lap restraint being checked by an attendant, then the car left the bay, immediately taking a five-foot drop before speeding into a tunnel decorated with African tribal wares.

Fake snakes, plastic vines, and bamboo spears piercing the inner sanctum of the tunnel were just a few of the props Clay noticed. They passed through a second tunnel with a spear piercing an unlucky explorer, which was a science skeleton dressed in faded, dusty clothes an explorer might wear.

An uneasy feeling hit Clay that had nothing to do with the scenery. The African tribal theme triggered a thought from his days in Japan.

"It can't be," he said under his breath as the train of cars reached the lift, which looked as though it would take them about sixty feet upward.

He spent most of the ride contemplating his past, and the possibility this theme ride was related to someone he wanted no part of. It dove through several more tunnels after spiraling downward from the top, then jerked from side to side on several sharp turns.

Sailing smoothly beneath two large manufactured temples, the cars took several more sharp turns, including one into another tunnel. A moment later the ride finished with another pulley drawing the cars up a hill, which was enclosed by walls and a roof.

Five Indian idols rested on each side of the cars during the ascent, each moving his two arms up and down ominously, as though carrying out a ritual. Strangely, each of the figures had one red and one blue eye. An evil voice said something about how the riders had invaded his land, and now they would pay.

A woman's scream followed that, which was part of the recording, barely audible over the clicks and clacks of the train being pulled upward by chain drive.

At the end of the tunnel was a villainous figure holding a pointed pan of some sort, painted to appear as though molten metal dripped from it.

Clay discovered cool water was actually the substance dripping from the bucket, but it was the eerie, glowing red eyes of the figure that stuck in his mind.

Several seconds passed as the cars stopped outside the station while another batch of riders was secured and checked before heading out. Once their train rolled inside the station, Clay lifted the restraint from his lap, then exited to his left, following everyone else, but lingering behind for a reason.

Once everyone was out of sight he leapt over the railing, quickly ducking under it to ensure no one took notice. Positive he was safe, he darted into the nearby woods, which ran parallel to the ride, and partly beneath the tracks.

Knowing he was requested to visit the area for a reason he carefully examined everything around him, seeing nothing unusual. Several speakers hung from nearby trees or posts, triggered to emit sounds of monkeys and other jungle creatures whenever the coaster train went by.

Keeping a safe distance from the track, Clay moved between trees to ensure no riders spotted him. He noticed vines growing up some of the trees, which appeared to be intentionally planted as part of the environment.

As a set of cars went by overhead, Clay pressed his back against a nearby tree. Once the danger passed he turned to resume his quest, spying an ominous sign tacked to a tree a short distance from him.

"No," he grumbled under his breath, assuming his worst fear had smacked him in the face.

There he spied a tribal mask tacked to a tree, black in color with gold trim, and beads of blue, green, and yellow speckled across its eyes and nose. Most tribal masks were elongated, but this one was perfectly round.

Clay walked over to the mask, surveying his surroundings. Knowing he was in no way visible to riders, he plucked the mask from the tree, suspecting it had nothing to do with the ride's scenery.

It was meant for his eyes only.

Looking around, he saw several other trees with similar masks of different shapes and sizes tacked to them. Grunting to himself he examined the mask further, finding no unusual markings on the back.

A sense of danger entered his mind with the same impact a hammer might have on a nail.

He turned just in time to catch an arrow in midair that would have otherwise pierced his chest. The sounds of rustling branches and the arrow sailing from a bow had alerted him to the danger, but his reflexes ultimately saved him.

Looking to the direction from which the arrow came, he spied a figure dressed completely in black, with a mask similar to those tacked on the trees. Wearing the traditional black garb of a ninja, the mask served for intimidation, made simply of thick paper.

Such tactics failed to phase Clay, and now he knew exactly whom he was up against.

With an exaggerated evil laugh, similar to those done by Geoffrey Holder in the 7-Up commercials when Clay was growing up, the man stood like a statue holding his bow in one hand. Before Clay decided how to respond, the masked man darted into the cover of the woods, having accomplished what he wanted.

To gain Clay's attention.

"Voodoo," Clay muttered the man's name under his breath.

It was the only name by which he had ever known the man, who was a true African-American. Voodoo was part of a neighboring clan in Japan, but he was the exception to the rule in his clan. Somehow the man had found himself welcome within a clan of otherwise native Japanese.

Perhaps it was because the clan was so small that they made room for him, but Clay knew when he met up with Khumpa and Kim that they were peas of a pod. It was only a matter of time before their corruptible natures encouraged one another.

And now he was confronted with two of the three being in close proximity.

Using his shirt, Clay wiped the arrow clean of his fingerprints, then tossed it to the ground. He now realized just how much danger he and his fellow officers were facing. Having no weapons of his own didn't bother him because he knew how to fight effectively without them. Still, he needed to warn Packard and the others.

Taking up his phone, he started to call his sergeant, then decided to track his adversary instead. Clay dashed across the open area beneath the metal tracks, hearing a rumble coming his way. Forced to duck behind a tree, Clay lost enough time that Voodoo was long gone by the time he entered the far edge of the woods.

"Shit."

Picking up his phone once more, he decided to phone Packard with the grim news.

CHAPTER 10

▼

Turpin had the option of entering the park like everyone else, or trying the employee entrance. Deciding he wanted his firearm with him, for a few reasons, he opted not to make a scene, and approached the guard shack in his rental car.

"Help you?" the guard asked, looking at the agent with a suspicious stare as he stood from his stool within the small structure.

Presenting his identification, Turpin decided not to bully the guard, but not to give up too much information either.

"I need to find a guest in your park," he said. "It's important, or I wouldn't be here."

The guard didn't seem to doubt him, but hesitated.

"You here about the incident this morning?"

"What incident?"

Giving a perplexed look, as though there was no other reason why a government agent needed to be there, the guard dismissed his words, shaking his head.

"Never mind. Need any help from our staff?"

"No. I should be able to find him on my own."

"It's a big park, sir."

"I'm aware of that, but I'll be fine."

Turpin kept his tone steady, never raising his voice.

The guard handed Turpin a map which seemed to cover everything both seen and unseen in the park. With reluctance, he reached for the button to raise the gate.

"I'll have to let my supervisors know about this," he said as though to imply Turpin wasn't going to be completely free to do as he pleased. "They'll probably want to have a talk with you."

"That's fine," Turpin said in compliance.

"Are you armed, sir?"

"I am. And, no, I'm not leaving my firearm with you."

"I wasn't going to ask you to."

Turpin gave as courteous a nod as he could muster, then drove through the raised gate, looking into his rearview mirror. He saw the guard immediately picking up the phone, suspecting he was going to be greeted by park security before he found opportunity to enter the park.

Knowing he was going to stick out because of his formal attire, Turpin didn't particularly want to go wandering through the park anyway. Behind the scenes help might be welcome, so long as they didn't ask too many questions, allowing him to conduct his own search.

Turpin pulled to the side of the paved drive, studied the map a moment, then decided to enter the corporate offices just up the road to seek some useful help. Coming from a city police background, he wasn't one to normally dictate a situation and smother it with possessiveness, but he needed to maintain a low profile this time.

A few minutes later he found himself trying the door to the main office, finding it unlocked. He stepped inside, finding no one inside. Feeling a suspicious tingle climbing his spine, the agent instinctively reached for his gun as his ears took in complete silence.

He started to call out, then thought better of it. Packard had hinted toward problems in the park, but Turpin figured the sergeant was being evasive for another reason. After all, the mess from the year before was wrapped up a little too well locally, but not from a federal perspective.

Walking along the carpeted floor he peered behind several cubicles, then reached the offices, finding his first person seated behind a desk. Wearing a polo shirt with the Great Realms logo on it, the man looked a bit surprised to see the agent.

"Can I help you?" he asked, standing up, but not leaving the protection of his desk.

His light brown hair was thinning on top, but he looked thick, as though he worked out. The agent guessed him to be in his early forties. Turpin also suspected he was a department head of some sort as he approached the man, offering his hand.

"Special Agent Jack Turpin, FBI."

The man shook his hand, but looked skeptical until Turpin produced identification.

"How can I help you, Agent Turpin?" he finally asked.

"You the only one here?"

"At the moment. We've got several at lunch, and most of them in a business meeting across the highway at the hotel."

"What's your name?"

"Adam Russell, sir. I'm the director of special events."

"Don't call me 'sir'," Turpin ordered.

"Yes, sir."

Russell flinched upon saying the word.

"Sorry."

"It's okay. Look, I'm here specifically to find someone, and I don't need attention drawn to myself. This means I don't want everyone in your offices knowing why I'm here, Adam. Are you able to break away from your work to help me out?"

A questioning look crossed Russell's face.

"Yeah. I'm just catching up some paperwork." His expression changed to one of concern. "We had an incident here this morning. Is that why you're here?"

"No. What *kind* of incident?"

"One of the rides had a malfunction, but we're not sure it was a malfunction at all."

"What happened?"

"A girl died when one of the seats fell about a hundred feet down. It separated from the housing lift, and some of the spectators said they heard a boom just before the seat fell."

Turpin thought back to what Packard said over the phone. If it was related to the year before, then terrorists were involved.

"I didn't *think* that sounded like a federal matter," Russell stated.

"But while I'm here, I'd like to have a look at that seat," Turpin said, thinking his experience might help them determine how the tragedy occurred.

And might answer a few of his own questions.

"Do you know where they took it?"

"I think they took it to the back of the wood shop. We have some storage space back there."

"How many people are out there right now?"

Holding up a finger, Russell picked up a phone, dialed an extension, and spoke momentarily with someone on the other end.

"Our head of security and a local detective are down there," he reported.

"Can you take me there?"

Russell shrugged easily.

"Sure. We'll take one of the carts down there."

"Carts?"

Without saying a word, Russell motioned for the agent to follow him out a back door where several carts like those used on golf courses were parked. They remained outside the main portion of the park where guests walked past by the hundreds, just beyond a white wooden wall taller than both of them.

Russell jumped into the driver's seat, openly anxious to help a federal agent. Turpin seated himself beside the man, wondering how much time he dared commit to this investigation.

"So, is it really exciting working for the FBI?" Russell asked once they were on the concrete back road toward the wood shop.

"Not as much as you'd think. There's a lot of paperwork, and a lot of time on the phone."

"But you're out here in person," Russell pointed out. "Must be something pretty important."

"You could say that."

"Ever shoot anyone?"

Turpin answered with a stern look, which Russell acknowledged by shutting up.

They passed several staff members dressed in blue or white shirts with the park logo. Most looked like teenagers, or perhaps college kids home for the summer. A few waved, while others appeared busy carting food or equipment to various parts of the park.

Having never given much thought to how theme parks really worked, Turpin had only been to one or two in his life. That was years ago, and much further south than his present location.

"How long have you been with the company?" Turpin asked.

"About ten years now. Its grown quite a bit since I came aboard."

"What exactly does your job entail?"

"Uh, well, I plan concerts, the parades we have in the park, and catered events for starters. I'm also kind of a liaison for the public anytime someone wants to arrange a special day in here."

"Special day?"

"Like sponsors who give us freebies to give out, or just to have their name on something we pass out. We work with a lot of local businesses because they support us."

"Does the town revolve around the park?"

Russell gave a half shrug with an uncertain look.

"I think the town is the size it is, and with the luxuries it has, because of the tax base the park provides. But it was here long before the park."

"You grow up around here?"

"I grew up around Louisville and moved up here after graduating from U of L, once I got the job at the park. My degree was in business, specializing in public relations, so it was a natural fit."

Turpin watched very little scenery pass them by. Most of the park's business interior was concrete, speckled with trees, shrubs, and the occasional building. Smells like cotton candy and popcorn entered his nostrils, passing by quickly. Overhead, the sun occasionally ducked behind several fluffy clouds, giving park guests some rest from the rising temperatures.

Taking longer than Turpin expected, the ride was smooth, but Russell had to slow or stop at every intersection to watch for pedestrians and other vehicles. Turpin examined everything they passed, looking for any signs of trouble, remembering Packard's vague warning.

If there was indeed trouble, he wondered why the sergeant hadn't contacted park officials, or local police. And if there was trouble, why was Packard still inside the park, and with his three officers?

Turpin's suspicions were raised, but he wasn't sure of whom they needed to be directed toward.

When they stopped in front of the wood shop he wasn't impressed. Little more than a pole barn, the shop appeared dingy because the original white paint had faded and chipped over the years.

A wooden sign hung over the door announcing the shop's specialty, but even its white paint and red lettering were faded. Turpin figured the park made plenty of excess funding for maintenance, but apparently the shops were neglected since they were out of sight.

"Not much to look at, but it gets the job done," Russell commented, stepping out of the cart first.

Turpin followed his lead, heading into the main shop, seeing a few men sawing and hammering, while several others sat at a table drinking soda and eating sandwiches. One even had a value pack from one of the booths inside the park.

Most of them shot the agent inquisitive stares as he followed Russell, as though they suspected a federal agent was there because of the earlier incident. Walking rigidly as usual, Turpin gave off an air of authority that was unmistakable. No one was ever going to deduce he was a banker or attorney upon first glance.

People foolhardy enough to poke fun at his accent, or his boots, quickly learned the stupidity of doing so. Turpin had lived too long to be belittled by people who had no comprehension of the hardships he had endured over five decades.

Russell led him across the long floor, which appeared to be covered with dust that mushroomed upward with every step they took, toward an area in the back. Separated from the rest of the work area only by an old blanket strung across a doorway, the storage area seemed equally bleak. The blanket provided privacy, but no form of security.

Brushing the cloth barrier aside, Russell led the way inside where two men examined the seat, now resting atop a sturdy work table. They looked up, staring at Turpin a bit longer than a few seconds with perplexed, somewhat unfriendly looks.

Russell cleared his throat to relieve the tension between everyone, then began introductions.

"Guys, this is Jack Turpin from the FBI. Jack this is Hugh Bryant, our head of security. And this is Brian Dorsett, one of our city detectives who occasionally does some security work for us."

Dorsett was a black man with an athletic build, smooth features, and hair trimmed almost to his scalp. Turpin shook hands with him first, then with Bryant, who also appeared to be in excellent physical condition.

Turpin guessed Bryant to be close to his own age because the man possessed a thick head of graying blond hair. Much like a hawk, his blue eyes displayed both confidence and a certain wariness whenever they surveyed his territory. He sported a gray mustache and goatee combination, wearing blue jeans with a button-up shirt containing no park emblems.

Apparently today was casual Thursday.

Unlike most of the security force, Bryant wore a photo identification clipped to his shirt, while most sported name tags like those found on fast food uniforms. Turpin suspected the man typically wore khaki pants or slacks once the regular season began, but the agent's focus quickly returned to studying his surroundings.

Both men wore firearms at their sides, which Turpin understood was a rarity in the park. Most of their security force consisted of kids armed only with mace and a radio. Only a handful of armed officers roamed the park to avoid concerning guests.

"What brings you out here, Agent Turpin?" Bryant asked, openly concerned that Turpin stood in his park.

Some security supervisors grew concerned when their turf was stepped on without them asking for help.

"I'm actually here on a different matter," Turpin confessed, "but thought I might be of help to you deciphering what happened to your seat."

"We're leaning toward foul play," Dorsett said, pointing to the charred marks on the back of the seat.

"Why exactly is the seat still here?" Turpin inquired.

"Because I'm the lead investigator, and it's just as easy for me to examine it here than at the police station."

Turpin grunted to himself, then drew close to the seat for his own examination. He saw four distinct char marks, one at each corner where the bolts had held the seat to the unit. With each mark was an indented portion of the metal, as though the explosions had come from behind the seat, forcing their way outward.

"Who has access to these seats?" he asked.

"Ride attendants, and pretty much anyone working in the park," Bryant answered.

"I mean access long enough to place devices behind this seat."

"I think the ride is accessed from the inner portion, so it would be relatively easy to conceal yourself if you made your way inside."

Examining the seat a bit more closely, he noticed bloody streaks along the sides, indicating it had not been cleaned. He wondered if any chance remained to lift fingerprints from the back.

"Are you saying it was definitely some kind of explosion?" Bryant questioned.

"Oh, most definitely. You two will have to determine who has access to that area, and when. Rigging four separate explosive charges wouldn't take an expert very long, but the ride would have to be inoperative, or they placed them there before, or after, operating hours."

Both Bryant and Dorsett shot him surprised looks, because he had confirmed in seconds what they had been tinkering with for almost an hour. Like puppies anticipating table scraps, they looked to him for further information.

"Can you tell me how you know for sure what happened to this seat?" Bryant prodded.

"Sure. My military unit practiced detonating charges and rigging bombs routinely, Mr. Bryant."

"Could you have a look at the ride itself?" the director asked somewhat anxiously.

"You two are on your own in this," Turpin said, noticing their posture. "My business here is something completely different."

Now their looks turned to hurt confusion.

"But if this was planned, that's nothing short of murder," Dorsett stated. "You have an obligation to stay and-"

"I don't have any obligation, son. I'm not a traditional agent, and what I'm here for far transcends even the bombing of a ride."

Both appeared stunned at his words.

"You've got a local police force and state police labs, just like anyone else, so you don't need me."

Bryant stepped forward, leaving his hands open near his waistline to express his exasperation.

"Then why on earth did you come out here to look at this seat?"

"Because it may be linked to the person I came here looking for. Not that I think he has anything to do with this, but I think someone else is after him."

"Do you need our help in your search?"

"No," Turpin said flatly. "I have Adam here, and that's enough. If I need something I'll be in touch."

Russell looked a bit flattered that an agent chose to keep him over trained professionals.

"Gentlemen, I wish you luck, but I have my own job to do."

Doing his best to overlook their flabbergasted stares, he turned away with Russell in tow, heading toward the cart.

"Where to, boss?" Russell questioned, trying to keep up with the agent's brisk pace.

"I need to make a call, then we're probably heading into the park so you can give me a little tour."

As they climbed into the cart Russell turned with a slight grin on his face.

"I feel like I'm part of an investigation."

"Don't get too used to it," Turpin warned. "My job doesn't include putting you in harm's way."

"This might get dangerous?"

"I just told your security guys that someone blew up part of your ride. No matter how you look at it, there's still something dangerous around here."

Russell didn't seem phased, as though Turpin was now his guardian angel. Like most people, he probably felt excited about helping a federal agent.

Feeling a bit guilty for not helping the park officials investigate the case, Turpin had little choice in the matter. His first and foremost assignment was to find Clay Branson. After that, what he did with his time was his business.

As they pulled away from the wood shop, Turpin plucked his phone from inside his sport coat, then looked up the next number he needed to call.

*   *   *   *

Sorrell had orders to visit a ride called Wrath of the Gods, which was close to the water park, and apparently shut down for repair.

Much like a Universal Studios ride, where passengers were strapped into one solid unit the size of two buses in width and length, the ride swung up and down like a pendulum, and even spun. Sorrell had only been to the park with his kids once when the ride was actually functional. Speculation was that the ride drew too much current, often blowing out its circuitry.

He knew of two access points to the ride.

One was the front entrance, which was sectioned off by park employees who kept vigil over the entrance. The other was the back entrance where employees went inside to work on the mechanical parts of the ride. He only knew this because the rear side was visible from a roller coaster he occasionally rode.

Once inside, he was supposed to await further instructions, but the whole notion of leading him and the group around felt preposterous to him. If they had demands, why didn't the terrorists simply make them known?

With only one real option of getting into the ride, Sorrell waited until no one was looking, then hopped the fence, knowing he was going to be visible from the peek of several nearby rides, no matter what he tried. Once he was far enough beyond the fence to avoid detection, he slowed to a casual walk, deciding to act as though he had a purpose for approaching the ride in plain clothes.

A fairly large, open area surrounded the back of the building that housed the indoor ride. No trucks were parked nearby, which indicated no one was working on the ride at the moment. Sorrell approached the back door, knowing someone, somewhere, monitored his every move.

He saw several exterior staircases which led up to the second and third levels. Each level had its own door as a separate access point to the ride's innards. Keeping it simple, Sorrell tried the door, knowing he had absolutely no skill in picking locks.

It opened.

Slipping quickly and quietly inside, he shut the door behind him, standing perfectly still a moment while his eyes adjusted to the dim lighting. To his left was a control room where operators started and stopped the ride. It had several monitors mounted above a desk, which seemed to be a security feature that alerted them if a rider was in danger.

An eerie quiet filled the ride's interior except for the sound of dripping water, which was part of the ride's theme.

Sorrell started to instinctively reach for his gun, then remembered it wasn't with him. Though not paralyzed with fear, he sensed something ominous about his current situation that gravely concerned him.

He discovered there was little about the ride that wasn't visible from the guest seating. Several gangway planks led to the mechanics behind the scenery, but they were narrow, and most of the mechanical aspects were high above, controlling the two large, metallic arms that maneuvered the mammoth car.

As he recalled, the ride started pretty gently, rising up, almost to the ceiling where the riders were confronted by the face of Zeus, who told them mortals were not allowed in his sanctum. A stiff breeze then hit them in the face as they tumbled over and over in the car while it plummeted downward.

Stepping carefully across the ride's floor, Sorrell recalled it looking as though it was made of plastic, molded to appear like a lava pit when the reddish lights shined upward from beneath the surface. Water colored by artificial lighting also spewed upward at the riders, representing bubbling lava.

Realizing he stood in an open space, completely vulnerable where everything around him was readily seen, he stepped back toward the entrance. If someone was indeed inside the ride, they were probably running around behind the scenes, along the rafters.

He ducked into a walkway where several computers stood silently, each with a blinking light, indicating they were in sleep mode. Sorrell walked through the entire labyrinth, cautiously looking around corners for anyone inside the ride.

Thoughts of leaving the building crossed through his head, but dedication to preserving human life and making Packard proud clouded his better judgment. By no means a perfect person outside of work, he upheld his law enforcement vows religiously.

After clearing the ride's first level, he looked up a stairwell leading to the second and third levels where employees controlled various mechanisms. Deciding the risk of stepping inside the off-limits building had just about reached a logical end, he stepped back. One more sweep of the main area would be enough to satisfy him before he left.

Sorrell walked to the center of the main floor once again, wondering what he was supposed to look for, or whom he might meet.

Looking around, he took in the ride's scenery, hearing a distinctive click that echoed throughout the building. He looked upward and around, seeing nothing in the windows used by employees to monitor the ride from behind the wall.

A thought suddenly occurred to him, too late, that one of the scarier parts of the ride was when Zeus' hand swept downward, missing the car by inches, then retracted out of sight.

He turned as the hand, connected to a full arm, began its descent, hitting him squarely as blinding pain shot through his body. The initial hit looked like a thousand flashbulbs went off in front of him, but it was the natural reaction to the body about to enter unconsciousness.

Sorrell had failed to cushion the blow in time, before the arm swatted him, sending him flying almost twenty feet across the room before the wall stopped him. Though he remained conscious as he hit the wall, a hard fall to the floor knocked him senseless as he raised his head, then slumped limply into unconsciousness.

CHAPTER 11

▼

Somewhat surprised at how well things were going so far, Bill made his way to the main offices, never suspecting an FBI agent was there just minutes before his arrival.

He worried about his cover story because anyone working in the main office was probably going to know he was lying. They likely knew everything that occurred in the park, but he was to the point that it seemed more intelligent to enlist the help of an individual. He simply had no idea who to trust.

Trying the doorknob he found it unlocked, letting himself in. A quick look around revealed no one in the immediate room. There was no secretary, because this was completely behind the scenes, and business meetings probably took place somewhere else.

Thinking he'd hit pay dirt Bill looked at the computers, trying to decide which might hold employment records.

"I don't even know what I'm looking for," he muttered, cautiously making his way around the first cubicle in case someone was still inside.

Considering the door was unlocked, he expected at least one person to be nearby.

Bill's only line of defense was the uniform he had borrowed from the hospital, which gave him the appearance of a maintenance man. Because of his confrontation with the park officer, the danger of other security officers finding him grew exponentially. If they found him, no story would seem believable in their eyes, especially if they bothered to check the facts.

Even if they failed to find the man, they were going to become suspicious that something had happened to him. Perhaps the man was a slacker, or security members maintained scattered contact with one another, which might buy him some time.

He finished looking through the cubicles, finding no one around. Thinking of justifications why the door might be unlocked, Bill reasoned that either people were nearby, or the office had a very light security risk. If that latter was the case, his search was about to be in vain.

Choosing a seat far away from the front door, with a title plate on the desk that informed him the desk belonged to human resources manager, he sat down. If anyone had access to employment records, it was this individual.

Bill scanned the monitor for any program that appeared pertinent to employment. When he found one, he clicked on it, opening some software that allowed him to navigate any way he chose.

"By name, seniority, position, or date hired. Aha."

He sorted the people by their hire date, starting with the most recent. Able to eliminate many of the employees by age, he was left with their position. Though it wasn't inconceivable the terrorists might work a booth or carnival game, he suspected they wanted roving positions with a bit more freedom.

Navigating the program rather quickly, he found the hiring for the current year wasn't complete, so he tapped the print button with the cursor. About five pages of employees, and all of their relevant information began printing beside his feet from an inkjet printer.

Sitting back in the chair, feeling satisfied he had a solid lead for the first time since arriving to the park, Bill put his arms comfortably behind his head, letting a smug grin cross his lips. The sound of a toilet flushing from a room less than ten feet away changed his mood completely as he scrambled to his feet, looking for an excuse as the door to the small restroom opened.

Bill chided himself for not checking all of the inside doors, but managed to make his way to a bulletin board before a woman emerged from the room.

Pretending to read a note on the board, he turned his attention casually toward her, finding her remarkably attractive. Shaped like an hourglass, she looked to be around college age, dressed in slacks and a shirt with the park's emblem on the chest. Bill had to pry his eyes away from her chest long enough to examine the smooth features of her face, highlighted by green eyes.

Her hair was dark and winding, reaching just past her shoulders. Her soft eyes were framed by lightly tanned skin that looked smooth, like satin sheets. Bill had just begun studying her flawless features when she addressed him in a slightly uneasy voice, since a strange man was standing in her workplace.

"Can I help you?"

"I was, uh, working on one of your rides and needed to call my boss about the paperwork."

Luckily his cell phone was in the truck, so his excuse was viable.

"You can use any of the phones," she offered, waving her hand like a game show model showing off merchandise.

She hadn't doubted him, which Bill considered a relief, because he had no desire to subdue a young woman.

Squeezing his way past her, Bill decided to use the phone beside the printer, hoping to mask the sound it made.

"So, what do you do around here?" he inquired, thinking she was probably cleaning up the restroom, or perhaps a secretarial assistant of some sort.

"I'm the owner's daughter," she replied, "but my official title is Director of Purchasing."

Bill tried to prevent his eyes from widening and jaw from dropping, but it was too late. Perhaps it was because he worked in a mostly male environment in his own department, but he would never have guessed this young woman to hold such a title.

"So you oversee the ordering around here? That's a pretty big task."

"It's not so bad," she replied. "I went to business school to earn my stripes."

Bill heard the subtle sounds of the printer pushing the paper through, and shooting ink onto the paper, so he decided to keep talking, though it was danger-ous to continue a conversation. If the young woman asked the wrong questions, he had no answers. Knowing her parents owned the park only made the situation more awkward.

"You get exclusive use of the rides?"

"Sometimes. Being in the front office has its perks. You ever ride the things after you service them?"

"I just do electronics," Bill lied without hesitation. "But I don't think I'd ride the things, regardless of what I worked on."

"Really? Where's your sense of adventure?"

"I guess I left it at home."

Bill heard the printer stop, but a glimpse told him a red light was blinking, indicating it was out of paper, or there was another problem.

"I'm not keeping you from anything, am I?" he asked her, hoping she might have something better to do.

"Not at all. After the day we've had here, I was about to head out."

Bill picked up the phone, looking to the buttons.

"Do I have to dial anything to get a line out of here?"

"No. Just dial."

She turned her back momentarily, which gave Bill enough time to fake a quick conversation, then duck down to look at the printer. He discovered it was indeed out of paper, but he saw no blank sheets around.

Cursing under his breath, he popped up from under the desk, toying with his wedding band to make it look as though he had dropped it.

His mind scrambled for a way to look for some paper, but his quest soon became hopeless, because the young lady already had her eyes fixed on him.

"Something wrong?" Bill asked, catching a look that bored straight through him.

"For starters, you didn't make a call," she stated. "None of the lines showed busy when you had the phone. So why don't you tell me what you're really doing here before I call security?"

Bill swallowed, wondering whether his next move was disclosing the truth, or going to jail.

*   *   *   *

Maynard considered it ridiculous that he was required to take a ride in the kiddie land, but as he drew near the Phantom Theater, he realized it was enclosed, dark, and he was about to be trapped.

He still considered it ridiculous that he was risking his life for people he didn't know, and he was about to be locked into a moving cart with no hope of escape. Why Packard didn't just go to the police felt suspect in his opinion. Maynard didn't believe the terrorists would do anything if local authorities were brought into the park.

Adding to his frustration, the wait for the ride was fairly long. A line wound itself around several rows of railing, but at least the room was air-conditioned. He felt his head throbbing as kids around him screamed.

For a kiddie ride, it seemed a bit intense.

And dark.

Everything inside the building was lit by tiny bulbs that flickered like candles. Several chandeliers loomed overhead, while organ music played in the background. Across the room, and above the crowd, a mechanically driven phantom played the organ, occasionally taunting the people below to enter his domain if they dared. The voice and music combined for a creepy effect, but Maynard was more worried about real issues.

With little else to do, except think, he began to weigh his loyalty to Packard against his own life. He wasn't about to be led around like some llama on display at a third-string farm.

Minutes later he reached the front of the line, seeing the cars that moved along a track in person. A metallic slot folded down over the lap of anyone inside, preventing them from moving or leaving the vehicle in any way.

Sensing danger, he apologized quickly to the teenage attendant, opting for the exit beside him.

As Maynard left he saw a young man watching the monitors, indicating the ride had cameras placed throughout. Maynard wondered what kind of trap he had just avoided as he slowly passed the monitors, seeing the brighter light of the outdoors ahead, at the end of a short hallway that led to a sharp turn.

Stepping outside, Maynard half expected his new cell phone to ring, but it did not. The sound of a strange siren entered his ears, coming from the direction of the main drag to his right. He turned, seeing a park ambulance, which appeared to be little more than a modified golf cart with added length, coming his way.

He moved aside, letting the two medics drive through, then wondered where it was going.

Casually, he followed the slow moving vehicle through the kiddie section, then into the area where the adult rides were found. It finally came to a wooden gate, where a security person opened for the medics, letting them through. Maynard drew close to the fence, able to see somewhat around the ride's side. The ambulance traveled beyond the building's corner, and Maynard ran out of unrestricted area to walk upon.

Returning to the front, he looked at the ride itself, noticing it was blocked and closed for the day.

"Wrath of the Gods," he said to himself.

A strange feeling occurred to him that one of his team members was injured, or worse, beyond that gate. He looked upward, noticing the sky grew a bit overcast, with ominous gray clouds in the distance. If the park was about to be struck by intense thunderstorms, he suspected attendance was going to plummet.

Working on a hunch, he used his own phone to dial Sorrell's number. It rang several times before someone answered.

"Hello?"

Maynard winced, not recognizing the voice.

"Is Ed there?"

"Uh, I'm afraid there's been an accident," the man on the other end of the line reported. "Are you a family member?"

"Well, no, but I work with him."

"I'm afraid I can't tell you anything more. It's the law, you know."

"I see. Thanks anyway."

Maynard hung up abruptly, clipping the phone to his belt.

"Fucking HIPPA laws," he muttered. "Christ, Ed, what did you get yourself into?"

He stayed near the fence a few minutes, failing to see anything down the path the ambulance had taken. Looking to his left, he noticed an entrance to a nearby roller coaster, guessing it probably had a high enough vantage point for him to see *something* behind the Wrath of the Gods ride.

A few minutes later he found himself atop the ramp that led to a roller coaster, with a perfect view of everything behind the other ride. The sound of the coaster cars pulling out barely entered his ears, but the distinct clickity-clack of the train being pulled up the lift was unmistakable.

As people passed by, wanting to ride the coaster, he leaned against the railing, watching the medics wheel a stretcher from inside the building. The distance was too far to see much detail, but he saw no body bag, and it appeared someone was strapped to the stretcher.

Beside the two medics, Maynard saw a man dressed in a suit who appeared Asian. Maynard had only the man's size and skin color to go by, but he felt uneasy, especially when he saw the man slip one of the medics some sort of paper.

Money?

The man on the phone hadn't spoke with an Asian accent, meaning the man he saw was born American, or there was someone else within their proximity. Looking down, Maynard found about a thirty-foot drop to the grass below. With little choice, he went against the flow of human traffic, making his way toward the exit, and ultimately the wooden gate where the medics entered.

As he reached the bottom of the ramp, rounding several rows of railing, he found himself changing his pace from a brisk walk to a more desperate jog toward the wooden gate.

He reached it before the medics, whom he had observed as long as the view allowed. When last he looked they were loading Sorrell into the ambulance, then turning around, apparently to drive him up to the gate, where they would probably meet up with an actual ambulance.

Maynard had yet to decide what he wanted to do. He only knew that he needed to confirm it was indeed Sorrell on the cot, and if so, he wanted to know his fellow officer's condition.

Beating up medics for information seemed excessive, but he questioned their integrity, and the authenticity of their position, considering he saw one of them receive something from the Asian man.

Having no answers was both frustrating and dangerous. Maynard had no idea who was on his side, preventing him from taking drastic measures of any kind. If he knew for certain the medics were on the take, and meant Sorrell harm, they would never reach his side of the gate.

A peek through the wooden slats revealed the medics were nearing the gate, but a glance to his right revealed two security personnel, both armed park officers, coming his way.

"Shit," he said to himself, quickly realizing their focus was not on him, but on assisting the medics.

Any heroic measures Maynard had dreamt up died with the arrival of the officers, but even as they met up with the medics, Maynard walked behind them, trying to listen to their conversation without being obvious about it.

Even as slow as the ambulance traveled, it made too much noise for him to hear their talk, unless he drew right beside them. He wasn't positive the officers hadn't seen him looking through the fence, so he decided not to chance it, breaking off to observe them from a distance.

Pulling out his own cell phone, he dialed Clay's number.

*   *   *   *

"We have a problem," were the first words Clay heard Maynard utter when he answered his own phone. "Well, maybe two."

Walking toward the main drag of the park, Clay had his own worries, like where his uncle might have gone.

"Spill it," Clay said.

"Well, I kind of ditched my assignment from the bad guys."

"You what?"

"It smelled like a trap, Clay. I wasn't going in there alone."

Clay sighed, though understanding what Maynard felt, after nearly having an arrow enter his chest earlier.

"What's the other problem."

"They did something with Ed. He's being wheeled out of here right now, and he's under the watchful eye of two park officers."

Saying nothing, Clay clenched one fist, incensed that the terrorists were trying, and succeeding, at harming his colleagues.

"What did they do to him?"

"I don't know. I saw the whole thing from a distance, and there wasn't much to see. He went into some building and got hurt, I think."

"But he's alive?"

"I think so. They didn't cover him, or put him in a bag."

Clay thought in silence a few seconds.

"What do you want me to do?"

"Nothing. If those fucks call you back, don't do what they ask of you. One of them tried to ambush me about half an hour ago."

"What about Ed?"

"Leave that to me, Rod. I'll call you back when I'm finished."

"Finished?" Maynard asked with a bit of apprehension in his voice, as though he thought Clay was about to hit the warpath.

In a manner of speaking, he was right.

He severed the call with Maynard, realizing his earlier call to Packard was little more than conversation. His sergeant had survived his assignment, which raised some questions about the terrorists' agenda. Killing all three of the officers was simplistic if that was their objective.

No, Clay decided, there had to be something deeper to their motivation.

Instead of calling Packard, he dialed the number for Bill's phone, receiving no answer once again. He wondered what his uncle could be doing that kept him from answering the phone. Instead of waiting to find out, Clay decided to search for Bill, or better yet, his utility truck, behind the scenes.

Bill had described the small truck earlier, and its decal, so Clay had some idea what to look for. His only dilemma was how to blend in with the working crowd, who probably knew one another particularly well. Taking a look upward, he decided the backs of the buildings along the main drag were plain facades.

If he reached one of the roofs, then chose a position with a good viewpoint, he could see what the medics were doing with Ed, then search for Bill's truck if necessary.

Hearing the sound of the small ambulance's siren enter his ears, he knew he had little time to waste. He hoped they took his fellow officer somewhere fairly isolated in case he needed to make a move.

A quick look around him showed Clay no one was looking in his direction except a small boy, so he leapt upward, grabbed a piece of drainage pipe hanging from the nearby roof, then used his momentum to land himself atop the false second story.

He saw the boy try telling his parents he saw a man leap to the roof, but they quickly dismissed it after seeing nothing when they looked. Grinning a bit to himself, Clay had already ducked behind a partition when they glanced his way.

Moments later the ambulance rounded the corner, traveling along the front of the buildings, which was the main drag near the entrance. Clay suspected they were going to take Sorrell behind the scenes near the front gate, so he jumped from building to building along the rooftops, careful to maintain his footing.

He had confidence in his ability to navigate the various pitched roofs, but a fall would certainly hurt, and land him in more trouble than Sorrell.

Some of the roofs were flat, since they had false fronts, and little or no real interiors, making his travel across them difficult at times. Most of them housed shops along the main strip, but the second levels simply held merchandise or provided scenery. Clay made certain he stayed far enough back that people walking past below him did not see a strange man walking the rooftops. Despite his caution, Clay managed to monitor the tiny ambulance as he crossed the tiles.

Eventually Clay reached the end of the buildings, able to observe the cart pulling into a gate, which one of the officers opened for them. The fact that the officers walked defensively with the park ambulance the entire ride worried him, but he suspected Sorrell was lured somewhere he wasn't supposed to be.

Once the entourage stopped on the other side of the gate, Clay positioned himself behind a ledge atop the building, eavesdropping on a conversation between one medic and a park officer.

"We have to get him medical attention," the medic said. "Somehow he got socked by that ride, and he's damn lucky to be alive."

"I don't care how hurt he is," the security officer said. "We're going to have the locals watch him at the hospital."

"He's probably no security threat. He probably won't wake up for days the way he's looking."

While the two men had been speaking, the second medic was checking Sorrell's vitals, which showed Clay at least a few of them were genuinely concerned for his fellow officer. So far they had given him no indication they were on the take, or meant Sorrell harm.

If their intent was simply to take him to the hospital, armed guards or not, Clay had no qualms with that decision. Sorrell's health was his primary concern, but he saw no need to take action based on their attitudes.

"His blood pressure and pulse are a little on the weak side, but he's still good to go. They on their way?"

Clay figured he was asking about medics from the local hospital.

"They're meeting us at the gate," the officer replied, nodding his head toward the employee and delivery entrance.

As much as Clay wanted to see Sorrell avoid any trouble, he was more concerned about the man's health. Rescuing his fellow officer from these men did no good if Sorrell died, or Clay had to worry about toting, or hiding, him all day.

Feeling a knot in his stomach, he watched them head for the gate, then darted across the rooftops the way he had come, looking for any sign of his uncle.

He was almost to the end of the row when he saw Bill's borrowed truck parked near one of the corporate office buildings. If he looked to his left, Clay saw the park itself, and thousands of people unaware that their lives were in danger. To his right was the corporate aspect, filled with business people and storage.

Somehow he needed to think of a way to save it all.

And his plan began with retrieving his personal items from Bill, once he located him.

CHAPTER 12

▼

"We have to get one last show in before the storm hits," Dave LaRue told his fellow actors as he stepped into the tavern.

Part of the elaborate set known as Frontier Town, between the main portion of Great Realms and the water park area, the tavern acted as a gift shop, bar, and eatery all wrapped into one.

"I don't think everyone's here," one of his fellow actors replied, sitting at a table, playing cards with some of the other actors, which was part of their routine to make the village seem real to guests.

Every ten minutes a train passed by, on the way to or from the water park. Guests had the option of stopping at the village for the live show, or to shop. Their other option was simply to remain on the train and return to the main park.

"See who you can find," LaRue told the three men sitting at the table. "The bosses want us to do one last skit before the storm hits, then we're free for the day."

With openly mixed emotions all three stood, then left the tavern in search of the other actors. While they were reluctant to hunt down the other actors, they seemed somewhat excited their workday was cut short.

Most all of them were regular employees during the summer, some fulfilling other duties aside from acting the part of cowboys and train robbers. Like LaRue, many of them taught at local schools, filling in their summer hours with extra pay.

LaRue looked around the makeshift tavern, seeing tables for playing cards or eating, a piano in the corner that played several western songs from the mining days, and an occasional burst of fog from a hidden machine to simulate a smoky bar.

None of the employees were allowed to smoke within any buildings, so the fog machine created a realistic setting while obeying park regulations. LaRue especially liked the old chandelier hanging above, tattered by the crew to look authentic after the park allowed LaRue to purchase it at a rummage sale.

A high school history teacher during the school year, LaRue became the unofficial leader of the bunch, simply because he had the most seniority. He made himself available to the employees, but he was also the one who had to bark the orders when there was work to do. His knowledge of history had actually helped the park expand what he originally considered a sham of a frontier village.

Though he didn't own horses or farm animals, LaRue lived in the country. Several friends lived on farms and ranches, so he learned quite a few tricks of the trade from them to research his role.

Only half the cast was available for work because their schools had let out sooner than others, or they weren't teachers. Some of the actors had *only* this job to get them by, while others worked part-time at the park, working midnight hours somewhere else.

LaRue had only about a dozen employees returning from the prior year, which disappointed him. He liked meeting new people, and getting to know them, but it took much longer to get everyone acquainted with the act when the majority of them were new.

While everyone gathered and organized he walked behind the bar, poured himself a glass of water, and guzzled it. Despite being May, and nowhere near the hottest days of summer, LaRue already found himself uncomfortable. Between his new beard itching, and the long-sleeved shirt he wore, along with a brown leather vest causing him to sweat, he was ready for his day to end.

Aside from him, only the bartender and a few guests roamed inside the tavern. The next train was only minutes away, with a thunderstorm following close behind.

LaRue typically played the part of a sheriff, because he wasn't good at acting mean like some of the other men. They got the part of the robbers, where there was more interaction with guests, so it worked out well for everyone.

Because of their appearance, the actors were not allowed to stray too far from the village. Kids often drew confused expressions when they spied men wearing Stetsons and toting revolvers. Granted, the revolvers were filled with blanks similar to what Hollywood studios used when filming movies.

Taking up his Stetson from the bar, LaRue gave a quick nod to the bartender, then stepped outside to see if his colleagues were anywhere close to ready. A thunderous rumble echoed in the distance, meaning they didn't have much time to get the show in.

Carefully setting his cowboy hat atop his balding head, LaRue looked sky-ward, seeing gray clouds rolling end over end in the distance.

"This may be an abbreviated version, Ted," he told one of the actors.

"That train'd better hurry, or we're gonna be treadin' water."

LaRue grunted to himself, seeing a few of the actors returning from the nearby buildings set up on the village's main drag. Stables, a jail, the tavern, a barn, and a general store were among the prop buildings built in the village. Behind the main drag where LaRue stood, a fort taller and wider than his own house loomed over the actors.

Authentically constructed entirely of logs to mimic the pioneer days, the fort had ivy growing along two of its sides. Two observation towers were mounted in opposite corners, giving it a genuine appearance, though LaRue knew the interior was little more than mowed grass from end to end.

A set of stairs stood along the side of one tower while the other had a ladder that led to a hatch on its inside, somewhat like a tree house.

Seldom was the fort used. More for scenery than practical use, several local movie producers had used it during filming, which made local reenactment groups happy.

In the distance LaRue heard the train whistle for the first time, which indi-cated they had about one minute to be in the vicinity, and about three before their act began.

He watched as his fellow actors scrambled from virtually every direction, won-dering where they had all been. Typically they remained nearby, ready to per-form, but he suspected many of them thought the act was going to be rained out, preparing to leave early.

Taking a quick headcount as the train rolled in, LaRue decided most everyone was present. All of his deputies and robbers were around, though he and the dep-uties had to hide inside one of the buildings until the robbers had harassed the train passengers a few minutes. Most of the actors dressed as towns folk, tending to the village's shops when they weren't participating in the acting.

Their number varied, depending on the number shoppers rummaging through the wares in their shops. At least one of them always stayed behind to make sure nothing was looted during the act, including the locker room area where LaRue and his actors changed.

It also served as storage for the costumes and props. The park maintained a strict policy about leaving their property unattended, so any props not belonging to actors were logged daily.

"Where the hell were you guys?" he asked Greg Linson, who usually played one of his deputies.

"We were in the old saddle barn," Linson answered.

The mammoth barn was used to store spare parts for the trains in one half, and to house indoor picnics in the other.

Because it had no windows, and only a door at each end for natural lighting, it gave LaRue the creeps whenever he walked inside alone. The entire exterior had been painted as a scenic mural with false windows in some strange pastel colors that irritated LaRue.

"What were you doing in there?" he asked Linson.

"Gomez and I were staking out some chicks crossing the railroad pass."

LaRue had forgotten his friend was such a pervert. Despite being married, Linson liked to shop for what he called "window candy" wearing bathing suits.

"One of these days your wife is going to step off that train and catch you in the act."

"She's caught me before, but I can usually lie my way out of it."

Another minute passed while the two men watched their colleagues badger the passengers, who were not allowed to leave the train yet. Whether they stayed in Frontier Town, or remained on the train to go elsewhere, they were treated to the show.

The path his friend had spoken of was an alternate way to the water park, which some people chose to take if they had seen the show before. The path linked the water park to the kid area, providing a short walk for those willing to get some exercise.

"Been a couple minutes yet?" LaRue asked.

"Close enough," Linson muttered. "Let's get this over with and go home."

Their act was still somewhat new to many of the actors, but each person knew who was supposed to get shot, who faked death, and who did the talking. For now, LaRue did most of the speaking, since he was the sheriff, and knew the role quite well.

Only one of the villains had any lines, and it was another friend of the history teacher. Danny Garrison was a fellow history teacher at a nearby school, and the two had been friends for years. Whenever LaRue couldn't make it to work, Garrison knew all of the roles, and knew to take charge of the actors.

Even during their performance, the two had a chemistry the other actors seemed to understand. Some of them felt pressured by the two teachers, but neither LaRue nor his friend ever put unreasonable demands on their summertime colleagues.

"I think these people have had enough of your banter, Black Bart," LaRue called to his good friend, who sported a five o'clock shadow throughout the summer for his part.

Garrison looked at him with a steely gaze, acting his part.

"Sheriff, me and the boys are just gettin' started. These good folks don't mind donatin' to the likes of me an' the boys."

"Come with us peacefully, Bart, and no one gets hurt," LaRue replied.

Garrison stared at him a moment, then jumped down from the train, sauntering two steps toward his friend before stopping suddenly, his open hand fixed atop his revolver as his fingers danced on the wooden grip.

Thunder rolled in the distance, causing virtually everyone to look, except for the trained actors. They knew not to deviate from their roles because they wanted the skit over. Half days of work were rare, so they took advantage of the situation, despite being an early date in the season.

Garrison spoke again, picking up the pace.

"Sheriff, maybe you should head back to your office and help old ladies cross the street, 'cause none of these people have a gripe with any of us."

LaRue looked to the people on the train. Some chuckled at his friend's comments while others appeared engrossed with the show. Several younger children covered their eyes, suspecting the gunplay about to ensue.

"This man had his gun out, did he not?" LaRue asked the train's general population.

A few people nodded, but of course the robbers had their guns out, because it was a staged robbery, even if they really didn't take anything.

"Bart, you're under arrest. Every time we have a group of tourists come through, you rob them. Your criminal enterprise is over."

"We'll see about that," Garrison answered, grabbing swiftly for his gun.

While some of the actors scattered for cover, others stood their ground, and some acted as though they were shot during the course of the next thirty seconds while gunfire rang out. LaRue followed the script as he planned it, shooting toward one of the robbers as planned, watching as he faked death. Garrison acted the part of a coward, running for cover behind people on the train, but when he stood up for a clear shot at LaRue, the sheriff aimed at his chest, pulling the trigger.

His friend stiffened, and several people near him acted appalled, as though something unexpected or disgusting hit them, then Garrison fell to the ground particularly hard. As the train conductor announced the skirmish was over, and the good guys had won, the train pulled away after a toot from its whistle.

As the train left the vicinity, LaRue watched the actors who had feigned death slowly rise from their positions, walking toward the locker room to gather their belongings.

Except for Garrison.

Lying face down on the dirt beside the railroad track, Garrison was perfectly still, even when LaRue walked over to him. Figuring his friend was playing a trick, his mind returned to the train passengers and their strange reactions when he fired at Garrison.

"Danny? You okay?"

When there was no response, LaRue knelt beside his friend, touching Garrison, then turning him over when there was no response.

Centered in Garrison's chest, near his heart, was a bloody spot, which bled through his shirt, and vest, because there was a hole all the way through both.

"Holy God," LaRue muttered, realizing instantly what had happened as his fingers poked through the holes, and into his friend's fresh wound.

He knew what he had done, but no idea how. All of their ammunition was supposed to be blank.

"Call 911," he ordered a nearby actor. "And get the park medics over here."

LaRue had basic first aid and CPR training from his school, but his mind froze momentarily, then he remembered to check for a pulse and breathing.

Leaning his ear down to his friend's mouth, he felt no breath, and saw no rise of the chest. It suddenly struck him he had just killed a human being, and someone he cared about very much. Deep inside he suspected it was hopeless, but the fact that LaRue would give anything to reverse what he had done compelled him to begin chest compressions.

Beside him, someone knelt down, giving mouth-to-mouth to Garrison. He didn't know who it was, and he didn't bother to look, because bringing his fellow teacher back was the only thing on his mind.

Everything else around him became a numb blur as he lost all sense of time and his surroundings.

$$* \qquad * \qquad * \qquad *$$

Bill barely heard the music playing in every speaker along the park's main drag, only because dead silence overcame the room he shared with the owner's daughter.

"I'm still waiting for an explanation," she stated, slowly edging her hand toward the phone, as though a warning for Bill to answer truthfully.

He had seconds to weigh the decision, but lying was not his strong suit, so he decided to come clean.

"I'm not sure you're going to believe anything I have to tell you," he began, still receiving a hard stare from the young woman, somewhat surprised at her bold nature.

He paused.

"But I don't have time enough to waste explaining everything, either," he added. "There are lives at stake, aside from the young girl who lost hers this morning."

"So you know something about what's been going on. But you're obviously not a cop, so who are you, and what are you doing here?"

Bill closed his eyes a few seconds, balancing his need for information versus getting this young lady out of his way, one way or another.

"Maybe I can be of help," a voice said from behind her.

Bill perked up, knowing his nephew had silently entered the building, even before he stepped around a partition that blocked their view of him.

"And who the hell are you?" the woman demanded, her hand starting for the phone.

Clay caught it before it touched the receiver, then gently led her to a chair. He produced his badge to her, and she seemed to believe it was authentic.

"I *am* a police officer, though my uncle here is not. My name is Clay Branson, and the man you've been conversing with is Bill. And you are?"

"Casey. Casey Trimble. My parents own this park. Are you two related to what happened this morning?"

Clay shook his head negatively.

"If we were directly related, we wouldn't be having a civil conversation with you. There are terrorists behind that ride's malfunction, and they've lured myself and three other police officers here for revenge on us."

"Then why not call the police? Or the FBI?"

"If only it were that simple," Bill scoffed.

Bill wondered if a bit of education might help.

"Do you remember reading about terrorists in Muncie, Indiana last year?" he inquired of her.

She thought a moment, then her eyes registered that she remembered.

"What of it?"

"We're the ones who lived through it," Clay answered. "The terrorists were targeting me, and now some of their buddies are planning to finish the job."

Putting her hands to her head, the young lady suddenly had a problem absorbing all of the new information.

"So let me get this straight," she finally said, looking to Clay. "These are terrorists like we see on TV, over in Iraq?"

"No. These are terrorists from all over the world who do what they do for profit. When they came knocking on my door last year, I was supposed to be the icing on the cake after they conducted their business."

"Icing?"

"They wanted me dead."

"I know this is a lot to comprehend," Bill stated, "but we don't have time to discuss all of this. What we really need is help from an insider."

An awkward silence filled the room once again.

Clay spoke first.

"Casey, we need your insight if we're going to catch these guys."

"How do I even know I can trust you?" she asked. "What if you're putting me on?"

"There's nothing standing between us and doing you lots of harm," Clay noted. "If you were an obstacle, you wouldn't be talking to us. We aren't the bad guys. If you agree to help us, Bill and I will explain everything to you as we go."

"If this is all true, I have to tell my parents what's going on, so we can evacuate the park," Casey said.

"The reason we haven't gotten other agencies involved is because the terrorists threatened to kill guests if we did anything except what they told us," Clay replied. "If you tell your parents, the terrorists will know we've alerted someone, and countless people will die."

Casey's expression showed her horror. Bill understood how she felt, knowing his nephew and the other three officers were sacrificing their well-being by obeying the mercenaries. Between the emotions that crossed her face, Bill sensed some mistrust, and rightfully so. He couldn't begin to imagine someone unaware of their situation comprehending the depth of the terrorists' hatred toward Clay and his friends.

Still, she seemed resigned to at least play along for the moment.

"How can I help?"

"You can start by finding me some paper, so I can finish printing off your employment records," Bill answered.

"Sure," she said, standing to pull some from a nearby desk. "You think they've had someone working here?"

"Probably *more* than one," Clay said. "They had access to the ride that malfunctioned. And I suspect they have lots more tricks up their sleeves."

"They don't make empty promises or threats," Bill informed her. "Last year they killed hundreds of people in our city, so just imagine the field day they could have here."

Now Casey looked concerned.

"I just feel terrible that we can't warn the guests."

"If we comply, I think most of the guests will be safe."

"Who is 'we'?"

"There are three other officers here with me. One of them came on a field trip with his daughter this morning, which is how this whole mess began. They were in line waiting for your ride when that seat dislodged."

Bill ignored their conversation momentarily, putting fresh paper into the printer, allowing it to finish printing the file.

"Bill, is my stuff in your truck?" Clay asked.

"Yeah. I grabbed quite a bit."

He looked to both his uncle and Casey.

"I need you two to figure out who is working behind the scenes for these bastards. Don't forget they paid off an FBI agent last year, Bill. *Anyone* could be on their payroll."

"Then I guess I won't have any trouble narrowing it down between the hundreds of employees on duty."

"Try people who returned from last year," Clay suggested. "And people who were here early this year, probably behind the scenes."

Bill sighed aloud.

"And where are you going to be?"

"I'm getting my gear and hunting down the two men I know are responsible for this mess."

Bill worried, because he knew Clay barely survived the encounter with his arch nemesis the year before.

"You going to be okay?" he asked.

"I'll be fine," Clay answered with no hint of doubt. "You two have the hard job."

Bill watched him leave through the door, then thought to grab the printout of the employee roster. He wondered how Clay planned on getting into his truck without the keys, but figured his nephew knew how to break into vehicles as part of his overseas training.

"Where is everyone?" he asked Casey, referring to the vacant room.

"Meetings. They won't be back for another hour or so."

"Good. Any ideas where to begin with your roster?" Bill asked, flapping the sheets of paper in one hand.

"Put them on that table over there," Casey suggested. "Each record indicates how long an employee has been with us. Mom and Dad made the program easy to use for tax purposes."

As Bill spread the sheets across the table, the phone rang, which Casey answered from the nearest desk.

She engaged in conversation momentarily, which Bill paid little attention to, until she spouted some words that peaked his interest.

"Oh my God," Casey stammered. "You're sure?"

A moment later she hung up the phone, looking down to the desk, as though searching the corners of her mind for an answer.

Or some form of consolation.

"What's wrong?" Bill asked.

"A man was just shot in our Frontier Town."

Bill immediately thought the worst, fearing one of Clay's colleagues was gunned down by a terrorist.

"One of our actors shot another man on his team."

"Shot…on purpose?"

"The details are sketchy, but I have to get over there and see what happened. My parents are on their way back from New York after hearing about the news this morning, so I'm basically in charge."

Bill snatched up the papers from the table.

"Something doesn't sound right about this," he said, following her out the door.

She turned to lock it, a worried look on her face.

"The actors use blanks," she said. "It's a show they put on a dozen times a day for the guests."

Casey led the way toward a small white SUV with the park insignia painted on both sides. She unlocked both doors, allowing Bill access to the passenger side. He felt somewhat better she trusted him enough not to drive away without him.

"You sure you want to be part of this?" she questioned him across the vehicle's hood.

"You're the most important person I know right now," Bill answered. "If anyone can help me find answers and keep other people from dying, it's you."

"Our security guys didn't want to say much until I got there," she said, climbing inside the vehicle.

"Be careful who you trust," Bill warned. "If the terrorists are behind this, they could have one of their own try and cover it up to throw you off track."

Casey's eyes misted, obviously from the overwhelming nature of what Clay and Bill told her, compounded by the absence of her parents and another park death.

"None of this is your fault," Bill stated in a collected, honest murmur. "I need you to stay strong, so we can catch the people who did this."

"Okay," Casey said, starting the vehicle, then driving them toward the accident scene.

*   *   *   *

Turpin couldn't believe he was at the theme park the one day every single thing fell apart. Now he and Russell were pulling into a lot beside the Frontier Town where a reported shooting over the radio caught their attention.

"I'm always the last one to hear about these things," Russell grumbled, pulling the cart to a stop. "If the Trimbles weren't out of town, I probably wouldn't be privy to this stuff at all."

"Kind of strange to have two accidents like this in one day, isn't it?" Turpin asked, stepping from the vehicle first.

"We've never had anything like either of these instances since I've been here."

Turpin followed him to a small crowd where he spied Bryant and Dorsett standing over what he presumed was a body beneath a white sheet. To the side, he saw a man pacing along the tavern's front entrance. Wearing traditional western gear from the Arizona or New Mexico area, the man quickly found a soft spot in the agent's heart, since Turpin hadn't seen a possible legitimate cowboy in weeks.

Noticing Russell was busy gawking at the covered body, the agent started toward the man, but Bryant's voice stopped him after two steps.

"Seems like trouble's following you around today, Agent Turpin," he commented.

Turning to face him, Turpin caught the grim stare from the security director. The agent wondered if Bryant remained sore after the agent refused to help, or he legitimately believed Turpin's presence somehow conjured newfound trouble. Bryant stood with his hands cupped on his hips, waiting for the agent to return verbal fire.

"It seems your trouble started before I got here," Turpin said. "But I can't help wondering if there's a common denominator."

Bryant appeared concerned, but his expression hadn't lightened, despite Turpin suggesting the park had an extended problem. Either the security director felt outclassed by the agent, or he knew something more than he indicated.

Turpin turned to approach the glum man standing near the saloon, but Bryant apparently wasn't done with him.

"I don't know what's so important that you couldn't be bothered when someone got blown up on one of our rides, but it seems to me you're not getting down to it."

Sighing audibly, Turpin turned around.

"What I'm doing here is *my* business, and if I felt a need to share it with you, I would."

"I'm just wondering why you keep following my troubles around if you have so many important things to do. I realize we're probably just novice police to you, but I would rather work with you than see you trailing my every move."

"What I'm doing here may have something to do with your two incidents. At this point I prefer to conduct my investigation separately until I know for certain."

Bryant grunted loud enough for the agent to hear.

"Have it your way."

Deciding further communication with the security director was a waste of time, Turpin approached the man in front of the tavern. He suspected the man witnessed something, or knew about the corpse.

Pulling out his credentials, Turpin introduced himself to the man.

"Jack Turpin, FBI," he said without offering his hand, because the man seemed jittery.

"Dave LaRue."

Turpin glanced inside the bar, seeing it vacated except for someone standing behind the bar itself.

"Can we step inside a moment?"

"Sure," LaRue said, still shaken up about something.

A moment later LaRue seated himself at a table inside the dim tavern upon the agent's request. Turpin took off his sport coat, draping it over the chair before sitting down across from the actor.

"What happened here?" he asked, looking to LaRue, who stared at the floor somewhat vacantly.

"I shot him," LaRue answered without hesitation, clinging to a ton of figurative mental baggage.

Turpin cleared his throat, unsure of exactly what to say next. It was readily apparent the man seated before him was no murderer, but there were questions that required answering.

"All of this is one big prop, right?"

"Yeah. We're actors who perform for the guests when they pass by on the train."

"And guns are part of your act?"

"Of course."

LaRue slowly removed the sidearm from its holster, setting it on the table before him. Turpin looked at it, then to its owner.

"You normally use blanks?"

"Yeah, but this time one of them wasn't blank."

Turpin's suspicion of foul play now proved correct. He felt sympathy for LaRue, but he needed to discover what happened, even if it diverted him from his primary assignment.

"Where do you keep your blanks?"

"Back there," LaRue said, nodding toward a room behind the bar.

"Show me," Turpin said, picking up LaRue's gun from the table as he followed the man toward the back.

When they reached the back room it looked like a cross between a sports locker room with carpet and a basement converted to a game room. Lockers, showers, and several dartboards caught the agent's eye immediately, but LaRue took him to a door at the far end of the room.

LaRue used a key to open the door, which contained a walkway lined with costumes, props, and several boxes along the floor.

"Our blanks are stored in these," LaRue said in a reserved voice.

Turpin knelt down to look, noticing the blanks looked similar to real bullets, except for the ends. Even so, if someone took for granted the bullets they loaded into a gun were fine, failing to examine them closely, they might never notice.

"Who else has access to this room?" he asked.

"Well, we usually don't leave it locked," LaRue admitted. "The only people who come back here are the people who work in this area."

"The actors?"

"Actors, two bartenders, and a few people who mind the stores. We're kind of our own little family back here."

Turpin heard a sniffle from the man as he finished the last sentence. LaRue was talking, but he still wasn't taking the death very well.

In front of the lockers were several benches where the actors set their clothes, or sat to change footwear. Turpin pointed to the one beside LaRue.

"Have a seat, and tell me exactly what happened."

Five minutes later, the agent had an idea what occurred outside the building, a bit surprised no one else had bothered to interview LaRue. He supposed their main concern was guest safety, and keeping the body from public view, because he hadn't heard a train come through since his arrival.

He had absolutely no doubt LaRue was innocent, because the man had nearly come to tears several times while telling his tale.

Realistically, the local police needed to interview him for themselves, then investigate the contents of the crates holding the remainder of the blanks. Several other issues remained unresolved, including possible security breaches within the park, and the fact that someone truly intended harm to an actor.

But which one?

"Is there any pattern to who gets what blanks?" he asked.

"No," LaRue answered. "We just come in and get six to load the firearms, and most of us have holders for twenty or thirty more on our gun belts. But the stuff on our belts doesn't get removed because it's just for show."

"Is there any order in which the actors retrieve their ammunition?"

"Not particularly. Some of us are usually here earlier than the others, but its basically first come, first served."

LaRue seemed to understand the agent's thinking.

"So whoever switched out the blank didn't have a specific target, did they?"

Turpin nodded affirmatively.

"Who would have motive to kill one of you? And why?"

LaRue shrugged.

"I wish I had an answer for you, sir. We've never had any trouble out here."

Suspecting the two strange incidents were related, the agent began formulating an idea of who masterminded what he now considered attacks.

He had a notion, based on what Packard said, that the park was under attack from terrorists, but he wondered why the sergeant failed to act on his information. The one thing Turpin knew for certain was that Packard knew more than he stated.

Perhaps some unknown circumstance forced the Muncie officer to keep his mouth shut. He recalled the file he read about the year before, when researching Clay Branson. The Koda was a sneaky group who attacked randomly, forcing Packard's task force to abide by their rules, to a limited extent.

If Packard had knowledge of a terrorist attack Turpin needed to speak with him immediately.

And until he spoke to the man, he didn't dare trust anyone.

"Come with me," he ordered LaRue as he stood.

Both men walked outside, finding several new faces standing beside the investigators and park employees. Bryant in particular seemed to burn a hole through LaRue with his stare, which quickly shifted Turpin's way.

"I need you to come with me, Dave," he said, walking over to take hold of the man's arm, as though prepared to drag him away by force if necessary.

"Alright," LaRue said without putting up a shred of resistance.

It was as though he didn't care what happened to him at this point.

Bryant now wore black leather gloves, which Turpin recalled from his police days served two purposes. They kept hands warm on cold nights, or prevented bruises from showing up prominently on suspects when they were punched to extract information.

He knew both purposes from personal experience.

Turpin intentionally shot Bryant a disparaging stare, indicating he didn't like the way the man handled internal security.

Bryant started to say something, but a disgusted look crossed his face, and he took LaRue to his marked police car.

Turpin watched him place LaRue in the back seat, thinking it was definitely an injustice if the man received greater punishment than his already decimated conscience.

"I hope you don't plan on torturing him to get a confession," he said as he approached the security director.

"Not that it's any of your concern, but I just want answers. I have two deaths in my park today and no real evidence about who's responsible. At this point I'm going to do whatever it takes to get answers."

Turpin looked to his gloves.

"The man is innocent of any wrongdoing."

"And you inferred that from a two-minute talk with him?" Bryant fired back, controlling his voice just enough that people nearby didn't hear.

"I'm trained to divulge facts quickly, Mr. Bryant. I don't go around beating confessions out of people to produce results for the public eye."

Bryant's face flushed red as he quivered with anger.

"I've worked with Dave LaRue for years. I don't think he has a thing to do with any of this, but I need the truth. I'm going to do whatever it takes to figure out what the fuck is going on inside my park."

"I have the authority to step in and take over your investigation if I think you're pissing in the wrong spots," Turpin warned.

"Coming from a guy who wanted nothing to do with this investigation an hour ago that's mighty wide of you. I just hope you aren't part of my problem, and if you are, I plan to expose the truth before you can cover it up."

Turpin simply shook his head in frustration, upset with himself for losing composure. Under ordinary circumstances he might be good friends with a curmudgeon like Bryant. At the moment he had neither the time nor the patience to carry on a conversation with the security director.

Returning his attention to the matter at hand, Turpin glanced at the body, then to the new faces nearby.

"Who are those two?" he asked Dorsett, who seemed a bit uncomfortable being in charge of the corpse.

"That's Casey Trimble," Dorsett said, pointing to the young woman. "She's the owners' daughter."

"That mean she's in charge today?"

"I suppose so. Her parents are on their way back from a business trip after hearing what happened this morning."

"Who's the guy?"

Turpin saw the man was wearing a work uniform of some sort, but it didn't look anything like the ones he had seen maintenance men around the park donning.

"Probably an outside maintenance guy. There are some problems the guys around here can't fix."

What Turpin really wanted to know was why Casey had an outsider, basically paid help at best, accompanying her through the park.

She seemed upset, but collected, especially when the man said something in a hushed voice to her. Turpin eyed him suspiciously a moment, wondering if this man was somehow related to the problems, perhaps forcing Casey to carry out his wishes.

Something about him seemed familiar, but Turpin couldn't quite place it.

At least not yet.

Thunder rolled in the distance, prompting the agent to notice looming gray clouds. He decided he needed answers soon, and to find them, he needed to find Packard or Clay Branson.

CHAPTER 13

▼

Packard spied Maynard from a distance as he waited beside a sub restaurant for his officer to arrive.

"This is fucked up," Maynard said, openly upset, as he drew near the sergeant.

"Hang in there, Rod. Clay just called to assure me they have the work files of all the current employees. His uncle is going through them to figure out who the bastards are."

Maynard took a seat at one of the covered patio tables with Packard as the rain cut loose from the clouds above. Many people had already started toward covered buildings, or exited the park, to weather the storm.

"So much for lots of cover to blend in with," Packard sighed.

Looking up, he saw dark gray clouds as far as the eye could see. The thunderstorm wasn't leaving anytime soon, but it was the cold chill Packard felt that bothered him. Air temperature had taken a dive, and he was stuck wearing shorts. To make matters worse, he would be drenched the second he left the limited shelter of the fabric umbrellas over his head.

"What happened to Ed?" Packard asked, never getting a very complete story from his officer during their earlier phone conversation.

"I'm not sure. I got there right when they carted him out of the building. They lured him in there and did something to him."

"But he was alive?"

"I'm pretty sure."

So was Clay, Packard thought. He felt terrible that Sorrell was injured, much the same way he felt responsible for Mitch Branson's death the year prior. After all, these men were his responsibility, much like teenage soldiers might be led by a young military sergeant into combat.

For a moment the sound of the rain spattering against the concrete around them was the only sound Packard heard. He observed several people scurrying for cover, while several others wore ponchos, or held up umbrellas.

"What are we going to do?" Maynard asked with concern. "By now they know I didn't go through with the ride they told me to."

"And it was probably a good thing. Now we know what they did to Ed, and if their objective is to kill us, they might leave park guests alone."

"Something tells me they aren't going to do that."

Packard suspected the same thing, but he was in no position to do anything about their activities. His hope was that Bill could discover who the renegade employees were so he could turn them over to the local police, or have Clay deal with them.

Under ordinary circumstances Packard might go after them himself, especially since he was thirsting for revenge, but he was weaponless, and to this point, lacking clues.

"What's this?" Maynard asked, staring down the main drag, where workers were reconfiguring their carnival game areas to withstand the rain.

And two park police officers walked toward them with a purpose.

It was obvious the park officers had singled them out for some reason, but the sergeant had no idea why.

"I don't suppose they're coming to warn us about the bad weather," Maynard commented sarcastically.

Packard wondered if speaking to two armed officers was wise, or if they were on a secondary payroll. Running served no purpose, regardless of why the officers were approaching them. Holding his hand out at a level position, he indicated for Maynard to stay put and keep quiet.

"If they become a threat, we'll have to take care of it," Packard grumbled just above a whisper. "If they take us somewhere isolated, they can do whatever they want with us."

Maynard nodded that he understood as the officers reached them.

Packard quickly observed the two men, realizing one was young, appearing grim and serious about his job, while the other was older, with graying hair and a more neutral expression. He wore a baseball cap to shelter his head from the rain, even though the younger officer carried an umbrella that protected the pair.

Tensing a bit, Packard felt prepared to defend himself if necessary, but there was no proof these two men were anything except regular park police.

Stopping short of the food booth, the older officer pulled a sheet of paper from his shirt pocket, looking at it before locking his eyes on Packard.

"You Tim Packard?" the man asked, obviously knowing the answer already.

Looking suspiciously at the park officer, Packard glanced to Maynard, who appeared ready to slug either man with just a word. Curious, and deciding a confrontation was not necessary just yet, Packard held out his hand to keep Maynard at bay.

"Maybe," the sergeant answered the initial question. "Who's wanting to know?"

"Agent Jack Turpin sent us out to find you."

Packard wondered how Turpin would know where to begin looking for him, but he suspected if the agent had a dossier on Clay, he probably knew everyone on the task force. He likely had photos of each member.

Since the agent had his number, Packard also wondered why Turpin sent park officers instead of calling. Perhaps he intended to meet the sergeant one way or another.

It plagued the officer that an FBI agent wanted to speak with Clay, but he had more pressing things to worry about.

"What does he want?" Packard decided to ask, rather than delay the inevitable.

From the corner of his eye, he caught a bewildered look from Maynard, who was obviously out of the loop.

"He wants to talk to you. He says he knows what's going on, and he wants to help."

Based on the officer's expression, Packard knew the man was nothing more than a messenger for the agent, and had no idea what the words actually meant. Turpin apparently wanted to help, and Packard needed a secondary source of information in case Bill failed to find any useful information.

"Where is he?" Packard asked the spokesman officer of Turpin.

"In our office. He said something about you being leery of FBI agents, so he offered to meet wherever you want."

Packard's mind raced for a solution that provided privacy and an opportunity to talk without people milling around. He suddenly regretted letting his kids lead him around when they visited the park.

"The candy shop on the main drag," he finally decided aloud. "Tell him I want him there alone, and I'll give him all the information he needs."

With nothing more than a nod, the one officer turned around, taking his colleague with him. Packard watched which direction they chose to walk, curious where the police headquarters inside the park might be located. They headed toward the center of the park, which undoubtedly led to the offices behind several walls along the main strip.

"And what am I supposed to do?" Maynard questioned.

"You're tailing me. I'll talk to Turpin, but I don't want you too far away, just in case something happens."

"Who *is* this guy?"

"A government guy who wants to talk with Clay."

"About what?"

"I have no idea. But that's part of what I'm going to find out."

Packard looked to his watch.

"We'd better get going," he said, knowing he was about to get soaking wet from the rain, which had barely let up from its initial downpour.

*   *   *   *

Ten minutes later Packard approached the candy store, which was lined from floor to ceiling, along every wall, with colorful candies. Bright yellow walls on every side of the store served as backdrops for the rainbow-colored sugar candies and chocolates that rested on clear shelves, or hung from small hooks.

Several people browsed, riding out the storm, within the store. Others stood nearby, wearing orange ponchos sold by the park at a premium because they forgot to bring their own.

Turpin was easy to spot, because no one else wore a dark suit or black cowboy boots within the park's confines. Packard supposed there was no such thing as casual attire for FBI agents unless they were on a special assignment.

Approaching the agent, Packard kept a safe distance, even when the man looked up from the array of bagged cotton candy to spot him.

"So what would you like from me?" Packard asked immediately, not offering a handshake to the agent.

"I'd like to know why two innocent people are dead inside this park," Turpin answered squarely, a grim expression across his face. "And I want to know why you haven't done a thing about it if you knew this was coming."

"Not quite four hours ago I was waiting in line to ride that tall thing in the distance with my daughter," Packard said, pointing toward the Skydiver ride which now served as little more than a visual attraction. "I heard a strange noise, then witnessed a girl, still strapped in the seat, come crashing to the ground not far from where we were standing. Before that, I had no indication anything was wrong in this park."

Turpin's lips formed a concerned, possibly doubtful position. He rubbed his chin as he thought of something, staring at the swirled lollipops before him.

"But after that happened, you knew something was wrong."

"The bastards called me, told me to have my men here within three hours, or they'd kill many more before the day was done."

"And it never occurred to you to tell the park officials to clear out the park?"

"There were rules. No police, no outside help."

Packard decided not to mention how Clay had enlisted outside help, just in case Turpin didn't completely side with him.

"And you complied?"

"Of course I complied. I went through this last year as I'm sure you're aware. These people didn't just walk into the park this morning and decide they were going to randomly kill a few people. They had this planned out and set up. For all I knew, they might have placed bombs at the exit gates, so I wasn't doing anything to piss them off."

"I know you're resourceful, Sergeant Packard, so I suspect you didn't just bring your three men into the park."

Packard gave no immediate reply, simply looking Turpin in the eye.

"Speaking of my men, I'm curious why you want to speak to Clay so badly."

"That's between me and him. My concern is for the safety of the people remaining in this park at the moment."

"This rain might be the best thing to happen," Packard confessed. "It's chasing away a lot of them without making it look like anyone told them to leave."

Turpin looked around the store cautiously a moment, shrewd as a hawk looking for a morning snack on the ground from high above. He seemed wary of being watched, which gave Packard a slight sense of relief.

"I need to know what you know," the agent finally said, apparently seeing nothing that alarmed him.

"I know I have one man on his way to the hospital, and me and my other two might join him if we follow any further orders."

Turpin's face corkscrewed into a curious look.

"They separated us and lured us into situations they designed, even though they said they wouldn't harm any of us."

"So they've been here some time, probably posing as employees," Turpin deduced aloud. "They could be absolutely anyone if the terrorists bought their way in here."

"You'll forgive me if I don't put my full trust in you, either," Packard added.

Turpin let a thin, quirky grin slip.

"The Bureau isn't perfect, but we don't have many bad apples, and it wasn't that long ago I was doing your job in Texas. Putting complete faith in me can only help you."

"You're not going to be much help tracking down terrorists in those duds," Packard pointed out. "You might as well have 'federal agent' tattooed across your forehead."

"If they're as well organized as you say, they probably already know I'm here, and they haven't done anything drastic yet. In fact, they probably suspect you've already talked to me, so time is of the essence my friend."

"Well, they've cut off communications with me, so I doubt you're too far off track. I'm open to suggestions."

"If they've infiltrated the park they have to have people working on the inside. I'll use some of my connections and look for people who stand out."

"What connections?"

"I met the head of security and a local detective this morning."

Packard returned a hardened stare, then shook his head.

"You can't trust anyone. For the right money, even high level people can be bought. Even FBI agents."

Turpin openly disliked the second reference to the agent who nearly got Packard and his crew killed the year prior.

"I'll do my part, and I'll be in touch," Turpin insisted.

Still putting forth a guarded front, Packard refused to be comfortable around the agent. He knew nothing of the man's agenda, much less where he came from. At this point he only had Turpin's word, and he knew that didn't always mean much.

Without a word, he started toward the door, but the agent's voice halted him.

"Oh, and tell Mr. Maynard when he shadows you he needs to be a bit more discreet."

Packard nodded sourly, then exited the candy shop, returning to the darkened skies and pouring rain that awaited him. The sound of thunder echoed in the distance while rain spattered off the blacktop surface, sounding like a thousand simultaneous leaky faucets.

Looking upward, he wondered what he was going to do while Turpin began an internal investigation. If the agent was truthful, which Packard suspected he was, he wished Turpin well in his search.

And his personal safety.

*   *   *   *

Bill and Casey had secured a conference room for themselves in the headquarters building, which overlooked the stores and mammoth water fountains along the main strip. As Casey spread employee records across the conference table, Bill gazed out the window at the guests flocking to the gates, ready to exit the park to escape from the terrible weather.

"You ready?" Casey asked, prompting him to turn around.

"Sure," he said, joining her on the other side of the long table.

Both stood over the papers, examining them.

"I've narrowed down the employees hired during the past year, but there are quite a few," she reported, pointing to several records highlighted in yellow.

"We're likely talking about male employees, possibly of Asian ethnicity, but not necessarily. Do you have photos?"

"Stored in our computers. Every employee *has* to have an ID made for access to the park."

"Do different badges allow various access points to the park?"

"To a limited extent, yes. Our regular employees have cards that get them inside the park, to their lockers, and to necessary buildings related to their jobs."

Bill thought a moment, deciding the terrorist group would never settle for limited access. They had to have at least one person working higher up, and he wanted an idea of who to look for.

"What's the next level of access?"

"There are only two more levels. The next is what most of our park police and office personnel have. They need access to these and other offices, so their cards work in those doors when the doors are secured."

"I take it the last level is full access, probably provided to you, your parents, and the head of security?"

Casey nodded.

"A few trusted employees also have those cards, but the total number of people is under a dozen."

Bill wondered how much access was truly necessary to rig part of a ride to explode, and to switch out a blank or two with real bullets.

"What kind of security do you have after hours?" he asked.

"We have two shifts of three guards who keep watch overnight. One patrols the parking lot while two monitor and walk the grounds inside."

Which meant, in theory, only one guard needed bribing to allow terrorist forces inside, if that guard had good information, or a detailed map for them.

Bill returned his attention to the employment sheets momentarily, until a tap on his shoulder startled him enough that he forcefully turned around. Staring directly at him was his nephew.

"I wish you wouldn't do that," Bill chastised Clay.

"Sorry."

"Did you find anything?" Casey asked the young officer.

"I'm striking out," Clay said, armed with several visible weapons, including a sword strapped to his back.

"How are you getting around without security stopping you?" she inquired.

"Rooftops."

Clay was visibly impatient with small talk. He had a reason for stopping in, which endangered his stealthy walk over the park.

"You mentioned something about an officer you subdued earlier?" Clay asked him quietly, so Casey didn't hear.

"In the parking lot near the storage building. He's locked in the trunk."

Clay nodded, starting toward the door.

"The keys are locked inside," Bill called out a warning.

"Not a problem," Clay replied, continuing on his way.

Watching his nephew leave momentarily, Bill was still amazed at Clay's various abilities, wishing he had time to master more of them. Casey returned to his side, touching his shoulder.

"You worry about him, don't you?"

"Yes, but not in the way you might think."

She gave him a questioning look, but Bill had no time to explain Clay's self-sufficient nature. Fully able to take care of himself, Clay had lost part of his emotional side during his stay in Japan. Bill doubted he was ever going to recover enough to settle down again, but he wasn't giving up all hope.

"What is Clay going to do? What was that about?"

"I ran into one of your park officers on my way in here. He basically admitted he was working for the bad guys, and wanted to put a bullet in my head. I got the better of him, and locked him in the trunk of his patrol car."

"Alive?" Casey asked hesitantly.

"Yes, but his physical well-being will probably depend on how he answers my nephew's questions."

She nodded, looking down to the papers spread across the table.

"Maybe he can get some information, but in the meantime, we might take some good guesses ourselves."

"I have a feeling before the day is done we're going to know who some of them are," Bill stated. "They can't hide for long, especially if they're responsible for two deaths."

Casey spent the next five minutes pointing out some of the older male employees who had access to more areas of the park. Bill looked over the sheets, but they were vague, and without photos.

"We need to look at their applications and their ID photos," he said.

"Why the applications?"

"See what kind of backgrounds they have. If they were dumb enough to put down military experience, or something useful in terrorism, I may be able to catch it. By the same token, I may be able to rule out some of them if their experience looks local and legitimate."

Casey gave a grin.

"You're pretty bright, you know?"

"That's what they pay me the big bucks for at the hospital."

"What is it you do?"

Not wishing to waste much time with his background, Bill kept his answer simple.

"I'm the director of maintenance."

"Wow," Casey said, snatching up the papers, leading him toward a nearby computer terminal.

She typed in several pieces of information, including names, and began calling up files on the employees they both thought met the criteria of potential terrorist aides.

Bill felt a strange pang in the pit of his stomach, wondering how much time they had left before the park felt the wrath of the men responsible for murdering two people. He hoped the death toll stopped at two, and his nephew, or someone, put a stop to the people creating such a ruckus.

CHAPTER 14

▼

Clay silently slipped through the parking lot toward the storage area his uncle told him about, finding no one outside because of the pouring rain.

Moving quickly between cars, he felt the rain peck at him through his soaked clothes. Keeping his concentration on the task at hand, Clay observed the area around him, seeing no park employees anywhere. He fully expected to see their security and police prowling the area, but things were remarkably silent.

With Casey's parents away on business, he wondered who was in charge of security and major park decisions. Someone wasn't doing their job very well, which led him to think at least one person had a secondary agenda.

And a supplementary income.

He felt several weapons beneath and against his clothing. A small pack strapped to his back held his *katana* and several other bladed weapons. Anyone who saw him might view him as a street performer or part of one of the park's shows before believing he was trained as an assassin.

Clay's instruction in Japan came in the form of tradition, rather than learning how to murder people in stealth. Several others didn't share his instructor's views, using their talents for profit and personal gain after leaving the *dojo*.

Approaching the police cruiser, Clay ducked beneath the top of the nearby cars, examining the trunk area, wondering if his uncle had secured the man enough that he couldn't reach the release cord.

Checking inside the vehicle first, Clay noticed the keys. In no mood to pick the trunk's lock, and without the benefit of tools, he took out a loaded punch he had bought years prior at a police convention. In his uncle's haste to grab Clay's equipment, Bill had left behind several key weapons and tools.

Masked by the sound of the weather, the shattering window fell inside once the loaded punch struck a lower corner. Clay reached inside, grabbed the keys, and used the remote to automatically open the trunk.

Taking hold of a short sword, he reached the end of the car, looking into the trunk with a stern look. A pair of eyes met his with initial relief, which quickly turned to distinct fear, as though the park officer recognized him.

In fact, Clay felt certain he was recognized.

"You're not going to kill me, are you?" the man asked immediately once Clay removed the gag from his mouth.

"That depends on you. You tell me what I want to hear and I put you back in here like I never found you."

"And if I don't?"

"I just gave you your best case scenario. Mess with me and I'll demonstrate your other options."

Without a word, the officer nodded in understanding.

"How many park employees are working for them?"

"Four that I know of."

"Who's paying you? An Asian, or a black man?"

"Neither," the officer answered quickly enough that Clay knew he wasn't lying. "It was a white guy."

The answer threw Clay completely. He felt positive Kim, or Voodoo, was masterminding the park's demise. His mind returned to the matter at hand, just in time to hear an arrow slicing the air, coming his way.

Clay turned to deflect or catch the thin missile, but he was not the intended target this time. He was unable to stop the arrow from piercing the corrupt officer's heart, ending the man's life, and preventing Clay from gaining answers to several important questions.

Based on the path of the arrow, Clay's eyes immediately went to the nearest building's roof, spying Voodoo there, lowering his bow. A throaty, evil laugh came from the man's mouth, covered by a dark mask, but as Clay reached for a *shuriken* to throw at him, Voodoo darted away.

This time Clay decided to pursue him, quickly slamming the trunk shut before he took off, knowing the officer was beyond his help. Voodoo often poisoned his arrows and darts, to ensure death, even if his mark wasn't perfect.

Sprinting toward the building, Clay leapt onto a car, which helped him propel him onto the rooftop, which Voodoo had already crossed. Now he was leaping to another building, but Clay took chase, pulling a short staff from a loop on his side, which contained a chain with a weighted end once the two halves of the staff were pulled apart.

He jumped to the next building, pulling the staff apart. He let the weighted end of the staff fly, catching Voodoo's right leg as the black man tried leaping to the next building. Caught by surprise, and having nothing to clasp while in mid-air, Voodoo fell between the buildings awkwardly flailing out of Clay's sight.

By no means did Clay expect to find his adversary helplessly in a heap, but when he reached the end of the building, Clay had to dodge the sharp edge of a sword thrust upward at him.

Deflecting it with a staff end, he jumped down, doing battle with Voodoo, sword against hardened wooden staff ends. Clay dodged a few jabs and thrusts from the *katana*, then used part of the chain to entangle the sword and pull it away from Voodoo.

While he was doing this, his adversary had pulled out a smoke bomb, throwing the tiny shimmering ball to the ground with a purpose. Clay barely saw the ball before it hit the ground, which prompted him to leap upward, thrusting a foot against one building for a further boost, providing a better view of which direction Voodoo chose to run.

Above the smoke, Clay was able to see the man dart toward the employee parking lot, which offered dozens of cars to hide behind. Several employees were entering the lot, either on break, or leaving for the day, so Clay followed Voodoo's lead, ducking behind several parked vehicles in pursuit of the man.

Already two cars behind his enemy, Clay watched Voodoo's every move, trying to monitor what the employees did. It certainly wasn't above Voodoo's methods to kill civilians to ensure his escape, or better his position by distracting Clay.

Depriving Voodoo of his best sword was a small victory, but Clay worried that the man had secret weapons stashed throughout the park. Now it was impossible to know who had helped the man, and in what way. Hopefully Bill had some ideas based on the employee records, to move the investigation along.

All three employees Clay had spotted made it safely to their vehicles, allowing Clay to creep one car closer to Voodoo. While in a crouched walk, Clay replaced the chain inside both ends of the staff, then closed it up, switching it with two small sickles from his compact backpack.

Once the three cars pulled safely past, Clay jumped atop the hood of the closest vehicle, darted across the top, then leapt to the next vehicle's trunk, planning on thrusting a sickle downward. If successful, the skirmish would end early, but Clay knew he was taking a chance of losing his adversary completely.

Taking one last leap, he swung downward while soaring between two vehicles, finding nothing below for the blade of his sickle to lodge into. Landing a second later, he looked around, listening intently for any sounds of movement.

Aware that his feet were vulnerable if Voodoo took to hiding beneath a car, Clay jumped up again, landing on the bumper of a nearby truck. Knowing the trained assassin remained somewhere in the parking lot, Clay decided to walk along the car tops, continuing his search. Darting across car tops kept him safe from ambush, but it also gave away his position. There was no way to silence his weight coming down on metal or fiberglass.

His archery skills were never topnotch when he was training, and Bill hadn't packed his bow or arrows, so Clay was left with shurikens, throwing knives, or blow darts for projectile weapons. None were highly effective against people trained as well as himself, so he needed to find Voodoo nearby, or risk losing him altogether.

Clay knew if he took down Voodoo, there was little other threat to him inside the park. Kim was a far better mouthpiece than a fighter, so Clay needed to live in the moment, seizing his one opportunity to end the overall battle before the death toll grew.

Reaching the last car in the row, Clay flipped defensively off the vehicle, twisting his torso in midair to land on his feet, poised for an attack. Seeing no threat, he crept along the line of vehicles, looking down each row for his intended target. He didn't expect to see Voodoo in the open, which left opportunity for the man to slip beneath a car, then crawl to safety.

Apparently the man didn't feel the same way, or felt threatened, because as Clay passed the next car, a short blade nearly lodged itself in part of his head.

This time, however, it was not Voodoo stabbing a weapon toward him, because the man dressed in black garb was Asian. A defensive glance behind him revealed that Voodoo had snuck up while Clay was distracted by the attack. Flanked on both sides, Clay now had to decide how he was going to battle two dishonorable men from his past.

*   *   *   *

Turpin had borrowed the services of Hugh Bryant, the park's head of security, once the scene in Frontier Town was processed and cleared.

Deciding to smooth over their earlier harsh exchange, Turpin apologized with what sincerity he could muster. He stated a desire to help Bryant find the people responsible for the two deaths, rather than take over the investigation.

Tension between them eased, but failed to completely dissipate after Bryant accepted the apology. He wanted more answers from the agent, but Turpin wasn't forthcoming, nor did he plan to be.

They set up headquarters in Bryant's office, initially finding two unarmed security personnel inside whom the security director immediately kicked out.

Several tense minutes passed between them as they seated themselves inside the office. Bryant peered outside the window momentarily as Turpin tried reading the man's thoughts. Both were too stubborn to instantly reconcile their differences.

Turpin swallowed his pride, deciding to break the ice, when Bryant spoke without turning from the window.

"I guess I don't need to call in any outside help if I have you here," the security director said before seating himself at a computer terminal, calling up employee records. "What exactly am I looking for anyway?"

"Employees hired in the last year who might be tempted to work for a terrorist organization."

Bryant simply looked to him with an incredulous expression.

"That's coming from left field, Agent Turpin. Mind explaining yourself?"

"I got a tip that your two misfortunes today may have been the work of an organization bent on creating terror."

Looking unconvinced, Bryant typed in a few code words that brought up the park employee roster.

"I'm not going to deny that the first incident looked staged to me, but I can't imagine how someone would have access *and* the knowhow to rig that ride to explode."

"Why do you think I'm asking you to look at the roster?"

"That's not what I'm saying," Bryant argued. "What you're talking about is a conspiracy that wouldn't be a one-trip mission on their part. And to begin with, they'd probably work on that ride after hours when we have only three active officers on patrol."

"So at least one of them would have to be on the take."

"Exactly. I might have an idea of who our rat is, too."

"Oh?"

Bryant typed in a name, bringing up a particular employee who looked like he was posing for a mug shot more than an employee identification badge. Turpin wondered if the man had experience posing for both kinds of cameras.

He appeared Caucasian, but his skin was tan, like he may have had a Hispanic or Asian mix from one parent. His black hair was thick, as was his jaw, but the brown eyes and his expression caused the agent to believe this man was incapable of feeling any kind of happy emotion.

Beside the photo was the name Hector Gomez. His age was listed as twenty-eight, and his height was just over six-feet tall. Little other information was available, because the park apparently did not enter facts from the paper applications they accepted.

"What's this guy's history?" he asked Bryant.

"I don't know him very well because he works the overnight shift," Bryant confessed. "I just know the other guys complain that he stays to himself and seems demanding about certain things when it comes to work."

"Such as?"

"His assignments. There were certain nights he wanted to patrol outside, and others where he wanted to patrol the grounds, leaving the veteran members to watch the monitors. No one on the midnight shift really cares which assignment they get, but the senior guys weren't happy when he came in and started throwing his weight around."

"You hired him, didn't you? What impressions did you personally get?"

"I'm not part of their interview or hiring process unless it directly concerns me, like my two assistant directors. It's typically a very hurried process done in late winter. If you have a pulse, and full springtime availability, you're pretty much hired if you show any kind of inclination to accept their pay and be nice to guests."

And anyone can fake being nice for an interview, Turpin thought.

"Where do we find this guy?" the agent asked.

"I doubt you have far to look," a voice said from behind the two men.

Turpin spun around to find Gomez pointing a gun in their direction, and one glance downward told him Bryant was equally surprised.

"Packard had to open his big mouth. He was supposed to keep things quiet, but no, he wanted to sell me out."

Turpin was now moderately confused.

"Sell you out? For what?"

"You're the one with all of the answers in front of you," Gomez said. "Why don't you tell me?"

"So you're saying Packard is the mastermind behind this entire thing?" Turpin said, making the doubt in his voice evident.

"He did contract work for the park so he could scout the whole place. It's in your system, I'm sure, but the two of you aren't going to have the chance to look up anything. He sent me over here to finish what I started."

Turpin's eyes had been searching for a way out of the dangerous situation laid before him. There was a chance he might be able to duck behind a nearby partition to draw his own firearm, but Bryant was trapped, with nowhere to go, even though he was armed.

If Gomez fired his weapon inside the room he risked someone hearing the shot. Turpin glanced over to Bryant, who had thumbed his radio's transmit button, keeping the appendage pressed downward.

Quickly returning his attention to their captor, the agent knew he had no good ideas. After all, agents didn't carry anything except cellular phones for communication, and his firearm might as well have been a mile away, because reaching for it meant certain death.

"You kill me, every federal agent in the state is going to be looking for your sorry ass," Turpin threatened, not backing down.

"I'm real scared," Gomez said with open sarcasm. "Packard and his crew took care of everything. I'll be on the next flight to Mexico while he's still trying to figure out what he wants to do here."

"Who is Packard?" Bryant finally asked.

"It's a long story," Turpin answered.

He returned his attention to Gomez.

"Do you really think I'm fool enough to believe a cop who lives over two hours away is responsible for two separate catastrophes here today?"

"It doesn't matter what either of us think, because you're both about to die."

A door behind the man opened, distracting him long enough for Turpin to push Bryant aside and draw his firearm, since the henchman had neglected to collect it. He likely figured no one would find them inside the security office, particularly in Bryant's personal office.

Stepping to the side, Turpin noticed the entering man who distracted Gomez was an Ohio state trooper who seemed perplexed by Gomez and some kind of fable the crooked employee quickly conjured. Turpin didn't dare call out, because Gomez had the gun hidden behind his back, and the trooper was directly between the admitted criminal and the only available exit.

Moving silently forward, Turpin had an idea about drawing close enough to physically overpower Gomez, but the man seemed to sense the movement. Instead of turning on the agent, he said something in a friendly manner to the trooper, then burst forward, pushing the man down before bolting out the exit.

"Stop him!" Turpin called to the younger man, who quickly regained his footing.

He gave Turpin a befuddled look, then glanced to the agent's firearm.

"I'm FBI," Turpin said sternly. "He was holding us hostage."

Without another word, the trooper took off to pursue Gomez. As Turpin turned to see if Bryant was unharmed, the director placed a hand on his shoulder.

"I'm good," he announced. "Let's go get that prick."

Turpin nodded, then both men raced out the door to catch up. It had been years since the agent engaged in a foot pursuit, and the rush of adrenaline felt good, particularly since he kept himself in excellent physical condition.

Following Bryant outside, Turpin felt his face immediately pelted by rain. Stormy weather had returned, creating a virtual blanket that made it nearly impossible to see more than ten feet in front of him. Amazingly, there was no sign of Gomez or the trooper through the rain. Turpin expected to see at least a bit of movement, however blurry it might be, to guide him.

"Let's split up," Turpin suggested, pointing out the direction he wanted Bryant to take.

Bryant nodded, shielding his face from the rain with a raised arm, then darted off to search for the two men.

Turpin took a more cautious approach, beginning to weave around the buildings and vehicles parked beside them, suspecting Gomez may have eluded or harmed the trooper. His senses were useless in the rain. He saw nothing, heard nothing except pounding rainfall, and felt only the cold metal of his firearm in his right hand.

Something about the situation didn't feel right, because he felt certain he and Bryant were close behind the two men when they left the security office. For them to be completely out of sight, despite the weather, seemed impossible.

Grunting to himself, Turpin proceeded with extra caution, wondering where the trooper's car had been parked.

A sinking feeling came over him as he pressed forward.

*   *   *   *

Bill and Casey had come across one particular file that caught Bill's attention for a few reasons. A man named Aaron Bekaert had come from Belgium to work on rides for the park, directly from the manufacturer who designed and created several of the park's metal roller coasters.

After reading the man's file, Bill discovered he hadn't actually been sent by the company, but volunteered to go to work for the park after deciding he wanted to leave his homeland. Paid rather well for his services, Bekaert performed the morning safety checks on several of the rides, often two-hundred feet off the ground.

Rather than visit the man at the metal shop, where he often worked, Bill decided to have Casey summon him to the main office. This would help them avoid confrontation in front of his colleagues, and give him a neutral environment for a formal conversation. Bill also liked the idea of having a confined space, in case the interview turned sour and he needed to defend himself.

"So your nephew is really a cop?" Casey asked while they waited for Bekaert to arrive.

"He is."

Bill caught a bit of a gleam in her eye, despite the dark circumstances surrounding them. He wondered if Casey had some form of puppy love for Clay, probably in the form of a sudden crush.

"I saw he was carrying weapons. Is he some kind of karate guy?"

Bill cleared his throat uncomfortably.

"Uh, he's a little more than that. He spent four years in Japan, so he's very well trained in a few of the arts."

"Arts, huh?" Casey asked, running her finger along the table, near the employee files, as she playfully went around the conference table.

In some aspects she showed full maturity, but in others, she was still a very young woman. After having sense enough to suggest Bill change his clothes, she was now distracted, asking about Clay.

Her father kept a closet full of spare clothes at the park, and Bill found some that enabled him to blend in as a businessman, rather than a mechanic. Casey thought it might be prudent to look the part if he was going to be her new assistant the remainder of the day.

"You seem to have forgotten our troubles rather quickly," Bill pointed out.

"I haven't forgotten. I'm just distracting myself momentarily with conversation. What are you going to do with Aaron?"

"Hopefully nothing. I just plan on talking to him."

"We call him the Belgian Bear. He's just a big lug."

"Does he speak good English?"

"He has an accent, but he speaks pretty well. Apparently he had learned our language before coming over here."

Bill looked to the man's record, which was limited, considering he was a recent citizen to their country.

"Is he a model employee?"

Casey took a seat across from him, growing a bit more serious.

"He gets to work every morning at the same time, gets along with others, and does the job well. He knows what he's doing."

"That's what worries me. He has intimate knowledge of every ride around here."

"I just can't picture him deliberately harming anyone."

Bill looked over the sheet.

"Says here he's never been married, has no kids. No attachments. He's my age, which makes me wonder if he's just a unique individual, or a perfect recruit for a terrorist cell."

Casey shook her head, openly set against any such thought.

"He's harmless. He sounds a little like a German, but he's absolutely loyal to my family. We've even had him over for dinner several times."

Bill didn't have time to waste, but he figured if anyone was capable of rigging a ride to explode, or tamper with other areas of the park, Bekaert fit the profile. He was running out of ideas, and with time against him, it seemed logical to start with a man who had both knowledge and unlimited access.

Taking a moment to look out the windows, Bill saw an incredible view of the main drag, which looked like a ghost town with everyone now indoors, or gone. A few umbrellas danced along the concrete paths, appearing as though they were floating, since Bill had an overhead view.

"Didn't your family ever prepare for anything like this?" he asked Casey, wondering why security was so lax.

"We don't have a huge budget, and the metal detectors seemed like enough of a deterrent," she answered. "I guess we never expected problems from within."

"You can claim you are a family business, but this is an enterprise to me. If it's impersonal enough that your parents don't do their own hiring, then it's become somewhat corporate, hasn't it?"

Casey lost herself in thought a moment, joining him to look out one of the floor to ceiling windows inside the conference room.

"When I was a kid it all seemed magical, and I just couldn't believe my parents owned it. I was the envy of every kid in school. It wasn't always easy, though. Dad fought to get loans for the new rides, but when they started to pay for themselves, it was almost an overnight turnaround from struggle to complete success."

She paused a moment.

"We never really expected anyone to try blowing the place up, or anything like that. The metal detectors took care of any threats we thought were coming, short of a crashing plane in here."

"Yeah, well, these people are great at blending in," Bill said, remembering how one of them infiltrated his hospital often enough to learn the layout a year prior. "It's not anything you or your parents did wrong."

A knock came to the door just after Bill said the words, and as he looked to see a solid man a few inches taller than himself standing at the doorway, he hoped Bekaert was as peaceful as Casey said.

Wearing overalls, Bekaert looked as though he might have been working on something in the shop. His brown hair appeared as though it had been caught in a crosswind, while his bright blue eyes went directly to Bill. They quickly returned to Casey.

"You wanted to see me, Miss Trimble?" he asked in a heavy accent.

"Have a seat, Aaron," she said, extending her arm toward a nearby chair.

He looked around the room as though he had never seen the executive conference room before. To Bill, he looked like a simple man with a gift for building and maintaining colossal rides. Though stout, and built like a bull, he was still small enough that he could reasonably climb around metal curves at tremendous heights in Bill's estimation.

"This is Bill, my consultant," she said, making Bill a happy man because she kept the rest of his identity secret.

Bekaert suddenly looked a bit concerned, as though he was about to be fired. He shifted uneasily in his seat, probably not accustomed to having a consultant around the family that had adopted him.

"Am I in trouble?" he asked hesitantly, openly unsure if he wanted to hear the answer.

"Not at all," Bill said evenly, trying to keep the man calm, beginning to suspect Casey was quite right about his qualities. "I just want to know if you've seen anyone tampering with any of the rides the past few weeks."

"No," he answered plainly. "I'm the one who works on most of them."

"What about the Skydiver?"

Bekaert's eyes widened a bit, realizing without a doubt why he was being interviewed.

"I work on it."

"What I really want to know is how hard it would be for someone to cause one of those seats to fall off."

Bekaert shrugged.

"If someone got inside the cylinder, they would be hidden. All of the screws and bolts holding the seats in place can be accessed inside of the cylinder."

"How often is the ride checked?" Casey asked.

He looked to her as though she should have known.

"I mean *really* checked," she clarified.

"We rotate which parts of the ride we check each day," Bekaert answered. "One part gets checked thoroughly each day."

He thought a moment.

"The inside cylinder was probably checked late last week."

"Is it possible a small explosive device might be overlooked?" Bill inquired.

"The bolts are covered with padding so we do not hurt ourselves inside the cylinder," Bekaert explained. "It is very tight in there."

Bill noticed how the man, like most immigrants, did not use contractions when speaking. His speaking was very plain, but straightforward. His eyes were constantly on either Casey or himself, which indicated he was being truthful. Now Bill regarded him as a useful informational source, rather than a potential suspect.

"Are you telling me four screws and bolts are all that hold those seats into place when they hoist people over three-hundred feet into the air?" he asked Bekaert.

"There is also a steel lip that connects the seats onto the steel cylinder."

Bill began to suspect someone with authority and access to every square inch of the park was responsible for the explosion, or very much helping the terrorists.

Casey had given him a rundown of who had such access, but he was able to rule out her and her parents, leaving a list about as long as the fingers on one of his hands. With Bekaert now eliminated as a suspect, he wanted to turn his attention to who was, and who wasn't, currently inside the park.

"Would you like me to show you the cylinder?" Bekaert offered, breaking Bill's train of thought.

"No, thank you," Bill replied absently, his mind still pondering his next step. "You've been a great help, Aaron. We may give you a shout later on if we need anything else."

Casey looked to him, as though surprised he took such initiative in the interview.

Bill had that quality, dealing with tough, independent men in his own department. He had to show leadership qualities, or risk being stepped on daily.

Bekaert slowly made his way out of the conference room, as though wondering exactly why he had been summoned at all.

"What now?" Casey asked once they were alone.

"I need to know the names of who has complete access to the park. And I want to know who is here at this very moment, and who isn't."

"What's that going to tell us?"

"Hopefully who is aiding the terrorists if someone isn't where they're supposed to be."

"I can find out who has been here today by calling up their employee cards. If they've been scanned at any access door, I'll know."

"Good."

Bill took a deep breath through his nose, sensing something wasn't right, as though danger lingered nearby. Unable to place the source of his discontent, he turned his attention to Casey, who had begun accessing a computer.

He hoped the truth came soon enough to save more of the people milling below them, unaware that any danger still lurked inside the park.

CHAPTER 15

▼

Instinctively, Clay should have sensed so much danger coming his way, and he knew the smart thing to do was to regroup and fight on his own terms. He also knew that running from the fight laid before him allowed the terrorists to keep the upper hand, because they would disappear to do more harm, hoping to draw him out.

This was his one chance to end the conflict, crushing the terrorist cell by killing its two leaders. Holding the two small sickles, he knew there were much better weapons for dealing with a one-on-two battle, but he was in no position to change weapons.

Voodoo and Kim were obviously ignoring the ritual known as *kuji-in*, in which warriors trained in classic ninja tradition used hand symbols before battle. The ritual was meant to heighten senses and enhance the body's physical and mental abilities. Clay practiced *kuji-in*, finding some use from it, but four years of training was a far cry from mastery of such a technique.

Apparently his adversaries had no use for ancient tradition.

Holding the sickles defensively before him, Clay glanced from one man to the other, wondering if they were going to attack, or simply wait for him to charge.

"What do you expect to gain here?" he asked instead, without so much as a blink.

Both displayed smirks, obviously amused that he would ask such a question, or that he didn't know the answer.

"Isn't it obvious?" Kim retorted.

"No. It isn't."

Clay shifted his stance, monitoring both men.

"Why this park? Why murder innocent people here?"

"Ask yourself what Sato would have wanted," Voodoo replied with a sneer behind his mask. "He wanted you to die as a failure, but we've done one better."

Clay was befuddled. What was that supposed to mean?

"When we get done with you, your name will be disgraced on a national level, and we'll be back to making money."

"This isn't a paid job?" Clay asked somewhat sarcastically. "I thought it was always about the money with your group."

"We're getting paid, but we took a significant cut on this one," Kim stated. "The chance for personal vengeance made up for the lack of funding."

Having heard enough, Clay readied himself for battle, thinking of a dirty trick he might use before either of his adversaries considered it.

"Your chance to run has come and gone," Voodoo noted. "Now only death is in your future."

"I'll be damned if I let you two chase me away," Clay replied sternly. "And I'll see you both in hell after I put you there first."

Wasting no time, Clay threw down a smoke bomb, but instead of retreating to safety, he charged Kim's left side, away from Voodoo, deliberately swinging the sickle in his left hand with precision aim.

If not for Kim sidestepping at the last possible instant, Clay would have struck the man's femoral artery, likely causing him to bleed out. Probably trying to avoid being hit at all, Kim had taken a half step back, causing the sickle to lodge itself in his thigh, doing a fair amount of damage, but not killing the man.

Not slowing one bit as he inflicted the damage, Clay left his sickle behind, leaping atop a nearby car, taking a defensive stance. Quickly replacing the remaining sickle to its holding pin at his side, he reached over his shoulder, slowly pulling out the *katana* to deal with Voodoo.

With stern eyes, and a calculated drawing of his sword, Clay showed he meant business, even as Kim limped off to one side, attempting to nurse his wound.

He struggled to pull the sickle's blade from his leg without further damaging the muscle tissue as his partner returned Clay's stare, the confidence ebbing from his face.

Clay had no idea what training the two men had done since his departure from Japan, so he didn't underestimate either of them. Giving them no time to recover, he charged Voodoo, who immediately placed his sword defensively before him, deflecting Clay's initial killing blow.

Exchanging a series of lunges and parries, the two engaged in combat, but Clay knew Kim was fully capable of interjecting himself into the mix at any moment. Keeping himself in a position to view both men, Clay realized the distraction was going to keep him from committing himself to finishing Voodoo.

If he had the capability in the first place.

Knowing he was never going to win the battle under the current conditions, Clay continued to parlay with Voodoo, feeling the second sickle at his side. He decided to take a chance which might end the skirmish early.

Or get him killed.

Acting more defensively, Clay backed off, waiting for Voodoo to take a predictable swing at him. When a one-armed swipe of the sword came his way, Clay flipped over the blade, landing behind his adversary. In the same motion, as he regained his footing, he held the sword as an extension of his own arm, virtually throwing a punch a Kim's neck, hoping to decapitate him.

Disappointment came in the form of Kim raising Clay's own sickle to block the blade, meaning he was alive, and recuperating.

Now Clay was caught between the two, in grave danger. A glance at Kim's face told him the man was in pain, and that something was drawing close to him from behind.

Suspecting Voodoo was no longer going to waste time in combat, he ducked to one side, witnessing a reddish mist emerge forcefully from Voodoo's mouth, spewing heavily into Kim's face. The Oriental man screamed in anguish as Clay took a shortened swing at Voodoo, slicing the man's upper right arm enough to cause continual bleeding.

He had heard rumor of the black man mixing in dark magic and trickery with his training, but he knew very little about the man's alleged black magic.

Until now.

Even so, he doubted the man used little more than minor biological warfare to gain unfair advantages over his adversaries. Kim was the recipient of the chemical weapon, and for the moment, he was completely out of the picture.

Clay engaged in sword play with Voodoo once again, deflecting several stabs and swings of the man's *katana*. He didn't lose complete track of Kim, but several quick glances let him know the man was incapable of attacking him, so Clay continued to wait for an opening that might allow him to injure or kill Voodoo.

The two wove between cars, artfully clashing their swords with precision accuracy and blocking techniques. Voodoo jumped onto a car hood, prompting Clay to take a swipe at his feet, which caused the man to leap over the blade. Clay then had to block Voodoo's blade, which came down toward his shoulder blade.

Spinning away from the car defensively, Clay blocked another swipe from the man's sword, then used his forearm to knock Voodoo's feet out from under him.

He landed hard on the car hood with a thud and a forced exhale of air from his lungs. Clay drew the sickle from his side in a flash, blocking Voodoo's sword with his own, creating the opening he needed to deliver a killing blow with the sickle.

Voodoo had enough presence of mind, and room, to maneuver if Clay went for his head, so he opted for a body shot, which would ultimately prove fatal. As he began swinging downward, a sense of danger came to him too late.

A gunshot rang through the air, bringing a sudden pain to his torso, as though he had been stabbed from behind. Never before had Clay been shot, but he now knew the sensation as the bullet entered near his left shoulder blade, exiting through the front in less than a second.

Unable to help himself, he lost track of the moment, looking down at his chest, letting a strange sound escape his open mouth. Just above his heart, near the shoulder, blood began pooling, then dripping, as he turned to see Kim holding a revolver pointed at him, with its dazed owner still trying to see clearly.

Clay refused to believe the man had stooped to such a level, knowing their training and its tradition dictated otherwise. Skipping over hand signs was one thing, but using firearms was completely taboo in combat.

What felt like a minute actually took place over a period of a second or two, then Clay's mind returned to Voodoo, and how the man was probably already delivering a killing blow. Ducking and rolling at the same time, Clay had no choice but to retreat from the fight, because he was going to bleed out before the opportunity to kill both men ever presented itself.

If not for Kim's disoriented state, Clay might have already been dead, but fate showed him good favor. He reached into his pocket, which prompted Voodoo to believe he was reaching for a smoke bomb, causing him to charge forward for the kill.

Instead of doing as he normally might, Clay pulled out a throwing blade, tossing it with skillful precision into the man's shoulder. This move granted Clay enough time to throw a smoke bomb, allowing him to duck under the nearest car before his adversaries knew where he went.

Blood droplets followed him like a breadcrumb trail, leaving him little time to escape the situation before they pursued him.

Torn between putting pressure on the wound and keeping his hands free to grab weaponry, Clay needed to ensure he was completely free before tending to the bullet hole. He continued rolling under cars, drawing closer to the park's employee gate, rather than the predictable nearby entrance.

Stopping at the last possible car, he positioned himself on his stomach to peer under the other cars in the lot. Seeing no feet, he knew the two men had taken to the tops of the vehicles, searching for him from above, ever so cautious because he might still strike their feet.

Another lucky break came his way, because he heard a door close in the distance, then several voices talking about trivial work topics. Several employees were leaving the park, either for a late lunch, or for the day. He saw two sets of feet drop in completely different areas, realizing Kim and Voodoo were close to finding him.

When he knew they were rolling beneath the cars for cover, he rolled to the outside of the vehicle he was hidden beneath, setting himself perpendicular to the tire. Obscured from their view, he remained perfectly still a moment, seeing a different door nearby that led inside the park. Beside it, however, was a steel trash bin, which granted him access to the roof if he had strength enough to make the jump, then run for cover.

He was amazed no guards were around, and even more so that the parking lot had no security cameras. Everything seemed too perfectly against him, but he was determined to overcome the odds if he was able to escape and heal.

Once he heard two cars start, he prepared himself for a running escape. It took only seconds for both vehicles to pass, then he regained his footing, sprinting toward the trash bin, hoping both Voodoo and Kim were too preoccupied to immediately notice him.

His luck, he soon discovered, had run out.

Despite a fairly quick run toward the door, he leapt atop the bin in one try, not slowing one bit as he jumped for the roof, clasping the ledge as an arrow soared through the air. The sound of the arrow's feathers cutting the air reached his eardrums an instant before the pointed object penetrated the hamstring muscle of his right leg.

The only thing stopping the arrow from going straight through was the brick wall of the building he scaled. Wincing in agony from the second wound, Clay struggled to reach the top of the building, then rolled quickly behind an air-conditioning unit to avoid further injury.

Realizing the arrow had a metal shaft, he wasn't going to be able to snap it in half, so he had no choice except to pull it through. Running already felt nearly impossible without the projectile lodged in his leg.

Gritting his teeth to keep from audibly giving his location away, Clay pulled the arrow through, gripping his own blood each time his hands changed positions. He half expected the two men to join him on the rooftop just long enough to kill him.

They didn't, which affirmed his notion that Voodoo was more than a little concerned he was a worthy adversary, hurt or not.

Tossing the arrow aside, once it was fully removed, Clay gingerly regained his footing, limping toward the main office area. He turned to make certain he wasn't being followed, unwilling to put his uncle, or Casey, in danger.

Knowing he was the only real threat to the terrorists, Clay felt terrible that he allowed himself to be so badly injured. With him effectively out of their way, they were free to traumatize park guests at will.

Picking up his pace, Clay clasped his shoulder, trying to stop the dripping of blood, fully aware that he was going to leave a trail regardless of what he did.

He quickly realized he needed to contact Bill for some assistance, or he was going to die.

CHAPTER 16

―――――――― ▼ ――――――――

"Something about this isn't right," Turpin said to Bryant as they returned to the security director's office. "Who the hell was that trooper?"

"I don't know," Bryant answered. "They sometimes send us troopers to work security at the front gate."

"*They?*"

"The state. We're pretty high on the revenue ladder, so they take care of us."

Turpin found concern over two issues. One, the trooper had never returned, or called in his location. Two, what Gomez said about Packard seemed somewhat staged, but required checking into, simply to clear the police sergeant, or add to the complex mess the agent found himself in.

Both men had checked around the immediate area, finding no patrol car. When Bryant radioed his men to look for the car, no one saw anything. Of course, the park was over three-hundred acres, and only half of the wooded area was cleared and used for the areas guests visited. Anyone who knew the private property well could hide.

Or lure a trooper into danger.

Turpin wanted to continue the search, but first he wanted to know if what Gomez said had any merit.

So far he had been selective with what he told the park's security director. Bryant forced the issue a bit harder when they were conducting a search, so the agent told him about Packard. He also pieced together some of the puzzle for the director, explaining that he was at the park for an entirely different reason, and Packard had been slow in feeding him information.

"Can you verify whether or not Packard was ever affiliated with the park, or contracted by it in any way?" Turpin asked Bryant, who seated himself at his desk.

Bryant replied with a stupefied look.

"You really believe that maniac was telling the truth?"

"It's doubtful, but he made sure to drop Packard's name, don't you think?"

"I see your point."

Bryant began typing something into his terminal, waited a few seconds, then turned to the agent as the computer's hard drive worked at a feverish pace.

"What is it?" Turpin asked when the man said nothing.

"You don't fully trust me yet, do you?"

"You know, this morning I was planning on meeting someone for a brief talk, then returning to California if I was needed for debriefing. I followed the individual I needed to talk to here, only to discover this is the worst day in history to visit the park. And to make matters worse, there have been two deaths and no stories that seem to match up. So, no, in answer to your query, I can't say I fully trust you yet. For all I know, you could be the leak who assisted Gomez and his crew in their activities."

"How can you say that after he held us both at gunpoint?"

"For starters, he didn't shoot either of us, and he basically threw a verbal dossier of his recent crimes our way. He didn't get hired on his looks, and I doubt he had access and smarts enough to enter all of the areas necessary to rig bombs and switch bullets."

Turpin's mind took a different direction.

"Speaking of which, what did you do with the poor guy who shot the actor?"

"Dorsett and I interviewed him and cut him loose. We know where to find him if we need anything else. I wasn't going to wrongfully arrest him like you thought."

Turpin grunted, though happy LaRue wasn't tormented extensively.

"Where *is* the detective?"

"Said he had to get back to his station to check on a few things. He was working with the coroner's office again after the shooting."

Turpin considered that plausible, but he was alarmed that the park was taking little action after the two incidents, especially if Bryant knew they were not accidents.

"So why aren't you closing the park, or warning guests about the danger?" Turpin inquired.

"Two reasons," Bryant answered quickly, and with a confident tone. "The owners don't want me to raise a fuss for any reason, because they don't want bad press. Also, today is a short day, so there isn't a whole lot of time left for anything to happen."

Souring at the words, Turpin let his expressions do the talking a moment before speaking again.

"It only takes a second for a bomb to detonate and kill hundreds of people. I don't think you have enough people to effectively check every inch of this park in that amount of time."

Openly unhappy about the comment, Bryant seemed resolved to stick with his decision, dictated by orders. As the computer beeped, both men felt the tension between them dissipate a little more.

After staring at his monitor a few seconds, Bryant's jaw dropped absently, even though he said nothing.

"What is it?" Turpin inquired, standing over the director for a look at the monitor.

There, before them was a standing order that Packard had been hired to join the team in a freelance capacity to tear down the condemned roller coaster. Along with the information was a computerized employment sheet, complete with his information, including an accurate photo.

"It says he was contracted to help tear down the Whirlwind," Bryant noted aloud.

"What would that mean?"

"It would mean he has an open pass to be here virtually any time of day, and that he'd have access to quite a few areas of the park."

Turpin's mind raced in a different direction because this was purely circumstantial evidence against Packard. Despite the sergeant not being open with him earlier, he doubted the man had anything to do with terrorist activity, based on Packard's history, and the fact that three of his officers had basically come with him.

"Who puts those into the computer?" he asked Bryant instead.

"I can't say specifically who does, because the park has a human resources department with several people in it."

Turpin wanted to call Packard, to see what defense the sergeant might offer, but he decided there was a more pressing issue that required his attention.

"I want to search for this Gomez and our missing trooper some more."

"My guys are on it," Bryant insisted.

"I'm not talking about the regular park areas. You have woods around here, and we now have evidence of terrorist activity that may go beyond two deaths. The only reason I haven't called in my people from the Cincinnati branch is because I'd have to go through a lot of red tape, and because I thought the local police were doing more."

"They *are*. Dorsett has local officers at the gates, and inside the park."

"The problem is already inside, Hugh. And now it's growing exponentially."

Turpin wasn't the least bit happy with the way things were being run. He understood that Bryant had standing orders, but the safety of park guests needed to be the man's first priority. If more guests died, and it came out that he knew about the danger, the park would be ruined, along with his career.

His own position as a rogue agent granted him certain privileges, but he wasn't supposed to make contact with local agencies unless dictated by his supervisor, or extreme circumstances presented themselves. In the midst of a confusing mess, he wasn't sure his story would make enough sense to them, because he didn't know the true identities of the terrorists involved, or if they truly were known terrorists.

So far he had two suspicious deaths and a man of international heritage who had momentarily held him at gunpoint.

"I want to continue the search before it starts getting dark outside," he insisted to Bryant, knowing the park was going to have lots of lighting, but the woods would not.

"You got it," the park security director said, likely realizing Turpin wasn't going to be swayed from his opinion.

"What do you have that can get us into the woods?"

"The woods have trails you can get through with a truck, Agent Turpin. If you stray from the trails, it's extremely dense, even on foot."

Gomez fled on foot, but the trooper's patrol car was missing, meaning it might be in the wooded area. Turpin was not dressed for trudging through the woods, nor did he anticipate time enough to explore over a hundred acres before dark.

"You know the lay of the land," Turpin said. "Let's go."

Bryant looked above his desk at several sets of keys lined in a row along pegs. He selected a set, picked them up, then led the agent toward the exit.

*   *   *   *

Bill had waited patiently for Casey to call up the files regarding who had accessed what doors, and when. The computer needed time to access every single person's activity, then Casey ordered it to narrow the category down to people who had access to restricted areas.

"It isn't inconceivable that someone stole an ID," Bill thought aloud.

"You make it sound like everyone on our staff is dirty."

"It only takes one or two, Casey."

She tapped a button, causing the printer to spring to life, making a clacking noise. It began printing as Bill heard a door close in the distance, somewhat subtle, as though someone was trying to keep it from making noise.

"What is it?" Casey asked, seeing his grave concern, obviously not hearing the sound.

"Someone just walked in. Downstairs."

Her look showed she was either very impressed with his hearing, or thought he might be clinically insane.

He walked across the room to examine the door, but a rap at a nearby window distracted him. Seeing nothing, he stepped to the window, carefully looking out one side to see if his ears had deceived him.

Seeing nothing except a concrete parking lot to one side, and the employee gate to the other, Bill saw grass beyond the lot, but no people. He was about to turn around when a torso dropped from above the window outside that looked very familiar to him.

"Clay?" he asked with surprise, quickly opening the window to pull his nephew inside.

Saying nothing, Clay seemed virtually incapable of helping Bill get him inside. He was weak, and bleeding, almost to the point of unconsciousness. He said nothing, only emitting an occasional groan as Bill cautiously laid him on the carpeted floor.

Casey remained at the computer, a concerned look crossing her face.

"I need towels and bandages," Bill told her. "Someone came in downstairs, so don't let them know about this if you see them."

She hesitated momentarily, looking down at Clay's battered form. He was still conscious, wincing from the pain.

"I'll be right back," Casey said before slipping past the door.

Bill watched the door close behind her, quickly closed the window, then focused his attention on his nephew.

"What the hell happened to you?"

"Voodoo and Kim," he said weakly. "Had to fight them."

"*Both* of them?" Bill questioned, knowing the traditions forbid stacked numbers in samurai warfare.

"They shot me."

A form of shock overtook him momentarily, but Bill knew Clay had mentioned several deviants from his clan, who used their abilities for personal gain. His concern shifted from how Clay sustained his injuries to how he was going to save his nephew.

"Trance," Clay muttered, beginning to slow his breathing, shutting his eyes.

Bill instantly knew what Clay meant, but doubted he had the ability to assist Clay into a virtual coma that slowed all body function, allowing the body to heal. It was typically a technique used to save a dying person from certain death, but in this case, he believed Clay wanted to slow his heart rate enough that the bleeding might stop, and his body might begin to repair itself without surgery.

Examining the wounds, Bill realized he had been shot in two different areas, the worst of the two being the shoulder area above the heart. Most of the blood loss came from that particular wound, and had yet to fully stop. Even dressing and a methodical slowing of the heart seemed like a risky alternative to surgery, but Bill also knew Clay was the only one capable of stopping the two men responsible for the day's chaos.

"Concentrate," Bill said, forming both of his hands into a hand symbol, like the shape of a spade, between them.

Clay drew a pained grin.

"You're killing me here, Bill," he said with a forced chuckle. "I'll do it myself. Just get me somewhere where no one will look for a few hours."

"A few hours?"

"Yes. And whatever you do, no matter what *they* do, don't be a hero against those two."

Giving a light squeeze to his uncle's right hand, Clay laid back, then exhaled what sounded like his last breath.

Ever.

An initial shock overtook Bill, but he quickly remembered his nephew talking about a technique where a trained individual could put himself into a coma extremely close to a dead state. Also, he suspected Clay would tell him if he were dying, at least to offer some kind of advice or warning.

"The Sleeping Phoenix," Bill muttered the name of the self-induced trance Clay had put himself into.

The Asian term eluded him, but he recalled Clay mentioning the trance was actually originated in Chinese culture, later used by the Japanese. Westerners such as Americans named it in novels and fictional stories as the Sleeping Phoenix. Bill hated using the American nickname created from ignorance, but he knew no other term for it.

Two hours seemed a bit short-term, even for a gunshot and an arrow wound, but he suspected Clay's intent was to curb the bleeding. Now Bill needed Casey's counsel about where to hide his nephew for a few hours.

Reaching up, Bill pulled the blinds down, and the drapes closed, so no one would suspect Clay had entered through the window. Hearing footsteps come his way, he peeked out the door, finding Casey had made her way back, carrying several blankets and medical supplies.

"You were right," she said, kneeling down beside Clay. "Adam Russell was downstairs, getting ready to leave."

Bill assumed this meant the man worked in the front office, but didn't feel a need to inquire.

Taking a few of the large dressings, he placed them firmly over Clay's wounds, letting them apply mild pressure while soaking up the excess blood.

"Is he breathing?" Casey asked with open concern.

"Yeah. It's hard to explain, but he's fine. I need to find somewhere we can put him for a few hours, where he'll be safe from prying eyes."

Casey continued to stare at Clay, as though looking at the first corpse in her life.

"He doesn't *look* fine."

Knowing the trance Clay had put himself into slowed down all vitals, enough that they were undetectable without medical devices, Bill had no way of proving Clay was alive to Casey. Clay was breathing so slowly, there was no visible rise of his chest.

He thought a moment, then looked to her.

"Got a mirror in your purse?"

She answered his question with a stare, then decided to search for the object as she reached for her pocketbook. A few seconds later, she found the object, handing it to Bill.

"Watch," he said, as though lecturing a school girl.

He held the mirror up for her to see, like a magician might before performing a trick. Holding the shiny surface in front of his nephew's face, Bill pulled up the mirror a few seconds later, displaying to Casey that the surface was fogged over from Clay's breathing.

"See, he's alive," Bill stated. "Now where can we put him so he'll recuperate without being disturbed?"

"There's a private screening room where my father watches videos on the other side of this room. It's totally secluded."

Looking around to ensure no one was coming or looking through the window, Bill removed Clay's weapons and pack, setting them directly beneath the window.

He took a moment to wrap Clay's wounds with cloth, over the dressings, readying him for transport, even if it was just a short distance. Behind him, Casey opened up the room, which was truly a secret, because no door was visible, leaving Bill to question how it opened.

Picking up Clay, he carried his nephew across the conference room, finding a soft sofa inside the screening room to lay him on. By no means peaceful looking, Clay appeared as still as a corpse, concerning Bill more than a little bit. Still, like his nephew, Bill knew the stakes, and decided to make use of his time by seeking the terrorists, realizing he was about the only person qualified to understand their nature.

Casey seemed to catch the concerned stare aimed at his nephew.

"What's wrong? You said yourself he's going to be fine."

"He will be, but I'm worried there's no one left to deal with the bastards hell-bent on ruining your theme park."

His own words gave him an idea.

When the Koda attacked Muncie the year before they had an agenda, and going after Clay was a secondary objective that could have been accomplished at any given time. He now wondered if summoning Clay and the other officers to the park was little more than figurative icing on the cake, giving way to a larger objective.

"Is there anyone who might want revenge on the park? A disgruntled employee, or someone who tried to purchase the park? Anything negative that's happened in the past few years?"

Casey slowly shook her head, trying to come up with something.

"Nothing stands out."

Then something clicked.

"The accident."

"Accident?" Bill questioned, rising from beside the sofa, leading her out of the secret room where they could talk, allowing Clay to rest.

Her face showed her doubt in what she had already termed an accident, and they both took a seat at the conference table before she explained the situation.

"Two years ago we had a teenager fall out of the ride known as the Whirlwind."

"I remember hearing about that on the news."

"Somehow the kid slipped out of the harness after the ride started."

"Didn't your employees check the harness before the ride launched?"

Casey shot him a scornful stare.

"Of course they did. Some people think there's an extra thrill to the ride if they release the restraints."

Bill had heard of a similar case at a theme park in Indiana, but couldn't recall the outcome. He only remembered a woman dying after undoing her safety belt and wriggling her way out of the lap bar to stand up for the coaster's initial plunge.

When the cars reached the bottom, she wasn't in any of them.

"The parents sued us, but we had videotape evidence, and a few witnesses that said the boy slipped out of his restraint," Casey explained.

"So you won the suit," Bill surmised.

"We did, but the family wasn't happy."

"Can't be easy losing a kid, even like that."

"No, but they seemed, well...bitter."

Bill was about to ask a few more questions when Casey suddenly stood up.

"Follow me," she said, leading the way out of the room, and eventually down the stairs to the offices.

There, they found Adam Russell working at his desk. Casey made some small talk with him, then he got up to leave, giving Bill a strange look as he headed for the exit.

"Did you tell him I was an axe murderer?" Bill asked when she returned, commenting loosely about the stare.

"Not exactly. There's something you need to see."

She walked over to a set of bookshelves, pulling out a scrapbook of some sort. Setting it on the table, she opened it, letting Bill examine the newspaper clippings throughout its pages. Covering every memorable event in the park's history, both good and bad, the book disclosed the details about the roller coaster accident, and the impending civil lawsuit from the family.

Several quotes from family members told of their pain, and how they held the park responsible for negligence that killed their son. Casey's parents also had several standout quotes, stating how sorry they were such a tragedy occurred, and how their employees had checked every car, and every person's safety restraints, before any coaster left its launch station.

"How could something like that happen?" Bill wondered aloud.

"Sometimes people want a comfortable fit when they ride, so they stick an arm or a leg in the way of the restraint which keeps it loose. He probably had it that way when our people checked it."

Looking at the photos, Bill had to question why anyone would want to chance a fleeting moment of euphoria on a steel coaster taller than most buildings. He also remembered what being a teenager was like, and though he was somewhat mature, and conservative, he had friends who did some of the wildest things he'd ever seen.

"No offense," Bill said, "but I can't see how in the world you won that court case."

Casey's eyes wandered to the nearest wall, as though she harbored some form of guilt. Obviously no theme park owner ever *wished* for an accident on his or her property.

"My parents had a good lawyer. He convinced the judge with the evidence we had that it was the kid's fault."

Though the court case outcome was a good reason for someone wanting revenge, Bill couldn't see why anyone would hire international terrorists bent on harming innocent people. It made little sense, but he saw no other reason why Kim and his colleagues specifically targeted the park.

Of course, it probably didn't take much of a reason for anything they did.

Something nagged at him to check the grounds with Casey, and especially the Whirlwind ride. He doubted answers would present themselves at the ride, but he wanted to see if there was any reason it might provoke a terrorist attack.

"We need to take a little field trip," Bill said.

He took a moment to return upstairs, collecting Clay's weapons, except for the *katana*, which he laid beside his nephew. There was another sword in the truck, but Bill didn't want to carry any weapons that might attract attention to him.

He doubted his nephew was going to need the weapons anytime soon, but if he did wake up, the sword was weaponry enough for self-defense.

"Where to?" Casey asked, following him, reluctant to ask more questions as they bolted out the employee entrance.

Bill noticed Adam Russell talking with someone on his cellular phone, assuming nothing in particular until he caught an unfriendly glare from the man.

He looked to Casey, but she was intent on following his lead. When she finally looked Russell's way, he diverted his eyes away from them.

"What's wrong?" she asked.

"Don't worry about it," Bill said. "I want to see the ride you got sued over. You said you were dismantling it, right?"

"Yeah. We can use one of the utility vehicles."

Now following her lead, Bill had a sinking feeling, as though everyone he encountered might be the enemy. Even though he knew who Clay had confronted by reputation, and from his nephew's stories of Japan, Bill had no idea who Voodoo and Kim were by sight.

Somewhat worried, he decided to save his judgment until seeing further evidence.

CHAPTER 17

▼

Packard and Maynard had left the meeting with Turpin somewhat disgruntled, taking to walking adrift through the park.

With the rain tapering off, more people began leaving their shelters. They were now on the rides, or wandering through the park.

The two officers had just reached the end of the main walk, near the entrance, when blue and red lights broke the otherwise dismal atmosphere around them. They came from behind the employee barrier, but the look Maynard gave his sergeant seemed equally strange.

"What are you thinking?" Packard wondered.

"Lights but no siren? Park police are going somewhere in a hurry."

"Park police only have blue strobes," Packard noted, recalling seeing one of their patrol cars when they entered the park. "That's either local or state boys."

Both men looked around, seeing no one gazing in their general direction.

"Fuck it," Packard said, starting toward the gate, which held no barrier, but rather two offset walls a person needed to pass between.

Maynard followed his lead, looking cautiously around when they crossed the threshold separating guests from employees. Packard barely caught a view of the police car as it passed through the parking lot, taking a trail that led from the lot into the woods surrounding the park.

"Come on," he ordered Maynard, seeing no one else around them.

Noticing the lights were no longer visible, Packard suspected the driver had just used them to get out of the lot in a hurry, then shut them down. When he reached the trail, it appeared sparsely used, but very dark, without any lighting. Tall trees loomed everywhere ahead of the officers.

Continuing down the path, Packard picked up odors of pine trees and grass, rather than the food scents everywhere else in the park. His eyes searched the area around them, wondering why a police cruiser would go down such a neglected area within the grounds.

It took only a few minutes of hurried walking to get their answer.

Ahead of them, still running, the police cruiser was parked in a small clearing. Making certain he wasn't seen, Packard ducked down as he walked, making certain Maynard followed his lead. Something felt wrong about the entire situation, because he now confirmed the cruiser was owned by the Ohio State Police.

"There's two people inside," Maynard whispered to him.

"I see that. Rod, can you get any closer without being seen?"

"Probably. You want me to identify the people inside?"

"No, but see if you can get anywhere close to the driver's side. I'll get behind the vehicle, so I can warn you if something changes."

Maynard gave him a skeptical look, but obeyed as the sergeant took up a safe position behind some shrubs, directly behind the vehicle.

He immediately noticed the two men in the car talking somewhat intensely, if not in a heated discussion. Hand gestures and bobbing of their heads were open indicators. He heard no sound, so the car windows were likely up.

Drawing closer to the car, Maynard stopped to look back at him, indicating he saw nothing unusual, or that he couldn't see anything at all. Packard held up his right hand, indicating for his officer to exercise caution. Of the three, Maynard was the quickest to leap into trouble, mainly because Sorrell was too slow to react, and Clay was a very reactionary person.

Still at a lack for answers, Packard knew he was pulling a desperate move, attempting to see what the state trooper was doing.

And with whom.

When the doors opened simultaneously, Packard thought for certain he or Maynard had been spotted. His heart skipped a beat, and his chest tightened, before realizing the two men inside the car were certainly having a heated argument.

"What do you mean the package isn't ready for transport?" the trooper asked the man who had been seated beside him.

While the trooper appeared to be a white male, the passenger, now out of the car and looking clearly unhappy, was Mexican or Arab.

"They haven't cleared the park yet."

"You'd think two clearly terrorist activities would be enough to convince that moron Bryant that the park needs to be evacuated."

"Everything is in place," the darker-complected man stated. "At this point, nothing can stop us from delivering the goods to our friends overseas."

"Then where did the FBI agent come from? That wasn't part of our plan."

"Neither was Nelson dying, but it couldn't be helped. He was about to blab to Branson."

It took less than a minute of conversation for Packard to understand neither of these men were on his side. One glance at Maynard revealed the wide eyes of his officer, meaning he too was very much surprised.

Packard had no idea what they meant about the dead man, or about what sort of goods they were exporting. It didn't matter, because he had a sinking feeling whatever they had planned was highly illegal.

A stiff breeze passed through the trees, causing the leaves overhead to dump their accumulated water downward. This caused Packard to miss the next line said in the conversation, but he quickly comprehended what they were talking about.

"Look, we have to get everyone out of the park, even if it means taking drastic measures," the trooper said.

A sinister smile crossed the other man's face. Packard had to wonder what their next plan entailed, thinking he probably couldn't stomach what they had in mind for the park, or its inhabitants.

"Voodoo just reported that Branson is as good as dead, so there's no threat left," the second man said.

"That agent might be a pain in the ass. We have to take care of him, make sure Branson is dead, and get rid of Collier. After tonight, we won't have to worry about taking orders from those two assholes."

A look immediately crossed his face, as though he should have known better than to mouth the last part of his sentence.

Who is Collier? Packard wondered. A number of unanswered questions floated through his mind, but he was in no position to call Turpin or Clay. If what they said was true, he doubted Clay was in any condition to answer a phone.

But how? Clay was the best fighter he had ever seen. Though Packard had never seen him kill a man, he had seen the aftermath of a gruesome battle in photographs. Clay wasn't responsible for most of it, but he defeated the man who was, letting Packard know exactly what he was capable of doing to other human beings.

As another swift breeze swept through the trees, Maynard took the opportunity to shift his position, since he had been crouched down the entire time. His knees were likely sore, but his movement didn't go entirely unnoticed by the two men beside the patrol car.

"You see that?" the second man asked.

"See what?"

"That bush over there moved."

Looking up, the trooper pointed to several tree branches blowing in the wind.

"Everything's moving, Gomez."

Shaking his head, the trooper seemed to have something on his mind.

"Maybe after we're all done with this I'll find out your real name," he muttered.

Refusing to believe his eyes had deceived him, Gomez slowly walked toward Maynard's position, causing Packard to quickly decide which course of action was most prudent.

Both men were likely armed, but he wasn't about to let them shoot Maynard like a dog without interfering in some way.

The trooper reached for his gun, and Packard saw Gomez's hand reach behind his back, probably for a weapon. His hand grasped the ground around him, finding a stone the size of a softball as the only available weapon. Clutching it in his left hand, his far weaker throwing hand, he prepared to use it if necessary.

Maynard knew the danger, not looking back to his boss, but ducking lower behind the bush, hoping they might not inspect too closely.

He wasn't that lucky.

Packard wondered if his officer was going to use the element of surprise, and attack one of the men, or simply flee into the cover the woods offered, hoping to avoid bullets.

Somehow doubting either man was a bad shot, he prepared to help his officer in any way possible.

Since neither man had his weapon fully drawn, Maynard chose to wait until the last second, then launched his fist upward, striking the trooper in the jaw. The move did little except stun the man, but it distracted Gomez enough for Packard to stand up and hurl the rock toward him before he could draw whatever weapon was tucked into his backside.

Striking him squarely in the back, Gomez's arm reached toward his wound, rather than the weapon, which Packard clearly saw was a revolver. Incapable of running well while wearing sports sandals, the sergeant decided to strike the secondary threat before he drew the firearm.

Charging forward, Packard threw a fist, catching the man squarely in the jaw as he tried pulling the revolver loose from his belt. Instead, the weapon flew harmlessly into the surrounding brush, leaving the men to decide the outcome with their fists.

Not hearing any gunshots, Packard figured the trooper didn't want to create a scene so close to the park, which meant Maynard was likely to escape. Despite his age, the man was as quick as a cheetah in the open plains.

He quickly found himself atop Gomez, his hands wrapped around the man's throat in an attempt to end their skirmish early. The opportunity to end a man's life by strangulation had never presented itself, and as Gomez fought and kicked, Packard began to understand the rush convicted serial killers talked about.

His feeling of empowerment lasted only a few seconds, because Gomez reached for a tree branch, poking it toward the sergeant's eyes. Releasing the hold, Packard rolled to one side, then kicked Gomez in the ribs, stubbing one of his toes in the process, though doing heavy damage to the man's rib cage.

Grunting in pain, Packard picked up another rock, hurling it toward the man, catching him in the jaw once more. Having no idea how dangerous his adversary was, Packard considered the idea of retreating, then decided it was a must as the trooper came into view, visible down the dirt trail.

Gomez was ripe to be finished off, but Packard wasn't about to take any chances, especially since the trooper had seen him, and already had his weapon drawn. Darting into the woods, the sergeant hoped to meet up with Maynard quickly, so they could figure out their next move.

Going deeper into the woods was dangerous, because it was getting dark, and the trooper had the false sense of legitimacy on his side if he wanted to call for a local task force to hunt down the two officers. Packard knew he was in grave danger, but he still had his phone with him.

Ducking behind a tree, he observed the trooper helping Gomez to his feet hurriedly, as though they needed to be somewhere right away. Feeling a bit safer, Packard crept closer to the scene he had just left, camouflaged by plant life. He watched the cruiser turn around, then speed toward the park.

"Rod," he muttered, feeling the trooper was pursuing his officer.

Or worse, the man had summoned Clay's adversaries for help.

*   *   *   *

Maynard had chosen to avoid the employee entrance he and Packard originally took, thinking the trooper might have called for park police. Instead, he darted across the parking lot, along the building, searching for another way into the park, or safety into the outlying woods.

Surrendering to park police didn't sound so bad, knowing the people after him were ruthless killers. He was only alive because of his quick feet, and because the men didn't dare shoot at him, fearing the attention.

Wearing steel-toed boots would soon wear on his feet, possibly causing blisters from rubbing friction. He cursed Clay and Sorrell for not letting him change at city hall as he ran.

A single row of employee buildings separated him from the guests, safety, and the soft music playing over the speakers. His run didn't slow for several hundred yards. Excellent conditioning from training with the SWAT team, and doing a lot more legwork with Packard, had paid off.

After the employee buildings came intermittent walls of vending machines, rides, restrooms, and mesh fencing. There was no evident way into the park, unless he wanted to scale something, which sounded fine, unless a guest saw him and reported him.

Feeling like a dog trapped outside his owner's property, he kept tracking the side of the fence, waiting for an opportunity to get inside. Several times the thought of phoning his sergeant occurred to him, but he wanted to be perfectly safe, and hidden, before attempting contact with anyone.

At a narrow end of the park, a wooden roller coaster roared overhead, shaking the tracks with a clacking sound that reverberated even after the linked cars passed overhead. A bit unnerved by the new experience, Maynard pressed forward, his heart thumping inside his chest.

Through a nearby fence, he spied several workshops which were little more than pole barns constructed relatively close to most of the roller coasters. Knowing exactly where he was in relation to the park, he decided to bypass the shops by going behind them. Carefully trudging through the woods, he had to step across the park's railroad tracks, then leap over several fences once he was sure no one was looking.

With coasters, trains, and walkers heading to the water park, he had all kinds of dangers around him. Heightened terrorist alerts had everyone calling for help, especially when they saw someone in a restricted area who didn't look the part.

At this point, Maynard had half a mind to find a way out of the park so he could retrieve his firearm from within the car. There were no more rules to follow, and since he was fighting for his life, the thought of having a weapon sounded ideal.

Finding himself safely across every public area except one, Maynard had to be careful, although he didn't think any guests were capable of seeing him in the thick brush. Near the winding entrance of the Expedition ride, he wove between trees and thick brush, keeping himself away from the steel railings that guided guests to the ride.

He vaguely recalled the coaster from a few years back when he rode it with his nephew several times. Somewhat isolated from the rest of the rides, and even the park itself, the ride twisted through a small area, and over itself several times. The area below the steel tracks was mowed as he recalled, so he knew better than to leave his wooded cover.

As he neared the ride, hearing the clicking and clacking of the roller coaster cars making their way up the first hill, he recalled the words exchanged between the trooper and Gomez. He couldn't believe Clay was dead or critically injured. The thought alone was virtually a crushing defeat, because Clay was always the foundation of their group.

When things got tough, Clay handled the situation, almost always by himself.

Crouching behind a bush, an eerie sense he was being followed swept over Maynard, but nothing was visible behind him when he turned around. He chided himself for letting his mind wander, but as he reached to move a branch aside, the distinctive sound of a twig snapping echoed behind him.

"You've got to be shittin' me," he muttered, turning again to see if someone had actually followed him.

No cars had moved in the parking lot, and he had kept careful watch behind him the entire way through the woods.

He wondered if park security had picked up on his movement, or if someone he never saw might have reported him. Either way, he planned to exercise extreme caution until he discovered who or what lingered in the woods.

Deciding that taking cover was his best option, he made his way toward the ride, careful to watch for video cameras, since many of the rides were observed for rider infractions. Steel rails, supported by huge wooden beams, comprised the majority of the ride, but there were two tunnel systems as well.

One was near the ground, toward the opening lift, with lots of props inside. Typically well-lit from abundant daylight, the wooden walls of the tunnel were shady and dark as dusk approached. Knowing that coasters typically came through every few minutes, Maynard stayed at the base of the tunnel, hidden from view, until a set of cars roared past him.

Peeking from his position, Maynard noticed only a few riders in the cars, meaning he was relatively safe to proceed into the tunnel without fear of being seen by scores of people. Inside, there was no safe haven that provided complete cover, but there was a door halfway up the safety inspection stairs beside the steel tracks that opened to the outside of the tunnel.

Maynard had spied it from a distance, noticing wooden stairs that led down to the woods outside the ride, which were obscured from the riding portion of the track.

Not taking time to look behind him, Maynard jumped into the tunnel, hoping to lure whomever stalked him into the open. After a quick dash up the stairs beside the rails, he found the door to his left, leading outside. Since the next roller coaster was not within earshot yet, he peeked out a crack beside the door, then glanced toward the bottom of the tunnel.

Nothing was visible from either front.

Unarmed, and getting a bit more nervous by the second, he made his way slowly down the wooden stairs as quietly as possible. He was about halfway down when the sound of cars rumbling along the track reached his ears.

"Shit," he muttered, finding the nearest shadowy area.

He pressed his back to the wall, hoping no riders noticed him.

Most of the scenery was along the opposite side, so most eyes would hopefully be fixed on the moving spears coming through the walls and roof. If he was extremely lucky, this set of cars might have no one on it.

In seconds it flashed past him, seeming to jolt, then press forward, as it reached the incline. The ascent began toward the end of the tunnel when a large chain pulled the string of cars up the lift. Sounding like a cross between a railroad locomotive and a giant zipper in action, the cars were caught by the metal teeth between the steel rails that kept them from ever falling backward.

Only two people were riding the coaster, in separate cars, and neither glanced his way.

Exhaling heavily to himself, Maynard looked to the bottom of the tunnel, then cautiously walked down the stairs, only to see the trooper step from around the corner, holding his gun in a defensive position.

"Fuck," Maynard said under his breath, dashing up the stairs, knowing the gun was about to be trained on his backside.

A shot rang out, the bullet struck the wood beside Maynard's left shoulder as he dashed up the stairs. Trained police officers yelled for suspects to stop, or at least identified themselves, when conducting a pursuit.

The side door most of the way up the stairs didn't come fast enough for Maynard as his hand fumbled, finding the knob awkwardly tilted upward. Apparently an old knob, installed when the ride was built, on a seldom used door no one really used, it was never a top priority in park maintenance.

And now it was keeping Maynard from reaching temporary safety.

Feeling his temperature rise, and sweat beginning to bead from his forehead, Maynard struggled with the door as the trooper's pistol took careful aim.

"Christ," he cursed, turning the knob as he tried holding it in a centered position.

In the back of his mind he wondered why he hadn't been shot yet, but from the corner of his eye he saw the man methodically walking up the stairs, like a serial killer from any string of horror films.

Suddenly the door burst outward, giving Maynard a taste of freedom. Slamming the door behind him, he looked wildly around him, knowing there was no chance of reaching the bottom of this new set of stairs before a bullet found him. Jumping was also no option, unless he chanced leaping to the thick branches of a nearby tree, all of which looked dead and flimsy.

Only one option remained, with seconds left to decide which direction to take. Hearing hurried footsteps on the other side of the door, Maynard ducked beneath the railing behind where the door opened. With no flooring on the other side, he was forced to cling to the wooden railing, leaning back slowly. Weathered for over a decade, with peeling paint, the wooden supports had bowed, leaving the cop a bit concerned for his life, considering the only object beneath him to break his fall was a partial tree stump.

Maynard had little time to worry about it as the door flung open. Holding his breath, able to see only the decrepit door before him, Maynard positioned his left hand near the door, waiting for it to close. In his right hand, the wooden railing felt virtually like putty, twisting and creaking lightly, as though the nails holding it might let loose any second.

He half expected to be shot through the door, but another coaster was coming through, meaning the trooper had to do something. Getting spotted was probably not what the man had in mind, and a second later, he shut the door behind him, distracted enough for Maynard to grasp his collar with a full fist, using his weight as he pulled downward.

In an instant it was over as the trooper tumbled over the side of the railing, losing his gun in the process. And just like that, Maynard had killed a person for the first time in his life.

"Holy," he said as the sound of the coaster cars climbing the first hill behind him entered his ears once again.

Shock overtook him for a few seconds, but he recovered quickly, ducking beneath the railing to the safety of the stairwell. Looking over the ledge, he saw the trooper's body lying awkwardly atop a rock, confirming what he already knew he had done.

He descended the stairs two at a time until grass was beneath his feet. Ignoring the body momentarily, he searched the area for the gun, finding it in a shrub before tucking it into his backside.

Freezing momentarily, he stared at the man's wide, lifeless eyes. Looking across the body, he saw bone fragments jutting from one elbow and a knee joint. Feeling more than a little disturbed by the sight, he used one arm, cautiously rolling the body off the rock before he vomited.

Nerves and the sickening thoughts had gotten the better of him, but he wiped his mouth dry, collecting himself before proceeding.

His next move was to search the man's back pocket, where he found a wallet. Maynard carefully pulled it out with two fingers. After, in essence, murdering a fellow officer of the law, he didn't want to leave evidence in case investigators dug into the case before he and Packard found a way to explain everything.

He swiped his hand through the other pockets, feeling a set of keys in one. He pulled them out, thinking he might check over the man's patrol car for information.

Maynard began to open the wallet, but instinct told him to tuck it away and leave the area before someone else came upon the scene. The trooper was likely not traveling alone, and there were at least two other terrorists still alive. His mind raced for somewhere nearby where he could slip into the guest area without being detected.

Remembering the metal rails he passed shortly before entering the ride area, he started toward them, through the woods.

An eerie sight froze him in his tracks as he came upon a tree with a tribal mask nailed to it. Painted black and gold, the mask had various colored beads covering its face. Two eye slots were carved from the wood, giving it a hollow, abandoned appearance. Maynard felt like it was watching him, so he quickly moved past it.

"Gives me the creeps," he muttered.

He had decided to call Packard once he returned to the park, and as he drew near a clearing a few minutes later, a noise sounded behind him.

Whirling around, Maynard thought it was possibly a branch falling from a tree he had passed, but he remained skeptical. Refusing to stop, he waited until no people were passing through the metal guide rails, then darted to get in line for the ride before anyone saw. Fortunately, the winding line to the ride was long, and seldom full of activity.

Already most the way toward the ride itself, and not wanting to arouse suspicion by turning back, Maynard decided to ride Expedition, then call his sergeant once he found some better cover.

CHAPTER 18

▼

Turpin had decided almost immediately that going into the woods was a grievous error. While there was still daylight outside, the dense trees refused to let any of it pass through their foliage. Another problem arose in visibility, because the trails offered limited sight distance, and to move on foot was both cumbersome and dangerous.

"Sorry this isn't very productive," Bryant apologized.

"I should have known better," Turpin said, feeling a pang in his stomach that came from both hunger and irritation at his luck.

Bryant had driven them almost a mile into the forest, and to Turpin's surprise, they hadn't seen a soul. He expected to find maintenance men driving around, or construction workers milling about, but the trail was devoid of activity.

"Let's turn back," Turpin said, knowing Bryant never wanted to make the trip in the first place.

It took a moment, but the security director found a smooth area beside the road where he was able to turn the small truck around.

"Do you act this mysterious on all of your assignments?" Bryant asked him once they were heading toward the park and better lighting.

"I'm an open book," Turpin answered.

"Not about why you're here you're not."

"Have you asked me anything else about myself?"

Bryant shrugged.

"I guess when you refused to answer *that* question I figured you weren't going to say anything else."

Turpin shifted in his seat, trying to manipulate some comfort from the warped seat cushions.

"I worked in Houston as a police officer, holding just about every position imaginable, including investigator and motorcycle patrolman. Toward the end of my career, I found myself in Iraq, serving my country after years of being a weekend warrior in the Army Reserves. Between that, I've had three marriages, lost half a dozen friends to cancer, and discovered I have a son I never knew about from my younger days."

"That must have been rough explaining things to him."

"I've never met him," Turpin admitted.

Bryant's eyes shifted a skeptical look toward him, then quickly returned to the dirt path ahead.

"How did you never know about him? If you don't mind my asking."

"My wife was murdered while we were separated," Turpin confessed easily. "They never found the men responsible, but *I* did. A case I had worked on went to court, and the mob boss behind it all had evaded arrest, but he knew I was getting close."

"I'm a little confused," Bryant admitted. "How could you have not known she was pregnant?"

"Because she hid it from me," Turpin answered. "Long before I went to Iraq, I spent a year overseas in Pakistan. When she and I were together and happy, there was no love greater than ours. But Maria could be vengeful sometimes."

Turpin paused, looking outside to the trees, and the increasing daylight as they neared the forest's edge.

"When she was murdered there was a delay in contacting me, because I had put down different beneficiaries on my paperwork before shipping out. I got back to discover she was dead, and there were no suspects. And her baby boy was put up for adoption."

"But you were the father," Bryant stated. "They couldn't legally deny you access to your son, could they?"

Smirking to himself, Turpin thought of the worst day of his entire life.

"Legally, Maria and I weren't married. I suppose you could call us common-law, but we had no paperwork to prove anything. When I got back, they said my boy was in a new home, and there was nothing they could do for me. The birth certificate listed my boy with her last name, so I had no legal leg to stand on."

"Did you search?"

"Eventually. I focused on who murdered my wife, and why. It took me a few months to find out the names of those responsible, and I took care of things in my own way."

He saw Bryant begin to ask something, then bite his lip.

Turpin remembered dishing out vigilante justice, but it never took away the hurt he felt because his true love was gone.

"Things just kind of snowballed, and I searched for my son the best I could, but there were no clues to follow. It was as though he had been swallowed up by a black hole."

He paused momentarily, feeling the hurt all over again.

"There was a time I thought he might know something about me, and maybe look me up, but he'd have to be in his twenties by now. He's either not interested, or he never learned about his real parents."

"What about DNA tests, or taking it to court?"

"Taking a government agency to court is, and was, a complete waste of time. I used every contact I had to find him, but Maria had been careful to illustrate what kind of person I was to her friends, who eventually became character witnesses. As much as we usually loved one another, she was capable of fiery hatred when she was mad at me. She never wanted me to go overseas, so I guess that was my punishment."

As they reached the edge of the woods, the sun began to break through the clouds overhead, but only to display beautiful red and orange tints as it began to set.

"If you retired from Houston, how did you make it on the FBI?"

"Long story short, they wanted an old coot like me to run errands for them and work on particular assignments that fell within my specialties."

"You must have quite a resume for them to pursue you like that."

"It reads like the obituaries, Hugh. My main reason for taking the job was to look for my boy, since I'd be traveling around the country and making new contacts. They keep dangling information in front of me like a carrot, but I'm working around their system on my own time."

An awkward silence filled the truck momentarily as the scenery changed from trees to concrete, and the smells of pine and cedar were replaced with cotton candy, popcorn, and pizza. The agent's mind returned to the task at hand, wondering exactly why his luck was so terrible. His assignment was to make contact with Clay Branson and return home with results.

The last thing he expected was a terrorist attack at a park he never planned to visit.

"My story isn't nearly as exciting," Bryant admitted. "I worked as a patrolman in Cincinnati most of my career. Did some investigation for a few years, but that wasn't for me. The position here came out of the blue and I had plans to retire in a few years anyway. There was no way I could keep my job over there if I took this position, but it's one of those things that just don't come your way very often."

"Once in a lifetime, eh? Most people in our field work security at schools and hospitals when they retire. You're telling me this job is worth the headaches over something like that?"

"Most times. They pay me more here than I ever made working in the field, but I work my ass off. Homeland security is a big deal these days, Agent Turpin. It's not easy working around the schedules of a dozen cops, a handful of local reserve officers, and whiny college kids. Every year I have to make it work, and until this year, it has."

"What happened today isn't your fault. You're dealing with people who extort money, kill people, and create wars for fun and profit. It's just bad luck that they chose your facility to do their business in."

Bryant grunted lightly, apparently not convinced by the words.

"I think of this place as my second home. Everything I do is what the Trimble family asks of me."

"Speaking of the family, who was that guy with the daughter earlier today?"

Bryant thought a moment, braking at an intersection. He waited, rather than driving onward, to converse with the agent.

"I'm not sure. I just figured he was a mechanic here to work on a ride. The way things have been, Casey might have needed to show him where to go."

"That something your security usually does?"

"No. Most of our mechanics are in-house, but the others who come here usually know their way around."

"And that situation didn't strike you as odd?"

Bryant turned, looking a little sour about the accusation.

"No, it didn't. Casey appeared perfectly at ease with the guy from what I saw, and she certainly would have flagged me down if there had been a problem. I know the Trimbles very well, Agent Turpin. I may not have your intuition and experience, but they treat me like I'm part of the family around here. If something was wrong, I'd know it."

"I'm starting to think your family business has too many branches to keep things safe."

"It has grown quite a bit the past few years, and maybe we haven't kept a lid on things like we should."

"Is part of your job description to modify personnel situations?"

"Unfortunately, no. They involved the kids in the business, and it created a bit of disorganization. My job has certain boundaries, which don't extend to the expansion of the business, even where safety is involved."

Turpin was wondering exactly what to do next when a call came over the radio about a fallen guest who had ordered chicken strips and bottled water within the past hour.

"Could be nothing," Bryant said optimistically.

"Or not," Turpin muttered under his breath as the security director steered in the direction of the reported incident.

*   *   *   *

When Bill and Casey pulled up to the ride, the sun was setting behind it both figuratively and literally. Only skeletal remains stood before them, beyond the gate lined with security tape.

Even as Bill stepped from the truck, his gaze failed to move from the controversial ride. Something about it sent a shiver up his back, even though this was his first time seeing it. Casey took his side, then he walked a step behind her as they approached the ride.

"Why is it just sitting here?" he asked her. "Where are the workers?"

"They aren't here today. My parents waited until just before this season started to make the decision."

"If the suit was so long ago, why wait this long? You're saying the ride was running up until this season?"

"It was. We knew it was safe, so we let it run, but the negative press from the family kept scaring people away from it. The rumors were hurting business."

Bill felt his face twist in confusion until Casey elaborated.

"You know how people will say a ride has killed three or four people, or that people have fallen out of it? My parents painted it, and even thought about changing the name, but nothing seemed to help."

"What's going to happen to it?"

"It'll stay here this summer, until it sells."

"Sells?"

"Roller coasters get transferred to different parks all the time under new names. Slap some new paint on them, and it's like a new coaster was installed if people don't know any better."

"I take it there haven't been any offers?"

"A few inquiries, but no real offers. I think most of the interested parties want the press to die down first."

Bill looked around the area, seeing nothing strange about the coaster, except that rails went skyward, only to abruptly end because parts of the system had been removed. Nothing about the launch bay seemed odd, except there were lighter spots in the floor where equipment had sat for years while the rest of the floor was scuffed and weathered by nature.

He began suspecting the ride had something to do with the terrorists being there, only because they had obviously been at the park in some form for months.

"Show me this storage area you talked about," he asked Casey.

A few minutes later they pulled up to a desolate area where metal rails were stacked atop one another, rusting openly from long since forgotten rides. Almost a dozen trolley cars were toward the back of the area, beginning to fade from sight because of trees and shrubs grown around and between them.

"What were those?" Bill inquired.

"We used to have a cable system throughout the park for tours. The cars worked on wires, going virtually everywhere."

"What happened to them?"

"Nothing really happened. My parents said there were a few close calls where people got drunk and nearly fell out of them. Basically their safety systems got outdated."

Able to relate, Bill looked at the heaps of rusting metal around them, not seeing any parts from the Whirlwind.

"Where is the Whirlwind being stored?"

Casey looked confused.

"I thought it was in the open. In fact, it was here just a few days ago."

Both looked around, seeing nowhere else the ride might be. The only building in the vicinity was a small wooden shack, barely large enough to hold a small tractor.

"Something isn't adding up," Bill thought aloud.

"There were some seats under a tarp out here, too," Casey noted. "They were here just a few days ago."

Though not a detective, Bill began piecing together a likely scenario of what the terrorists might be doing. Since most of them were foreigners, he wondered if they had ideas of stealing the roller coaster, then transporting something illegal inside it to another country.

Other than the path they had come from, there were no tracks or paths in any other direction, meaning whoever had transported the parts elsewhere wasn't under suspicion.

Or had phenomenal timing.

"How much of the coaster has already been taken down?"

"About half of it. Why?"

"I may have an idea of who has it, and why."

"I might too," a voice said from behind them, startling them both.

Bill whirled defensively, wishing his senses were as attuned as Clay's. Mastery required lots of time he couldn't spare for practicing the arts.

"Tim?" Bill asked, recognizing Packard from a few meetings with his nephew, and from the newspapers.

"Uncle Bill," Packard said, obviously mimicking what Clay usually called him.

A few seconds of silence passed, then Casey appeared confused, shifting her eyes between them.

"This is Clay's sergeant," Bill explained to her. "He was here when the accident happened on your ride this morning."

"And we may be in for a bigger accident if we don't get the park cleared out," Packard said.

"Why's that?" Casey asked.

"My other officer and I just overheard a conversation between two of the terrorists in the woods. They have some plan to move something out of here tonight, and they're about ready to do whatever it takes to get everyone out of here."

"This place would be locked down if they did anything drastic," Bill said. "How the hell would they expect to get anything done?"

Packard shrugged.

"Something tells me they have this planned out pretty well. This park should have been closed after that incident this morning, but now *two* people are dead."

"I'll tell Bryant to evacuate the park," Casey decided aloud.

"Will he listen to you?" Bill questioned.

"He has to. When my parents aren't here, I'm in charge. Right now he's just going by a standing order."

"I thought Clay came with two of your officers," Bill said, feeling a bit concerned they weren't around.

"Ed got injured in one of the rides. They carted him off to the hospital. And Rod was just with me when the terrorists spotted us spying on them. I don't know if he made it or not. I don't dare call him because he might be hiding somewhere, and I don't want to give away his position."

Casey took hold of her radio, turned it on, then walked off by herself to contact Bryant. Packard gave Bill an uneasy stare, as though he suspected the worst had yet to come.

"The terrorists said Clay was as good as dead," he reported. "Have you seen him?"

"He's alive. The bastards shot him with an arrow and a gun."

"Is he okay?"

"He'll survive. We left him in the office to recuperate and stop the bleeding."

Packard's expression was a mix between shock and deep concern.

"He'll be okay," Bill assured him. "He knows what he's doing."

"I hope so. Because without him, we might get buried out here beside these old rides."

Packard's cellular phone rang by his side. When he looked at the identification bar, some relief openly crossed his face.

"Rod," he answered. "You okay?"

A minute passed while the sergeant engaged in conversation. Bill overheard something about a state trooper being dead and an identification mixup of some sort.

"What's the word?" he asked Packard once the man was off the phone.

"Rod was chased by a state trooper, who seemed to be one of the cronies, but when he searched the man's wallet he found the name was Collier. He and some Gomez guy talked about killing a man with that name before they left the country."

"What do you think it means?"

"Rod seems to think they have the real trooper under wraps somewhere and this guy took his place. Makes sense to me, because even if one of them got surgery to look like the man, there's no way you could learn what those guys do in a short time. They probably kept him around for information."

Bill felt a bit skeptical, but he also knew the terrorists the year prior were equally inventive.

"What is your officer doing now?"

"He wants to go to the trooper's address and check it out, but he doesn't have a ride. Ed had the car keys, and he's at the hospital."

Casey returned to the fold, overhearing some of their conversation.

"I can loan him a park vehicle," she said. "Did you say the name Collier?"
Packard nodded.

"An uncle of the boy who died on Whirlwind had that name. And he was a state trooper stationed in a different part of the state when the accident happened."

All three exchanged worried glances, knowing the conspiracy was unfolding, but answering fewer questions than it opened.

"Call your guy and have him meet us near the front gate," Bill said. "We've got to get everyone out of this park and figure out where those pricks put the Whirlwind pieces."

"There was a guy working on it today when the terrorists ordered me over there," Packard revealed.

"What did he look like?" Bill asked quickly.

"White guy. Had kind of a scruffy beard I guess. He didn't strike me as odd."

"Casey just told me no one was working on the ride today."

"I didn't see him work. He was on break when I met up with him."

Now Bill felt more confused than ever. He didn't know exactly what the sergeant was talking about, stating the terrorists had issued him orders, but he could learn about it on the trip to the front gate.

"Let's get back," Bill said to Casey. "We can swap information and figure out who else to trust."

Casey nodded, leading the way to the utility vehicle. Bill took one last look at the desolate dumping grounds behind him, concerned about the lack of forthcoming answers. He turned to follow Packard and Casey, wondering how things had gone so badly for Clay and the others.

*   *   *   *

"What was that about?" Turpin asked Bryant once the security director finished speaking with a female voice over the radio.

The two men had reached their destination, where the sick guest was reportedly growing more ill by the minute. Casey's transmission was the order to evacuate the park. With one word over the radio, Bryant's security force would deny access to rides and walkways, informing people the park was closing for the day.

Strangely, the security director had requested five more minutes from the person on the other end of the radio.

"As you probably heard, that was my boss giving the order to clear the park. I want to see this patient before I make any rash decisions. If there's any chance it's a biological contamination there's no way in hell I'm letting people out into the public."

"You can't hold thousands of people hostage in here, whether it's chemical or biological. There's more danger to more people if you keep them inside."

Bryant shrugged helplessly.

"Damned if I do, damned if I don't. Let's just see what we've got first."

Both men stepped from the vehicle, finding a small crowd centered around one of the food stands. As they pushed their way past several employees and concerned guests, Turpin found something far worse looking than he expected.

A man in his early twenties was lying on the ground, with labored breathing, sweating profusely. What appeared to be red sores covered his face and arms, causing Bryant to wince slightly before turning to the agent.

Two park medics were talking to the man, checking his blood pressure while preparing to move him onto their tiny ambulance.

"What do you make of it?" Bryant whispered.

"It's not food poisoning," Turpin mumbled back, making a point that this was likely another action taken by the terrorists.

Bryant appeared incapable of taking action for a moment, openly perplexed by the scene before him. Turpin had to assume the man was trained in dealing with everything from drunken guests to mass casualty incidents. Deeply suspecting the man was poisoned by something, Turpin was determined to stick to his guns about letting the other guests leave the park.

"What did he eat?" Bryant asked one of the food court employees.

"Just chicken strips and bottled water," the young vendor manning the food stand in question answered, still wearing a striped apron and a paper hat.

He appeared to be a real life cartoon character with red hair, and freckles covering his arms and face. Turpin figured him to still be a high school kid based on his appearance and how shook up he seemed to be.

"Is there any of it left?"

"No. He threw it away over there," the employee said, pointing toward a trash can, "but there were too many containers to know which ones were his."

Bryant cursed under his breath.

"No one else has fallen ill?"

"This is the first one we've had," one of the medics answered.

"Get him out of here and get the rest of these people out of the park," Turpin insisted, using his official tone toward Bryant, keeping a hushed voice as he led the director away from the crowd.

"What about all of these people? They've all been around him."

"If I give you my take on this, will you trust my experience?"

Reluctantly, Bryant nodded. By no means a spring chicken in police work, even the security director appeared befuddled by the new turn of events. Turpin doubted the Cincinnati police department handled too many mass casualty incidents.

"I think someone tampered with one particular bottle, putting some kind of chemical around the bottle neck. There's a clear liquid compound that will dry on contact, releasing itself when it comes in contact with moisture from someone's lips. *That's* what I think happened to him."

"Will he die?"

"Probably. I'll tell the medics what I think it might be, but there's no guarantee, even if they rush him to the hospital."

Turpin wasn't trying to be pessimistic, but he had seen chemical killers before. They were deliberate, created to make a point.

And a scene.

Not only was this going to be more bad press for the park, but now gossip was going to spread uncontrollably throughout the grounds amongst guests and employees.

Bryant stared at the man a moment, as though silently giving him last rights, then issued a command over the radio for his security force to evacuate the park at a normal pace.

"I hate doing that," Bryant muttered when he returned to the agent's side.

Sweating a bit from the forehead, the security director took off his yellow windbreaker, laying it across one arm.

"I know you've got orders, but human life is worth more than profit."

"Maybe so, but what if our problem escapes with the crowd?"

Turpin shook his head.

"I think we're about to get to the root of our problem. There's something they want from this place, because they've been extremely low-key. If their objective was bloodshed and mayhem, things would have been much worse."

Watching momentarily as the medics loaded the stricken man onto their ambulance, Turpin considered calling Packard, but decided to wait a moment.

"How long will it take to get everyone out of the park?" he asked Bryant.

"Could take up to an hour, but probably about half of that."

"I want you to keep *your* staff here, along with the medical guys."

"What about the firemen?"

"You have those, too?"

Bryant nodded.

"We keep four on-duty firefighters in the park daily. They're local guys who work here on their days off from the city fire department. We have one pumper truck here in the park, with a seventy-five foot ladder on it for certain rescue situations."

"How well are they trained?"

"They have medical training, and they can all do high angle rescues in case we have problems on the taller structures."

"Keep them here. I want to talk with their officer as soon as we're done here."

"You got it."

Turpin looked around, seeing people everywhere. To his left was the famed observation tower, and to his right was the kiddie area, with lots of miniature coasters and rides. Knowing there was one piece of information missing that might solve the entire mystery for him, he thought about the day's events. Everything pointed to an inside job, larger than Gomez or any one crooked officer could handle.

Few people had access day and night to the park. The owners, their daughter, Bryant, and perhaps a few of the maintenance men. It took vast knowledge, or at least someone to supply the knowledge, to blow up a ride section and replace bullets halfway across the park.

Rigging an explosive also required knowledge. The kind of knowledge Turpin remembered learning from his military days.

Staring at Bryant, he felt positive the man probably had some sort of military background because of how he conducted himself. Rigid and straightforward, Bryant had people skills, but they seemed somewhat forced, as though he wasn't accustomed to dealing directly with the public.

Turpin remembered having issues dealing with the public when he came home from his deployments. He never let his guard down, but relating with the public required more subtlety in the States than in the Middle East. Bryant's job required a police firmness while wearing kid gloves around paying guests.

As the security director interviewed a few of the workers, Turpin gave the appearance of casually walking around, but studied the man from a cautious distance. Bryant had been holding his windbreaker over his right arm, but when he shifted it to the other arm to jot down some notes, Turpin saw something interesting.

For the first time that day Bryant's sleeves were rolled up, and as the security director scrunched up the sleeve on his left arm to keep it in place, the agent's keen eyes spied contrasting colors on his flesh. In gold, barely visible beneath the sleeve, was the bottom of an anchor tattooed on the side of Bryant's arm. Though the gold showed well against Bryant's flesh, Turpin only noticed it because of the black outline surrounding it.

Above it Turpin observed traces of much more black ink, leading him to believe the tattoo was a version of the eagle and anchor combination many sailors in the United States Navy associated with their job.

Turpin had several friends who served in the Navy, making him highly familiar with the symbol. He suspected the artwork was customized for Bryant because it didn't look much like any of the rate badges worn on Navy uniforms.

Whether or not Bryant was a SEAL in the branch remained undetermined, but Turpin now knew something about his temporary colleague that raised his suspicion.

Knowing better than to ask the man directly about his service record, Turpin decided to make a phone call when the opportunity presented itself. Diverting his attention elsewhere before Bryant noticed his prying eyes, Turpin thought he saw a shadow move across the roof of a nearby candy store.

He stared a moment, but saw nothing else. The movement reminded him of his primary objective, which had been buried in the pile of problems mounting around him. Turpin wasn't about to put meeting Clay Branson above thousands of lives, regardless of his orders. He was no longer a military man, and though he believed in following orders, he wasn't a machine, capable of turning off emotions.

Returning his focus to Bryant, he considered the man to be an incredible actor, or innocent of any involvement with the day's crimes.

Once the medics had the man loaded on their ambulance, Turpin walked over, pulling one of them aside.

"Sir?" the man asked, apparently already knowing the agent's credentials.

Word traveled fast, even in a theme park.

"I think what this man got into is a strain of VX," Turpin informed him.

"The nerve agent?"

Though impressed the medic knew about the deadly compound, time prevented him from engaging in a lengthy conversation. The chemical had a list of exposure symptoms that read like a bad combination of the flu and vertigo. Developed in the United Kingdom during the Cold War, the controversial chemical had allegedly been used during wartime in the Middle East.

Lots of other nerve agents were available to terrorist sects, such as the 'G' agents, but most of these known chemicals were gases, more effective in airborne outbreaks. A Japanese religious sect known as *Aum Shinrikyo* used Sarin, a form of the agent titled GB, in an apartment complex in 1994, and a Tokyo subway in 1995, with modest success.

Unlike those agents, VX evaporated very slowly. Often developed in a gel form, it didn't dissipate in sunlight like most nerve agents. Turpin couldn't see any way the terrorists might use a gas-form nerve agent in bottled water or chicken strips.

"Someone probably put a gummed form of the chemical on the bottled water he bought," he explained to the medic. "His hands, mouth, and even his face may have traces of the chemical. He needs *immediate* transport to the hospital, and anyone who comes in contact with him needs to take precautions."

Somewhat stunned that a biological warfare agent had infiltrated the park, the medic slowly took in the revelation, nervously licking his upper lip.

"I think the stuff is mostly isolated to him, but you need to get his clothes off and take precautions for yourselves," Turpin advised.

"You're pretty sure that's the stuff?" the medic asked, obviously hoping Turpin was blindly guessing.

Turpin had already developed a theory that the man touched the tainted bottle, then handled the chicken strips he ate with the same contaminated fingers. Surface contact typically created a number of terrible complications, but ingestion created an entirely worse scenario.

"Pretty sure, son. If it's not VX, it's something almost as bad. You'd better get moving, or he ain't gonna make it."

Giving an understanding nod, the medic jogged over to his partner, whispered something in his ear, and jumped into the ambulance's left seat. They drove away almost immediately as Turpin watched the second medic radio someone as a distressed look crossed the man's face.

If anyone else had secondary exposure, the effects would likely be mild. Getting everyone out of the park made more sense than a quarantine in Turpin's experience. He let out a deep breath through his nose, hoping against all odds the victim survived the incident.

He hoped the medics used his words of wisdom to better his care, rather than taking too much time to protect themselves by donning excessive gear.

As Bryant busied himself with the interviews, Turpin walked toward a nearby ice-cream stand to get a chocolate cone before they closed for the night. He was in no mood to be denied, after eating virtually nothing all day, so he was willing to pull his identification if they said they were closed.

He considered the water might not be the only thing poisoned, but figured the terrorists wouldn't waste time tainting a variety of foods. His stomach had grumbled several times, so Turpin decided to take his chances.

Smirking to himself, he wondered if pulling his identification might earn him a discount. He quickly felt guilty about thinking such things when a man fighting for his life still remained within his sight down the concrete path. Turpin learned shortly after joining Houston PD to forget about the everyday tragedy he saw through callous jokes or focusing on his family, but today even that didn't feel appropriate.

CHAPTER 19

Packard and the others met Maynard near the front gate before Casey led them back to the office area for some privacy. The disguised evacuation went smoothly because most guests seemed to figure the park had a shortened day anyway, so leaving an hour early was no big deal.

Casey found an unmarked vehicle for Maynard to use, then informed the gate guard to allow him to leave. She explained that most of the unmarked vehicles were the same make and model, so the security people knew what they looked like.

With Maynard on his way to investigate the trooper's residence, the three remaining people had to decide on their own courses of action.

"Here's a gun I took from Clay's place," Bill said, handing a semi-automatic pistol to Packard.

Taking it, the sergeant felt a small wave of relief come over him. He had been risking his life, running through various areas of the park without any protection. With Clay out of commission, any true investigation fell to him, because he had no idea who to trust.

"Can I see Clay?" he asked Bill and Casey, wanting assurance his officer was fine.

Losing Sorrell was one thing, but Clay was the only one capable of dealing with the ultimate threat. He wanted to assess his officer's injuries in person.

"I suppose so," Bill answered, as though skeptical it was in his nephew's best interest.

All three walked upstairs to the conference room, then back to the room where Clay was placed atop a sofa. When Packard first spied his officer, he felt positive he was looking at a corpse. He had seen his share of dead people, most of which had pale skin and an eerie calmness surrounding them that had nothing to do with them not breathing.

To him, Clay looked exactly like that.

"You're sure he's okay?" Packard had to ask.

"He is," Casey answered. "Bill already proved it to me."

Packard knelt beside Clay, taking a look at the bloody gauze on his shoulders, then looked up to Bill with concern.

"When will he wake up from this?"

Bill answered with a helpless shrug.

"I only know what the concept is. It depends on how bad his wounds are, and when his body decides it's healed enough."

"We're up a creek," Packard said. "If we don't trust anyone, we can't be calling any police. If there's any chance that was a trooper, or they made someone up to look like him, then we can't trust any agency."

"What about that agent?" Bill questioned.

"After what happened last year, I'm not sure I fully trust him either. There's just too much coincidence that he came looking for Clay today, and he came all the way out here."

"Then what do you propose?"

"That you and I strike out on our own and start looking for some answers."

Casey looked less than pleased about being left by herself, and said as much with a sigh.

"It's too dangerous," Bill informed her. "Besides, we need someone to stay with Clay in case he wakes up. We'll be in constant contact with you."

"And just how do you plan on getting around the park without security throwing you out?"

Bill looked to Packard.

"She's got a point."

"I don't have a problem with staying here," she said, "but you won't get fifty yards out there without someone from Bryant's force stopping you."

"Are you going to suggest something, or is this your way of telling us you want to tag along?" Packard asked.

"There isn't much I *can* suggest. Bryant just made a standing order that all of his people, the medics, and the firefighters are to stay behind. Every other employee is ordered to leave immediately once their posts are cleared."

"I don't suppose there's much chance of us being convincing park employees," Packard said with a groan.

He was beginning to see only one alternative, but it involved trust. As much as he hated the idea, he decided to call Turpin to meet with him. He could use police intuition to quickly discover if the agent was there on his behalf, or with evil intent.

"I'm going to call the agent," he informed the others.

"You really don't want me tagging along that badly?" Casey asked, openly upset.

"Someone has to stay here with Clay. We're going to need to know the second he wakes up, if there's still time to do anything."

"He's been doing fine by himself," she argued.

"Yeah, but when he wakes up, he's not going to have any idea where we are, or what the terrorists are doing. It'll be up to you to keep him informed."

She looked doubtful, thinking Packard was telling her a half-truth, as though she were a child.

"If you talk to him while he's like that, he'll probably hear everything you say," Bill confirmed. "He told me it's like a comatose state that brings the mind and body together in perfect harmony so they can heal."

"Pardon my French, but that sounds kind of like bullshit," Packard said. "I know the boy is capable, but you can't just heal your body by concentrating on it."

Bill lifted his hands helplessly.

"He never said it was perfect, but if you take a look at his shoulder you'll probably find the bleeding has completely stopped because his heart is barely working."

Caught by his own words, Packard hesitated, then returned to Clay's side, lifting the cloths to find the blood dried on the material, and the wound already beginning to heal. He suspected it wouldn't take much activity to rip the injury open again, but the flesh and blood had formed a clot that kept Clay from bleeding out.

Of course blood also stopped flowing and clotted completely when a person died.

Packard grunted to himself, then returned to Bill.

"I'm calling Turpin. We don't have time to waste if the people are going to be out of here within the hour. It'll be dark right after that, and we still don't have a clue where the parts to the ride are."

Bill nodded.

"If you think you can trust him, go ahead."

"At this point, we don't have much choice. I just hope he trusts me after this morning."

Packard stepped out of the conference room, into a hallway, before locating the agent's cellular phone number in his phone's menu. He pressed the send button, then listened to two rings before a somewhat familiar voice answered.

"I'm not sure I should be talking to you, Sergeant Packard," the agent's soft drawl came across the phone, despite a less than perfect connection.

Packard suspected the building prevented good cellular connections, but was more concerned about Turpin's statement.

"What's that supposed to mean, Agent Turpin?"

"About an hour ago a man affiliated with the terrorist group inside the park told me you were part of their organization."

If the words were meant to stun Packard, they failed. He half expected some kind of twist from the terrorist organization involving him and his officers.

"And you're going on hearsay? I thought better of you, sir."

"The problem with his statement is that we looked employment records up in the park computer and it says you were contracted to do work on a ride."

Packard let the statement sink into his mind a few seconds, turning to see Casey and Bill engaged in minor conversation in the other room.

"That sounds a bit impossible, considering I visit this park about once a year with my family."

"Lucky for you that's kind of what I was thinking. The problem is I haven't been able to act on some of my impulses or finds."

"I want to meet up with you," Packard said, cutting to the chase. "We've made some discoveries on my end."

"We?"

Packard cleared his throat.

"My officers and I," he told a partial truth.

"Who's with you right now?"

"I'm with Clay Branson's uncle and Casey Trimble, the owners' daughter."

A pause separated them momentarily over the phone.

"Okay," Turpin finally said. "Where is your officer?"

"Clay is indisposed momentarily."

"You realize my job was to come to Muncie and meet him, right? Now, thanks to these sons of bitches my day is ruined, and I've been thrown in the middle of a terrorist plot unlike anything I've ever seen. If we're going to get through this I need complete honesty from you, and we need to meet face to face."

"You know where the employee offices are?"

"Yes."

"Meet me inside the offices in five minutes. Maybe we can find a solution to *all* of our problems."

"I hope so. Do me a favor and ask Miss Trimble about her security director, and especially his background. I'm having my own trust issues at the moment."

"Will do, Agent Turpin. See you in five minutes."

"I'll be there."

*   *   *   *

It took Maynard longer than he expected to find the state trooper's address, partly because he miscalculated the flow of traffic, and because he missed his turn.

East of Mason, a small town near the theme park, the address was just outside the town in a small but expanding housing community. He pulled the borrowed car in front of the house, seeing no other vehicle in the driveway, and no sign that anyone was home.

Having no useful information about the man, he began to doubt the theory that the terrorists might have kept him alive for information, and perhaps the real Darren Collier was already dead at the base of a roller coaster. If so, kicking in the back door seemed logical, but Maynard decided to be cautious, just in case Packard's hunch was right.

Sitting in the car momentarily, he weighed his options.

Knocking on the door would likely result in no one answering.

Kicking it in was reckless, though there was something to be said for the element of surprise.

Snooping around the property would alert anyone inside, or result in neighbors calling the police to report a trespasser.

Since he had no idea where the patrol car was parked, he had foregone searching for it, which meant any evidence it held was staying put.

Fingering the keys he lifted from the body, he decided to jump the fence to look for a door out back, hoping he guessed the correct key quickly. If not, someone behind the door might lie in wait to shoot him.

Stepping from the car, Maynard surveyed the area around him, seeing no one outside, and few cars in any driveways. Feeling somewhat safe, he carefully walked up the short driveway, noticing every window in the trooper's house had dark curtains over it. Either the man was a bachelor with bad decorating sense, or someone had something to hide.

Finished with gray wood siding, it loomed at two stories with an attached garage and length enough that Maynard suspected it held a minimum of three bedrooms. He wondered how much Ohio troopers earned as he approached the wooden gate that surrounded the property.

Through the slats, he spied an in-ground pool in back, and beside it a small dirt hump. It took a moment for him to get around the fence before finding a spot he could climb over. After a quick look around, he scaled the fence and found himself in the back yard, quickly running in a hunched manner toward the back door.

A closer look at the dirt hump allowed him an educated guess that it might be a dog, because it was the right size. Stopping at a corner of the house, he fished the keys from his pocket, trying to guess which one might unlock a door. Several had inscriptions which ruled them out immediately, but he came across one that looked like a familiar doorknob company.

He finished examining the set, picking out several that looked like solid possibilities, then approached the back door, quietly jiggling the first key into the lock.

It refused to turn.

Trying a second key, he received the same result, causing him to wonder if *any* of the keys worked.

Growing a bit concerned that someone inside might hear him, he tried the third key quickly, finding it turned in the lock, allowing the door to swing inward.

Immediately pulling the gun from his backside, Maynard stepped cautiously inside, finding it dark because no lights were on. Odors of stale, and possibly decaying food entered his nostrils, as though no one had taken out the trash or cleaned up after dinner for weeks.

He quickly shut the door behind him, standing still a moment, listening for any sound as his eyes adjusted to the dim lighting.

Only thin streams of light entered around the windows from the dark blinds, or the cloths that covered some of them. Appearing somewhat makeshift in nature, the cloths were blankets or table coverings hurriedly thrown over the windows. Maynard drew close to one, finding it hung by thin framing nails carelessly pounded into the window's framework.

A strange feeling of endangerment came over him, as though he had just sprung a trap.

Making the situation worse, he stood in the center of the house, with a hall-way to explore on either side of him. Standing in what he considered the family room, he was able to see the kitchen in front of him, toward the front of the house, and a living room immediately to his right. A hallway continued on the other side of it.

Beside him a console for a home security system hung near the back door. For some reason it wasn't armed, which raised his anxiety that someone was inside the house. With his eyes adjusted to the weak lighting, he took half a step forward, then froze in place as someone passed in front of him, stepping into the kitchen.

Holding his breath from sheer fright of being discovered, he watched the man walk into the kitchen, then begin searching the cabinets for something to eat. Maynard stepped back, into the shadows, monitoring the man and his actions momentarily.

Since the man's back was turned, Maynard found himself unable to see any features. He ducked behind a nearby lazy chair, wondering if this man was possibly the legitimate owner, or perhaps the trooper's roommate. He considered the possibility of the trooper having a life partner, but something felt out of place, because this man didn't seem to know where things were located.

Maynard's initial shock had caused him to miss most of the man's features when he passed through the room, but now he saw the man had dark hair and fairly light skin. It was possible he was Asian, but the officer's attention focused on the man's backside where a pistol grip jutted upward from the man's belt.

Dressed in an old flannel shirt, some sort of olive green work pants, and industrial brown work shoes, the man was definitely a different nationality. Maynard verified the fact when the man turned around, based on his olive complection. As he gathered the components for a sandwich over the next few minutes, Maynard observed he wore a black patch over his right eye.

"Great, a pirate," Maynard said mockingly to himself, watching the man whistle something to himself, then leave the kitchen the other way.

He settled into the living room, turned on the television, and flipped channels for something to watch.

Assuming the man had come from the other end of the hallway, where a prisoner might be held, Maynard snuck the other way, noticing the man had turned on the surround sound.

So much for low key, he thought, wondering why terrorists would bother covering all of the windows if they were just going to make noise.

Of course this individual was probably left behind for a reason.

Covered by darkness that his adversaries had already created, Maynard made his way down the hallway, finding every door closed except the one at the end. Suspecting his luck wasn't good enough for him to find what he was looking for in the open room, he started reaching for the closest doorknob.

Stopping as his hand touched it, he decided to walk the extra fifteen feet to look, finding a wooden chair beyond the opening as he drew to one side. Beside the chair's feet he saw what appeared to be human feet, bound by thick rope.

Cautiously taking a look behind him, Maynard saw no activity, and the television was still blaring, which prevented him from hearing anything if the man came his way. Deciding it was in his best interest not to stand in front of an open doorway, he looked inside the room, finding a pair of eyes meeting his own.

There, a man who looked exactly like the one he had killed less than an hour prior, started to say muffled words through the gag in his mouth until Maynard held his own forefinger up to his lips.

Stripped down to his underwear, the man was bound and gagged with added humiliation from the heartless terrorists. Considering the house was cool, Maynard assumed the man had to be extremely uncomfortable.

"I'm here to help," he said quickly, noticing the man was bound virtually everywhere with the thick rope, and handcuffed to boot.

Inside the room was a single lamp with an exposed lightbulb. Maynard found no other light sources around, but it was enough to allow him to see most everything around him.

Now racing against the clock, he had to decide whether or not to untie the real Collier or deal with the henchman first. He liked two-on-one odds much better, but didn't want to be looking over his shoulder every few seconds while he untied the trooper. He usually had a jackknife with him, but left it in their unmarked car when he reached the park earlier that morning.

Nothing remained in this room except a dresser, which he rummaged through quickly, finding underwear and socks.

"Is there a knife around here?" he asked Collier.

With a tilt of his head and a muffled sound, the trooper indicated the adjacent room might have something in it.

Taking another look behind him, then a few steps forward, Maynard confirmed the henchman continued to watch television, though he had turned it down, likely realizing the risk.

Maynard stepped into the room like a cat avoiding a flea-ridden carpet. With both windows covered, the room had absolutely no light. Deciding to chance it, he flipped on the light switch, quickly rummaging through dresser drawers, then a corner desk after having no success. There, he found a pair of scissors, deciding it was the best sharp edge he was going to find without venturing through the house.

As he neared the door Maynard flipped off the switch, then listened momentarily for movement in the hallway. He heard nothing for a few seconds, but as he reached for the doorknob, the television suddenly went silent. Cracking the door slightly ajar, Maynard listened to the terrorist speaking on a cellular phone down the hallway in broken English.

He seemed to be questioning an order for some reason, and the officer wondered if he had just been asked to murder the trooper ahead of schedule.

"Great," Maynard muttered, hoping to avoid confrontation altogether, or at least until it was no longer avoidable.

He had no good way of sneaking the trooper outside, but he didn't feel much like killing another person.

Another moment of eavesdropping allowed the officer to decide Collier was about to be murdered unless he intervened. The guard hung up the phone, then began gathering belongings inside the living room, placing them in a bag. He also used a rag to dust the area clean of his fingerprints and trace evidence.

Waiting until the man had his attention occupied for a few seconds, Maynard exited the secondary bedroom, shut the door, and snuck into the other room. First, he used his personal handcuff keys to undo the cuffs binding the trooper's wrists.

Maynard then placed the scissors in Collier's hands before peeking out the doorway just enough to see that the henchman was nearly done with his cleanup.

"Try and free yourself," Maynard told the trooper. "He's cleaning up, then coming down here to kill you. I'll be in the closet, so keep him distracted."

Collier nervously nodded with wide eyes, but seemed intent on complying.

A closet with slotted sliding doors was completely hallowed out, allowing Maynard easy access to the inside just before the henchman made his way down the hall.

Pulling the gun from behind him, he made certain the safety was off, then held it in a ready position, unsure of whether the man with the eyepatch even planned to speak before pulling the trigger.

A fine line of right and wrong, moral and immoral, kept Maynard from simply shooting the man once he was within view. He needed proof that the henchman was evil, simply to justify shooting him in his own mind. Still, he needed to protect Collier because it was the right thing to do, and the trooper probably had some of the answers Maynard needed to hear.

Able to view Collier through the blinds, he found the trooper nearly halfway through the process of cutting the rope. Like Maynard, he listened intently for the man's steps down the hallway. From his position in the closet, Maynard barely had a view of the door, and nothing beyond it.

With no television blaring in the background, Maynard heard when the steps finally came closer, then watched with anticipation as the man entered the room, raised his firearm, and pointed it deliberately at Collier's head without a single word.

Acting without hesitation or thought for his own safety, Maynard shouldered his way out of the closet, surprised the henchman, and shot directly at the man's heart while still in motion.

Though his shot wasn't perfectly on target, it proved to be a slower mortal wound.

After slumping against the wall, the terrorist dropped his firearm, then slid down to the floor, a bloody streak following him along the wall. He began what medics called agonal breathing, which is comprised of strained breaths, either from heart trouble, bodily fluids leaking into the wrong areas, or fluids entering the throat from the bottom up.

In this case, he seemed to be choking on his own blood from internal injuries.

Taking hold of the scissors, Maynard freed Collier within a few seconds, then helped him out of the chair.

"I haven't stood since yesterday," the trooper revealed, trying to slowly rise from the chair. "I've got that numb tingling in my legs."

"What the hell is going on around here?" Maynard inquired, barely able to pry his eyes from the dying terrorist, whose one good eye looked upward at him, as though inquiring why he deserved death.

"I was about to ask you if you had any answers. How did you even know where to find me?"

"Let's just say I saw your evil twin an hour ago. I'm Rod Maynard with the Muncie Police Department."

Collier looked at him with some recognition in his eyes.

"They had a guy made up to look like me," he said. "They kept me alive for information, but I never got wind of their plans. And aren't you a little out of your jurisdiction?"

"It's a long story. You never heard anything from the terrorists? No idle talk?"

"I just know they were setting me up for something. And some other cop, too. They thought they could make everyone think I snapped because my nephew was killed at the park a few years ago. I didn't see how they could get away with it."

"You'd be surprised."

Maynard took notice of the man's lack of attire.

"Once your legs get the feeling back you might want to get some pants on."

"I plan to," Collier said. "We have to call the authorities to let them know what happened."

Saying nothing, Maynard gave him a look that indicated otherwise.

"Before we do anything I'll fill you in on what happened today. Calling other cops might be a bad idea at the moment."

Collier began painfully walking toward the next room.

"Well, it's going to take me the better part of two minutes to put some pants on, so you've got plenty of time to get me up to speed."

Nodding, Maynard wondered where to begin.

CHAPTER 20

▼

Packard observed Turpin when the agent stepped through the door of the lower offices. He walked somewhat like the sergeant expected, with a stiffness that came from being a Texas lawman.

Wasting little time, the two shook hands before they even exchanged words.

"We need to make this quick," Turpin said. "I only have a few minutes before my shadow comes looking for me."

"I get the feeling we each have half of the puzzle, so I hope we can figure some things out," Packard noted. "First, my officer and I overheard a conversation an hour ago between two of the thugs who said they wanted to eliminate you, kill a man named Collier, and said Clay was as good as dead after he fought two of his old adversaries."

"For some reason they want you to take the fall," Turpin said. "They've gotten into the computer system here and created files linking you to work done at this facility."

"They also want the park completely cleared out, because they plan on moving something out of here tonight."

Turpin tapped his chin with a forefinger in thought.

Casey stepped behind Packard, despite his request that she and Bill stay upstairs. He had no right to argue with her, because she legally had ownership over the park.

"Can I trust Bryant?" Turpin asked her, obviously knowing her somehow.

"I think so. He's been with us a few years now."

"Can you tell me if he was ever a Navy SEAL, or what his military background is?"

Walking over to a computer, she began typing in several commands.

"What are we going to do about this?" Packard asked the agent. "Now that the guests are out of the park they no longer have leverage."

Turpin sighed, then gritted his teeth.

"True, but until we know where they are, or what they're doing, we'd be giving them ample opportunity to escape while we search."

Casey returned, standing between them.

"He was in the Navy, but he was a lieutenant. Our records showed he went to officer school after some college classes."

Turpin grumbled something under his breath, apparently having little respect for military officer schools.

Or perhaps the Navy.

Packard had more pressing concerns than figuring out the agent's motivations and pet peeves. He wanted to start looking for the terrorist camp before dusk overtook the entire park.

An idea suddenly hit him.

"Is there lighting in any of the uncleared acreage?" he asked Casey.

"In certain areas. Usually just the places utility trucks might go, like near the rides, or back where we have the haunted trails in the fall."

"Where are you going with this?" Turpin inquired.

"We think they stole half of the ride that's been dismantled, and now it's nowhere to be found. If they plan on moving it out of here tonight, we simply have to look for any lighting outside the park."

"And how do you propose we do that?"

Casey looked at him with a wry grin.

"The observation tower of course."

A few minutes later the three of them stood inside the elevator car on their way up to the observation tower platform, which was a full twenty-six stories high. It allowed for a fantastic view of the entire park, and even some regions surrounding it.

Before leaving, Casey had checked over Packard's alleged employment records at the park, finding some facts that left the sergeant uneasy. The times he supposedly clocked in were all times he was doing task force work by himself, away from others. Therefore, he had no alibi for any of the instances.

And worse, it meant he was being spied upon for over a month in Muncie.

He and Turpin had discussed more of their finds, and some information, but nothing that seemed vital to solving the mystery around them.

The three discovered somewhat quickly that the view from the tower became obscured by tall trees, particularly in nearly dark conditions. The elevator doors opened, allowing them to step onto the platform floor. Constructed of a metal grid pattern, the floor felt incredibly sturdy under Packard's feet.

Surrounded by wrought metal bars, the tower kept guests safely within its confines. A sign warned potentially mischievous guests and children not to throw anything from the tower.

"It's hard to see, but a single light source should show up through the trees," Packard thought aloud.

"Not if they've planned on us looking for them," Turpin replied. "We may have no choice but to call in any and everyone to search."

"We can do that, and we might stop whatever they're doing here," Packard said. "But the two leaders aren't ordinary men. If we let them go, they'll pack up and move on. Then someone else will have to deal with a death toll and terrorists with no conscience. They aren't trained like you and I, Agent Turpin."

Turpin gave him a suspicious look.

"Then tell me, how *are* they trained?" he asked, still wearing a bit of a smirk, trying to get Packard to confess something.

"I think you already know. And the only man who can stop them is temporarily incapacitated."

A call came over her radio for Casey, which she answered immediately.

"This is Casey. Go ahead, Hugh."

"I need to speak with Agent Turpin. Have you seen him?"

She looked to the agent, who nodded it was okay to tell him.

"I'm with him on the observation tower. We'll be down in a moment."

Packard walked around the platform a moment, suspecting the terrorists were far too smart to remain in the open. They had some sort of inside help, deeper than Gomez, because their ability to hide and maneuver seemed too perfect. Someone with vast experience around the park had aided them.

As he stared into the dark woods ahead, seeing a star-filled sky as a backdrop, his phone rang beside him.

He looked to the number, seeing it was Maynard. He pressed the talk button, anxious to speak with his officer.

"Good to hear from you, Rod."

"Good to be alive, Sarge. You were right. I have Collier right here beside me."

"Then who is that body you left behind?"

"That's the million-dollar question."

Packard had told no one about the body, figuring it was more trouble than they needed if police and coroners came inside the park to examine it. Only dental records or DNA evidence might tell them its identity, and both methods took too long to attempt for the quick answers he needed.

"What do you want me to do?" Maynard asked.

"Stay away from the park, Rod. Keep him with you, and don't go to the authorities just yet. I've got the FBI agent with me, and he's going to take charge."

"Staying away was my original plan. I thought I might check on Ed while I was out and about."

"Too dangerous, Rod. If they start missing Collier, they'll be looking everywhere. They were setting him up for the fall, and *me* as well."

"You?"

"They had evidence planted in the computers that I worked here in the park as a freelance repairman."

A momentary silence crossed the line.

"That doesn't seem feasible, considering you always had witnesses around you back home."

"Well, conveniently, they have my clock-in times here at times I wasn't working, or around people at home. They've been spying on us for months, Rod, waiting for this thing to come to a head."

"Not good."

"No, it's not. Just lay low with our state trooper until we get things figured out around here. Right now he's the best piece of evidence we have to put this shitball together. I'll call you when I have something more."

"Okay. Be careful, Sarge."

Packard hung up the phone, finding both Turpin and Casey looking his way.

"Good news?" Turpin inquired.

"Sort of. Things just got a little more complicated."

"How so?"

"We figured out something about the trooper you saw chase Gomez out of the office earlier."

Turpin raised an eyebrow.

"He wasn't really a trooper at all."

"But he had the marked car and uniform," the agent argued.

"Yeah, because they were holding the real deal hostage while one of them posed as him for the past week or two."

"Of course," Casey said. "They were setting him up for the fall, because his nephew died on our ride a few years back. He transferred here around the time of the trial, so it would all make perfect sense."

"If they got away with it," Packard added.

"Then where's the real trooper?" Turpin asked.

"With one of my officers."

"And the fake?"

Packard swallowed hard, not wanting to divulge the information. At least not in full.

"Well, he's no longer with us."

Turpin's expression went from concerned to furious within a second's time. Packard suspected he was upset because this had not come up earlier in their conversation.

"We have another corpse lying around this park and you decided not to inform me?"

"I never said it was inside the park," Packard stated, trying to backpedal a bit.

The agent looked at him the way a parent does when he doesn't believe what a child is telling him.

"Look, it's another hangup I didn't need to deal with," Packard said sternly. "Police would have stormed this park in force."

"I'm beginning to think you lack trust in me," Turpin replied. "I wouldn't necessarily say calling in the locals is the best thing to do."

"My lack of faith in you is founded in what happened to *me* last year, Turpin. I'm willing to trust you because I have little choice."

"I know what happened last year, but I also know if you had called me sooner, we might be a leg up on these bastards. I'm not enjoying the mind games, trying to figure out who's on my side any more than you are."

Casey cleared her throat so both men heard.

"While we're up here arguing about who to trust and who might backstab everyone else, the bad guys are getting ready to leave with my parents' roller coaster parts."

Packard looked to Turpin, who returned an equally hard stare.

"What do you suggest we do next?" he asked Casey, since she was the only park authority available.

"I suggest we get everyone around here to start searching the park. No one knows the park better than our own employees, and most of them love overtime."

"We can't ask them to do that unless they know the danger," Turpin noted aloud. "We're dealing with trained killers."

"Then we tell them what they need to know," Packard suggested. "And we tell them not to engage anyone they don't know."

Turpin looked less than pleased about the plan, but knew they needed manpower without involving local or state police.

"What about her?" the agent asked of Casey.

"She stays with Clay to make sure he's apprised of our situation if he wakes up."

"But he has his uncle for that," Casey insisted, obviously wanting to be part of the action.

She didn't strike Packard as someone who wanted constant protection, and showed no signs of being worried about her own well-being.

"You're staying with Clay and that's final," Packard insisted.

"But my parents own this park. I can call the authorities if I want to and ignore whatever you say."

Packard equated the statement to a child throwing a tantrum, but Turpin handled it before he was able to speak.

"You can do what you want to, but I'm a federal agent, and even if you call someone I'll be in charge of this scene," he said slowly and softly through his drawl. "Little lady, the best thing you can do is just what Sergeant Packard asked of you. It won't be any less important than what we do, and we'll keep you informed of whatever we find."

She seemed to agree, especially after he said updates were forthcoming.

"As for you and me, we're meeting with Mr. Bryant," Turpin said, directing the statement toward Packard. "We'll reorganize our search, then see what we find."

Nodding in reply, Packard felt pessimistic about their chances, thinking the terrorists had planned everything too well to slip up now.

Still, he followed Casey and Turpin into the elevator car when it returned to them.

*   *   *   *

When Casey returned upstairs to the conference room area, Bill was gone. She searched the area, calling his name every so often, but no answer came.

After looking upstairs and down, she checked on Clay, finding him in the same condition as before. He breathed so slowly it was impossible to tell if he was really alive, but she remembered Bill proving it earlier.

Carefully peeling back the dressings on his shoulder, she found the bloody cloth entirely dry, as was the wound. She grazed her finger along the dried blood, finding his skin cool to the touch. Where the bullet had exited the skin felt lumpy because of clotting and miniature skin flaps on the sides of the hole.

He failed to stir one little bit, as though he saw no reason to wake up.

Or no threat to himself.

"I wish you would wake up," she told him just above a whisper. "If nothing else, I could use the company."

Casey jumped a bit when the cordless phone rang on the conference desk in the main room behind her. She rose from her knees to walk into the room, picking up the receiver as she looked out the window. A perfect view of the nighttime lights along the main drag revealed a complete lack of activity, which felt completely abnormal to her.

Usually at least a few employees remained visible, but the concrete and buildings appeared perfectly quiet.

"Great Realms," she answered generically, not knowing the caller's identity.

"Casey, it's Mom," a familiar voice stated in a somewhat annoyed tone. "Your father and I are on our way to the park. We've been held up for over an hour in traffic."

Casey had spoken to her parents twice during the afternoon, updating them on the situation, but assuring them Bryant had things under control. Their confidence in him kept them from openly worrying, but Casey had neglected to mention some of the worst details.

She wanted her parents home safely before telling them about the shooting death and the grave possibility that terrorists had planned to decimate their park months ahead of time.

"How are things at the park?"

"We've sent the guests home early."

"We planned for the park to close by six anyway, didn't we?"

"Yeah, but I had a talk with Hugh."

Casey let her statement end there.

"Is there something you're not telling me, dear?"

"A few things have happened, but nothing I can't tell you after you get here. I'll have Hugh brief you once you get here."

"A few things, eh?"

Casey cleared her throat purposefully as she wandered toward the screening room.

"I don't want Dad crashing the car trying to get here. We'll tell you everything when you arrive."

Suddenly she felt relieved that reporters hadn't badgered them heavily about the deaths. One good thing about owning a theme park that covered hundreds of acres was guaranteed privacy in the wake of a tragedy.

News crews were not allowed inside the grounds without permission, which Bryant had certainly not given, so any video footage would show the park from a distance, or file footage might be used. If the real story got out, every news hound within a hundred miles would want an exclusive.

"Is Daddy there with you?" Casey asked to be sure.

"Of course. He's driving, and cursing at the traffic."

Growing more disturbed by the moment at the sight of Clay's unmoving body, Casey stood, walked out of the room, and into the conference room. A glance out the windows showed a continued lack of activity along the main drag.

"When do you think the traffic will let up?" Casey inquired.

"It's hard telling. The radio reported an overturned semi ahead, so it may be awhile."

Casey thought she saw a shadow pass outside the window to her right. Though it was dark outside, light from a lamppost passed through the window, and this time through the drawn blinds. Thinking it was odd that something could disrupt light on the second story, she drew closer to the window.

"Mom, I gotta run. Call me when you get in."

"Okay. Love you, Casey."

"Love you, too."

Casey hung up the phone, then peered around the side of the blinds.

Suppressing a gasp with her right hand, Casey drew back from the window after seeing at least four men dressed in dark garb climbing the building toward that particular window.

Each had a pack on his back with handles sticking out. They all wore some sort of dark mask to conceal their faces, or at least toboggans to cover up their hair.

Something had likely led them to Clay, whether it was a blood trail, an educated guess, or someone she trusted who leaked his secret hiding place. He was in no condition to fight, much less wake up, but she recalled Bill stating something about Clay's subconscious hearing everything around him.

Dashing for the secret room, Casey dropped to her knees beside his resting place, catching her breath a few seconds before speaking to him, shaking him lightly.

"Clay, if you can hear me, this is Casey. There are men climbing the building, and they're coming to get you. You've got to wake up! Do you hear me?"

She expected some response, like him waking up groggily as her parents had on Christmas morning when she woke them.

But nothing changed.

"Please wake up," she virtually pleaded, shaking his closer arm more violently this time.

When nothing changed, she looked behind her, seeing men climbing through the far window effortlessly, as though the locking mechanism never existed. One by one they climbed through, staring intently at her.

And their primary target.

"No," she murmured, wishing the terrifying situation before her was nothing more than a bad dream.

With deliberate purpose, mixed with caution, six men stalked toward her from the opposite end of the hallway. Even from the distance equivalent to half a football field she saw they held weapons. Not guns, but silent weapons like Clay and Bill had toted.

Their intention was obviously assassination, but she kept her wits, running toward the side of the door, throwing it closed to give her more time to think. Feeling certain she was on her own, she backed away from the door, looking around, knowing there was no escape. She felt like a cooped chicken waiting for the foxes to arrive.

Looking and listening intently, she took one more step back, bumping into something solid she hadn't expected. Whirling around, she saw Clay's blue eyes boring through the door before looking a bit more softly into her eyes.

"Take cover, and no matter what you hear, don't come out," he said just above a whisper with a stern, almost big brotherly tone.

Color had returned to his face, and his wound showed no sign of bleeding. In his right hand Clay clutched a long sword, which appeared to be the only weapon he had against the likes of six assassins.

He moved her toward the back of the sofa with considerable ease and amazing gentleness. Without so much as another word, he approached the door, turned his head downward, and to one side, then raised it again. She wondered if he heard anything on the other side, because she certainly did not.

Casey watched as he assumed a martial arts position, holding the sword in one hand, then opened the door, darting into the hallway in a virtual blur.

All six men readied their weapons, but Clay's instincts were unlike anything she had ever seen. He ducked the swing of one sword, then whirled to avoid a bladed weapon that looked like a miniature sickle to her. Delivering a back kick to the man with the sickle, Clay sent him flying hard against a nearby wall.

Afraid of hitting one another, the men attacked one or two at a time, which gave Clay far too much opportunity to defend himself. Ducking, weaving, and dodging from side to side as various bladed weapons came his way, he occasionally found opportunity to get in a kick or punch.

At one point the men closed in on his position with readied blades, but Clay had enough room between the table and large windows to dash toward the clear surface. Casey wondered if he planned to bust through the surface, leaving her to fend for herself, but his feet touched the window in succession, as the blades jabbed toward his backside.

She couldn't believe he built up enough speed in two steps to rebound himself from the window, do a back flip, and land atop the table, but that was exactly what she saw.

Clay then jumped down to safety, leaving all of the men wedged between the table and windows, allowing him to defend only one side.

For some reason he was not using his sword, which Casey guessed was because he outclassed the would be assassins so badly.

Clay refused to kill the men, when she saw several opportunities for him to do so. Despite regarding herself as a novice in the world of martial arts, Casey knew Clay passed up several chances to better his position.

As though watching an action movie, Casey was drawn toward the door, watching Clay move like lightning, striking the men with fists and feet repeatedly. Though wearing them down quickly, he was in danger of reopening his wound.

Framed in the doorway, Casey was mere steps from the action, causing one of the armed assassins to take notice. Clay took notice as well, striking the man from behind with a vicious blast from his forearm to the head.

"Stay in there," Clay ordered, slamming the door shut on her.

When he turned around, all six men were to their feet, poised for combat, but growing tired simply from him parrying their blows. He knew they were Kim's flunkies, thinking they were learning the secret art of *ninjutsu*, when in reality they were puppets he created for disposal on missions like this.

Either Kim believed Clay had let himself forget most of his knowledge, or let himself go physically, because these men posed little threat to him. Yes, their weapon handling was dangerous to most adversaries, but they had no knowledge of the senses Clay possessed, or how to fight as a unit.

Clay charged through the middle, three men to each side of him, flipping through midair as a *katana* and a *sai* sliced at where his abdomen would have been. Landing in the position known as *jumonji no kamae*, otherwise known as the offensive posture, Clay launched a straight kick behind him, breaking two of the charging attacker's ribs.

Effectively he was down to five enemies.

Another charged at him, but Clay caught his arm, which held a pair of short wooden staffs connected by a chain. Taking the weapon, Clay struck the man stiffly in the head with his own weapon, then tossed him aside.

Down to four.

He had two reasons for not killing his adversaries. One, he didn't want to leave any kind of evidence trail, because he figured Voodoo and Kim had set his group up somehow. Clay had no desire to fall into their trap by committing murder.

Secondly, he wanted at least one of them conscious for questioning. He had no idea if they spoke English or not, but imagined Kim required it, because they needed to blend in within any given situation.

At this point the four remaining capable men began eyeing one another as though contemplating escape. Perhaps they realized Kim had set them up, or that they had no chance against a seasoned warrior in top physical condition.

Regardless of what they thought, Clay had decided none of them were leaving the room unless they planned on smashing through the large windows two stories above a hard concrete surface.

Intentionally motivating the four men to change their minds, Clay sheathed his sword, sliding it into the sturdy sheath strapped to his back without so much as a glance behind him.

All four were armed with various weapons, and it took only a second for the two closest men to charge him with a *sai* and a short sword. Clay anticipated their movements, ducking the sword while blocking the sharp end of the *sai*. Grabbing the same attacker by the hair, he jumped atop the long conference table to distance himself from the others, thrusting the man's head against the cured wood surface.

In virtually the same movement, he grabbed both of the man's arms, twisting them as he landed on the other end to pull them out of socket. A sharp painful scream emitted from the man's mouth, but he quickly silenced himself, sliding off the safe end of the table to distance himself from the battle.

Taking up the *sai*, Clay motioned for the other initial attacker to charge him with a hand motion, which the man did after a few seconds of intimidated hesitation. As soon as the man sprinted around the table, Clay saw his eyes divert in the time it took to blink toward the other two attackers.

About to be attacked from the front and behind, Clay focused on the first man temporarily, deflecting the sword attack with his borrowed weapon, punching the man in the face, then kicking him in the shin. Sensing a weapon coming toward him instinctively, Clay leapt atop the table, avoiding a bamboo pole with a bladed end.

The blade lodged itself in one of the chairs, giving Clay time enough to strike the attacker in the head with his foot. With the short sword now swinging at his feet, Clay let his feet leave the ground, landing in a handstand with only his left arm. He deflected another attack with the *sai* in his right hand, then swung his feet around, kicking the short sword attacker in the head.

Buying himself just a second or so, Clay landed on his feet, wasting no time in launching an attack against the second of the three capable men, since the other remained trapped behind him. Less than two feet existed between the table and the wall to Clay's left. Unlike the other side, the opposite walls consisted of covered metal.

Kicking the bamboo staff from the man's hands, Clay caught it, swinging it like a cheerleader might twirl a baton, striking the man's head once more. He clutched the weapon stiffly, jabbing the man in the stomach before delivering a debilitating blow to the man's temple.

Two left.

As the man slumped unconsciously against the table, Clay spun to block the short sword with the staff, then kicked the man in the abdomen. He ducked a blade aimed for his head from behind, and jabbed the *sai* behind him. Another scream filled the room because the weapon had lodged itself in the man's thigh, near the large artery running through his leg.

Another enemy down.

Pulling the weapon free, Clay watched the droplets of blood pass by his face in midair as he swung the weapon to block the short sword once again. Fenced within the tight area, Clay fought the man using the staff, dropping the *sai* atop the table just in front of him.

Parrying a few swipes of the sword, Clay forced the sword upward, exposing the man's face enough to allow an opening. Grasping each wooden end of the staff, he thrust it upward, catching the man on the bridge of his nose, causing it to gush blood. Clay then clasped the hand holding the sword, stabbing him through the shoulder with the staff's bladed end, pinning him against the wall.

Whisking the *sai* from the table, Clay ran the sharpened blade through the other shoulder, drawing a painful cry from the man now helplessly trapped.

Reminded of the constant throbbing in his own shoulder, Clay knew blood ebbed from the wound once again. Any movement compromised the wound, but the few hours of rest gave him enough remaining strength to finish the task at hand.

Without bothering to look around him, Clay focused intently on the man's face, clutching his jaw forcefully with his hand. If anyone stirred behind him his heightened senses would alert him before danger struck.

"Tell me where Voodoo and Kim are," he demanded.

Instead of answering, the man showed complete disrespect by attempting to spit on him. Clay squeezed his jaw even tighter, preventing the intention from being carried out.

"You can answer me, or we can play rough," Clay said sternly, twisting one of the blades with his free arm, drawing a pained cry.

Wearing a black winter cap atop his head, the man had shown his face and identity from the beginning, apparently suspecting no one was going to live to identify him. Clay forcefully tore the hat from his head, then twisted the other blade for effect.

"In the woods," the man stammered after holding out a few seconds, speaking excellent English.

"You're going to have to do better than that."

"Maybe he can tell us where they're taking half of a roller coaster," Casey said, stepping up from behind Clay.

He had heard her footsteps, quiet as they were atop carpet, but sensed no danger approaching, so he never diverted his attention from Kim's thug.

"I've apparently missed a few things," Clay noted aloud.

"A few. They've managed to steal half of a roller coaster from our park, and we have no idea where it is. And it seems one of them disguised himself as a state trooper and got himself killed by your buddy."

Pausing a few seconds to think, Clay decided on his next question.

"So where is the cargo? And who is the mastermind behind this whole thing?"

"I don't know," the man insisted.

"One more chance, or I can stick these blades in far more painful places."

Quickly rethinking his situation, the man dispelled the answer hurriedly.

"The cargo is in transit. It left the park earlier today."

Clay looked to Casey, who shrugged helplessly.

"It's possible. We haven't checked on the parts in a day or two."

"Where is it going?" Clay asked, returning his attention to his captive.

"New York City. They have a buyer overseas."

"A buyer for our coaster?" Casey asked, raising her voice in utter surprise.

"No, a buyer for their product," Clay said darkly, allowing his eyes to bore into the man before him. "You're going to tell me everything, or your life span will see its end within the next five minutes."

CHAPTER 21

▼

Before leaving the house with Collier, Maynard decided to search the place for any evidence that might help put things in perspective.

It sounded more and more like the terrorists had an airtight plan to frame Packard and the state trooper for murder and terrorist acts. Keeping the state trooper from calling in other authorities was no easy task, but Packard had assured Maynard the FBI man was taking charge of the operation.

While Collier finished getting dressed, Maynard searched the kitchen for any information that might prove useful. Nothing obvious was lying around, and it seemed improbable that Collier's jailers would put anything inside drawers and cupboards.

"You sure we shouldn't call anyone in on this?" Collier asked, returning to the kitchen, now dressed in full uniform.

He had apparently decided to prepare himself for anything, just in case they needed some local authority.

"Not until my sergeant gives the okay," Maynard said, still rummaging through the counter top's stack of loose papers, most of which looked like bills.

"I take it the bad guys didn't pay your utilities for you," he noted, picking up a late sewage bill.

"And I think the pricks ate me out of house and home."

"I'm looking for any kind of note or plan they might have left behind. Did they change guards on a regular basis?"

"At least four or five times a day."

Maynard sifted through the paperwork, seeing nothing useful.

"What are you hoping to find?" Collier inquired, following him into the living room.

"Anything that might tell us about their plans. Locations, their cargo, anything."

Collier stood there a second, as though still absorbing the fact he was free, and wasn't going to be murdered like a dog.

"You okay?" Maynard asked him.

"Yeah. I think so."

"Good. Grab any extra guns and weapons you've got."

"Expecting trouble?"

Maynard thumbed through some booklets and papers atop the coffee table, seeing nothing helpful until a sheet of torn paper caught his attention.

"Trouble seems to follow me and my crew."

"What's that?" Collier asked as Maynard scooped up the sheet.

"A phone number. Your writing?"

"No. Must be something they brought in."

Maynard didn't recognize the area code, but the number itself seemed to be within the United States, based on the number and order of the digits.

Plucking his cellular phone from his belt, Maynard started to look at his list of contacts, planning to call Packard when the doorknob to the front door turned.

Less than ten feet from them, both officers knew it was shift change for the terrorists, quickly exchanging concerned glances. Collier reached for the service weapon at his side, but Maynard held up a foreboding finger, wondering if there might be more than one of them. If the dead man failed to contact them by a certain time it was possible they came looking for him.

With Turpin by his side, Packard had the ability to check the phone number Maynard found, and trace any phone calls made from Collier's residence. It was enough to break the case wide-open and put them a step ahead of the terrorists, but such knowledge was worthless if neither of them made it out alive.

"Back door?" Maynard asked in a hushed whisper as someone fidgeted with the key at the front door a moment.

Collier looked at him as though he were insane, and Maynard understood the man's desire for revenge, but other lives were at stake. At this point no time remained to retreat from the room and escape cleanly, so Maynard quickly motioned for Collier to take cover behind the front door. In the meantime, he hid behind a nearby chair, pulling the recovered gun from behind him, holding it in a ready position.

Having no formulated plan worried him, because he didn't know how the trooper planned to react, and the last thing either of them wanted to do was shoot the other. Being next to the front window, Maynard had just a second to peek outside the blinds, behind a hung blanket, to see only one man attempting to enter the residence.

Holding up his forefinger for Collier to see, he watched the trooper acknowledge the sign, then stand down slightly. Neither was in great position to mount an attack when the terrorist guard finally entered the household, but Maynard crept to the edge of the chair, hoping Collier made the first move.

In mere seconds it was over as the man stepped inside, looked around for his friend, and received a pistol whipping to the back of his skull. He fell to the ground in a heap as Collier stood over him with a hardened look.

"We need to secure him," Maynard suggested. "We can't have him coming to and calling his buddies."

"Securing doesn't seem right after what they did to me."

Maynard hesitated, formulating his words before he said them.

"Killing him doesn't make things right, Trooper Collier. It makes you a murderer, and twice today I've had to kill in self-defense. We have hundreds of people counting on us to disrupt their plans, and no time to waste. Understand?"

Collier nodded slowly as a car motor started outside, drawing both of them to the window.

One look outside revealed that the relief guard had a driver, who was now prepared to leave the premises.

"Was he leaving anyway, or waiting for his buddy to come out first?" Collier wondered.

"I don't know, but we need to deal with him."

"How long do we wait for him to come inside?"

Maynard growled under his breath. Time was the one luxury they did not have.

"Keep an eye on him," he finally said, referring to the fallen guard. "Tie him up with something and watch for his buddy."

"What are you going to do?"

"I'm calling my sergeant so he can have the FBI guy trace this number and monitor any calls made from your house since you've been held up."

Collier looked concerned, as though not wanting to handle another intruder by himself, or uncertain about doing two dangerous tasks at once.

"I'll be in the kitchen if you need me," Maynard assured him. "Just find some rope and a gag and deal with our number one problem. His buddy probably won't come in right away."

Seeming a bit more reassured, the trooper kept vigil over the door, keeping his firearm in the trained ready position.

"You had a whole spare uniform?" Maynard questioned as he looked for Packard's number in his phone's contact list.

"Of course I had another uniform. The gun belt is my original issue, which I retired a few years ago."

It took two rings before Packard answered the phone on the other end.

"What have you got, Rod?" he asked immediately.

And somewhat impatiently.

"I've got a phone number one of the assholes left here at the house. Thought your FBI guy might be able to trace it."

Maynard read it to him, looking out to see Collier now securing the intruder with some sort of twine that looked better suited for arts and crafts than binding a human being.

"Anything else?" Packard asked.

"A thought. You might have him trace any outgoing calls from this residence as well. If they *have* cell phones, I haven't seen them."

"Good idea. You two aren't still there, are you?"

Sighing through his nose, Maynard didn't want to take time to explain, but he wasn't about to let Packard think he was incapable of following orders.

"We had company. One of them is still waiting outside in a car."

"And the other?"

"About ten feet from me. He'll be down for awhile."

Silence crossed the line a few seconds.

"You got it handled?"

"We're holed up. If he steps inside, he'll be joining his buddy on the floor."

"Then get your asses out of there."

"Will do."

Maynard wanted to ask how the search was going for Packard, but figured the sergeant had more pressing issues than giving him a news brief.

"Give me the phone number there," Packard requested.

Maynard requested the number from Collier, which the trooper replied loud enough for Packard to hear on his end.

"We'll get on it," Packard said.

"Good luck."

"You too."

Packard severed the call, leaving Maynard holding the phone, feeling helpless because he wasn't part of the group carrying out what he considered the real work. He wasn't lacking for excitement, because he suspected he was about to confront another terrorist. These men were flunkies for the real masterminds.

"I don't like waiting like this," Collier said when he returned to the living room.

"Me neither, but we're not going far after we get out of here. My job is to keep you out of sight and safe until they clear things up at the park."

"You don't think I can do that myself?" the trooper retorted, not watching outside vigilantly as he had been.

"They got you once, didn't they?"

"That was different. I wasn't expecting a welcoming party when I got home from work."

"You're lucky to be alive at all."

Collier cleared his throat, returning his attention to the car outside.

"If they hadn't been so ignorant about how my job works, they wouldn't have needed me for information."

Maynard still found it highly irregular for the terrorists to keep him alive, but he supposed it was all part of their master plan. These weren't the suicide bomber type of terrorist. They thought and planned beyond all other groups, and for their own agenda.

"Here we go," the trooper finally said, observing through the blinds he carefully moved aside.

"When he comes through the door, we both punch him in the gut and then you can put him out."

Collier nodded, pulling an extendable metal baton from his side.

Casually walking toward the door with mild irritation written across his face, the terrorist appeared to be of Middle Eastern decent. The scowl on his face was quickly erased when he entered the door, because a throaty, pained groan came from within. Collier tackled him to the floor, crossing the back of his head with the baton.

"Nice job," Maynard said.

"You too. What if their buddies come calling for these two?"

"We won't be here, and hopefully these two aren't worth the time for their bosses to track down."

"Where are we going, exactly?"

Maynard shrugged.

"Anywhere but here. You're the only person who can actually testify to the truth in this whole mess."

"I feel like a witness in a mafia trial."

"The mafia doesn't have anything on these guys. Grab whatever you need, because we're getting out of here in two minutes."

Collier went through the wallets of both intruders, snagging some cash when he found it.

"The sons-of-bitches took my wallet, so the least I can do is repay the favor."

"Oh, yeah," Maynard said, reaching into his back pocket, pulling out the trooper's billfold. "I got it back for you."

Collier took back his wallet, then looked at the money from the two intruders momentarily, as though deciding whether or not to put it back.

"Fuck it," he finally said, pocketing the money as he opened the front door. "If I can make one request, I'd like a hot shower and a decent meal."

"Whatever you want, buddy. I'd say you've earned it."

*   *   *   *

Bill had taken it upon himself to explore the park, taking to the areas behind the scenes, and the woods beyond those. Armed with many of Clay's silent weapons, and a gun from his personal collection, Bill had given himself the unenviable task of avoiding park security while searching for Clay's attackers.

After seeing several search parties pass him without success, he began to wonder if Kim's group was actually brazen enough to remain inside the park. After all, if they had the coaster parts, there was little or no reason to remain behind. And if they needed anything else accomplished, they had devoted henchmen to put at risk.

Stealing the coaster was only half their plan, however. The other half involved ensuring Clay's death, which made Bill regret leaving his nephew behind. He knew Clay's heightened awareness kept anything dangerous from getting too close, but Bill's own senses warned him of impending danger.

Nowhere near as attuned with the surrounding environment as his nephew, Bill still had a little awareness of impending danger, and it was virtually ringing in his ears. Approaching the underside of a wooden roller coaster, he remained crouched as he walked, cautiously eyeing the terrain around him.

His glasses were steamed up along the top edge because of the sweat dripping down his forehead, and his body heat rising from running, crouching, and other movements. It wasn't hot outside, but he had traveled nonstop to where he now stood.

Because of his conditioning, little energy had been expended, but he suspected his journey was far from over.

Looking up, he saw little else aside from painted white beams, intersecting and crossing one another in such a way that they supported the tracks above them. Several spotlights from the side illuminated the boards, allowing Bill to see most everything around him.

Without so much as a bush or patch of weeds around him, Bill took cover beside one of the larger support beams. Standing perfectly still a moment, he listened to everything around him, hearing too much silence for his taste. He expected to hear bird calls or activity from within the park, but no sounds came forward.

Until the sound of footsteps lightly treading behind him barely reached his ears.

Whirling around, Bill saw an Asian man standing before him holding a *katana*, his eyes boring into the American.

Not entirely surprised to see Kim standing before him, Bill quickly composed himself, though wondering if he had anywhere near the skill to battle the man. Clay never told him much about his adversaries. They were simply figures mentioned in some of the stories he told from his stay overseas.

"You're not going to shoot me?" he asked, referring to the cheap shot Kim and Voodoo took on Clay.

Kim sneered.

"You're just as arrogant as your nephew. Don't think for one second we haven't planned on murdering you as a trophy."

Bill pulled his own *katana* from the small pack strapped to his back, drawing a mildly surprised look from his newfound adversary.

"Then let's not waste anymore time talking about it."

Of the two possible dangerous confrontations, Bill knew Kim was the lesser of two evils. Clay had spoken of him as being better with his mouth than a sword.

"You're not going to have your buddy shoot me from behind, are you?"

Kim simply smirked with confidence.

"No. I believe you won't be any trouble for me. Besides, my friend has his own agenda. Your nephew has no doubt murdered the six men we sent to assassinate him, so Voodoo will take care of the scraps before he leaves."

Bill masked his concern, but wondered if Clay had overcome his ailments to defeat six men. With Casey, Packard, and Turpin temporarily away, he wondered if they might be casualties upon their return to the conference room.

Putting all negative thoughts out of his mind, Bill concentrated on the threat before him, visualizing the weapons strategically placed throughout his own clothing and pack. Clay taught him to observe his adversary's stance in order to best pick a suitable defense. He also said any opportunity to catch an opponent off-guard was an opportunity worth taking.

Bill raised his sword, beginning a charge all at once.

His initial slice toward Kim's head was deflected, bringing them into a bladed exchange in which they took turns aiming for various body parts. Bill fought off several quick advances, waiting for an opening.

Kim leapt atop one of the nearby beams, walking along its narrow surface like a cat, holding his sword out to one side, inviting Bill to attack him.

Even with limited training Bill knew better, so he pulled a smoke bomb from his nearest pocket, throwing it against a nearby rock to conceal his next move. The notion of retreat never entered his mind, but Kim predicted his attempt to draw close from behind, blocking the overhand slice with his *katana*.

With no time to block a return swing by Kim, Bill had to duck, or discover how it felt to have his head cut in half. He suspected the pain would last less than a second, but he wasn't done with Kim just yet.

Kim was quick, which Bill expected because of his slender, small form, but sparring with Clay had taught him to anticipate. Clay had also reminded him on several occasions how sharp his bladed weapons were, by simply grazing his uncle's skin with one.

If paper cuts were capable of killing a human being, Bill now knew how death would feel.

Though it required no pressure for a sharp blade to split skin open, it required little more effort to sever tendons and bones. Bill stuck his blade up defensively, blocking an attempt by Kim to disarm him.

Disliking Kim's slight advantage on the high ground, Bill backed off slightly when their swords parted. Both took a few seconds to stare at the other, deciding how to best attack.

"You haven't killed me yet," Bill noted.

"Perhaps I'm going to flay you slowly."

Or perhaps you're stalling, Bill thought.

Obviously Voodoo and several henchmen potentially remained, so Bill felt uneasy about standing in such a wide open space. Bill read and retained history quite well, recalling how many times pride had thwarted the efforts of heroes and conquerors. He had no intention of letting his own ego keep him from retreating, or at least examining his surroundings better.

Several branches snapped behind him, causing him to spin around for a look. Immediately he realized park security, or someone searching the grounds, was coming his way. When he turned around, he spied the back of Kim as the man darted for cover in the opposite direction. Cursing under his breath, Bill followed him, not because he wanted to pursue the man, but because it was the only safe direction left to choose.

A few seconds later, he turned around, seeing a search party of three armed men enter the space where he and Kim had just fought, looking suspiciously around. His time was limited, because they were surely going to unleash the entire security force into the area. Looking around, Bill secured all of his weapons before dashing into the thicker brush for a hiding spot.

He found good cover centered in a thick bush, observing the security force, able to hear their conversation. Discovering his initial instincts proved correct, he weighed his options, which included an unprotected dash toward the offices, or hiding out where he crouched.

After hearing Kim's words about his nephew, he decided to risk making his way to the offices, knowing Kim might ambush him, or the security force might shoot at him. He had his phone, but compromising Clay wasn't something he wanted to chance. Without a sound, he left his position in a full sprint, looking for the closest feasible area to jump the fence.

*   *   *   *

Packard wasn't sure why Adam Russell remained inside the park when everyone except security was ordered to leave, but he was suddenly glad. Turpin had apparently worked with the man earlier in the day, and now they had him searching computer files for any information about the company taking apart the Whirlwind.

Knowing he and the agent had limited computer skills, the sergeant watched Russell's fingers dance across the keyboard, calling forth screen after screen of information. What might take himself or Turpin hours to produce, Russell accomplished in minutes.

"Isn't there paperwork for construction?" he asked Russell.

"There is, but it's locked up in the human resources office."

"Shouldn't be a problem," Turpin said, holding up a key.

"Where did you get that?" Packard questioned.

"I got it from Casey's office."

"And I thought you Bureau types were ethical."

Turpin smirked, walking toward the human resources room as Russell contin-ued to open files on the computer. Packard got up to follow him, wanting to see any new leads for himself.

"You sure we can trust him?" the sergeant asked in a hushed voice once they stepped inside the room.

"I'm not sure who we can trust, but I've got to put a little faith in someone who has ten years with the company."

Packard walked to the filing cabinets, finding one marked "Contractors" before opening it. Inside were bids and packages, but he discovered a file specifi-cally dedicated to the Whirlwind. He pulled it out, finding a company name and some paperwork, but nothing of immediate help.

When he found Bill and Casey at the coaster graveyard, he recalled Casey mentioning no one was currently working on the project, which left him wonder-ing about the man he spoke to earlier.

"Something is missing," he stated aloud.

"How's that?" Turpin inquired.

"The guy I saw at the Whirlwind ride said he was full-time in the park, hired to take it down, but no one is currently working on the project."

"If he works in the park, he could be doing some of the odd jobs."

"Or maybe he works here, but lied about working on that particular project."

"Why?"

"I don't know, but someone doctored the computers in a few different ways, and the only people who have that kind of access level are the owners, Casey, and a few select others."

Turpin pulled out a seat from behind the desk, sitting in thought a moment.

"Everyone else in this scenario has nothing to do with the park," he deduced. "The owners are gone, conveniently I might add. Casey isn't a likely suspect."

"There aren't many left, are there?"

"No. And I can't rule out Bryant completely."

Appearing as suddenly as an apparition, Bryant stood at the door.

"Considering I'm right here, and not fleeing the country, I think you can rule me out," the security director stated with a stony face.

Packard and Turpin exchanged uneasy looks, knowing Bryant's statement made sense. He had every right to be upset with them, but they were looking at saving lives.

"The only reason I wasn't here sooner was because my staff needed me to look at a disturbance under one of the coasters," he explained. "Turns out someone, or a few people, were under there for some kind of meeting."

"Surely they aren't stupid enough to stick around here, knowing the park is closing," Turpin suggested.

"All's I know is someone besides my people were under that ride. And for the record, I don't have the ability to change anything in that computer. I can barely read and write e-mail."

"Welcome to the club," Turpin said.

"Then we're looking for someone who has access, information, and motive," Packard suggested. "Can we get a look at the files for people who have higher access codes?"

"Sure," Bryant said almost eagerly, probably ready to clear his name.

All three men returned to the room where Russell had finished calling up all of the files for construction and demolition during the past year. The screen showed several photos, and a biography for the Whirlwind coaster.

"Sit tight, Adam," Bryant said, taking a seat beside the man to call up his own information.

In a matter of seconds, despite limited typing skills, Bryant had called up everyone above a Level 5 grade in the park.

"Level 5 is access to pretty much everything important," Bryant explained. "Everyone else is limited to their working area or the public areas inside the park. No one below that level could alter anything inside the computers."

"So everyone we see here is a potential suspect," Turpin determined aloud.

"Except me," Bryant insisted.

Turpin grinned, slapping the security director gently on the shoulder.

"Okay, Hugh. Except you."

Over the next five minutes Bryant led them on a virtual tour of everyone with high access levels. The number was limited, but the computer system ran unusually slow according to the director. He cussed at it a few times, but the computer didn't seem to care.

Packard simply watched the staff photos attached to the profiles, which Turpin seemed more interested in reading about. He saw no one familiar until the profile for the human resources director popped up. Something instantly struck him, as though he had seen the man before, but it wasn't until the computer advanced to the next file that he figured out how he knew the man.

"Go back," he told Bryant. "Who is that guy?"

"Steve Koop. He was our director of human resources until about a month ago."

"What happened to him?" Packard inquired.

"He went on medical leave. Colon cancer as I recall."

Packard recognized him as the man sitting on the launch deck for the Whirlwind ride. In the photo he had no beard, and appeared far less tanned. He suddenly suspected Koop had spent the past month somewhere far more sunny than Cincinnati, because the Midwest had yet to reach peak tanning days.

"He's the one I talked to when I visited the Whirlwind ride."

"When were you planning on sharing this information?" Bryant asked testily.

"Whenever I chose to trust you, which wasn't until about two minutes ago."

Turpin cleared his throat, as though trying to settle a skirmish between children.

"You're sure it was *him*?" the agent asked.

"Positive."

"What did he say?"

"He said he was working on taking apart the ride."

"That's *it*?" Bryant asked skeptically.

"Pretty much. He admitted he was a regular in the park and gave his take on what you planned to do with the ride, but nothing else."

Everyone stood silently a moment until Russell spoke.

"We have a camera in that area, don't we?"

"True," Bryant agreed. "Everyone's been too busy to watch the monitors today."

"Maybe what he wanted was proof that Packard was in the area," Turpin suggested. "It's hard to push him as a criminal mastermind without proving he was in the park, observing what's turning out to be the focus of the terrorist plan."

Packard came to realize that without Turpin's presence, he might have been linked to terrorist activity without much hope of proving his innocence. Not knowing their ultimate plan ate away at his insides, but knowing the key players gave him hope that they might be caught and punished.

"Is that area videotaped all day long?" Turpin asked the director.

"Yes. I'll have my people pull the tape."

"What reason would Koop have for joining terrorists?" Packard asked.

"Profit," Turpin answered.

"I never did like him much," Bryant stated. "He always acted like he was better than the rest of us."

Packard noticed Russell nodding in agreement.

"There were reasons he didn't get to touch the Trimble checkbook. I never dealt with him unless I had to."

Despite the new developments, Packard wanted to know what they planned on stashing inside the roller coaster hull, and its intended destination.

Answers weren't forthcoming until Clay walked through the front door with Casey in tow just a few seconds later. The airy sound of the glass door opening drew everyone's attention, but Packard focused on the blood dripping down his officer's hand. He saw no cut, so he wondered where Clay had been.

"I'm glad you're all here, because we have a bigger problem than we ever thought," he revealed in a calm, collected manner.

*   *   *   *

Clay only recognized Packard in the room he now found himself in, but he knew Turpin had to be the FBI agent his sergeant mentioned. Casey had quickly informed him who Russell and Bryant were behind the glass door, before they entered the office.

"I can't even begin to explain what could happen if that roller coaster sets sail," Clay stated to the group. "The only good news is it may not be far along."

"How did you find all this out?" Bryant asked skeptically.

"I got one of the six men who just attacked me in the conference room to spill the beans."

Everyone looked at him as though he had imagined the attack and created a fabrication. Undaunted, he continued.

"If they escape with those parts, they'll leave the country with one of the most dangerous assassination tools in the world."

Now everyone looked completely puzzled.

"I'll keep it simple, because we don't have much time. Does everyone know what the liniment DMSO is?"

Everyone except Russell nodded affirmatively.

"Apparently Kim and his group have contracted someone to create a new strain for use as a weapon."

"How so?" Packard questioned. "That stuff is fairly harmless."

"Not completely," Turpin replied before Clay had an opportunity. "There have been documented cases where it has harmed human beings in certain conditions. When introduced into the bloodstream, it creates a new compound, and if it is reintroduced to the air at a cooler temperature, it can be somewhat toxic."

"How do you know this?" Bryant asked.

"There was an emergency room case somewhere in the Midwest where almost an entire emergency room full of people fell ill after an innocent shot brought the transformed chemical into the air. Nurses and doctors collapsed, and they quarantined the place until a Hazmat team found the cause."

"So by itself, can it be life-threatening?" Bryant further inquired.

"Not really, but in the right scenario, it incapacitates people."

"And it makes a great compound to build from," Clay said. "They've apparently found someone who took its properties and worked up a more dangerous strain. Now they have an undetectable chemical someone can absorb inside their body, then open up at will to disable or kill everyone around them."

"And one of their people just told you this in conversation?" the security director asked with heavy skepticism.

"He had lots of prodding, believe me."

Casey nodded affirmatively in his defense.

Turpin now addressed Clay directly.

"Son, I need to sit down with you when this is all said and done, but for right now, what do we need to do to stop these bastards?"

"If at all possible, we need to identify the truck that picked up the roller coaster. How well do you track delivery trucks when they come in here?"

Bryant answered.

"We don't write down plate numbers or anything like that, but we have cameras all over the park, and a storage library where we keep the tapes for a month before rolling them over."

"Then I need you to start searching for any kind of vehicle on those tapes capable of carrying out the coaster parts. There's no other way in and out of here is there?"

"Well, the delivery trucks don't actually go through the area where employees and repairmen go, which actually makes it easier to track, because they have their own entrance."

"Good."

"What else did you find out?" Turpin asked.

Clay paced for a moment, trying to recall every detail.

"I know the truck had to make a stop in town to pick up the chemical. The way it sounded, it was already going to be packaged and ready for immediate use."

Turpin drew a strange look across his face before Clay virtually saw the light-bulb appear above his head.

"A medical facility," he said. "They need it in ointment form, or maybe some kind of inhaler, so they need a place that can make significant amounts in secret."

"No pharmacy can do that," Clay deduced. "I need to know where they took Ed this afternoon. Did they call any of you with an update?"

Everyone shook their heads negatively, leaving Clay to recall the writing on the ambulance.

"I think it said 'Urgent Care' on the side."

"They serve the Cincinnati area," Bryant said.

"The hospital?"

"No. Typically the medical centers. They do a lot of patient transport, but they also move organs and blood sometimes."

"Can you get to work on finding out which centers they serve, and where the ambulance took Ed this afternoon? Something tells me he was their excuse to pick up the chemicals."

Bryant appeared unhappy.

"How can I monitor tapes and check out your leads?"

"Have Tim and Casey help you."

"Does your buddy have a cell phone?" Turpin asked Clay.

"He should. Why?"

"I can have my people trace his signal and triangulate his location within a few blocks."

Packard stepped forward.

"I'll get you the number. Let's just hope the thing is still on, or his captors didn't ditch the thing."

Everyone stood silently a moment until Turpin looked at Clay.

"What about you?" he asked.

"They have unfinished business with me," Clay answered. "They aren't going to leave this park until I'm six feet under. Or they are."

"I'll go with you."

"No. You wouldn't be any help to me, and I think you already know that."

Turpin returned a strange smirk. He did indeed know he was no help, which meant he was there to talk with Clay about something the officer had no interest in discussing.

His thoughts suddenly turned to someone *not* in the room.

"Where is my uncle?" he asked Packard, uncertain whether or not anyone else present knew Bill except Casey, whom he'd already asked.

"He was gone when we got back."

Clay closed his eyes, sighing inwardly. The thought of his uncle attempting heroism plagued him, because Bill was typically not the type to chase adventure, and this was the worst possible time to start.

"If he gets back here, don't let him leave again," Clay said, shifting his eyes between Turpin and Packard.

"We can't hold him here," Turpin said.

"Then charge him with trespassing or something. I can't afford to worry about him with what I'm about to do."

Turpin looked grim.

"And what is that exactly?"

"Put a stop to all of this."

He turned to go, stopping as he held the door halfway open to turn around.

"I'll be in touch. If you find anything, act on it," he said to Turpin. "We don't have time to waste, even if I find the men responsible. Oh, and you can send all of the park employees home. No sense in endangering their lives needlessly."

Turpin nodded, though openly unhappy about the situation.

CHAPTER 22

▼

For hours Sorrell had been unconscious, in the hands of two men posing as ambulance drivers. For all he knew, they were the real thing, but their intentions seemed quite villainous, because the one time he awoke they knocked him upside the head, sending him back into blackness.

Now light returned to his eyes, but it was fuzzy, like a photograph taken while moving. Plastic odors filled his nose, because every medical device around him appeared sealed in clear wrapping.

Before, he felt vibrations, because the van was moving. He had studied his environment only a few seconds before being rendered unconscious. The back of the ambulance looked familiar, but he was strapped down to a mobile cot, his hands taped securely to the sides.

"Shit," he muttered, realizing the van remained still, but he was helpless to free himself.

Worse than being strapped to a cot was the pain lingering in his body from the earlier accident. Unsure whether or not any bones broke during what he now deemed a setup, he looked around for a way to undo or cut the binding straps.

Feeling like an upended turtle, he stretched his neck, desperately taking in his surroundings. Police officers encounter ambulances routinely during their shifts, so he recognized this ambulance as authentic. Both of the men transporting him were gone, and one look out the small windows in the back led him to believe they were parked at a hospital or medical center.

A concrete loading ramp took up most of the view, leading him to think it unlikely they were parked at a factory or government building. Their purpose for staging at a medical center eluded him, but he had no intention of sitting around to find out.

Weighted down by sticky tape, his hands had a range of about two inches in any direction. The tape had little give, wrapped several times over, meaning it needed to be cut, or torn from one edge to the other by hand.

Sorrell chuckled in frustration, knowing his bad luck led him into the strangest of situations, never giving him an easy way out.

Several of the fingers on his right hand patted down his right side, finding the small pocketknife he often carried still inside the front pocket. Unfortunately his fingers were unable to move anywhere near the pocket opening. Only his thumb had any chance of reaching the pocket, but as he stuck it inside the opening, he realized it came up inches short of touching the blade.

"Shit," he muttered again, using his thumb to put pressure against the pocket itself, attempting to tear the threads that bound it to the blue jeans he wore.

With limited mobility, his thumb found great difficult in simply snapping the first few threads, but in the process his arm brushed against his jacket pocket, touching his cellular phone.

Groaning, he figured his true salvation was more difficult to reach than the knife. Sorrell attempted to shift his entire body to one side, hoping to dump the phone from inside the pocket. Like a stubborn pet, the phone refused to obey, remaining lodged inside his jacket.

He felt somewhat like James Bond, attempting to escape inevitable death, but keeping his cool like the fictional agent wasn't easy. He struggled against the tape, realizing its purpose was to restrain unruly patients in the field.

It worked perfectly.

Using his arm, he bumped the phone, attempting to dislodge it from whatever lump kept it in place, whether it be the jacket's inner lining or his belly. Overturning the cot was an idea, but he wanted to feign unconsciousness when the two men returned, so he decided against such a plan.

Faking was the only logical defense, because his body felt battered, and his head was painfully ringing as though someone had taken a baseball bat to it. His vision seemed perfect one minute, then fuzzy the next.

Twisting his right hand, he began to feel the tape stretch a bit, allowing him to reach the phone, through the pocket's outside layer, enough to bump it.

After several unsuccessful attempts, he moved the phone toward the pocket edge, then managed to pluck it with the only two fingers capable of reaching the pocket's opening. He slowly moved it into his hand, careful not to dump it on the floor, then used his thumb to flip it open.

One look at the phone told him it had a strong signal, but a weak battery.

He quickly scrolled through the list, finding Maynard's name in the phone list, then hit the send button.

During the two rings it took before his colleague picked up, Sorrell turned up the volume, allowing him to hear better, since he was incapable of moving the phone to his face.

"Ed?" Maynard's voice asked skeptically from the other side.

"Rod. They've kidnapped me and taken me to some medical place."

Silence a few seconds.

"You okay, buddy? You didn't look good when they wheeled you out of the park."

"I'm not kidding, and I'm not okay. They've got me strapped down to the medical cot. I'm still stuck in the ambulance."

A few more seconds of silence.

"Okay, Ed. Do you know where they've taken you?"

"No. I can't see shit. I just see a concrete loading ramp of some sort out the back window."

"I can't help you if I don't know where you are," Maynard said with unusual desperation in his voice.

Sorrell had no further information for his friend, but it mattered little as the two men appeared from somewhere behind the ramp.

"Shit!" Sorrell exclaimed. "They're back, Rod. Just keep quiet and listen until I get something more for you."

"Gotcha."

Quickly placing the phone inside one of his jacket's rumples, Sorrell faked unconsciousness as the two men opened both rear doors. He swallowed quickly, feeling his body begin to sweat from sudden tension. After all, he had no idea if they were simply going to dump him off, or put a gun to his head.

One of the men climbed inside as the other handed him a large case. Sorrell barely saw anything, because he dared not open his eyelids beyond a millimeter for a peek. He saw a loading cart of some sort beside the second man containing several more boxes. They were picking up something, but he had no idea what.

"You're going to have to move fat boy out here so we can load the rest of these boxes," the man standing outside the ambulance said.

"Hold your horses," his partner snapped, opening one of the boxes to pull out a small tube that looked as though it might hold ointment for chapped lips. "I need to put this stuff on before we cart our *patient* inside. It'll take a few minutes for this stuff to work."

On him? Sorrell wondered, knowing they meant him, but doubting the gel was for his benefit.

He felt his jacket sleeve raise on his left arm before something cool was rubbed all over his forearm. He wanted to resist, but maintained his cool, and the charade, knowing any attempt to fight or escape was futile.

Nothing felt different after the cream was applied, making Sorrell wonder exactly what they were doing to him.

"Those dumb fucks think we're paying them under the table for making this stuff," the second man said. "We'll be paying them alright," he added with a sadistic chuckle.

Sorrell didn't like the sound of his words, but took note that neither man had a foreign accent. It gravely concerned him that Americans were willing to help terrorists and betray their country for money.

Perhaps the plan had deeper origins than he knew about, because terrorists thought far enough ahead to place their people in the right posts.

The outside man looked at his watch.

"If we don't hurry up, we're going to miss our rendevous with the big truck."

"We've got time. They aren't going anywhere without us. And if Kim thinks he's going to double-cross us, I've got a preventative measure for that, too."

Sorrell wished for the ability to reach up and slap them both upside their noggins before shooting each of them. Considering he had no weapon, and his arms were held in a grip as strong as a vise, he had little choice but to wait.

"How long does it take that stuff to set in?" the second man asked of the liniment.

"A few minutes. It would have been a lot more fun to use the capsule, but you need a willing suicide killer for that."

Sorrell caught the meaning of the words, realizing they were about to use him as some sort of biological weapon. Now the lives of others rested in his ability to escape or discover his whereabouts.

"Let's roll," the first man said.

A few seconds later the cot began rolling toward the back doors as they wheeled Sorrell inside the rear entrance.

"Go ahead and load the cargo," the first man ordered. "I'll take our tourist here for his last ride."

As they entered what appeared to be a hospital, Sorrell opened his eyes a bit more, realizing his guide was focusing on the route. While there was no overhead sign stating what building they were in, Sorrell caught a glimpse of someone's name tag, which had a company name on it.

Pathologist Medical Supplies.

PMS? Sorrell couldn't help but wonder, despite the dire circumstances.

His original assumption of being inside a medical center or hospital died the moment he spied the patch sewn upon the passing man's lab coat. He wondered how this man was even getting away with bringing a patient inside the building, unless some strange protocol allowed such a thing.

A few seconds later the cot stopped, and the man stepped inside a room. Sorrell heard some conversation, deciding this was his one opportunity to communicate with Maynard.

He kept his voice just above a whisper, speaking toward the phone as he turned it to face him.

"Rod, if you're there, they've got me in a building called Pathologist Medical Supplies."

He heard no answer.

"Rod?" he asked a bit more desperately, though still in a hushed voice.

One bar of battery life remained, but the phone beeped, indicating it was nearly dead.

"I'm on my way, Ed," Maynard's voice finally said. "I'm with a guy who knows the area very well, so we'll be there in a few-"

Giving one last beep, the phone died, causing a disgruntled grimace from Sorrell as a tear welled up in one eye. He thought about the wrongs in his life, which included not spending enough time with his kids, missing church a few times a month, and keeping incriminating secrets from his wife. He hoped it wasn't his destiny to die helplessly, like a cow sent to the slaughterhouse.

Then a flicker of hope, combined with anger, moved his thumb toward the pants pocket once more, tearing the thread with more ease this time.

Motivated by survival instincts, he knew if he failed to get the knife free, he was destined to die, and take several lives with him.

It took only a few seconds to rip the pocket enough to pluck the knife with his fingers, but maneuvering it to open the blade proved more difficult. Careful not to slit himself as he opened the blade, Sorrell used the knife like a handsaw, slicing back and forth into the tape binding his right hand, watching it peel the substance back as though it were butter.

In mere seconds his right hand was free, but at the same time, the door opened, and his captor appeared. Sorrell feigned unconsciousness again, clutching the knife in his right hand as he prepared to mold his own escape plan.

Then carry it out.

*   *   *   *

Bill wondered if he might be centered in the North Pole's Christmas Village with all of the lights gleaming around him. Absolutely every light inside and around the park seemed to be on, aiding in the search for terrorists.

Losing the security force seemed a bit too easy, leading him to wonder if they were called away, or found more pressing issues. Without the burden of having to crawl around or hide from them, he was free to track Kim once more.

Despite the lights illuminating everything around him in detail, the park now felt like an abandoned town. Rides, concession stands, and games of chance were completely open to vandalism or theft, except no one was around to partake in such activities. Bill suspected very few true criminals remained inside the park, but those few posed the greatest threats to the guards.

He felt bad carrying most of Clay's gear with him. His nephew would probably want it if he woke up, but Clay knew there was more weaponry waiting inside the pickup truck if he needed it. Though an underlying concern for his nephew kept him from devoting full attention to his current search, Bill fought to remain focused.

Ducking under several branches, Bill drew close to the tall grass just outside a mesh wire fence. His chin touched a few of the blades, discovering they had water droplets on them, which likely came from the earlier thunderstorm.

Consciously regulating his breathing, he looked around him, seeing no one inside the fence, but a surveillance camera monitoring the premises. He had followed broken limbs, branches, and grass blades to his current location, but now he saw none of those things in any direction.

Looking upward, Bill found the fence close to ten feet in height. At the top was a single strand of barbed wire, which failed to intimidate him after Clay's lessons about overcoming obstacles.

With little hesitation, he scaled the fence as easily as a squirrel navigates tree bark. Reaching the top, he put one arm over the dangerous wire, vaulting himself over in one move before leaping to the ground.

Starting his search anew, Bill questioned why he was tailing a man with equal, genuine weapons training as his nephew. Clay readily admitted his training was a watered down version of old Japanese ritual, but Kim was no slouch. He was young, knew his weapons, and had experience using them.

Bill assumed the man had likely taken lives, but no proof existed. Either way, he began questioning his own sanity for tracking a known terrorist.

All around him he spied ideal places to hide. Mobile carts, shadows, game areas, and a few small rides were just some of the cover Kim might have sought.

Staying in the open felt impractical, so Bill moved closer to the building which took up the equivalent of two city blocks, exhibiting games of chance on the outside. He guessed the interior served as a combination of storage and the arcade that took up the center of the complex.

Reaching to his side, Bill plucked a bamboo staff nearly two feet in length from a holding clip. Known as a *tenbin*, used historically in Japan as a rod to balance buckets of water on the shoulders, it also provided concealed weaponry for farmers in the homeland.

Bill twisted the staff's ends, then pulled them, to reveal a chain inside. Everything he knew about swordsmanship was defensive, which meant beating Kim with a blade might take forever, or never happen.

Nearly finding his skull detached from his body once gave Bill insight about which weapons to use against the Korean native. As he drew near the building, seeing stuffed prizes swinging gently above him, Bill wondered if Kim might have held back, luring him into a false sense of security.

Music still played softly in the background, but Bill relied on his eyes and the internal mechanism that warned him of danger to protect him. As he stepped beneath the awning that protected vendors and players from the elements, Bill felt the hairs stand on the back of his neck. Something behind him went unseen as he stared out at the well-lit walkway.

Sensing no immediate danger, he turned, seeing nothing in the blackness behind him until a pair of eyes slowly opened, giving him his first indication Kim had been lying in wait, meditating. Bill swallowed hard, knowing this was his final battle with the Korean. Yes, there was room to retreat, but Kim knew how to use throwing weapons, which would likely incapacitate him.

Standing above Bill, atop a counter used to hold prizes, Kim remained frozen like a statue momentarily, as though trying to provoke drama from the dire situation.

From total blackness, Kim stepped forward, revealing his form, and all of the weaponry held by the small pack strapped to his back. Dressed from head to toe in black, he blended in with the background, barely visible, as though a black light illuminated his silhouette. He wore the traditional garb of a ninja, including the hood.

Only his eyes gave him away.

Meant to intimidate, the clothing did little to phase Bill. Without removing his eyes from his adversary, Bill pulled the two ends of the bamboo staff apart, twirling the chain so it wrapped itself around his left wrist.

He wished he knew the mystic hand symbols samurai warriors used to enhance their minds and call upon unseen elements, but Clay had never taught them. Based on the way Kim and Voodoo attacked Clay, Bill doubted Kim was willing to undergo the ritual two warriors usually exchanged before combat.

Like a shadow coming to life, Kim emerged from the black painted background, slowly drawing a short sword from a sheath at his side. Bill clenched the bamboo rods, then lightened his grip, remembering to keep his fingers nimble and ready for anything.

Spatters of rain dropped around them, smacking Bill in the face as his blue eyes locked on his target. He refused to attack first, knowing Kim had likely thought of every conceivable defense against his limited offensive moves.

When Kim leapt down from the stand, his blade moved with such swiftness that it seemed to cut the raindrops. Even through fogged glasses Bill saw many details, blocking the initial attack with the chain, wrapping it around the sword swiftly.

He only managed one quick wrap, which wasn't enough to keep Kim from yanking the sword back. Bill now realized his choice in weaponry was capable of blocking most any sword attack, but there were very few ways to inflict pain or kill with a chain.

Of course he expected no life and death battle to last just a few seconds, but his decision-making needed work. Clay had never gone over strategy with him, so Bill was forced to wait for an opening.

He blocked a few more swings and slices from the short sword until Kim leapt atop the table for the high ground. Instead of foolishly chasing him, or backing off, Bill pulled more chain from the bamboo ends, hurling it around Kim's legs into a loop. As it completed a full circle he tugged on the chain, tripping up his adversary.

Kim landed hard, but the surface sounded like wood to Bill, who worked around metal and wood shops in his profession. He knew the sound wood made when struck, and he also knew Kim wasn't going to be injured by the surface.

Keeping hold of the staff's other end with his left hand, he reached behind him for a *sai* with the other. Completely metal, the weapon looked similar to a fork, with the middle of three pointed ends longer for effective defense and stabbing. Dyed a dark brown color to keep it from reflecting light, the weapon provided several offensive techniques.

Bill decided to use the simplest attack of all, stabbing downward before Kim fully regained his senses. Reflexes alone kept Kim's arm from being impaled by the weapon's center blade. Instead, he received a gash from one of the sharpened prongs on one side.

Reactively swinging the sword, he forced Bill to pull up the chain in defense. With no time to wrap the sword again, Bill took two steps back to retreat from the deadly blade, leaving the *sai* stuck in the vendor stand. Plenty of other weapons remained strapped to his back, but he hated the idea of leaving his nephew's property behind, primarily because they were his personal favorites, and he didn't want security finding them.

Kim attempted to stand, looking down in surprise because the loop remained around his ankles. He seemed to contemplate the danger of his bad luck, too late to act because Bill tugged the chain again, yanking Kim completely off the stand with a thud as the rain began pouring harder around them.

A passing storm began unloading sheets of water upon the dueling pair, leaving Bill's visibility slightly impaired. Everything around him looked black and white, mixed with small streaks of color as though Bill were driving at night with bad windshield wipers.

Fighting back the urge to find new shelter, he drew the *daito* from its secure position at his side. Slightly shorter than a *katana*, but longer than the *wakizashi*, the *daito* was the ninja's choice of blade in the feudal days.

Knowing a semiautomatic gun remained tucked behind him in his belt, Bill refused to reach for it, hating the idea of cheating in an authentic bladed fight. He also suspected Kim wasn't incapacitated enough for him to successfully draw *and* fire the weapon.

He watched as Kim undid the chain from around his feet, knowing an experienced warrior like Clay would likely take advantage of the situation and charge his adversary. Bill wasn't as nimble or lightweight as his nephew, so he opted to stay back and take his chances when Kim regained his footing.

Holding the chain as he rose from the ground, the Korean native threw it down disgustedly when he stood erect, his eyes narrowing with hatred, boring into Bill. Separated by thousands of rain droplets and less than a car's length, the two men raised their swords, prepared to kill the other.

Or die trying.

CHAPTER 23

▼

Sorrell clutched the knife, but kept it tucked beside him as a man dressed in a lab coat followed his captor out the door.

"You can't be bringing patients in here," the man said.

"We just had this talk. I just need to leave him here a few minutes while I drop off the cargo."

"This is bullshit!" the lab worker said, restraining his voice to their proximity. "It's bad enough you can't even pay us in full, but now you want to leave your luggage here too?"

"Ten minutes is all it'll take for me to run the stuff over there and get the rest of your money."

Shaking his head defiantly, the man seemed to sense a ruse, which Sorrell already knew about. He hated biding his time, but stalling gave Maynard time to find him, if his partner actually knew the location. Sorrell simply hoped this new quarrel might set him free.

"No. I want your partner to stay here until you get back with the money. We haven't slaved for two months, hiding from our boss, forging records, and stealing chemicals for you to fuck us over now."

Sighing through his nose, and openly displeased, Sorrell's captor put his hand on the cot. His plan seemed to be crumbling all around him, and Sorrell knew he had little time to waste. They had some kind of schedule to keep, so he doubted the fake EMT was about to put up with lengthy delays.

"Okay," the man finally said agreeably. "Stick my patient in there for a minute and I'll get my partner. You can use him as collateral until I come back."

Sorrell felt his heart skip a beat, then thump in his chest. The moment to act had arrived, because he was about to be wheeled five feet away to his death, or attempt to free himself.

Using the only free appendage available, he thrust the knife upward, landing it squarely in his captor's chest, just above the heart. While the man stumbled backward, gasping and flailing, Sorrell busied himself, attempting to tear the rest of his restraints by hand.

Tearing them from edge to edge now worked because he had the free hand. Sorrell worked feverishly, swinging his left hand from the bonds a few seconds later.

Staring up, he saw the man in the EMT uniform now clutching the knife in his chest, bewildered that his plan had backfired. Sorrell's thighs and feet remained strapped against the cot, so he only monitored the man a few seconds, watching him pluck the knife from his chest. He stomped toward Sorrell with evil intent, but the other man stepped in his way, obviously finding the scene disturbing.

For his trouble he was slammed against the wall with a hard shove, leaving Sorrell to once again fend for himself.

Abandoning the restrictive straps a moment, Sorrell caught the man's hand as the knife plunged toward his throat. Physically stronger than the pretend medic, Sorrell remained dizzy and weakened enough that they seemed evenly matched.

Sorrell used both hands to hold the knife a safe distance from his throat, but the medic began turning the blade toward Sorrell's wrists instead of plunging it downward. He didn't have enough force to cut the officer deeply, but Sorrell suspected the man simply wanted to draw blood because of the chemicals flowing through his system.

Changing his plan drastically, with little room or ability to move, Sorrell pulled the man downward, biting his right hand. Screaming in pain, the man released the knife, which fell into its owner's hands. Quickly slicing through the tape restricting his legs and feet, Sorrell regained his footing as the man's partner stepped through the nearby entrance.

"Shit," Sorrell muttered as the man seemed to mouth the same word.

Realizing the initial help from the building's employee was a one-time thing, because the man looked more concerned for his own well-being now, Sorrell darted the other way.

Because he was lumbering and slightly overweight, he realized he wasn't going to get far, and they couldn't afford to let him leave the grounds alive, so he needed a plan. His left leg was in agony from the injury sustained inside the park.

He suspected a hairline fracture, but knew there wasn't ample time to evaluate the limb.

"Keep them here," he heard the first medic order his partner.

Nothing had changed. This man still wanted Sorrell as some kind of human bomb to kill the workers. Reaching a hallway with several people crossing from one end to the other, Sorrell waited until no one was looking, then darted into the nearest room, hoping for vacancy.

Since no lights appeared to be on, he took a chance, discovering his luck held out. An office with a desk, chair, and filing cabinet, it offered little in the way of hiding, but had a lock affixed to the doorknob.

Sorrell locked the door, left the light off, and slumped in the nearest corner. His injured leg felt as though someone had lit it on fire, but he endured the pain, remaining quiet and still.

Barely able to see anything out the window from his position, he noticed the man enter the main hallway, look both ways, then curse to himself before turning around. Anyone who spied him would surely question why he was so far inside the building, and he probably had no ready excuse.

He wasn't about to report a missing patient, since he clearly wasn't supposed to bring anyone into the building with him.

"What exactly *is* this place?" Sorrell asked under his breath.

It looked very much like a laboratory with everyone wearing lab coats. He slowly stood, noticing several rooms down the hallway contained test tubes and beakers. It appeared the company manufactured and experimented in medicines.

Sorrell ducked behind the door when he saw someone walking his way. The person passed without incident, forcing him to realize he needed to move or eventually be discovered.

In the opposite corner, a phone atop the desk caught his eye, but he couldn't remember Maynard's number. Everyone's phone numbers had been programmed into his cellular phone for so long that he never memorized them.

"Fuck."

About to give up hope, Sorrell's gaze went to the front entrance where he saw Maynard walk through the front door with a state trooper. Ecstatic, he realized the cavalry had arrived, along with some form of guaranteed safety.

Maynard approached the secretary at the front desk, so Sorrell decided to leave the safety of the room to rendezvous with his friend before the creepy medic returned. In a sense, Sorrell needed a safe environment, but he also wanted Maynard to help him catch the men who had brought him to this facility.

Sorrell placed his hand on the doorknob with the intent of yelling to Maynard before his friend had opportunity to leave, but as the door swung open, the medic came around the nearby corner. With barely enough time to save himself, Sorrell spied a blade in the man's right hand, slamming the door shut as the man thrust the knife inside first, desperately trying to cut the officer.

Now Sorrell knew his instincts were correct, compounded by the conversation the two men had in the back of the ambulance. If any of his blood was exposed to normal air, he and everyone around him who breathed in the new chemical compound were doomed.

If Maynard hadn't seen the strange actions of the medic, the man's agonizing yell surely got the attention of Sorrell's partner and the trooper. Unfortunately, Sorrell hadn't disabled the medic's arm because the knife continued to bob back and forth from a rotating wrist. Pushing against the wooden door for his life, Sorrell couldn't lean forward too much, because he understood the results of getting slit.

Sorrell breathed heavily from the activity, feeling sweat drip from his forehead as his head pounded, bringing him near the brink of unconsciousness. His injured leg kept him from putting significant force behind his efforts, so the door began slowly giving way. The fight for his life seemed nearly over, with him teetering on the losing end.

A quick glance to his right showed Maynard and the trooper drawing their weapons, aiming toward the man. Sorrell heard them shout warnings, but his mind was racing too much to understand their words. Until the knife dropped to the floor, he had no intention of relaxing.

"Don't kill him!" Sorrell shouted to Maynard, who seemed to pick up on his words through the barely open door. "We need him alive."

Unfortunately the man also heard his words, because he thrust himself against the door, sending Sorrell stumbling backwards until he crashed against the desk in a heap.

Instead of running, or surrendering, the man seemed intent on killing Sorrell, even if it cost him his own life. Sorrell looked up to the man towering over him in a flash, ready to slash him with the knife as though he were a gang member with a switchblade.

"The knee!" Sorrell shouted to Maynard, who had a firearm pointed at the man's torso.

Maynard fired, collapsing the man beside Sorrell, who tried scrambling to his feet, but failed because of his injury. The trooper helped Sorrell up, barely pulling him out of the knife's range before it sliced through the air where his knee had been a second earlier.

"Drop it," Maynard said. "You aren't getting out of here."

"He has a partner," Sorrell said as the trooper reached for something on his gun belt.

"I'll die before I let you pigs take me into custody," the man spat from the ground, blood splattering off the shiny tile floor from his fresh gunshot wound.

"That can be arranged," the trooper said, "but I have a better idea."

He extended an ASP baton, striking the man's knife hand with the metal weapon, knocking the knife to the ground. Sorrell quickly slid his foot over, stepping on the blade, then drawing it toward him as it scraped along the floor.

Together, Maynard and the trooper subdued the man as a crowd gathered around the room. They cuffed him, then harshly threw him against the wall.

"Keep an eye on him," Maynard told the trooper, who was already beginning to search the man for additional weapons.

Maynard motioned for Sorrell to leave the room with him.

"Where is the partner?"

"Back here."

Sorrell led the way, quickly navigating the hallways toward the back rooms.

"We have a problem, Rod."

"I'm just glad you're okay, buddy. Whatever it is, we'll deal with it."

"Well, I can't get a scratch on me, or something pretty bad will happen."

Maynard gave him a quirky look, as though suspecting the penalty might be a lashing from his wife.

"They rubbed some kind of chemical agent into my skin. The people here made the shit for them, and I'm their guinea pig."

"What happens if you get cut?"

"Everyone around me dies. The chemical gets into the air and the new compound formed from this stuff mixing with my blood turns toxic."

Sorrell didn't stutter because he was gravely concerned.

Maynard instinctively started to take a step back, stopping himself as Sorrell took notice.

"But you're okay right *now*, right?"

Sorrell nodded.

"I'm scared, Rod," he confessed. "I don't know what this stuff will do to me."

Maynard nodded, calm as ever, although he stopped to rub his head in thought.

Or mild frustration.

"Where is the other guy?"

"He's either back there with the guys who made the stuff, or he went back to the ambulance."

"Where's that?"

Sorrell pointed to the hallway just ahead.

"Everything is down that hallway."

Maynard put an assured hand on his shoulder.

"Stay here. I'll deal with them."

"We need them alive, Rod. Those guys made this stuff. They've got to know how to neutralize it."

Although Maynard didn't look confident about the impending outcome, he gave a nod that told Sorrell he wouldn't let him down.

"Alright."

Sorrell couldn't help but watch his colleague walk down the hall, then turn. He followed Maynard, although he remained a safe distance behind. He heard Maynard yell some commands once he stepped inside the room where the manufacturers were housed, suspecting his partner had caught them all together.

Sorrell reached the door a few seconds later, finding Maynard had them all at gunpoint, apparently waiting to sort out true criminals from possible innocent bystanders. In there, the medic stood with them, hands in the air, a gun at his feet.

Unlike his partner, he had no wish to die for his sins.

"Who's the trooper?" Sorrell inquired.

"It's a long story," Maynard replied without taking his gun, or his eyes, off the room full of people.

"I take it this means we're calling in the locals?"

"I suspect Collier isn't going to put if off any longer. I'm more worried about Tim and the guys still inside the park."

Inside the park?

Sorrell had almost forgotten about that nightmare. If the others were still hostage to terrorist demands, he doubted a favorable outcome, even if he had just helped foil some of their ultimate plan.

*   *   *   *

Inside the Great Realms offices, Turpin found several things going his way.

Bryant located the videotape with a truck entering the park, then leaving through the same gate with a covered load. They captured the license plate number, giving the agent something concrete to call local police and federal agents about. Knowing the truck might be anywhere between Cincinnati and any port along the East Coast, he suspected he might still need a small miracle to find it.

While he made the call to the local FBI branch about the truck, Packard received a call of his own, which he seemed anxious to share with the agent. As Turpin finished speaking with an agent in the Cincinnati branch, the police sergeant paced and fidgeted at the door of the office Turpin chose for some privacy.

"What is it?" he finally asked Packard after hanging up the phone.

"My other officer just called. They now have four men in custody who were involved with our terrorists."

"What happened to keeping the trooper safe?"

"That went out the window when my other officer called for help. This whole thing is over the deadly chemicals Kim and Voodoo had locals manufacture for export inside the stolen coaster."

Turpin thought the entire ploy sounded ridiculous. He knew most countries had strict enforcement about importing and manufacturing chemicals, but stashing deadly toxins inside steel coaster parts seemed excessive. Then again, port laws were more strict in European and Asian countries. A roller coaster probably seemed completely unthreatening to port police ordered to check suspicious loads.

"What else did he tell you?"

"The chemicals were made locally, and they are a strain of DMSO. They were going to use my injured officer as a lab rat, but Rod got there in time to stop them. They're treating Ed for his injuries and the chemicals the pricks rubbed onto him."

The agent's mind raced momentarily, trying to get a grasp on the situation.

"So they can cure him?"

"Basically they gave him a neutralizing compound that counteracts the DMSO strain. He'll be kept under observation the next twenty-four hours, under quarantine, because they can't risk him getting cut and infecting others."

Packard had a mischievous grin on his face, as though he had saved the best information for last.

"What?" Turpin asked impatiently.

"The two fake medics who took Ed out of here were supposed to meet with the lab techs, get the chemicals, and kill the techs by cutting Ed open. None of this happened, which means the chemicals are still at the lab."

"Okay. So we've got the chemicals."

Turpin thought about it a few seconds longer.

"And *they* don't."

"Right. And they were supposed to meet up with our big truck just outside of Cincinnati to pick up and pack the chemicals. That truck may still be waiting at their rendezvous point."

Packard slid a sheet of paper across the desk with the address and name of the hotel where the meeting was supposed to occur.

"I'll call the Cincinnati branch and have them intercept that truck right away."

"Rod said the locals were storming the chemical facility," Packard stated. "I guess that means we won't be keeping things under wraps any longer?"

"No, we won't. I'll take responsibility for that, but we still need to clean things up around here. And that means I need to know the location of the fake trooper's body."

Packard shrugged lightly, not from reluctance, but because he didn't seem to know.

"My best guess is under the Expedition ride, because that's where Rod said the man chased him. Why do you need to know that now?"

"Because I'm going to examine it. Maybe he was supposed to meet up with the others, and just maybe he has some paperwork to bolster our case."

"It's not safe out there if Clay's enemies are still running around."

"I don't much care. And that's another reason I wish you'd leveled with me in the first place. If we had known what we were up against, we might have been able to stop them."

Packard initially looked confused at the statement, then shook his head negatively.

"You can't just stop people like that with guns and manpower."

Turpin drew a grin.

"You take me for a fool, Sergeant? I know who those people are, and believe me, we have people who can take care of them. The reason I'm here is to woo your officer away from you so he can make a bigger difference for his country."

Packard looked away a few seconds, then seemed a bit angered.

"It seems I wasn't the only one hiding things. What else do you know, Agent Turpin?"

"I wish I had more time to go into this, but I don't, lad. My direct supervisor pieced a few things together about the attack in Muncie last year, and the death of a well-known drug lord in Chicago. Seems the man caused you some grief last year and almost killed you and three of your officers."

A stunned look crossed Packard's face, because no one knew about that incident in his mind. Turpin suspected the truth came from the drug trafficker's big mouth before he was permanently silenced. Even the most professional criminals tended to brag about their biggest feats to someone. A kingpin named Salas made an abandoned vegetable vending stand look like Swiss cheese before hastily leaving the scene a year prior.

Turpin suspected the sergeant's entire sting operation was going bad when his informant was gunned down by the drug lord's henchmen. Witnesses claimed they saw the henchmen immediately turn their guns on the building where Packard and his officers hid themselves for a good view, but all four officers survived the onslaught. They were never officially linked to the scene, and the informant's body was never found, leaving them in the clear.

Packard had done a good job of covering up the incident, but the witness statements and the fact that the sergeant's informant became a missing person gave Turpin enough facts to piece together a scenario.

"You don't own a sword, do you?" Turpin pressed, referring once again to Salas's death in Chicago.

Packard exhaled a heavy sigh, apparently turned off by the conversation's direction.

"No. I don't."

"Then I guess that makes you innocent in that Chicago murder, doesn't it?"

Packard looked displeased, though Turpin was uncertain if it was because he was there to recruit Clay, or because the government knew so much about the sergeant's unethical justice.

"Don't worry, Tim. I'm not squeaky clean either, which is why the government recruited me after I retired. And Clay can always decline without penalty."

"Without *any* penalty at all?"

"What I know stays with me. I remember what it's like to put the bastards away, only to have them running free an hour later because they were in someone's pocket. In a perfect world, we wouldn't have to jump through so many hoops to get a conviction, Tim. And I'd be home riding my horses right now instead of chasing chinks around a theme park."

Turpin plucked his sport coat from the seat behind him, finding it wet from being exposed to the rain for so long. Without putting it on, he checked to ensure his firearm was secure at his side.

"I'm going to find that body," he informed Packard. "You've got my number if anything new comes in, but I don't plan on being long."

"Just watch yourself."

Turpin gave a courteous nod, hoping he came across as genuine with the sergeant. He understood the frustrations that came with policing a city. In his thirty years of police work in Houston he discovered most of the new laws did not benefit officers in any way. Criminals were given more rights on a yearly basis, and he found himself powerless to keep the worst of the lot behind bars.

On his way out, Turpin stopped to see Casey a moment, who stayed with Bryant to review more tapes. Russell remained in the office as well until Turpin deemed it safe for him to leave.

"I need your help, young lady," the agent said to Casey in his soft drawl, carefully touching her on the elbow to lead her away from Bryant in the room where they had watched tapes the better part of the last hour.

"What can I do for you?" she asked once they were in the main hallway.

"I need to know where the Expedition ride is."

"I can show you," she offered, reaching for a windbreaker.

"No, no. Just point me in the direction."

Instead, she pulled out a map, pointing to their location, then showing him the ride.

"It's probably better to drive over there," she suggested. "Or you can take one of the carts across the park."

Turpin looked outside, noticing the rain had once again diminished to a strong drizzle. He had no idea how to navigate the dirt roads surrounding the park, so he decided on the cart.

"I don't suppose those things are enclosed?" he asked her with a crooked grin.

"No, but they do have roofs."

She handed him a set of keys from a nearby key rack.

"Number 18 is right outside. They drive like golf carts."

Turpin turned to leave, but Casey touched his hand.

As he turned around, she gave him an unexpected hug.

"Be careful," she whispered in his ear.

"I will," he promised, wondering what exactly prompted such emotion from the young lady.

He had worked closely with her the past few hours, so perhaps the stress of the situation worried her. Most people shied from federal agents, but she seemed openly glad he accidentally stumbled into her park on the worst day in its history.

"I'll be back," he promised her, feeling as though he had found the granddaughter he never had.

He wasn't too young to have grandchildren, but they wouldn't be nearly her age. His thoughts drifted to the possibility of having a son somewhere he had never met, but they returned to the task at hand.

"Stay close to Tim and Hugh," he instructed Casey like a good grandfather before pushing the door open to the cold and wetness awaiting him outside.

*   *   *   *

Several minutes later the agent found himself at the gate leading into the Expedition ride. Casey had taken the time to inform him how to make his way around the ride without getting on or near the tracks earlier in the day.

Following the gates that led to the launching area, Turpin looked around, hearing commercials from the television sets bolted overhead. They focused on different areas of the park in the commercials, then the programming changed to music videos. It took just over a minute for Turpin to near the launch bay, where he stepped under the metal railings and into the grassy surroundings.

Though his original intention was to wear his sport coat to keep his white dress shirt from making him highly visible, he opted to grab his black leather jacket from the rental car before leaving. He didn't like the glossy sheen on the jacket, but it felt much more comfortable and warmer than the sport coat.

While fetching his jacket, Turpin had also taken time to call Tom Diersen back at the Cincinnati branch. He informed the agent to concentrate on hotels and motels in and around the city. Diersen informed him they needed more time to access phone records from the trooper's house and the phone number Maynard provided through Packard.

The attempt to triangulate Sorrell's cellular phone failed, but Turpin now knew it didn't matter. Diersen inquired about the special status attached to Turpin's identification number, which Turpin replied he wasn't at liberty to say.

In a sense, being a rogue agent felt similar to '00' status in the James Bond movies. It didn't give him a license to kill per se, but he had privileges usually allowed to only the highest government officials. He doubted the *suits* liked any federal agent sharing any part of their privileged status, but Turpin didn't much care about their opinions.

Stepping through the gate rails, he immediately realized the rain had soaked the ground, leaving it slick. Using the rail to steady himself, Turpin regained steady footing atop the grassy soil, switching on the powerful flashlight Casey loaned him for navigation through the dark woods.

He already had doubts about searching for the body with so much danger around. Not only were terrorists probably still in the park, but the overcast sky provided no moonlight, and a hazy fog diminished the effectiveness of every light inside the park. Still, he made his way through the darkness, following the lightly-worn trail carved by employees down a slight embankment.

Reaching the bottom, he saw the ride's tracks ahead, realizing the area wasn't as vast as it appeared on Casey's map. The ride was designed to take up a small area, the tracks overlapping one another, making several passes in the same area. He drew near the bottom, shining his flashlight toward a small grove of trees near one of the ride's enclosed areas.

A face suddenly appeared in the beam, startling him as he froze where he stood, his heart thumping in his chest.

Breathing a sigh of relief with reserved caution, Turpin discovered the face was a tribal mask affixed to a tree. It's vacant eyes stared back at him, giving him an eerie feeling, as though someone might be watching his every move.

Turning off the flashlight, Turpin discovered the few lights still switched on from the ride provided ample lighting to see his way under the Expedition. He stared upward, noticing several lanterns along the first lift, which blinked off and on, as though a warning to riders they were entering a dangerous area.

If only they knew, he thought.

A flash illuminated the sky in the distance, letting him know another storm approached from the west. Keeping his right hand atop his firearm, Turpin made his way under the ride, and under a few trees, as everything around him grew darker. The blinking lanterns provided only intermittent dim light, but he refused to turn on his spotlight just yet.

Thunder rumbled in the distance, keeping him wary of his surroundings. Virtually blind and deaf due to the conditions, the agent moved some shrubbery aside with his arm, approaching one of the enclosed tunnels the roller coaster ran through. There appeared to be three of the tunnels, and each had a tinted light glowing from special bulbs inside.

A blue glow led him toward the closest tunnel, but as the thunder ceased momentarily, he heard a different noise behind him. Quietly turning around, Turpin looked upward first, seeing the first lift with no one nearby. Getting shot from above was his worst fear, but being gutted with one swing of a sharpened blade was a close second.

Focusing his attention on the clearing ahead, he saw a lighter color than the vegetation that consumed much of the ride's underbelly. The poor lighting gave him fits until he neared the object, deciding that it was gray in color, appearing to be a body. His foot had lifted for another step when he saw someone knelt beside the body, rummaging through its pockets.

He doubted the looter was a park employee, and if that proved the case, the man would have ample opportunity to explain himself. Somehow Turpin doubted the man worked for the park.

"Freeze!" he yelled the cliche phrase, dropping the flashlight as he pulled his firearm from its holster with rehearsed swiftness.

Instead of complying, the man bolted toward the other side of the ride, where more rails passed and looped around one another. Turpin had the choice of searching the body or chasing the culprit.

Picking up the flashlight, he decided he might do both.

Dropping to his knees, the agent quickly picked up where the other man left off, sifting through pockets quickly from experience. The only object he found was a folded piece of paper in one shirt pocket. Looking at the dead man's lifeless eyes, he considered it fitting the imposter died in such a way.

"Serves you right," the agent said to himself, stuffing the paper into his own jacket pocket.

Grunting to himself, he stood. He gave a cautious look around the area, then backtracked the way he had come. Instinct told him chasing the man was highly dangerous, because the man seemed to know the park well enough to disappear within seconds. He was no ninja, because he surely would have attacked the agent without hesitation.

Turpin's educated guess told him the man was Gomez, because he was still unaccounted for, and apparently was not one of the men taken into custody at the lab. Maynard certainly would have reported such a find to Packard, who suddenly seemed loose-lipped about his findings.

As he darted up the hill toward the railings near the ride's entrance, Turpin decided if the intruder was Gomez then he was sent there by his superiors to retrieve something. If that held true, he would choose confronting the agent rather than returning to Kim and Voodoo empty-handed.

Ducking through the railings more carefully this time, Turpin picked up his pace, wondering if Gomez might try disabling the motorized cart. Though it was improbable Gomez could beat him back taking a longer route, the thought plagued him. He picked his pace up to a steady jog, which he did most days, keeping him in shape.

During the past ten minutes Turpin had experienced the two downfalls to wearing his favorite kind of footwear. Poor treading on a slippery hill was something he expected due to the slick soles, but he absolutely detested running. Not only were the heels noisy, but they were elevated, making any pace faster than a walk feel awkward.

When he reached the cart almost a minute later, Turpin glanced around once more, seeing no one else. An instinctive alarm rang in the back of his mind, warning him not to simply jump in the cart and drive a predictable pattern to the offices.

Suspecting Gomez was armed, he slipped into the driver's seat, taking a different route entirely, weaving between the many rest areas with trees and benches as he drove. He changed his mind about returning to the offices, thinking he might endanger the few people remaining in the park.

If everything went according to plan, he would eliminate Gomez as a threat to anyone left inside the park's boundaries.

No matter the cost.

CHAPTER 24

$$\blacktriangledown$$

It required very little of Clay's investigative intuition to figure out Voodoo's desired meeting place for their confrontation.

All bets were off after his two arch enemies shot him, completely shattering the traditions they once studied overseas. Clay sensed they had abandoned their scruples for business and profit, using their training as a tool, rather than a way of life.

He approached the Expedition ride from the rear, discovering more tribal masks tacked to the trees, as though placed there to form a makeshift welcoming committee. Feeling indifferent about their presence, Clay knew it was more smoke and mirrors from Voodoo. He recalled hearing stories about Voodoo's power over people, making them sick or blind through his will alone, like some witch doctor.

Looking upward, Clay found an eerie scene, like a bat looming atop the ride's crest. He knew immediately Voodoo stood there, patiently waiting, meditating his mind into the calm, ruthless machine necessary to battle the officer. Clay knew no fear, only wanting to kill this man, because no other option remained.

Jailing Voodoo endangered innocent lives, while incapacitating him could never leave Clay the satisfaction of knowing citizens were safe. Once again the fate of hundreds, perhaps thousands, rested on his shoulders.

"You always were too melodramatic," Clay said to him, although Voodoo didn't appear to hear his words, simply looming above like a gargoyle.

Several seconds passed as Clay slowly knelt on the moist ground. Now dressed in traditional black garb, he wore a full mask to conceal his identity from cameras and anyone who might happen to see the impending fight.

"And you were always one to preach," Voodoo replied without opening his eyes, now spreading his arms out as though sprouting wings to fly down. "Your ambition to do right by your master blinded you to seek a better life for yourself."

Closing his eyes, Clay continued to sense everything around him, his senses finely attuned with the environment. If Voodoo even flinched Clay would detect it.

"My master took us in as strays," Clay retorted, breathing in deep, controlled breaths. "Perhaps your clan was designed for murder and mayhem, but my *sensei* took in strays. He left us better people than we ever could have become on our own."

"Your master was soft. *You* are soft. What kind of man leaves his wife and child to die at the hands of strangers?"

Clay felt his blood boil as the words entered his ears, but he calmed himself quickly, knowing Voodoo wanted him upset. Was there no limit to the man's treachery and manipulation? Taking in another deep breath, Clay focused on the moment ahead, knowing he had Voodoo all to himself, doubting Kim dared interfere a second time.

"Are you going to debate this all night, or are we going to get down to business?" he asked the terrorist leader.

"There's nothing to debate. I'm simply giving you an opportunity to learn what you've missed by taking the easy path."

"Easy path?" Clay asked with skepticism, standing as he touched his pack from top to bottom, making certain every weapon was available to him.

He had placed the remaining weapons from Bill's truck into the pack, which gave him a larger variety than the first time he confronted Voodoo.

"If you think upholding the law and saving lives is the easy path, I have news for you. What you do costs lives, and fulfills only one agenda. Your own."

Voodoo gave the same evil, deep laugh he had that afternoon.

"Is it wrong for me to seek wealth? You don't understand how many nations want to change the world for the better. And how do you jumpstart the process?"

Clay refused to answer.

"By taking out political figures and leaders."

Another pause ensued, which only raised Clay's ire. He didn't particularly care about the details, because he wondered deep down if Voodoo might be stalling.

"We developed the perfect mix of chemicals for assassination purposes, but we needed an unsuspecting way of transferring them overseas. Who would bother to dig inside roller coaster parts? If you tear it apart, you ruin the value, opening yourself up for a lawsuit."

Clay was listening, but this was information being sorted out by Turpin and the others. He wanted to get down to business, but Voodoo continued to stall.

"We planned it perfectly. Open air contamination for groups or enclosed areas, or capsules designed to look like teeth. One bite and they filled the air with toxic gas, leaving only the source with the antidote alive. If all went well, your friend Sorrell took at least two people with him when he died."

Clay looked upward, a scowl etched across his face as the raindrops pelted him. Voodoo remained frozen like a statue, now staring skyward as lightning flashed behind Clay. The brief illumination gave the officer opportunity to see Voodoo had a fair number of weapons with him, which came as no surprise.

Sick of mind games, Clay stood before drawing a collapsible bow from his pack. He unfolded it into position, then fired an arrow toward his adversary. Voodoo caught it as Clay expected, but the point didn't seem lost, because the man reached for a *shuriken* star, hurling it toward Clay's right eye.

Simply moving aside to avoid the predictable path of the flying weapon, Clay watched Voodoo leap from the coaster's crest, grabbing hold of a horizontal board halfway down to slow his fall. He did this several times, clutching the boards just long enough to slow his descent until his feet touched the ground.

Taking only about five seconds to reach the ground, Voodoo reached for his *daito* while Clay drew his over his shoulder. Without another word, both men assumed offensive stances before charging one another.

Their swords clashed once, bouncing harmlessly away as the two men regained their footing. Clouds moved overhead, providing moonlight for their critical skirmish.

For almost thirty seconds they took turns attempting slashes and thrusts to soften one another up for the killing blow, but neither gained an advantage.

During the last exchange their swords glanced off one another, sending each of the wielders whirling back to defensive positions to analyze their tactics. Clay drew the shorter sword, deciding to double his offensive flurry by using two weapons. He watched Voodoo back up a step, prepared for the incoming attack.

Clay took notice that Voodoo stood beside the coaster's wooden beams, so he ran past his adversary in a surprise move, propelling himself off one of the boards toward Voodoo. While in midair Clay spun his body like a whirlwind, effectively making the blades act in conjunction like a blender.

Anticipating the move, Voodoo took a step to the side as he used his sword to deflect the killing blows from Clay. Landing with one knee on the ground, Clay held both blades at his sides with caution, staring up at his enemy.

Voodoo refused to give in, charging toward Clay with his *daito* swinging from side to side. With two swords Clay found blocking the assault somewhat easy until Voodoo made a pass toward his wrist which Clay had a fraction of a second to block. He lowered the hand just enough to avoid losing any body parts, but his *daito* was knocked beyond his reach, sticking into the ground several feet away.

Making a mental note of its position, Clay continued to battle Voodoo with his shorter sword, avoiding several deadly swings. Voodoo jabbed at him, but Clay caught his arm as he launched an open right palm into his enemy's face, sending him reeling toward the wooden cross-sections of the coaster.

After such a bold move Clay expected him to charge again, but Voodoo took off through the woods, waiting until he reached a safe distance before turning around.

Pulling a knife from inside the top of his garb, Clay threw the short, stubby knife at Voodoo, but the man caught it with incredible dexterity in his right hand. Giving another evil laugh as he turned, Voodoo disappeared as the woods swallowed him whole.

Without much thought, Clay pursued his adversary, striking a thin wire with one of his feet as two small darts flew from a nearby tribal mask's eyes toward him. The noise of their launch, like that of a blowgun being used, reached his ears. He ducked the darts, suddenly becoming wary of his surroundings and the true purpose of the masks.

Clay suspected booby traps were all around the tribal masks, but his primary concern was tracking his adversary in case any innocents remained inside the park. As he picked up his second sword he trekked into the woods behind Voodoo.

"Traps be damned," he muttered, wary of his surroundings.

More careful this time, he took off in a run as he chased Voodoo to whatever twisted location the black warrior chose next.

*   *   *   *

Bill found Kim to be far less accommodating than before when he tried to engage him in battle.

With so many carts and benches around, Kim simply ducked and wove between them. At first, Bill wondered if the Korean was cowardly, but decided this was a clever ploy to anger him and force him into a stupid move.

To test his theory Bill reached for a *shuriken* star from his belt, throwing it with surprising accuracy at Kim's chest in one motion, considering he had never thrown one. Proving him right, Kim easily deflected the star with his sword. Instead of contemplating why Kim might stall, Bill charged forward, surprising the Korean with a sword attack.

He took three solid slashes that Kim blocked with ease, despite the concerned look in his eyes. Bill backed off, glad he had established himself as an aggressive fighter so the Korean wouldn't underestimate him.

His primary concern was keeping all of his limbs long enough to kill Kim, or let Clay finish the job for him. Hope remained that his nephew was alive and well. Clay was tough, so he doubted even six poorly-trained men could murder him.

Circling around his adversary, Bill picked up one end of the chained weapon, hurling it toward Kim's face, forcing the Asian man to block the wooden staff end with his sword. The move worked, but left him vulnerable to attack from Bill, who ran passed him, grazing the side of his stomach with the *daito*.

Blood oozed from the five-inch line across Kim's flesh, much like a giant paper cut. Properly maintained swords knew few boundaries when it came to their sharpened blades cutting through organic materials.

Kim looked disgustedly at the wound before turning his furious countenance toward Bill. This time he charged forward, but as Bill prepared to block a sword attack, Kim slid along the ground like he was playing baseball. Letting his sword go to one side, he pulled two stubby knives from inside his clothing, slashing the insides of Bill's thighs.

Though Bill had miscalculated the initial attack, he recovered enough to leap over some of the blades' reach, or his femoral arteries would surely have been lacerated. Such an occurrence meant certain death from bleeding out, virtually leaving him helpless as blood gushed from his legs.

The two painful streaks along the insides of his thighs convinced him that Kim was out of practice, but still knew how to instantly kill. He rethought his strategy, backing away slightly as crimson droplets fell from his legs, dissipating instantly within the rainwater puddles beneath him.

"You see, you still have much to learn, American," Kim sneered with an ugly scowl. "We'll see to it that you are buried beside your nephew."

Bill now understood one wrong move meant the end of his life. Clay had taught him to be wary of his opponent and that person's arsenal at all times. He watched as Kim drew a pair of *sai* from his pack, twirling the metallic weapons with speed and grace. Two lessons Clay had never gotten around to teaching his uncle were how to twirl weapons and how he stuffed so many weapons into his pack and his garb.

At least I know the important stuff, Bill thought. Using the weapons was important, but Bill still couldn't believe he was actually engaged against a real ninja, even if Clay said their teachings weren't traditionally complete.

Kim suddenly stopped twirling the weapons, then charged Bill with them. He swung them downward like lawnmower blades toward the older man, but Bill blocked both weapons with his sword, kicking Kim squarely in the chest.

He hated exposing his leg even for a second, but Clay told him to use quickness and power in every blow to avoid injury. Much to Bill's surprise it actually worked.

Not wasting a moment, Bill attacked with the sword, putting Kim on the defensive. His sword was blocked several times, but he swung close to Kim's left hand, knocking the *sai* loose from the man's grip. As the weapon flew harmlessly to one side, the right hand stabbed toward Bill's chest.

Unable to block the move with the sword, Bill's only defense was throwing back his left shoulder to lesson the blow, which missed his heart. Instead, the *sai* plunged into his shoulder, tearing muscle tissue as it reached several inches past the flesh.

Quickly withdrawing, Bill held up the sword defensively. A sinister grin replaced the scowl Kim wore on his face earlier.

"Not so easy is it? You think I lack the knowledge to kill you?"

"I think you're afraid," Bill said, trying to stall momentarily to evaluate the damage to his shoulder. "You and your buddy are afraid Clay is going to kill you both, so you sent your hired goons after him."

"He is not as perfect as you think. Does he spend countless hours a day training?"

Before Bill answered, Kim revealed his own thought.

"He does not. What he has failed to realize is that his clan never respected him or liked him."

Bill didn't care much for small talk, but he realized Kim was leading to a point of some sort. He knew only what his nephew told him of his time in Japan. Clay seldom revealed much about his life or training overseas, but occasionally he told stories that tied in with Bill's training.

"You and Sato were jealous," Bill stated. "Isn't that why you're here? Isn't that why Sato was here last year?"

"Not at *all*. Do you really think we needed to come all the way over here to conduct our business? Hardly. Our objective was to disgrace then kill your nephew any way possible. Our missions here were just a bonus, a way for our organization to make money and frame your nephew's friends for misconduct."

Bill felt blood ooze down the side of his leg. He was growing weaker by the moment, which he now realized may have been Kim's intent.

Even so, he wasn't about to force an attack until he needed to.

"So why now? Why do this again after Sato failed? Wasn't he the best in your clan?"

Kim paused, still grinning somewhat.

"I do this because I am ordered to. I am a businessman like Sato. And like our master, Ryo Nosagi."

"Don't you mean ex-master?"

Drawing an even larger grin, Kim slowly shook his head negatively.

A cold chill ran down Bill's back as he realized what Kim had just implied. Rain continued to pelt his numbing face.

"No," he muttered to himself. "You're lying."

"You think so? Do you really think Nosagi took in all of us strays out of pure kindness?"

Wheels churned inside Bill's head, thinking about everything Clay had ever said about his former master. Clay never said one bad word about the man, so why was Kim trying to poison the Nosagi's good name?

"Who arranged Clay's marriage? Who pushed he and Eri together? And who do you think ordered Sato to kill Clay's beautiful wife and son?"

Bill shook his head, his thoughts returning to the memories of Clay's pain over the years. His nephew had endured so much, finding only a little peace when he killed Sato the year prior.

"Why?" Bill stammered.

"Because Clay was supposed to aim his hatred toward Sato, which we could have used to our advantage. Instead, he chose to *chase* Sato."

"So all of this was to corrupt Clay because he would have nothing left to live for?"

"In Japan, we were taught honor is everything. When one has no master, and no family, he may become wayward. We thought your nephew understood that."

Bill couldn't believe what he was hearing.

"We Americans think a little differently," he said. "Clay wouldn't become a rogue just because he lost his family."

"Oh, but you should have seen how happy he was, and then how devastated."

Now Kim was mocking Clay, relishing the moment.

"But why come over here to kill him at all?"

"Because Nosagi was betrayed by two of his closest pupils who threatened to tell your nephew the truth. We found and murdered one, but the second has never been found."

Bill understood completely. He felt a bit weaker than just minutes before, realizing Kim had stalled long enough to bring him closer to the brink of unconsciousness. A lightheaded feeling was next, then a complete inability to react.

Looking down, he saw the puddle now colored purplish-red. The overhead lamps created a shimmer that moved with the ripples created by each falling blood droplet.

"If Clay finds out Nosagi is alive, and what he's done, he'll kill him."

Kim laughed as though the notion Bill spoke was complete insanity.

"Nosagi will live out his days as he sees fit, running his empire from his new island home. Clay is no match for his former master, even if he somehow survives us."

Us.

Bill realized if he died at Kim's hands, his nephew would have two evil men tracking him down. He prayed his nephew was alive as his hand reached behind him. Kim's eyes studied him like a hawk surveying a mouse scurrying about for cover, likely wondering which weapon Bill planned to pull out next in his doomed attempt to survive.

When the handgun pointed directly at his chest after Bill swung it around, Kim had only time enough to give a shocked expression before Bill fired five consecutive rounds into his chest. They happened so fast that Kim never hit the ground until all five bullets were in him.

Feeling somewhat lightheaded, Bill stumbled over to Kim's body, wondering if he possessed the ability, like Clay, to put himself into a trance. He doubted it, but for good measure he fired two bullets into Kim's skull.

"You should have killed me when you had the chance," he commented toward the fresh corpse.

Usually a very technical personality, the maintenance director felt a tear come to his eye as the emotion of almost dying, along with the new danger his nephew faced, caught up with his mind.

Bill made his way over to one of the vendor stands, looking behind the front facade for something to help cover his wounds. He found a few towels, which saved him from tearing up his own clothes. Tearing them into thick strips, he tied them around his legs. With the bleeding controlled, he took a seat on a nearby bench.

"I've got to clean this up," he thought aloud.

Picking up the weapons made for a much easier story to tell authorities when the time came. Bill doubted they would believe a story about sword fighting in the middle of a theme park that ended in gunfire. He planned on picking up Clay's weapons and returning them to the truck while he thought of a good cover story.

Even as he stood from the bench to recover his borrowed weapons Bill wondered if he dared tell Clay about his former master. On one hand, he knew Clay would immediately seek revenge against Nosagi, which Bill wholeheartedly justified. It also placed Clay in grave danger if he challenged Nosagi on the man's home soil.

Another option existed in which Bill took this newfound information to his grave. Doing so also put Clay in extreme danger because Nosagi would continue to have the element of surprise. Without Clay knowing, Nosagi could send assassins at will to eliminate his former student.

Bill limped forward, picking up the *daito* and *tenbin*, as heavy thoughts plagued his mind. Feeling a bit weak, he took a seat on a nearby brick centerpiece before carefully rotating the chain into the wooden ends of the *tenbin*. He stopped, staring forward at the arcade, then to Kim's body.

His thoughts returned to the dilemma plaguing his mind as overwhelming concern for his nephew caused him to stop restoring the weapon to its original state.

Sighing aloud, he wanted to search for Clay, but working at a hospital gave him experience enough to know he wasn't going far on foot. A bloody trail had followed him from the battle sight to the area where he now sat.

Clay called him a technical man, meaning Bill thought and lived logically compared to other people. He was right, but Bill looked down to his hands, which trembled noticeably. Not only had he just survived something he should not have, but he had killed a man in the process. He never went to church, and seldom prayed, but he suddenly felt a bit more religious.

Taking a deep breath to calm down, Bill relegated himself to fixing the weapon, because he wasn't going anywhere until help came his way, or the bleeding subsided.

*   *   *   *

Turpin had taken an unusual route around parts of the park toward the offices. He worried somewhat that Gomez might have contacted his employers, but he suspected those men had their hands full.

Deciding to confuse Gomez even more, Turpin abandoned the cart near the observation tower, despite light showers still dousing the park. He walked toward the other side of the tower, which housed a flavored crushed-ice vending stand.

Standing perfectly still, hidden in the shadows, the agent observed the area around him.

The sound of gunfire entered his ears after he jumped inside the cart, but it sounded distant. Knowing the security force was gone for the evening, he wondered who might have fired a weapon. Bryant and Turpin surely hadn't left the offices, and he doubted Clay Branson had any need for a weapon.

Clay's uncle, on the other hand, might have found a firearm of some kind.

Ahead of Turpin stood all kinds of shops down the main strip. At the end was the part of the office that housed the conference room. Beyond that area he knew the metal detectors and turnstiles for ticket takers remained vacant, though he couldn't see any details because of the rain and low lighting.

To his left, his right, and behind him, concrete paths led from other areas of the park. He wasn't able to see behind him unless he compromised his position. If Gomez headed for the offices or chose to look for the agent, he needed to pass through the area.

With the motorized cart a short walk behind him, Turpin suspected he was leading Gomez into a perfectly devised trap. The only other way to the offices required a roundabout path the terrorist aide was unlikely to take.

Curious about what information the sheet of paper contained, he dared not look. One second of distraction might prove costly with hired killers roaming freely through the park.

Several minutes passed with eerie inactivity around the agent. Turpin grew concerned that Gomez may have fled the park, returned to his employers, and worse yet, gone the long way around to reach the offices.

Packard and Bryant were capable of defending themselves, and both men were armed. Turpin worried mostly about Casey being the only civilian inside the park, since Russell had left for the day. She was their responsibility, but he wondered if they had kept her conveniently close by for too long.

Surveying the area directly ahead of him, Turpin finally saw a shadow emerge from a sidewalk path, all the way down the main walkway. Too far away for Turpin to positively identify, the shadow appeared from behind the furthest shop, stepping cautiously into the open.

He headed directly across the walk toward an entrance that led behind the village facade.

And into the offices.

"Damn it," Turpin said, rising from his hiding spot.

He carefully looked around before heading down the left path to intercept the unidentified person. In a crouched run, he freed his weapon from the holster at his right side, keeping it in a ready position.

Drawing closer to a collision course with the mysterious figure, Turpin felt his heart thump inside his chest. His position with the Bureau seldom put him in foot pursuits, despite his job involved tracking and detaining criminals who evaded capture.

He typically planned accordingly to catch them by surprise, eliminating their opportunities to run.

A combination of the weather and the giant fountains to Turpin's right covered the sound of his boots atop the concrete path, but the man he tracked somehow saw or sensed the agent's presence. His head turned sharply as Turpin drew within an accurate firing range.

He recognized this man as the same person looming over the body under the ride. Whether or not he was Gomez still eluded the agent, considering he only had Packard's description as a reference.

When the man saw him, his eyes widened as both men stopped in their tracks. Turpin raised his gun without a word, sending the man in a frenzied dash toward the closest safe harbor.

The fountains.

Surrounded by a wrought iron fence, six fountains stood twice as tall as any man, surrounded by smaller fountains that reached about waist-high. The man leapt over the short fence, dashing into the water before scrambling for cover behind the active fountains.

Not only were the fountains large, but the spray they emitted gushed over each side, creating a mushroom appearance of translucent liquid. Gomez immediately sought refuge behind the first fountain as Turpin jumped the fence, careful not to lose his gun.

He stepped down the concrete embankment, jumping into cold water that reached his knees, immediately soaking his legs and his cowboy boots, weighting him down.

As a precautionary step he holstered the gun, not wishing to be ambushed by Gomez. He felt confident the man was no match for him in hand-to-hand combat, so until he found the terrorist, Turpin decided to exercise caution.

The six fountains combined to sound like a waterfall, filling his ears with noise that potentially endangered him. If he failed to see *or* hear the younger man's activities, Turpin suspected he might take a bullet somewhere above the waistline. He had little doubt the man was armed, since employees and police officers weren't required to pass through metal detectors like guests.

Packard believed the man had posed as an employee, if this was indeed the same person.

Instincts told the agent he was tracking Gomez.

Turpin made his way around the first fountain, covered by its eggshell color and the gushing water. Lights from inside the fountains changed color every ten seconds or so, illuminating the entire set with every color from orange to green within a minute.

Controlling his breathing, Turpin listened for any sounds beyond the fountains as he stepped around the far side of the first structure. He gave a quick glance to his right before proceeding to the next fountain, realizing he was completely open to gunfire almost four seconds as he fought his way through the water.

Luckily none came his way. He suspected the man he tracked had enough worry to keep him from making any sudden moves.

Each large fountain had four regular lights around it to keep the structure itself illuminated. Turpin noticed one of the lights turned almost ninety degrees away from the fountain as he rounded the corner, setting off a danger signal in his mind.

Doubting the park would let the light sit awkwardly, he suspected Gomez had accidentally bumped it as he rounded the structure. What struck Turpin as odd was that the light was on a corner that led back toward the first fountain, meaning Gomez was attempting to escape.

Or doubling back to kill the agent.

Turpin ducked down, creeping back the same way he had just come. He instinctively reached for his gun as the man came into view through the water. Through the flowing liquid it looked as though Gomez was melting, but Turpin saw enough to know he didn't need his gun. The last thing he needed was to attract the man's fellow conspirators, if any remained.

Nervously looking around, the man had no idea the agent planned to ambush him until the one second he had to save himself passed. As Gomez looked behind him, Turpin struck like a boa constrictor, positioning himself behind the terrorist aide as he spun him to a helpless position.

Gomez raised the gun from instinct alone, his back drawn tightly against the agent's chest. Turpin's arms assumed the correct position around his victim's forehead and chin as the gun raised, twisting with enough power and agility to snap at least one vertebra that connected the skull to the spine.

Releasing his grip as though he held a stinky garbage bag, Turpin allowed the body to collapse straight down.

"Sorry, kid, but you were playing for the wrong team," he said, letting the body slump into the water where it immediately began floating away.

Turpin had enough evidence against the terrorists without Gomez, so the man became expendable. Capturing and restraining him was a danger the agent dared not afford. Now completely soaked from bursting through the cascading water to attack Gomez, the agent shivered slightly from the cool air. He quickly recovered the other man's gun before trudging back to dry land.

Stepping over the short railing, Turpin looked around. A stiff breeze blew several leaves across the concrete walkway at the park entrance, but no people were visible. Several of the store windows displayed mannequins wearing the park's merchandise, giving the agent a strange feeling.

He had seen several movies with similar settings where a character survived a bizarre holocaust or meltdown to find himself alone. Though he was very much accustomed to being alone, he drew some comfort in knowing others were never very far from him. It kept him human in a job that demanded he occasionally cast aside his emotions.

Taking a deep breath, the agent began walking toward one of the gates leading to the corporate offices. He balked momentarily, wondering if anyone had checked out the gunshots he heard halfway across the park. Deciding no one else was available to check the area, he sighed aloud, trudging toward the disturbance.

He wondered where Clay, his primary objective, was located and if the young man would survive the evening.

CHAPTER 25

▼

When Clay caught up with Voodoo, he found himself just outside the construction area where the Whirlwind's framework barely showed against the park lighting. Despite its white color, the coaster's metal railings disappeared into the darkness beyond the launch area until Clay stepped inside.

Directly above him a security camera mounted to a light post monitored his activity. He considered throwing something to disable the camera, but decided he hadn't stepped fully into its view, so he tossed down a smoke bomb. Before the smoke dissipated Clay was beyond the camera's range, already tracking Voodoo.

Clay found few hiding places around the roller coaster. He cautiously examined the launch area, then checked the back side. Beside the large wooden deck, where the attached cars once started their journey up the railing, Clay noticed a small barn that housed two other sets of inactive cars. He saw no sign of his adversary, so he moved on.

His eyes were adjusted to the darkness when he left the launch area, stepping onto the metallic stairway that paralleled the coaster tracks to the crest of the first hill. Stairs were necessary for daily and weekly maintenance checks, also serving as an emergency exit if the cars stopped halfway up the lift.

Looking upward, he noticed all of them appeared to be in place, since the entire first lift was still in place. Most of the removed pieces came from the far end of the Whirlwind.

Though he had never experienced a modern coaster stopping anywhere once it started, he knew they had safety checkpoints periodically along the tracks to monitor the cars.

He didn't like the idea of isolating himself on the stairs, but he was determined to flush out Voodoo. The man's actions irritated him, distracting him momentarily from the task at hand as his feet touched the fifth step. Alerted to the danger almost a second too late, Clay darted up another step as a sword's tip pierced the metal grid pattern of the fifth step where his feet had just touched.

Clay decided to race down the stairs to confront Voodoo until the man cut off the exit at the lift's base. He held his *daito* directly in front of him as he carefully ascended the stairs. Clay drew his own sword, prepared to end their skirmish quickly, despite the close quarters.

Seconds later he found himself blocking predictable swings from Voodoo, since only two effective directions of attack remained. Both men knew an overhead attack was easy to block, so Voodoo only swung from the sides, hoping to catch Clay lingering a split-second too long.

Believing another dimension of Voodoo's attack was forthcoming, Clay dared not look behind him as he faced his adversary, stepping backward up the metal stairs with the utmost faith they were all in place.

Until one came up missing.

When Clay's foot fell through an opening where a metallic step was once mounted to the roller coaster's structure, he had a fraction of a second to react. Failure to react meant a fifty-foot drop, leading to serious injury or death.

Instead of letting his sword go completely, or grabbing the step in front of him with a free hand, Clay stuck the sword vertically behind him, letting the blade penetrate one of the mesh gaps in the step behind him.

The rest of his body fell through the slim opening as he watched Voodoo lift his own sword overhead, preparing to plunge it downward into Clay's neck or chest.

With both hands wrapped around the sword's grip, Clay relied upon the *tsuba*, the sword's square hand guard, to keep his hands from sliding down the blade. He swung his legs through the thin opening, kicking the side of Voodoo's sword as it came down toward him. Though Voodoo retained his grip, his arm flew wide, giving Clay enough time to fully swing his body up through the opening. Using his momentum, Clay flipped backward to the step above the opening, blocking Voodoo's next sword attack before drawing a knife from his side.

He ran the short blade across Voodoo's abdomen, but the man saw it coming, so the wound looked like little more than a glorified paper cut.

Clay took one more step upward, regrouping as Voodoo stared intently at him through his black hood. He pulled out a smoke bomb, threw it down against the step he stood on, then disappeared from Clay's view.

"Shit," Clay muttered under his breath, not seeing his adversary anywhere on the stairs.

He defensively whirled around, but Voodoo had not flipped above him either. If Voodoo hadn't gone to either of those places, that left only a risky jump off either side, or a leap through the missing step.

Shifting his feet toward the outside of the step he stood upon, Clay avoided the blade punching upward to disable either of his appendages. Voodoo stabbed upward several more times from his new perch under the stairs, but Clay avoided his attacks with nimble foot movement. He then leapt to a lower step with a flip some gymnasts might envy, landing catlike on his feet.

Instead of risking a return leap through the opening, Voodoo let his sword fall to the ground below, then went hand over hand along a thin rail until he reached a pole. A support pole of some sort for the Whirlwind's thicker metal beams, it touched the track base, reaching all the way to the ground. As he reached the vertical beam, Voodoo used it like a fire pole, sliding toward the grass below.

Not wishing to lose his adversary again, Clay dashed down the steps while trying to monitor Voodoo's movements. Clay finished the race second as he spun around from the steps, seeing no trace of his enemy.

"Damn."

Voodoo had only one realistic route to take if he wanted to avoid combat, which took him through the woods. Clay suspected he was doubling back toward the Expedition ride where booby traps and tribal masks lurked in the shadows.

A fairly worn path led the officer to a mesh fence that led outside the main park area. He ran up to the fence, seeing no movement anywhere along the metal, or the barbed wire above. If Voodoo had climbed the fence he suspected it would still be shaking slightly from supporting a human form.

Surrounded by bushes, Clay listened intently the next few seconds, hearing nothing. He rotated slowly, keeping his feet centered in the same area for a defensive move whenever Voodoo attacked.

An attack seemed inevitable, so he worried about his feet being exposed.

His worries proved well-founded when Voodoo took a swipe with a short sword from inside a nearby bush. Only the movement he'd waited to hear alerted Clay in time to jump out of harm's way. He scaled the fence, stopping halfway up to observe the ground below. Voodoo emerged suddenly from a different bush, grazing him along the arm with his sword's blade.

Clay groaned in pain, but held onto his own sword, immediately swinging toward his adversary, backing Voodoo away from the fence. Jumping down, he continued to battle Voodoo, putting the man on the defensive. As Voodoo defended one of his swings, locking their swords momentarily, Clay kicked him squarely in the chest, sending him soaring backward until he landed atop a shrub.

Raising his sword over his head, Clay came down with a killing blow that missed because Voodoo rolled off to one side, deflecting Clay's sword with his own. Standing a safe distance away, Voodoo held his hand out before him, luring Clay closer, then blew some sort of orange powder that hit the officer in the face.

And more importantly, his eyes.

Clay's eyes immediately burned, but instead of swinging wildly with his weapon, he listened intently, not trusting Voodoo to battle him honorably. He kept his weapon close to his body, prepared to defend any kind of cheap sword jab.

He heard only the man's sinister laugh, then the sound of Voodoo scaling the fence. Clay dropped his sword as he attempted to flush his eyes with only his hands. Natural tears began to form, but a minute later when he opened them his vision seemed fuzzy. He felt strange, as though drugged somehow by the mysterious powder.

Against the odds, he took up his sword, putting it into its scabbard before climbing the fence. Halfway up, he decided not to simply follow Voodoo into his trap. Dropping down, Clay ran the other way, following the conventional path toward the Expedition ride. At least two drinking fountains stood between his position and the ride, providing ample opportunity to flush out the chemicals in his eyes.

Without full vision, a drugged feeling overtaking his senses, and preset traps lying everywhere beneath the Expedition ride, Clay knew the hazards of following Voodoo.

He also knew the consequences if the man escaped, so he stumbled forward. Clay fought to consciously keep himself running in a straight line as he emerged from the grassy underbelly of the Whirlwind to the concrete walkways of the regular park.

Instinctively he knew the chemicals were only going to affect him more violently as adrenaline shot through his body, but he had little choice. If he failed, Voodoo would have opportunity to murder Bill, Casey, and everyone else inside the park before he disappeared to whatever remote area he chose.

Clay was determined to keep that from happening.

*   *   *   *

Packard finally had an understanding of most everything the terrorists had planned. With four people arrested at the lab and enough witnesses to piece together the entire scenario he felt better, but still worried.

Two of his three men were fine, but he wondered if Clay had made the right decision by tracking Voodoo in his injured state. Bill had voluntarily helped the group, so Packard prayed no harm came to him. The sergeant still carried guilt from Clay's cousin getting killed the year prior.

No one was going to side with a man who called his officers a state away to ask for their assistance because terrorists demanded it.

Unless everyone came home.

Bryant and Casey continued to work at the computers, digging up pertinent information for Turpin, since he had taken command of the park as his own crime scene.

"He's been gone too long," Casey commented as she printed a file from her computer station.

"Who?" Bryant questioned.

"Agent Turpin. Well, *all* of them."

"He knows what he's doing," Packard said. "And Clay isn't going to let anything happen to us."

"What could possibly happen to us that hasn't already?" Bryant asked, not turning around from the computer terminal.

Packard shook his head, looking away. He knew the type of men from Clay's past were trained beyond anything he or the security director could stop. Unfaltering devotion motivated his top officer to do whatever it took to solve any problem, or to protect his own. Rather than let Kim or Voodoo escape, he would likely take his own life if it meant ending theirs.

He had already checked both entrances to the building, making certain they were locked. Knowing locked doors were useless against the likes of Kim and Voodoo, Packard still believed several other threats possibly remained.

"I still can't believe they did all of this just to smuggle chemicals in our roller coaster parts," Bryant said when Packard paced the floor nearby. "Why go to all that trouble?"

"They're a different breed," the sergeant replied. "To them, being dishonored is something we compare to being a rapist or a murderer over here. They want to run Clay's name through the mud as icing on the cake."

"He's an American," Bryant noted. "What would he care?"

"More than you know, Hugh."

Bryant shot him a quizzical look before returning his attention to the monitor.

So far as Packard knew, Bryant had never seen Clay's silent weapons. It seemed like everyone else left in the park knew he was something more than a city police officer, but kept quiet about what they had seen.

He had mixed feelings about Turpin recruiting his officer. He felt selfish for wanting to keep Clay around, but at the same time the two had grown somewhat close. Still, he wanted to see the young man make the right choice, and if he had the opportunity to help others on a national level Packard saw no reason to refuse.

The manner in which Turpin arrived kept Packard guarded against the possibility the agent wasn't everything he claimed. Perhaps his timing seemed the most awkward, but Packard had little doubt he was legitimate.

Despite the agent reminding him of some of the old-timers on his own department, Packard sensed Turpin was a dangerous man. The Bureau's regulations, last he knew, accepted no one under the age of twenty-three, and no one older than thirty-seven. He also felt relatively certain field agents were assigned to other positions before reaching Turpin's age.

He didn't dare ask Casey or Bryant about him because they seemed rather fond of the agent. The security director was close to the agent's age, and the two had apparently found some parallels in their careers to talk about.

Packard began wondering how they were able to remain focused on their tasks with three allies still in danger.

All three turned their heads at the sound of a door closing behind someone. At the closer of two doors stood a man with a purpose.

And a pistol.

"Koop," Bryant said with disgust.

"Thanks for the warm welcome, Hugh," the man replied sarcastically.

"You've got a lot of nerve showing your face around here."

"Doesn't seem I have much of a choice, does it? Months of planning went down the drain when the two buffoons Kim hired got their load confiscated at the drug lab. Without those chemicals ol' Steve here doesn't get paid. And if I don't get paid, I can't pay for the plans I've already made on an island that shall remain anonymous. Which, in turn, means my life isn't worth shit anywhere."

Packard noticed the man meant business, despite his lightly comical way of telling his tale.

"Pointing a gun at us isn't going to do you any good," he told Koop.

"No, you're right. That's why I have Mr. and Mrs. Trimble under my loving care. I seem to have intercepted the lovely couple as they tried to make their way inside."

"No!" Casey said, leaping from her seat.

She tried running at Koop, but Bryant caught her by the arm, pulling her back to safety.

"What do you want, Koop?" the security director demanded.

"I propose a trade."

Packard knew the man wanted money or the chemicals. There was no way any police agency was about to let the chemicals fall into the wrong hands, but he suspected Koop had evil intentions if he didn't get his way. After all, he had nothing to lose, and running would end in his eventual capture.

"What do you want?" he asked of Koop.

"I want out of this country, and I want money. And since little Casey here doesn't have her hands on the family checkbook, and is an only child, I'm willing to take her and leave her parents to pay for her safe return."

"You bastard!" she screamed at him. "Take me. Just let them go."

Bryant looked extremely concerned as the new stipulation was announced.

"I can't let you take her," he said to Koop.

Raising the gun, Koop pointed it at Bryant's chest.

"I can take her, or you can take a bullet. Considering our past working relationship, I'm not so sure I don't want to put one in you anyway."

Stepping forward, Bryant apparently wanted to test Koop's intentions.

"Step down, Hugh," Koop warned. "You aren't going to be the hero today. Then again, you never were much of anything in Cincinnati, were you? You never made rank over there, so you thought you'd come over here and be top dog, right? I guess you're going to have to settle for being a failure all of your life."

"You fucker," Bryant said angrily, controlling his tone. "There was a reason we never let you have any control around here. We never trusted you."

"No, but I was smart enough to hack into your precious computer system and set things up the way my new employers wanted them. Just another failure under your belt."

Bryant's lips quivered angrily, then folded inward in disgust. Packard suspected the man was literally biting his tongue to prevent saying something ultimately regretful.

Packard decided to protect the security director by speaking.

"We can work something out. You don't need to take Casey."

Koop looked at him like a person might stare at a coworker who just told a tasteless joke.

"You don't think I'm that stupid, do you? I wasn't the one eating every shred of information put in my hand this afternoon, Sergeant. Now if you two gentlemen will excuse me, I'll leave with my favorite park employee. I expect you'll both expedite the negotiations for me once I'm free and clear."

Packard saw Bryant scowl again, understanding what failure on one's own turf felt like. His hope of buying some time fell through, but he had one last question to ask that seemed quite pertinent to their situation.

"Where can we find the Trimbles once you leave?"

Bryant continued to keep hold of Casey's wrist, not surrendering her to Koop any sooner than necessary.

"I'll send them your way. Gentlemen, I would love to continue this conversation, but I have money to recoup, and very little time to do so."

He paused, motioning for Bryant to let Casey come toward him. She left his side hesitantly until Koop motioned with the gun for her to stop several feet away from him.

"I need your weapons, gentlemen," he said, pointing the gun at Packard, then toward Bryant.

Packard complied immediately, knowing Koop wasn't naive enough to believe either wasn't armed. He looked over, seeing Bryant hesitating, as though he harbored some heroic plan of action. When the security director looked his way Packard shook his head negatively at the man, indicating it was foolhardy to act.

Thinking better of his situation, Bryant undid the safety loop over his firearm, carefully removing it before placing it on the floor. Packard also placed his on the floor before him.

"Kick them over," Koop instructed the two officers.

They complied, sending both guns past Casey where they came to rest near Koop's feet. He picked them up, tucking both firearms into his pants along the back side.

Packard wished any of the three missing people from their informal task force would return to stop Koop before he stole Casey away. Forced to watch helplessly, Packard saw Koop grab Casey's wrist, forcing a scream from her before he dragged her toward the door.

Bryant started forward, but Packard raised his arm, catching the security director along the chest because he saw something from the corner of his eye that indicated Koop's escape was doomed.

"Wait," he said in a hushed voice to Bryant. "There's no need."

As Koop stepped through the door, turning to make certain he wasn't being followed, Turpin stood up from behind the door, clocking the man in the head with a weapon.

Packard walked to the door as Koop slumped to the ground, giving them another witness to the truth.

"Nicely done," he told Turpin.

"Wouldn't have been necessary if you two had been more careful."

"He had a key," Packard said flatly. "The doors were locked. We were busy digging up your evidence."

Bryant shot him a questioning look, since the sergeant actually played no part in searching for evidence, short of the occasional suggestion.

"Where are my parents?" Casey asked no one in particular, obviously desperate to see them alive and well.

All eyes turned toward the parking lot where Bill came forward with an older couple. Casey ran toward them, brushing Bill on the shoulder carefully with one hand before hugging each of her parents.

Packard noticed the slits along Bill's pants, even before the man walked over to join him.

"What have I missed?" he asked.

"This was pretty much it."

"Who was that guy?"

"Our human resources director who got dicked out of his payoff from the terrorists, so he opted for Plan B."

Bill looked at the man, now being cuffed by Turpin.

"And I thought our human resources people were bad."

Chuckling, Packard observed the agent picking up Koop before dragging him inside the main office. He looked to both men as Bryant joined them, leaving Casey to speak with her parents.

"I think it's time we call in the locals," Turpin said.

"Your call," Bryant said.

The agent nodded in understanding. He had taken over the case during the afternoon, so everything fell on his shoulders.

"We're going to have to weave quite a tale," he said.

"We don't have to do much of anything if you keep control of it," Packard suggested. "A lot less messy that way."

"I can do that, but we have to handle this delicately. One wrong word about how this whole mess was handled could get us *all* into trouble. I didn't exactly follow protocol by my agency's standards either."

Turpin looked to Bill.

"Where were you?"

"I confronted Kim before I found Casey's folks in the parking lot. They were tied up in Koop's van."

Everyone looked at him, waiting for the answer they really wanted to hear.

"Oh. Kim won't be bothering anyone, including Clay."

The way in which he stated the last remark led Packard to believe Kim was confirmed dead.

"You can find him on the walkway over there," Bill added, pointing to the area.

Turpin glanced with a quizzical look on his face.

"Will he have several bullets in him?" he asked Bill.

"Yeah, but I lost count."

Everyone around him let satisfied expressions cross their faces.

"Let's get those cleaned up," Bryant said, looking toward the man's injured legs. "We've got a med kit over here."

Packard waited until they left before addressing Turpin.

"How long can you give Clay?"

"Not long. I can sweep some things under the carpet, but there's only so much liability I'm willing to shoulder."

The agent's hardened meaning came through his soft drawl. Despite his professionalism and knowledge, Turpin harbored some secrets. Packard understood all about keeping skeletons in the closet, but he wondered how secure Clay's future was if he accepted the offer.

"You been swimming?" Packard inquired.

Turpin returned a crooked grin.

"Let's just say your pal Gomez won't be bugging us any more."

"That leaves just one."

"Yeah. It does."

CHAPTER 26

▼

By the time Clay reached the wooded area surrounding the Expedition ride he felt worse than ever. He thought he had avoided breathing the substance when Voodoo first blew it toward him, but now it seemed mere contact with his skin caused the symptoms.

Washing his face did nothing to help the dizzy feeling overcoming his body, but he was able to see somewhat clearly again.

Maintaining his balance distracted his senses from detecting danger, but when his foot triggered a wire, Clay ducked an arrow that would have gone through his neck with ease. Lodging itself in a nearby tree, the arrow vibrated momentarily, appearing as three objects for a few seconds until Clay's vision returned to normal.

He remained sprawled atop the ground momentarily, collecting his wits before continuing onward. Not knowing Voodoo's location made the journey tougher, but now he wondered if the man was cowardly enough to avoid battle altogether.

Obviously Voodoo feared him, based on the number of traps placed throughout the wooded area.

Like shooting someone in the back, killing in an honorable battle without any contact was considered very dishonorable. In feudal Japan such an act was reason enough for suicide because a person would be openly disgraced by his fellow sect members.

Clay intended to make this an assisted suicide for Voodoo.

"You can come out and fight, or you can live in shame the rest of your days," Clay said loud enough for anyone in the vicinity to hear.

"Afraid of impaling yourself on one of my traps?" Voodoo asked, emerging from nearby shrubbery.

"Hardly. At least I have some respect for death. And for life."

"You don't know how to live," Voodoo said as he stepped forward, then took a defensive stance, holding a sickle in each hand.

Clay had seen him use sickles on practice dummies in Japan, recalling how the man chipped off almost a dozen parts of their wooden limbs in seconds.

"You live in yesterday, dwelling over the loss of your wife and child. It's time I sent you to join them."

As though on cue, both men charged forward, their weapons connecting as they jumped past one another.

Clay landed in the shrubs where Voodoo launched himself from, finding a new injury on his left thigh from one of the sickles. His defenses had barely been too slow because of the drugs infiltrating his system.

Sensing the hesitation, Voodoo immediately attacked again, bringing both sickles toward Clay from virtually every direction within a few seconds. Blocking the attacks, Clay knew what kind of danger his body's weakened state placed him in.

"Do you feel it?" Voodoo taunted. "That feeling that you're on the verge of dying? Don't worry. Many men, women, and children have felt it before I ended their miserable lives."

Grunting angrily, Clay attacked him with the sword, nearly losing one hand as he knocked one of the sickles away, while the other sickle slashed down at his fingers. Removing the endangered hand from the sword, Clay clutched the sword with his other hand, cutting cleanly at Voodoo's skull.

Voodoo ducked as their weapons scraped against one another. He then kicked Clay just above the waistline, sending him rolling backward through the nearby brush.

And another snare.

Landing close to the ground, Clay looked above him as two spiked boards crashed against one another. Judging the height of the trap around where his neck might have been, he felt thankful this trap was undone. Had he been standing, Clay doubted he could have escaped the device unscathed.

Springing to his feet in one motion, Clay snatched his sword from its lodged position in the earth, attacking Voodoo before the man recovered his second sickle. Voodoo blocked the blade with his weapon, punched Clay in the chest, then flipped backward to avoid a calculated slice of the sword.

Voodoo dashed forward next, aiming the sickle's blade toward Clay's thigh, but the officer dove over the weapon, tucking his head as he rolled through the blow and onto the ground. He stood, fighting off more of Voodoo's attacks as their weapons made clanking sounds every time they touched.

Catching the blade of Voodoo's sickle along the edge of his sword, Clay spun around, kicking his adversary in the face, sending him reeling into the shrubs. He pressed the attack, but as he swung downward with the sword, Voodoo used the sickle to knock it from his hands.

Now Clay found himself dodging several swings from the short weapon until one tore a deep scratch along his chest, shredding his black uniform as it left a trail of red.

Anticipating the next swing of Voodoo's weapon, he caught the man by the arm, using an open-palm strike against his nerves. This action rendered Voodoo's arm useless the next few seconds, forcing him to drop the weapon.

Neither had a ready weapon, so they fought hand-to-hand, each dodging one another's blows until Clay caught Voodoo's stunned arm. Raring back, he threw the arm against a nearby tree, then kicked the area where he anticipated the arm would remain.

His kick broke the sapling in half, but Voodoo had retracted his arm in time to keep it from further harm.

Again, Clay realized his reflexes were slowed just enough to keep him from finishing the battle by Voodoo's witch doctor tactics. He felt his senses returning as the dizzy feeling left his body. Perhaps dousing his eyes with water helped him avoid further illness, or the lack of inhalation kept his immune system functioning properly.

Either way, he felt ready to end the skirmish.

Clay spun around with another kick, hitting his enemy in the side of his head. Voodoo returned an attack of his own, punching toward Clay, who kicked as more of a defense than an attack. Voodoo caught his leg under one arm, prepared to snap it with a viciously forceful elbow until Clay drew himself in close enough to chop the side of Voodoo's skull with a sharp blow from the side of his hand.

Both fell back from one another, staring intently.

Voodoo plucked one of his sickles from the ground before coming at Clay, but the officer leapt upward, grabbing a tree branch to pull himself above the attack. He then kicked Voodoo's back as the terrorist passed by, hurling him into a thorny bush.

Clay let himself drop to the ground, picking up his sword before looking for his adversary. No sounds entered his ears, and Voodoo had now disappeared amongst the shrubs surrounding the ride.

Tired of playing mind games, he cautiously entered the brush, looking around as he held his sword close to his body. Prepared to defend himself in an instant, he knew Voodoo had to be frustrated that his attacks continued to fail.

Much to Clay's dismay, he finally succeeded, lodging the blade of a sickle in Clay's thigh as his other hand came down with a blade aimed at the officer's upper body. Despite the sudden surge of pain in his left thigh, Clay blocked the blade with his own sword. His free hand struck Voodoo in the face, then reached for a tribal mask hung directly behind him. Clutching it on the narrow side, he also used it as a weapon, turning to use it as a makeshift fist by pounding it into Voodoo's eye socket.

Clay watched as he darted further into the woods, quickly taking chase. If he hesitated, it gave Voodoo ample time to evade the traps because he knew their locations. Wondering just how many surprises remained, Clay stopped suddenly, realizing the bushes in front of him had stopped moving.

Meaning Voodoo also stopped moving.

Or found some high ground.

A chain wrapped itself around Clay's neck from above as Voodoo hoisted him upward by tugging on the opposite end, draped over a large branch.

With only a few seconds to react, or risk his circulation being cut off to the point that he became incapacitated, Clay used his fingers to create some slack between the metal and his neck. His sword fell harmlessly to the ground as Voodoo likely hoped.

The chain also served as a weighted anchor, allowing him to swing his legs upward, kicking Voodoo's fingers, then his face, dropping him to the ground.

Clay also fell, landing hard because Voodoo had hoisted him twice his own height into the air. As he hit the ground Clay rolled into a tree. His back ached, but he took up his sword once more, standing to confront his enemy again.

Despite standing in one of the dimmer areas beneath the ride, Clay noticed light shimmering off several objects in the less dense woods ahead of him. Taking a step forward, he knew the remaining tribal masks awaited him inside that particular area. Voodoo, now to his feet, intentionally stepped backward toward the area, his eyes giving a sinister look that indicated he was smirking beneath his hood.

He was inviting Clay to certain death.

After feigning a charge toward Voodoo, Clay pulled a stubby knife from his pack. Deciding to make his last knife count for something, he threw it at the largest portion of Voodoo, watching it sink instantly into his adversary's torso.

Voodoo pulled it out with disgust, throwing it back at Clay who caught it without injury, predicting such a move from the man. Now willing to retreat, Voodoo darted into the area overrun with tribal masks.

Clay watched his adversary's every step, missing the same trip wires when he crossed areas Voodoo skipped over. When Voodoo finally stopped in the clearing's center, Clay confronted him. Both took offensive postures, looking far more fatigued than when they began their skirmish across the park. Voodoo pulled his last sword from the pack strapped to his back, putting them on even footing.

Without a word the two sprinted forth once more, their swords clanging as they clashed in midair before each man landed in the opposite starting spot. They engaged in more swordplay until their weapons locked against one another one final time.

Clay dug into his physical reserves, kicking Voodoo in the chest, then whirled around to kick him in the face. As he anticipated, Voodoo's fatigue caused a mistake as he held his sword out to one side, instead of defensively near his chest.

Capitalizing on the error, Clay brought his own sword at an angle across Voodoo's chest, cutting an inch deep through the man's torso. As the man brought back the sword to prevent more damage, Clay turned his weapon to the correct angle, thrusting it smoothly upward, severing Voodoo's primary sword hand in the center of his forearm.

Though neither blow proved fatal by itself, or in conjunction as it seemed, the fight was in essence over. Absently pulling off his mask, Voodoo stared at his fallen hand, lying on the ground beside him, with bewilderment. It still clutched the sword, looking ready for action as though it might be popped onto his wrist with the right magic.

Knowing the man's illusions and parlor tricks were completely fake, Clay had little doubt Voodoo's thoughts now focused on saving his own life. He stumbled back, running toward the other end of the woods with little thought about his intended path.

Without looking, Clay slid the sword into its scabbard along his backside, watching his enemy run through the shrubs ahead until a strange noise echoed through the wooded area.

A dozen or more metal spikes flew through the air like arrows, each landing in a different area of Voodoo's body. Everywhere from his knees to his shoulders, the spikes made themselves at home, lodging themselves deeper than any cut Clay had inflicted.

A pained look crossed Voodoo's face as he stared almost vacantly toward Clay. The metal weapons were likely poisoned, meaning no matter what trick Voodoo attempted, nothing could save his life.

He slumped to the ground, landing hard on his knees before falling forward. His face embedded itself into the ground as his hand continued to bleed several seconds before the leaky crimson pool ceased.

Feeling the ends justified the means, Clay went about carefully picking up the nearby weapons discarded during the battle. He hoped Voodoo was the last of the bad apples from his past. Kim was far more dangerous in a scheming sense, but Clay doubted the man stuck around past the afternoon, likely leaving the dirty work to Voodoo.

He made a mental note to tell whomever took charge of the entire park fiasco that several traps remained near the Expedition ride. Local authorities probably had people skilled in disarming bombs and traps.

Weakened and bloody, Clay staggered toward the main strip. He hoped to find friendly faces awaiting his return. After surviving such a gruesome day, he needed some good news.

CHAPTER 27

▼

When Clay finally limped onto the main drag, he saw blue and red lights flashing outside the main gates, but no activity inside the park.

Packard and Bill spied him first, rushing over to assist him. Packard took his side, guiding him toward the main offices while Bill removed all of the weapons, whisking them away toward his truck.

"I'm not crippled," Clay told his sergeant, who insisted on aiding him as though he had a broken ankle.

"Play along," Packard said. "Turpin's covering our asses, so we've got to make it look good."

Clay chuckled to himself, wondering how the agent planned on explaining the day's events to local authorities. Virtually no move the officers made was by the book, they were over a hundred miles out of their jurisdiction, and at least two dead bodies remained inside the park.

"Turpin said he can cover up a lot of the stuff, and he says Bill should never have been here. He isn't sure he can cover that up."

"I wouldn't have brought him if I'd known he was going to run off like that. How the hell is Turpin going to cover up the video evidence?"

Packard shrugged.

"He can have Bryant destroy the video evidence. All those cops out there have been ordered to sit tight and guard the perimeter until Turpin comes up with the right angle to tell them."

"Any sign of Kim?" Clay inquired.

"Bill killed him," Packard whispered as they neared Casey, her parents, and the agent.

Clay felt proud and confused at the same time, wondering how his uncle had survived such an encounter, much less eliminated one of his arch enemies.

When Casey spotted Clay she immediately ran over, throwing her arms around him, not letting go as she spoke.

"Thank you for everything," she said, her head resting against his shoulder.

"You're welcome. You won't have to worry about any of those creeps invading your park again."

Casey lifted her head, smiled warmly, then kissed him on the cheek.

"If there's anything I can do to repay you, just let me know."

"Maybe a free pass, so we can spend the day together," he suggested, bringing a glow to her cheeks. "This time we'll do it without fending off bad guys."

"Consider it a date," Casey said before returning to her parents.

Clay wondered if two families might eventually sue the park for the deaths of a guest and a park employee, gunned down by live ammunition. He didn't consider either incident the park's fault, since the terrorist group infiltrated the employee roster with falsified documentation.

When Bill returned to the fold a moment later, Clay noticed a somewhat distressed look across his uncle's face.

"What's wrong?" he asked.

"Nothing," Bill answered, though obviously troubled by something.

Packard left Clay's side to ask Turpin something.

"You can tell me," Clay insisted once they were alone.

"Maybe someday. It's nothing."

Bill tried to look reassured for his nephew.

"Really. It's nothing."

Clay decided to drop the subject, ready to return to a normal life.

"I really appreciate you coming out here to help," he told Bill.

"As long as we don't all go to jail, I'll say it was worth it."

Grinning, Clay placed a hand on his uncle's shoulder.

"How did you deal with Kim?"

"We tried it the traditional way, but when it came down to it, about seven bullets did the trick."

"Seven, huh? Sounds like you were kind of angry."

Bill shook his head.

"Nah. Just thorough."

Clay wanted to question his uncle more, but Turpin approached them. The agent offered his hand, which Clay readily shook.

"I take it you've taken care of our problem?" the agent asked.

"The park should be safe for habitation, if that's what you mean."

"You've proven to be exactly what my boss thought you were."

Clay said nothing, giving the agent a cagy stare.

"I've been sent here to recruit you for a rogue agent program the FBI started in Los Angeles."

"I've never heard of such a thing," Clay replied.

"That's the idea, son. I don't need an answer right away, but my boss wanted you to hear it straight from the old horse's mouth what you'd be getting into."

"Which is?"

Turpin looked around, apparently seeing too many people nearby for his liking.

"We're going to be here awhile, and there's going to be a long trip back to Muncie afterward. I think that'll give me plenty of time to explain my job to you."

Clay nodded in agreement.

"I'll be all ears."

Turpin gave him a crooked grin before looking over his shoulder.

"I'd better get to fixing this mess. I'll need you and your uncle to show me where all of these bodies are, so I can come up with a good story for the locals. The press isn't going to leave this one alone for weeks."

As the agent left to sort out the details, Bill gave him a playful nudge in the ribs.

"FBI? That's incredible."

Clay shrugged off the notion, unwilling to commit to any new job until he heard the details.

"I can't imagine living in California, Bill. It would be a paradox compared to what I had in Japan."

A thought suddenly came to him.

"Did they find the six thugs I left upstairs this afternoon?"

"They found some blood and blade marks in the walls, but the guys were gone," Bill answered. "Think they're a danger to society?"

"Probably not. They were just puppets."

Clay suspected they fled the park and never looked back. Kim had set them up for failure, and they achieved the expected results. He doubted they would be scared straight by the experience, but they weren't going to be tutored by Kim or Voodoo any longer.

Packard returned to Clay's side after a brief discussion with Bryant across the lot.

"You going to take it?" he asked.

"I don't know a thing about it," Clay answered honestly. "California is a long way from here."

"You'd probably do your country a lot more good working on a national level," Packard said thoughtfully.

Clay chuckled briefly.

"You pushing me out the door?"

"Not at all. I'm just saying you've got to do what's best for you. I'll still have my goof ball and the bulldog."

Nicknames and comradery were two things Clay knew he would miss if he left his department. Working for the Bureau sounded like a dream come true, but he needed to weigh the pros and cons before committing to anything.

"Is Turpin really going to get us out of this scot-free?" he asked his sergeant.

"Sounds like he has the angles covered. Maynard and Sorrell assisted with an arrest in Cincinnati that gives us more witnesses than we need. With you and your uncle wiping out the rest of the clan, I guess that turned out to be a good thing."

Packard folded his arms, openly happy Kim and Voodoo were no longer threats to anyone.

"My daughter didn't have to see that shit this morning," he commented. "Those two were monsters, weren't they?"

Clay nodded.

"We're damn lucky there weren't lots more casualties."

"I hope you don't have any more bad apples from your past."

"Me too. And if there are any, I hope they've learned their lesson."

"What's that?"

"If they want to kill me, they need to keep it simple."

Packard grunted to himself.

"You know, I hate to tell you this, but even you won't live forever. Maybe it's about time you give up some of your extracurricular activities and try some different ones."

"Like?"

"Dating."

Clay looked over to Casey. Her parents were busy speaking with Turpin momentarily, so she returned a somewhat affectionate gaze. Her eyes drifted toward the offices, indicating she wanted him to meet her inside for some time alone.

"You know, Sarge, I might just do that."

CHAPTER 28

▼

ONE MONTH LATER

Clay followed Casey into the grassy area in Frontier Town as they planned for an early morning picnic. Now in regular season, the park opened every day for business, leaving them the option of eating before or after regular hours.

Despite hosting one of the previous month's tragic events, Frontier Town provided one of the few accessible scenic, grassy areas inside the grounds. Venturing into the woods meant battling ants and other insects for unblemished food, while the rest of the park offered only blacktop views or chlorine smells from the water park.

"I can't say I've ever had a picnic breakfast before," Clay teased as Casey began unfolding the cloth after pulling it from the basket.

"We're lucky to squeeze this in, Clay. I wish we could have the park to ourselves."

He laughed lightly.

"I don't think your parents are going to close the park all day for us. They'd probably have an angry mob at the front gate."

An hour remained before the park opened, so Casey had the train conductor drop them off as he tested out the steam engine for regular daily use.

Clay's hectic schedule kept him from visiting Casey sooner, but he called her several times to reassure her that he hadn't forgotten. They had also traded e-mails, which allowed them more personal contact when they found time to correspond.

"I'm glad we finally got to do this," he said.

"Me too. I wanted to thank you again for saving our park."

"It wasn't just me."

"I know, but you didn't have to come here from Muncie and risk your life the way you did."

Clay stared at the blue skies with fluffy clouds occasionally floating by. The day looked nothing like the overcast, stormy day when the terrorists invaded the park.

"If I hadn't come, a lot more people might have died. You have Agent Turpin to thank for sorting out that mess and making us all smell like roses."

Turpin had indeed laid all of the blame on Kim, Voodoo, and their henchmen. He cleared Packard of any wrongdoing, spent hours interrogating the remaining culprits for confessions, and kept Bill in the clear. He attributed the terrorist deaths, along with the fake trooper, to the terrorists turning on one another, despite knowing otherwise.

"Speaking of our favorite agent, are you going to take that new job?" Casey inquired with a flirtatious smile.

"Probably not," Clay answered truthfully. "It sounded like quite an adventure, but I'm happy where I'm at."

She continued unpacking more things from the basket, giving Clay a moment to enjoy the sunny sky, thinking what a paradox the day seemed compared to a month prior.

"How's the park been doing?" he asked as Casey handed him a breakfast burrito.

"The media gave us favorable coverage, despite the two deaths. I don't think we're going to be sued, but you never know. Business has been pretty good, despite the gas prices."

"And the Whirlwind?"

"In storage where it belongs. We've had three parks call to make offers, so it will probably have a new home by next summer."

"That's great," Clay said without too much enthusiasm.

Casey caught the lack of emotion.

"Something wrong?"

"Not really. I just keep thinking there was something more to this whole mess that we didn't find out. Before all of this, Bill and I were close, but now I only see him once a week if I'm lucky."

"Give him time," Casey encouraged, drawing closer to him with a glass bottle of orange juice. "That day was hard on all of us."

Clay nodded, but didn't agree in reality. He felt certain Bill had learned something that fateful day he had no intention of sharing with his nephew.

Based on what Turpin told him, Clay put together a likely scenario that Bill crossed blades with Kim until the Korean said something unruly. Bill claimed he used the gun in self-defense because his legs were so badly hurt from the knife wounds, but Clay suspected something deeper provoked his uncle.

"When are you going to teach me some of that karate stuff?" Casey asked, picking up a strawberry as she playfully danced it near Clay's mouth.

He took a nibble, grinning genuinely for the first time in what felt like forever. Years had passed since he went on anything he considered a real date.

"You wanting to help me battle more bad guys?"

"You answer a lot of questions *with* questions," Casey observed.

"I'm inquisitive."

Casey looked at him with a skeptical look.

"I think you have things to hide."

Clay snatched a strawberry from the nearby bowl before addressing the statement.

"It's not that I hide things. People around me aren't always safe."

"Why?"

"Those guys who invaded your park a month ago were people I knew from Japan years ago."

Casey appeared somewhat stunned, as though she wondered how he became involved with terrorists.

"It's hard to explain, Casey. We were all trained the same, but a few pupils used their training for evil. Like the two men here last month."

She finally breathed outward, showing relief.

"But I'll teach you anything you want to know. I'm not sure about how often I can commute here."

Casey laughed, her hair brushing against the picnic cloth.

"Maybe we can get you a job over here."

Now it was Clay's turn to be amused.

"Director of terrorist affairs?"

Casey drew closer to him, running her finger up his chest. He hadn't felt this comfortable since the first time he made love with his wife in Japan. Clay had no intention of removing any clothes in the middle of a theme park, but Casey had intelligence and an undying spirit he found exhilarating.

"You'll have to cook me a traditional Japanese dinner sometime," she said. "I used to love it when my parents took me to Chinese restaurants."

Clay winced a bit.

"There's a difference, but I can actually cook quite a bit of both menus."

He was about to ask her something when the train whistle tooted in the distance, indicating it drew closer once more.

"Probably my father sending Marty to check up on us," Casey surmised.

"Aren't you a little old for babysitting?"

She sighed.

"Not when it comes to my father."

Instead of passing through, the train slowed to a complete stop at Frontier Town with two passengers. Two men stepped off the train before the locomotive slowly built up speed enough to leave the station. It gave several clacks as it heaved forward, rocking gently from side to side like sheets in a gentle breeze.

Clay and Casey stood to greet Bryant, who had accompanied a bearded man Casey instantly recognized, but Clay did not.

"Dave," she said, approaching the man to throw her arms around him.

Bryant shook hands with Clay.

"Good to see you again," the security director said with the first smile Clay ever recalled seeing from the man.

"Likewise," he replied. "Things been smooth around here?"

"Sure have. And that's how I like it. I didn't take early retirement to do real work."

Both men chuckled easily.

Casey continued to speak with the other man, seeming to console him in some way.

"Who is that?" Clay inquired.

"Dave LaRue. He's the man who shot his buddy last month. Today is his first day back to work since the accident, and Casey had something special planned for him."

On the same day as our picnic? Clay wondered.

Bryant seemed to read his sour expression.

"We didn't know Dave was coming back so soon until last night," the security director explained. "Casey had a memorial built for the guy who died where the tombstones are."

Bryant pointed to the area behind them.

"Won't that make things a little awkward?" Clay wondered, staring at a large marble stone with engraved words along its smooth side.

"Hopefully not."

Casey walked LaRue over toward Clay, then introduced them. They quickly exchanged handshakes before strolling toward the memorial.

All four stood in front of the stone, reading the inscription.

For Danny Garrison.
A man who touched countless lives,
Supporting students, school, and family alike.
You will be in our hearts always, Danny,
Because God needed a good entertainer
In Heaven.

"It's beautiful," LaRue stammered, tears welling in his eyes.

"Dave? You okay?" Bryant asked, obviously concerned.

"Yeah," LaRue said, wiping his eyes.

Knowing the story behind the accidental shooting, Clay felt somewhat uncomfortable being present as an outsider at such an important, though tiny ceremony. He couldn't imagine how it might feel to accidentally kill a fellow officer, drawing the only parallel he knew.

"It's good to have you back, Dave," Casey said, putting her hand gently on his back.

"Thanks, Case," he said, using her nickname. "It's good to *be* back."

He sounded genuinely glad to be around his second family, but Clay sensed incredible hurt within the man. Unlike Kim or Voodoo, LaRue was a man of principles and kindness. He and Garrison were casualties of different kinds the month prior.

"Can I have a minute?" LaRue requested, indicating he wanted to be near the memorial alone.

Bryant strolled along the railroad track, observing the large wooden fort as Casey took Clay by the hand, leading him the opposite way.

"It took a lot of support from my parents and the employees to get Dave to come back," she explained. "No one thinks any worse of him after what happened."

"It would be wrong if they did."

"The park is a better place to visit if Dave is here. He has a passion for entertaining guests, and he's like family."

Clay felt the connection between all of them. Like a small town, everyone seemed to know everyone else.

Perhaps the park wasn't as commercialized as he originally thought.

"Maybe I'll use that season pass a little more often," Clay thought aloud.

"You'd better. I don't like riding the roller coasters alone."

Clay found an instant connection with Casey that seemed to carry him through the bad times at work. He decided to make more time for her in his life, because he wanted to be around her, around the family atmosphere that made her such a good person, and away from the past that continued to haunt him.

He pulled her close, giving her a kiss on the lips, despite the unusual timing. She melted instantly, moaning slightly as their lips gelled like waves cresting over shoreline boulders.

When they separated, Casey gave him a satisfied look, somewhere between friendliness and true love. Clay instantly knew he was right where he needed to be in life and his new relationship.

Perhaps at long last his bloody past could be laid to rest. He wanted to be a new man. He wanted to start a family. Most of all, he wanted to begin living before he grew old and died.

Looking into Casey's eyes, he believed for the first time in a long time his goals were within reach.

978-0-595-40231-1
0-595-40231-3

Printed in the United States
54189LVS00002B/25-45